The ~~~~ Beneath

Matthew Palmer

Special Thanks To
Dad, Mom, Persie, and all my closest friends

1

Why We Run

      He sat back in the wooden chair, sipping at the cup nestled in his calloused hands, light and soft against his skin. The warmth of the tea poured into his body and settled in the pit of his stomach. Steam rising from the wooden cup tickled the dark stubble above his lip and along his chin. A noise at the front of the shop alerted the man in the seat, and he lowered his cup onto the table, his head swiveling to meet the sound.

      The door swung open wildly and smacked against the wall nearby as a small figure stood in the light flooding in from outside. The inside of the little tea shop was illuminated by swinging paper lanterns, showing off the lush yellows of the framing and the solid brownish green of the paint. From the doorway, the figure stepped into the shop, their brown hair matted in sweat to their forehead. It took a moment for the man in the chair to realize, but the figure that stood before him was but a young boy, dark tan skinned with almond shaped eyes of a brown color.

      "Listen up! I want the owner of this crummy shop to come out, right now!" The boy screeched, baggy trousers flapping in the wind from outside, held up on his waist by a thin string. Several people in the room looked to one another, shrugging to themselves, and resumed their conversations. "Hey! I'm not playing around!" The boy shouted again, stomping on the ground with a foot. In a quick motion, a knife flew across the room and embedded itself into the wall next to the boy.

      "Why are you in here again?!" The elderly owner shouted. "I told you last time! You won't get any money! Get a job! You'll get nothing from me!"

He scratched at the wispy gray hair atop his head and fiddled with the little knives in his hands.

"Ha! It'll take more than a couple toothpicks to stop me this time!" The boy jumped onto one of the tables, just as another knife flew by and struck the shop's stone floor beneath him, producing a tiny spark, invisible to those not carefully paying attention. The man in the seat with the tea cup, however, was paying very close attention to every single movement between the boy and the owner, his bare feet pressed firmly onto the floor. His green eyes were fixed now on the boy, who he noticed had the hair just above his ears and down and around his neck shaven down to fuzz, the hair above that wavy and short, parted slightly to the side.

"I have half a mind to get the authorities involved! They'll send you to prison for good this time!" The owner threw another knife, this one landing just in front of the boy's wooden sandals.

"If you can catch me, old man!" The boy jumped from the table to the next, and people started clearing out. There was an old couple that left first, then a younger woman with a baby, and then a family of four that shuffled out the doorway. But, the man with the tea cup sat and sipped, watching the scene for himself. The boy jumped again from table to table as knives flew past his head and became lodged in the walls. Charging for the owner, the boy slid over the counter into the kitchen, where he was met with a dead end by the back of the kitchen, where the owner now cornered him. The other man was now standing by the counter, watching as the owner twiddled a knife in his hand, his back turned to the man at the counter.

"I've got you now, boy. You will get no money, and you will never come back to my shop!" The owner pulled his arm back, ready to throw the knife, but he fell backward suddenly, hitting his head on the counter and then slumping his body down onto the ground. The boy looked to the man standing by the counter, who had a scowl on his face. He took this event as a sign, and promptly ran out of the shop, bounding into the forest.

Shortly after entering the forest, something from below grabbed his leg. The boy looked down, and his eyes met with a cluster of rocks surrounding his ankle, locking him to the ground. "I'm sorry okay! I-I didn't mean to cause all that! I just wanted some money! Please!" The boy pleaded with his hands clasped together, assuming the owner or an authority was nearby, waiting to kill him or take him away, as footsteps rang in his ears. As for the rocks, he figured them to be some sort of trap rigged by either culprit. "Don't kill me!"

"Oh, stop groveling. It's a little pathetic you know," a voice said, letting out a hearty laugh. The rocks retreated into the ground and the boy turned around to see the man from the shop who'd watched him, now walking up to him. "Next time, ask nicely for the money and maybe you won't get knives thrown at you." The boy looked at the man and cocked his head to the side with an eyebrow raised.

"How'd you do that? With the rocks? You have a little creature under there that grabbed my leg?"

The man ran his fingers against the fuzz on his face and thought for a moment. "I can't trust you enough to tell you. How could I? I've just met you, and you did just try to rob a friendly tea shop."

"You call that guy friendly? He tried to kill me!" The man raised his eyebrow and frowned at the boy. "Right, I did try to rob him. But still!" The boy protested.

"How about we start with your name." The man walked over to a nearby willow tree and sat at its base, his robe resting in his stillness.

"Why should I tell you my name?"

"I did save your life back there."

"What do you mean?" The boy thought for a moment, before realizing. "You tripped him?" The boy exclaimed. "Well, I guess that is fair." He kicked a pebble at his feet across the ground, his eyes set on the grass and dirt below. "My name's Lao."

"I knew a boy named Lao." The man muttered, moving a tiny pebble through his fingers.

"Really?" Lao turned to him, his eyes wide.

"Yes. We were in camp together as kids. I never saw him after that though," the man said plainly, an inkling of sadness dancing within his voice.

"Oh." The boy quickly redirected the conversation. "So, how did you do the thing with the rocks?" Lao walked to a tree adjacent to the man and slid down, sitting just next to a boulder. Looking to him, waiting for an answer, Lao saw the man put up his hand slightly, flick his wrist and hand, and then felt a sharp sting hit the side of his head. "Ow!" The man was now smiling, his hand returning to his side. "You… you did that."

"Is that a question or a statement?" The man nodded, his hands moving in a rhythmic motion as a pebble floated in front of Lao's face.

"You're a Mystic?" Lao shouted, standing up and smiling. The pebble jumped toward him, hitting him in the center of the forehead with a loud tap of his skull. "Ow! Again?" He exclaimed, rubbing his forehead with his palm.

"Not so loud. You know what will happen if I'm found out. I need to know if I can trust you." The man said, walking to Lao.

"Yeah! You can trust me!" The boy had an air about him. It was not only shady, but innocent and naive as well, and while it didn't sit well with him, the man nodded his head and began walking into the forest, followed closely by young Lao. "So what's your name? Where are you from? How do you do the magic thing? Oh! Is it like with your brain, like you think really hard?" He questioned, one after another after another.

"I will answer all of these to you if you answer me one question."

"Sure! Anything!"

"Why do you run?" The man kept walking, smiling to himself with his hands in pockets on the sides of his robe.

"Huh?" Lao's head tilted again in bewilderment.

"Why do you run away? Those who are on the run believe they have a reason to run. I run because I have a destination, a motive. What's your reason?"

"I don't know. I guess since I don't really have a home. I've kinda had to run from place to place and steal to get by. It's not fun."

"It doesn't sound fun."

"Yeah." Lao muttered, kicking a pebble across the ground, where it skittered across the dirt and clicked against a tree.

"You look very young, especially young to be on your own like this. I hope I don't scare you; I am some magic man you just met in a forest." The man looked to Lao and smiled, chuckling to himself.

"It is kinda weird." Lao smiled too, continuing to walk until the two of them reached an old, seemingly abandoned shack.

"Welcome to my house!" The man said jokingly, gesturing to the building with his hands, now freed from his pockets.

"It looks… cozy." Lao said, standing still and scanning the house. It was certainly old, rotted wood pillars at the front porch, dusty bamboo framing, and crummy cracked stone lining the outside and inside walls.

"You can leave if you want. No reason for you to be staying with some weird man."

"I don't really have a place nearby, so I might as well stay here for the night. Thank you."

"Not a problem. I have a bed in there and I can make some soybean soup if you want." At the mere mention of food, Lao's stomach began to growl, bubbling in his chest.

"That sounds perfect."

"Good." The man smiled. "Oh, and to answer your first question, my name is Shen Jin, pleasure to meet you."

"Nice to meet you too, Shen. If it's okay with you, I'm going to take a walk around, get some air." Lao said, turning away from Shen.

"Not a problem. But do come back before dark. It's dangerous out here at night." Shen turned away and headed into the house.

Lao began walking deeper into the forest, finding a small patch of bamboo growing near a creek. The ground underneath him crunched as soil and rocks shifted under his sandals as he walked into the bamboo, pushing some of the stalks out of his way. Sounds of flowing water filled Lao's ears from the pond nearby, calm and soothing, and soon, another sound filled the air. A faint scratching seemed to be coming from somewhere outside the bamboo patch, which Lao was now standing in the center of. Listening carefully, making no sound other than the occasional shifting of his feet, Lao could make out that the sound was getting higher, climbing almost into the air. The next sound he heard was the subtle flapping of wings, and a crash against the bamboo stalks.

Lao jumped back, his spine brushing up against one of the stalks of bamboo. The crashing continued as the noise sifted through the stalks of bamboo, pushing them out of the way one by one. Whatever was making the noise was getting closer. It was scratching at the bamboo, clawing at its surface, grabbing onto each stalk with an iron grip as it pushed it from its way. More and more, Lao's heartbeat picked up, and he looked around him frantically, looking for a way out. But, the sound seemed to be coming from all directions at once. He thought for a moment, and ultimately decided to fight. Or, at the very least, try to.

     He crouched down and looked around on the ground, figuring there might be some kind of rock or a stick he could use to defend himself. To his luck, he found a fallen bamboo stalk lying on the ground. To his misfortune, however, the thing making the sound and chasing him, had also found what it was looking for. As Lao grabbed the stalk of bamboo, he felt a stinging sensation in his shoulder, and he cocked his head around to see a mess of dark brown feathers on his back. Instinctively, he brought the bamboo around and poked the creature on him, and it released its grip on his shoulder, leaving gashes and blood.

     Lao turned around and saw the creature, a juvenile hookbeak, about the size of a piece of firewood. Its eyes were black and beady, staring him down while gripping onto one of the bamboo stalks with its scaly yellow legs and sharp talons. A rat-like tail coated in feathers whipped around from its rear end, and it clicked its sharp beak with the black hook at the front of it. Quietly, the creature let out a low squawk that resembled a growl, and within seconds, it lunged forward at Lao.

     Its small wings flapped in small bursts as it weaved through the bamboo after the evasive Lao, who was actively backing away through the bamboo, and swinging his newly acquired weapon in the direction of the creature. Its jaws snapped and the scratchy tongue behind its beak longed for a taste of flesh. It moved closer, and Lao saw an opportunity. He swung the bamboo, striking the creature in the wing, and he could hear a faint snap as the fragile bone broke under the weight of the hit. The hookbeak let out a loud screech and its talons grasped one of the bamboo stalks near it, crawling up to get away from the boy who crippled it.

Lao stumbled out of the bamboo and collapsed into a mess of heavy breathing, sweat and blood running down the side of his arm and his back. He took a moment, controlling his breathing the best he could. In through his nose, which wasn't much air, out through his mouth, and soon he just gave up and breathed solely through his mouth, which slowly brought his heart rate down. He stared down at the stick of bamboo in his palm, and noticed a large crack traveling half the length of it. He made little sound, other than a sigh of relief, figuring the hookbeak had left, injured and likely to die.

Lao gathered his strength, gripped the bamboo in his hand, and used it as a walking stick, making his way back to the house. On his way, he could feel the blood leak from the wounds on his back and shoulder. Thankfully, the talons had only sunk just barely into the muscle, the blood pouring out at a slow rate being just an annoyance to the boy. That is, until he reached the house, when the real annoyance presented itself.

"Lao! What did you do?" Shen shouted, running out of the house, now wearing a simple olive green leather tunic that clung to his frame. He draped one of Lao's arms over his shoulder and neck and aided him in walking into the house.

"I was by the creek," he began, breathing heavier again, the blood loss catching up to him now, "I was attacked by a hookbeak. It's gone now." He dropped the stick of bamboo at his feet just before the two entered the threshold of the shack.

"I didn't know they were this far from the mainland. In any case, I told you to be careful! You didn't listen!" Shen walked over to a wooden cabinet, opening it and reaching his hand inside. A moment later, he pulled out a roll of bandage cloth and a small woolen pouch filled with something.

"I was careful! Or at least I tried to be," Lao muttered, sitting down in a rocking chair. He gripped the fabric of his shirt and pulled it off of him, feeling the blood on his back and shoulder stick to the cloth. The blood had started drying now and the wounds began closing, if only slightly. Shen walked back over to Lao and began wrapping the bandages around his shoulder, going in a circle around his armpit, shoulder, and arm, covering the entirety of the wounds in cloth, which immediately began soaking up blood that had not begun drying yet.

"If you were really careful, you wouldn't be in this situation, Lao."

"I'm gonna be okay, right?" Lao said, a hint of panic creeping into his voice.

"Yes. It might scar, but you'll live." Shen finished wrapping the wounds and flicked his wrist, a small sharp rock coming up from a bowl on the table nearby, using it to cut off the cloth from the roll. He then flicked his wrist back in the bowl's direction, placing the rock back inside it. "There. You're all patched up." Shen walked to the still open cabinet and placed the roll of cloth back, then came back to Lao, opening the woolen pouch.

"What's that?" Lao piped up and tilted his head slightly.

"A healing mix of herbs. Here, eat some" Shen said, handing Lao a small pinch of the green leaves.

Lao took them reluctantly, nibbling on one of the leaves, and immediately, he felt his tongue gather a bitter and vile taste. "Ugh! This is so gross!" The skin between his bushy eyebrows crinkled as his face wore an expression of disgust.

"Oh yes, it's terrible. But it will help fight off infection. Now, eat it." Shen walked over to a section of the floor, pulled up one of the floorboards, grabbing a small blanket, then placed the floorboard back. He walked over to Lao, and wrapped the blanket around the boy. "Here."

"Thank you." Lao said, sighing as he munched on the leaves, his face still in a state of disgust. "Hey, Shen?" Lao's head looked up from the ground and he choked down the chewed up leaves, which had become a fine paste in his mouth.

"Yes, Lao?"

"What's your destination?" Lao settled into the rocking chair, shifting back and forth as the blanket covered him, warming his body up.

"What do you mean?" Shen was in the kitchen now, a bronze pot of boiling water on the metal grate above a small bed of hot coals as a makeshift stove. He carefully grabbed a handful of little soybeans from a small cup next to him on the counter.

"When you asked why I was running, you said that you were running because you had a destination. Where is it?" Lao's voice was laced with a kind of whimsical curiosity which reminded Shen of himself in a way.

Shen thought for a moment. His mind began to jump from memory to memory in his head. He saw his parents, his father, a stoic and brooding man, and his mother, a beautiful and simple woman. That memory faded into the next, where Shen saw sheer darkness, a neverending blackness which filled his eyes, while his ears were filled with a loud knocking sound. This memory faded too, into the next, which showed Shen the face of a little boy, no more than three, waving goodbye with Shen's mother next to him, a familiar face to Shen. "My destination is an island off the southern coast of Vasai, called Sukoshi. As for why I'm going there, I would prefer to keep that to myself, for now."

"Vasai? How are you gonna get there? They aren't letting anyone enter or even leave that isn't with the shipping companies or a merchant."

"How do you know that?" Shen stirred the brewing soup in the pot and mixed in some soft spice leaves that smelled of a fragrance somewhere in between lavender and cilantro.

"You hear a lot of things living on the streets."

"Right, I suppose so. So I assume you've seen all the Vasai soldiers posted at the docks."

"Yep, as well as the Batung soldiers on the northern side of the island; one of them tried to arrest me."

"For what?"

"I stole some jewelry from a corner shop. It was worth about 200 Yin, and I couldn't go to jail." Lao stood up for a moment from the seat, and began pacing around in the living room, feeling the creaking wood underneath him. He thought back to the time he stole the jewelry. He'd swiped it from the counter as the old woman running the shop was talking with another customer. A few moments later, she noticed it was missing and called over a pair of soldiers. The next thing he knew, Lao was in a little holding cell on the north shore of the island, surrounded by flimsy bamboo bars.

"I suppose it's understandable. I don't blame you, Lao."

"Thanks, I guess." Lao shrugged and sat back down into the chair, his memories now fading into the blankness of his subconscious. Shen walked over to the boy with the bronze pot in one hand held by the handle, and a small bowl and broth spoon in the other hand, held carefully balanced in his palm.

"Here," he said handing Lao the bowl and spoon, which the boy took willingly into his small hands. Shen began to calmly pour some of the soybean soup broth into the bowl in a steady stream. The brownish tinted liquid now rested in the bowl, giving off steam carrying with it a sweet and flavorful aroma.

"Thank you, Mr. Jin."

"My pleasure." Shen smiled brightly, his eyes squinting just a bit, and he returned to the kitchen to get another bowl, pouring out some soup for himself.

Lao took a small sip at the broth spoon filled with the soup, and the warmth began moving down his throat and into the base of his stomach. "Mm, this is delicious. I haven't actually had soybean soup before."

"It's very healthy, and filling. Please, eat, you'll need the nutrients in the herbs to fight off infection in those wounds. After you're done, please put the dishes on the counter and rest. Tomorrow, I have to go down to the docks at the north gate and try to get some information."

"Information for what?" Lao asked, gulping down another spoonful of soup.

"First, I must find a way to get to Shuijiao Island, just west of here. Then, from there, I travel to Lujing."

"And from Lujing you get into the mainland."

"Exactly. How did you know that?"

"I'm from a small town on the mainland."

"Why did you leave?"

"I'd rather not talk about it." Lao shifted a bit in his chair as he slurped the rest of his soup right from the bowl, cupping his hands around the bottom and tipping the now lukewarm liquid into his mouth.

"I understand."

"If you'd be okay with it, I'd like to go with you to the docks. I wouldn't mind joining you on your trip to Shuijiao Island. As long as you keep the soybean soup coming," Lao said, smiling as he set the bowl onto the counter in the kitchen and walked back to the chair.

"You're welcome to join me. But, I can't promise you'll get more soup until we get to Shuiijao. We will have some tree nuts and berries though."

"I guess that works too." Lao chuckled to himself, the chuckle then spreading to Shen, who let out a hearty chuckle under his breath.

"Lao, if you don't mind, I'd like to ask you something."

"Sure," the boy said.

"What do you know of it, the Mystic cleansing, I mean."

"Not much at all really. My mom used to tell me stories about the Mystics when I was little. She said they were people with special powers, and that they were sought after and killed. But, other than that, I don't know much."

"Thank you. I was just curious. Get some rest, now, we leave tomorrow," Shen said, smiling a little to himself. A few minutes later, Lao settled onto the rigid couch with scratch marks all over, leaking cotton stuffing, and dozed off lazily into sleep. At the center of the living room, Shen sat, legs crossed, eyes closed, hands held close to the fire he'd been nursing as Lao fell asleep.

Shen took this time to think to himself. He breathed calmly, inhaling through the nose, exhaling through the mouth, his hands now resting on his knees. He thought for a moment about what it was he was doing, squatting in some shack instead of living peacefully back home with his mother and father, had they been alive. Shen laid down against the wood, a rug draped over his body as a blanket, and he was lulled into sleep by the faint sound of the crackling fire, popping quietly with each ember.

Across the Water

    Lao awoke in a state of disarray, blanket wrapped in his legs, and his body sprawled out on the floor below the couch. He swiveled his head around, a sharp pain brewing in his neck. His eyes rested on Shen in the kitchen, carefully packing leather pouches into a larger animal hide bag. "Shen, what are you doing," Lao asked, his voice wavering with a yawn. He brought his legs over the edge of the couch and they fell to the floor, still wrapped in the blanket, his heels hitting the hard floor with a thud. "Ow!"
    "Careful, you might get a splinter."
    "Because that's the least of my worries." Lao said, pointing to the bloody bandages along his chest and shoulder, his other hand occupied in trying to untangle the mess of blankets at his feet.
    "Don't get snappy." Shen finished putting the things into the bag and placed the flap over it, then brought it over his head, tightening the leather strap around his waist like a belt, the bag resting gently on his side. He walked over to Lao and lightly tapped the floor with the balls of his feet, raising a small rock spike that pierced through the blanket and ripped it just enough for Lao to wiggle free. The dazed Lao was now wide awake, stood a few feet from Shen, against one of the walls.
    "What was that?!"
    "You were stuck, I got you out."
    "You could've killed me!" Lao shouted.
    "Oh please. It was nowhere near you."
    "It was right near my legs!"
    "Quit whining, we have to go."

"What? Why now?"

"We were followed. They're nearby. We have to go soon. Here" Shen said quickly, tossing Lao a spare leather tunic of a pastel green color. "Put this on, and put the hood up." Fiddling with it in his hands, Lao felt the hood at the back of it with one of his hands, the smooth fabric brushing against his skin.

"By who? What's going on?" Lao stuffed his arms into the sleeves and pulled his head through the neck hole of the tunic, then draped its baggy cloth hood over his messy hair, the tiny hairs at the back of his head and around his ears brushed by the fabric.

"Vasai soldiers, and they looked angry." Shen began wrapping an olive green scarf around his neck, a bundle of cloth around the ends of which dangled behind him and rested on his back. Embroidered on the scarf was a little insignia that Lao took notice of; it was a simple crest with the image of a bright green creature inside it. The creature looked to be some kind of large rodent with scales along its arms, legs, and body, essentially everywhere but the underside of its belly. Its head had a relatively thin snout with a small nose at the end of it and a white line down its forehead. Lao thought for a moment if he should ask Shen about it, but decided against it.

"Open up in there!" A voice cried, followed by the sound of banging on the front door of the shack. Shen placed a finger to his pursed lips and stepped for an open window on the other side of the room. Lao followed calmly, trying his best to keep quiet. This would not work however, as Lao passed over the floorboard which housed the blanket given to him, producing a loud creak. In reaction, Lao ducked his head, his eyes squinting, his mind hoping with everything the soldiers at the door didn't hear the sound. "We're coming in!" The shout was brief, and was followed by the hefty sound of the rickety door busting down off the rusted hinges.

"Run!" Shen shouted, jumping out of the window and turning around to help Lao out. Lao looked back, making eye contact with one of the soldiers. This one was a fairly burly woman, her brown hair cut short at the shoulders and her muscular arms occupied by a thick bow, an arrow at the ready. As his eyes met the head of the arrow pointed at him, Lao turned and ducked, the hood falling behind his neck as he crouch-ran toward the window to Shen.

"What did I do?" Lao screamed, getting halfway to the window. A few moments later, the sound of the arrow releasing filled Lao's ears. In a quick motion, initiated before the soldier had even released the string, Shen flicked his hand up, a wall of dirt and rock raising behind Lao. The arrowhead embedded itself into the wall, piercing through only a bit, only the tip of the arrowhead showing on the other side.

"Let's go!" Shen moved his hands, hurrying Lao out of the window. He flicked his finger in the direction of the wall, and pieces of it flew toward the soldiers on the other side each time he did. Lao jumped out the window, his leg catching the sill and tripping him, and his face came to the ground. Shen knelt down and helped the boy up, rushing him away from the shack, heading north.

"You won't get away!" The female soldier shouted, running out the front door of the shack, then around to the side Shen and Lao departed from. The male soldier with her ran around the wall of earth, rubbing his forehead which bore a slight red mark on it as he climbed out of the window to follow after his partner. Both of them bore the light tan skin of the Vasai people, glinting with sweat in the sunlight as they ran after them.

"Come on, Lao, faster!" Shen looked back and saw the female soldier ready another arrow, running at a fair pace. He stopped briefly and raised his leg up with a bent knee, a rock rising from the ground. He then moved his hand forward with an open palm, the rock now careening toward the soldier and knocking the bow from her hands. The arrow released from the string as it fell and embedded itself into a nearby tree. Shen turned back around and noticed Lao was a couple feet away, running for the exit of the treeline.

Shen quickly caught up, using rocks under his feet to propel his movement slightly. The two got out of the treeline, their eyes scanning the area before them. They both saw the docks, a wooden pier of a light birch wood swarming with people carrying nets of shellfish and sealed wooden crates of seemingly anything. Lao smiled, and Shen followed, but this was short-lived, as a voice broke the silence from behind them.

"Put your hands up and I won't shoot!" The female soldier held her bow, arrow at the ready, her aim directed right at the center of Shen's torso. Her partner came up behind, a short spear in hand, pointing toward Lao. "We know what you are, dirtskin." The soldier spat.

"You know nothing," Shen muttered through gritted teeth. His eyes glanced over at Lao next to him. He observed a terrified look on the boy's face, and his memory flashed to a single image: a young boy taken kicking and screaming by a figure dressed in shining armor. The image faded, and Shen smirked, back still turned to the soldiers. He brought his leg up slightly behind him, a rock of fair size coming up from under each soldier. "Run! I'll hold them off! Get help, quickly!"

"But-"

"Go!" Shen snapped and turned around to face the soldiers, his eyes set on the female soldier, now backed up against a tree. Lao ran away down the hill, almost tripping and tumbling, but caught himself, as Shen fought with the soldiers. "You won't kill me that easily."

"I've killed many before you. I'll kill more. I'll make sure your kind is wiped from the face of the planet." The female soldier readied another arrow, and Shen noticed the arrowhead. Its material did not shine in the sunlight leaking in from the east, in fact, it was rather dull. Taking a chance, Shen flicked his wrist, and the arrow moved, flying toward the male soldier. Unable to react in time, the arrow pierced into his ankle, going straight through.

"Agh!" The soldier screamed, clutching his leg frantically, his spear on the ground next to him. The female soldier, hair now in her face, huffed and readied another arrow, this one's tip gleaming in the light.

"You will die!" The female soldier shouted, bringing her arm back toward the quiver at her back.

Shen jumped and kicked forward slightly, a rock launching into the soldier's stomach. She was knocked back, her spine colliding with the tree behind her. She slumped down, sliding down and dropping her bow. The male soldier managed to pull himself up, only to see three figures coming from behind Shen.

"Are you alright?" Lao shouted, running up to him. Behind the boy, two Batung soldiers in dull bronze armor and helmets with bright green feathers on them ran up to the scene.

"What happened, sir?" One of the soldiers, a younger man with blue eyes, pale tan skin, and auburn hair peeking from his helmet, walked up to Shen, his sword drawn.

"That one," Shen pointed to the female Vasai soldier knelt down against the tree, "she stole my bow and attacked me! She's a Mystic!"

"He's lying! He's the Mystic!" She threw her arm wildly and Shen flicked his fingers toward him, a rock flying into his chest from next to where the soldier was standing. "I-I didn't do that! I swear! I-" her rambling was quickly interrupted by the young Batung soldier walking over and hitting her in the head with the handle of his sword.

"She's telling the truth!" The female's partner cried, his leg bleeding from the wound.

"He's in shock, officer, she shot him. It's a lot to take in, the betrayal of your own partner."

"No! No!" He cried for a few more moments, before ultimately passing out from blood loss.

"Dawei, take him to the infirmary to the south, and get rid of her. I'll help these two," the younger Batung soldier said. He took the quiver of arrows from the female soldier and the bow, then walked them to Shen, handing them over. "Here you are, sir."

"Thank you, officer. Can I get your name?"

"Yes, sir. The name is Chang Wen."

"Why thank you Chang. This is my little brother, Lao."

"Hi," Lao muttered, almost tripping over the single word.

"You look familiar, kid." Chang eyed Lao up and down, his shining eyes moving along with the boy's height. "Might just be me. Where are you two headed?" While Shen draped the quiver over his shoulder and neck, bow in hand, Chang placed his sword back into the holster on his side.

"We need to get a boat to Shuijiao." Shen said, then pondered for a moment, creating a lie in his mind to tell. "My wife is waiting for us there."

"If you're from the mainland, what brings you here?" Chang raised an eyebrow, unsure of the truthfulness of the man before him.

"We're here on business. I'm a hookbeak hunter." Shen adjusted the leather strap of the quiver along his chest, a few arrows shifting around inside.

"Oh. Well, I commend you, I don't have the guts to kill those things. They're vicious." Chang brought his brow back down to normal level, resting a small amount above his eyes. "If you want, I'm supposed to be heading back to

Shuijiao myself tomorrow, but I can talk to the dockmaster about getting over there today."

"You'd do that?" Lao perked up, his brown eyes darting to Chang.

"Yeah. It wouldn't be too much trouble. Consider it payment for turning in that dirty Mystic." He gestured his head in the direction of the unconscious female soldier. A sinking feeling found its way to Shen's chest, which he quickly tried to shake off. Chang noticed the discomfort in Shen's face, and nudged him. "You alright, sir?"

"Yes. A bit tired is all. Thank you for the concern, officer."

"Please, you don't have to call me officer. I am only a private, after all." Chang explained.

"Then I'll just call you Chang."

"That works. Now, let's try to get you two to Shuijiao before nightfall." Chang led the two down the hill to the docks, where Lao scanned his eyes around the waters and on the wooden planks, scouring them for anything interesting.

The young boy noticed sailors and merchants hauling wooden crates to and from boats and the main warehouse at the back of the dock to the far left. Sailors were cloaked in leather clothing, coupled with iron boots that shone with dim light in the sun, while the merchants wore simple woolen clothing in varying colors of white, brown, and olive green, along with leather pants. There were a few fishermen too, tossing nets into the water and dragging them back, fiddling with the little fish the nets caught.

Water brushed up against the dirtied sands below the docks, going around the wooden supports and pilfering through the holes in the sand made by little sand crabs. Looking out onto the horizon, Lao saw only water, tinted a deep blue, with a slight brown tinge, waves forming and dissipating with the winds. "Lao, are you alright?" Shen placed a hand on the young boy's shoulder, and Lao noticed they were atop the docks now.

"Erm, yes, just a bit tired, Shen." Lao did his best to come across as Shen's younger brother, changing his tone ever so slightly, which, while not all necessary, fooled Chang enough.

"Don't worry, kid. When we get on the boat, I'll try to keep the talking to a minimum so you can rest a little."

"That's very kind of you, Chang," Shen said.

"Again, sir, it's no problem at all."

The three of them arrived at the boat, which Shen thought of right away as 'a bit rundown.' The front paint was partially chipping, the dark green color fading away into the water it rested in. The rest of the wooden vessel seemed rickety on the surface, creaking with each little wave that passed by under it.

"Are you sure it's safe, Chang?" Lao questioned, scratching at the back of his neck with two of his fingers.

"I've taken five full-sized adults across before, kid, I think she can handle the three of us. Now, excuse me while I go talk to the dockmaster." With a nod, Chang went toward the main warehouse, stepping with a carefree stride that offset the rugged look of his dirt-stained armor. Once he got far enough from them, Shen and Lao began speaking in hushed whispers.

"Are you alright, Lao? Any cuts? Bruises?" Shen asked, taking Lao's chin in his hand, moving his head around to try to get a better look at any injuries hidden from view. Lao shook this off, pouting.

"I'm fine, Shen!" He whisper yelled. "Really, I am. Those soldiers didn't hurt me at all."

"Promise?"

"Promise." Lao tucked his hands into the pockets of his tunic, feeling a little notch of leather with his fingers.

"Alright. When we leave, I want you to settle down and rest. You still have that nasty shoulder wound."

"I know. Besides, I wasn't lying when I said I was tired."

After a bit of silence between the two, Chang came back, helmet held at his side. "Alright. So, we got the go ahead to go to Shuijiao. That's the good. The bad, is that I'm going to have to do a mandatory mark check on both of you. The dockmaster gets real picky about it, and I wouldn't want to make the guy angry."

"Of course. It's completely understandable, Chang." Shen began taking off the scarf around his neck, holding it softly wrapped around his wrist. He then turned around, back facing Chang, and tilted his head downward, looking at the ground in front of him. Carefully, Chang stepped up behind Shen, examining the back of his neck, noticing the beige skin throughout, with maybe a freckle or two here and there. All along the neck, there was only the beige color, nothing more than skin. After Chang had stepped back from him, Shen took the scarf from his wrist and placed it back around his neck, the fabric brushing softly against his skin.

"You're good, sir. Now the little guy," Chang turned to Lao, "Lao, please turn around for me?" He asked, bending his knees only slightly to get at Lao's level. With minor hesitation, Lao turned his back on Chang and pushed the hood out of the way of his neck and onto his shoulder. Again, Chang took great care in looking him over, brushing his fingers over the dark tan skin, finding nothing but the flat color, free of imperfections. "All good, little man." Chang ruffled his fingers through the boy's hair, messing it up slightly.

"Thank you, Mr. Wen." Lao said, turning back around to face him. Lao stood confused, scratching at his hair and fixing it, wondering what had just happened. For now, though, he decided to deal with it later, once the three of them arrived at Shuijiao.

"Now that we got that out of the way, let's get going. Shen, sir, if you and the little one could get in the boat?"

"Certainly, Chang." Shen said, and looked to the boat. Walking over and stepping in, he was careful not to knock around the two adjacent oars firmly held to the rim of the boat. He then took a seat toward the back of the vessel and aided Lao in getting in. Lao shook, a minor fear of falling in the water, while Shen held onto him, helping him into the boat where he would sit next to Shen.

"All good?" Shen and Lao nodded, almost simultaneously. Chang then hopped into the small wooden boat, rocking it side to side in the water, a bit of water splashing the inside of it. There was a certain smell to the water. It was neither earthy nor salty, but a combination of the two. This combination of smell tickled Lao's nose as the boat rocked underneath. "Let's go then!" Enthusiastically, Chang took the handles of the oars into his palms, clutching them firmly with his fingers, and then began to move his arms up and down, the boat lurching forward onto the waves.

It was a little bit into the ride, a good amount of time, before Lao settled in and fell asleep. He was laid down softly at the back of the boat, in the crook between the back and the furthest back seat. It was not the deepest sleep, but it was sleep nonetheless, and the gentle rocking and calm waves helped keep him in that state of slumber as Chang and Shen talked amongst themselves. "So, Chang, how did you come to join the army? You are freshly enlisted I assume?" Shen asked, his back leaned against the side of the boat sat in the middle seat.

"Not enlisted, sir, I was conscripted." Chang kept his eyes focused forward, steadily rowing along, the heads of the oars cutting through the waters with ease as they pushed the boat along. As Shen was about to speak, Chang interrupted. "And before you ask, yes it was because of what I did." Shen knew, from his travels throughout the mainland, that if one was convicted of murder with good reason, they would be given the option to either spend thirty years in prison, or be conscripted to the army.

"I see." Shen placed his hand to his stubbled chin. "Then, may I ask why you did what you did?"

"My mother and father are old, very old. They can't fend for themselves. One day, a group of bandits came and they took my mother from the village. So, against my father's wish, I went to their camp, and I killed their leader." Though his back was turned, Shen could feel the pain and the regret, all through the young man's voice. "I know what I did was wrong. I know that. But I chose the army because I figured I could actually make a difference. I could kill the Mystics that plagued the world."

With that final note, a sinking feeling arose in Shen's chest, and stayed with him as he spoke in return to the young soldier. "I don't fault you for your decision. If it were my family, my mother, perhaps I would do the same."

"You know, sir, you don't look very old. But yet, you're as wise as if you've been through a whole lifetime."

"You're right Chang. I am only thirty years old, a fraction of my life as a whole. But I've been through many things. I've learned that, in life, everyone goes through a fire. The fire can cook, provide people with a necessity in life. But, the fire can also destroy, burn all it touches to ash. It's what you do when you encounter your fire that decides who you are." Shen's words resonated within Chang, snaking their way into his ears and in two directions, one through his chest, ending up in the heart, and one through his head, landing firmly in his mind, forever burned into his memory.

"Wow. I never really thought of that."

"I could just be babbling, honestly." Shen chuckled, running his fingers through the scarf around his neck. For a longer time now, the two of them remained silent. Every now and then, though, Chang would glance back at Lao, smile at the sleeping boy, and then his eyes would go to Shen, content and staring at the waves ahead, at the horizon with the sun perched slightly above it. Chang's blue eyes would then turn back along with his head to the water ahead, at the path he was subconsciously following along with.

After a while, as the sun began to dip into the horizon, Shen became curious. He eyed the back of Chang's neck, noticing the very pale tan skin, and wondered about its reason, before asking outright. "Chang, I don't mean to be rude, but you don't look like someone from Batung."

"You're fine, sir, not rude at all. My mother is from Ogon and my father from Vasai. You'd be surprised how many other soldiers ask me that." Shen put the answers in place, and then painted a mental image of Chang's parents in his head. He imagined a frail old lady, graying hair once blonde, pale skin like fired ceramic, typical of the Ogon people. Then, he imagined a stoic old man, light tan skin, a spear with a fish at its top firmly gripped in his hand. "Say, now that you bring up looks, you don't look all too Batung to me either."

It was true. Shen had a combination of Vasai and Batung heritage, making his skin a beige color, not too dark to be Batung, not light enough to be Vasai. "Yes. Well, like you, my parents were not from the same place either. My mother came from Vasai too, actually, and my father was from Batung."

"Good to know," Chang smiled and looked back to meet his eyes with Shen's, then turned back around to face the water once more.

Soon, just as Shen's head began to lull off into a daze, the boat was thrashed at the side with vigor. This alerted him immediately, and his head darted to Lao, who was now awoken from his rest. "What's going on?" The young boy asked, rubbing at his eyes with the backside of his hands.

"I don't know. Stay close to me, Lao." Shen looked to Chang, who stopped rowing, his eyes peering over the edge of the boat and into the depths below. Shen looked around, seeing jagged rocks a dark gray, waves crashing up against them, around the area of the boat. But the rocks were not the cause of the noise or the hit on the boat. As Chang's eyes scanned the water, nothing showed itself, until the soldier realized the large shape passing by. He could only stand and watch, motionless, as the shape turned a narrow end toward the boat and hit its side once more.

This time, teeth sank into the wood, a circular pattern poking into the inside. Shen quickly grabbed a hold of Lao, keeping him in the dead center of the boat while Chang grabbed for the sword at his side. In the swift motion it took the soldier to pull the blade from its holster, the thing latched to the side of the boat began tearing and shredding at the wood, pieces and shards splintering out and into the water around, until the inside of the boat began taking in water. The smell returned, not earthy nor salty, and it was not just in the air, but at the feet of Lao, Shen, and Chang, who had his sword in his hand firmly gripped at the handle.

"Get to a rock, now! I'll hold it off!" Chang stabbed at the thing on the side of the boat, and Shen grabbed Lao, putting him onto his back, then jumped into the water, making a splash that came up into the two's faces. As this happened, Shen felt the quiver of arrows slip off his shoulder into the murky depths below, and realized his bow was still on the boat. In spite of this, he remained focused on the rock ahead.

"Lao, hold on tight!" Shen began to swim vigorously, pumping his legs with the rapidly strengthening waves and spreading his arms with each stroke until he reached the rock. Carefully he set Lao down and then sat at the edge of the rock, his scarf falling to his side on the ground. At the back of his neck, Shen could feel water dripping down through the center of his back, taking with it a slightly grainy substance.

"Chang!" Lao shouted. Shen's green eyes darted to the boat, only to find it in pieces, with Chang treading water in place, sword nowhere to be seen.

"Chang, get to the rocks!" Shen took off the heavy leather tunic that had soaked up water, unlacing the front, letting it fall to the ground behind him. His body, average and slightly muscular, beaded sweat and was coated in a thin layer of water, bare and facing the cool breeze.

As Chang began to move his arms forward toward the rock that Shen and Lao were on, another shape circled under the water around him. This one was more narrow, a streamlined body and long narrow front end. The other shape had a more large and bulky shape, almost fat. The new shape's narrower end quickly turned toward Chang's left side, then emerged from the water.

It came out in a full jump, its smooth gray skin glistening with the combination of sunlight and water. A dolphin, it seemed, until Shen looked to the mouth. Protruding from it were teeth lined on each jaw like a woodcutting saw, sharp, jagged, and bright white. This was a sawtooth dolphin, staring down Chang with its beady dark blue eyes.

Shen then deduced that if this was a sawtooth, then the thing that tore the boat to shreds must have been a shredfish. It was a creature, about as large as the boat, with a head the size of a melon. It had a fat body, wrinkled and scaled, and pectoral flippers that guided it, along with the large tail fin at its rear. The key thing about the shredfish that Shen had heard from the fishermen throughout his travels, was the mouth. The shredfish, with its circular mouth lined with rows of razor sharp teeth, would tear apart wooden boats, leaving the contents inside to be eaten by the sawtooth.

"Chang! Hurry! Now!" Shen shouted, a weight crushing down on his chest as his heart sank in fear. Chang paddled hurriedly, his feet kicking, arms flailing, until all of a sudden he stopped. The sawtooth had gone back under the water, and couldn't be seen by the likes of Chang, nor Shen. With a violent thrashing, the creature latched onto Chang's side with its jaws, beginning to tear apart the flesh, leaving blood to pool in the water.

On instinct, a rush of feeling going through his head, Shen stomped his bare foot on the ground, a rock raising up from in front of him. Lao gasped audibly, and he brought his knees to his face as he sat, keeping his eyes closed with his head down. Then, with a swift motion, Shen raised a pillar of the ocean rock from under the creature, tossing it up into the air. The sawtooth wriggled and squirmed, water flying from its smooth skin just as a rock flew from Shen's position, this one sharp and jagged like a spear, piercing through the creature's body.

It dropped, lifeless, into the water below, where it was promptly consumed by the shredfish lurking in the depths. Shen then looked to Chang, who was on his back, facing the sky. He jumped into the water, paddling quickly over to the soldier through the bloodied waves, and scooped him up with his arms, carrying him carefully back to the rock. Back turned to Lao, Shen scrambled to grab his bag, which had fallen with his tunic to the ground.

Lao brought his head up from his knees, gazing at Shen, who was now patching up the soldier with cloth, slightly water-stained, and he noticed something odd on the back of his neck. Right in the center, surrounded by the beige skin, was a green circle, only about the size of his small fist.

Shen finished patching up Chang, tying off the bandage on his left side, then put the cloth back into his bag, nestled among herbs and pouches of berries and tree nuts. As Chang came to, his blue eyes fluttered open, and Shen set him down. Suddenly, the soldier grabbed him by the neck, a loose grip of only one hand. His face became red, his eyes gleaming in the dwindling sun.

"You filth." Chang shook vigorously, fingers clutching at Shen's throat. "I should've known you were one of them. I should've killed you… I should've killed you while I had the chance." He managed to puff out, strained, each muscle in his neck bulging with a seething anger, before his body relaxed and his mind went black. Resting at his feet, the soldier let go of his grip on Shen, unconscious, bleeding from the wound in his side.

With a somber look on his face, Shen turned to Lao, and simply spoke, low and firm. "Don't be scared. He didn't hurt me." After that, the two sat still on the rock, staring out at the waves, taking in breaths of the earthy and salty smell of the waters around them.

Night Sky

The sun held its place, only dipping part of its bottom into the horizon, a blue hue coating the sky above them. Shen sat on his rear, bare feet pressed against the wet rock, knees bent with his arms at his side. Lao sat similarly, though his feet were cloaked in wooden and leather sandals, and his arms were wrapped around his knees, his head in the crook of his elbows.

"Why did he do that, Shen? Why?" Lao brought his head up, looking to his companion, whose eyes were fixed toward him.

"He had to. He had to hurt me. I'm a Mystic, after all."

"But why, Shen?"

"If I could answer that, I would. But I can't, and anyway, now is not that time. Now, we have to go to Shuijiao before it's too dark. I can see it from here." Shen pointed across the water, a long swim to be sure, but it was manageable. "If I've read the map correctly, that is." Lao brought his head up more, and his eyes met with the horizon, just barely picking up the sight of the island's edge.

"You have a map?"

"It's in my pack. Never travel the world without a map." Shen lightly patted the leather bag at his side, and smiled warmly in Lao's direction. Lao chuckled a little to himself, but quickly stopped in a matter of moments.

"Shen?"

"Yes, Lao?" Shen stood up, grabbing onto the mess of leather at his feet that was his tunic, and wrapped it around himself, shoving his arms through the sleeves. He grabbed onto the bag too, and tied it around his waist once more, where it rested on his hip.

"How are we going to get to Shuijiao? We can't swim, that thing will get us. And we don't have a boat anymore, so how are we going to get there?"

"I have an idea. It will make me look very ridiculous, but it'll work, if all goes well."

"How sure are you?"

"As sure as sure can be." With that, Shen got down on both knees, and began rooting through the bag at his side. He went through pouches of herbs, tea leaves, bits of metal, a sizeable pouch with about twenty little silver coins, Yin, as the currency was called, until, at the bottom of the bag in a little nook, Shen seized a small stone. Its surface was smooth, like cloth to the touch, and shone with a divine light. Inside, as could be seen through its clear surface, there was an explosion of color. There were beautiful bits of orange and pink, blue clouds billowing through green pillars, all swimming within the little rock.

"What's that?" Lao was stood upright now, balancing himself, while slightly wobbly, on scrawny legs.

"Hang on. You'll see in due time." With an aura of mystery at his side, Shen leaned over the edge of the water and with the little stone in his palm, he dipped his hands just below the surface. He felt the cool water brush past his beige skin and saw little salt crystals dissolve in foam against the creases of his palms. Soon, there was a thin, and very thin at that, coat of salt crystal around the outside of the stone Shen held in his hand.

"Um, Shen? What is this supposed to-" Lao was cut off as his jaw dropped and his eyes went wide, fixated on the water in front of Shen. Rising from the seafoam was an enormous sea turtle, glowing yellow eyes with no pupils, great amounts of algae growing on the back of its shell like a carpet. Its face bore scars like teeth marks and tentacle prints, showing history of attack on attack upon its skin. A mighty beak stood at the front of its head, golden, with white whiskers on the sides of its mouth, lightly bouncing with the waves.

"Hello, friend," Shen said, petting the creature's head, laden with patches of brown scales and long dead barnacles. Shen then began to make a quiet clicking, coming from deep inside his throat up to the front of his teeth. Lao raised an eyebrow, not being able to decipher a word of what the two were saying, if they were saying anything at all. There was more clicking, and then it suddenly stopped, and the creature opened its beak. Shen placed the smooth crystal, glinting with light, into the turtle's mouth. It took a few moments, but the turtle finally closed its beak and turned its shell toward the rock. "Alright, get on." Shen said, beginning to lift Chang onto his back once he had rounded up all of the supplies onto the turtle's shell.

"You're taking him with us?"

"Of course."

"But…" Lao began, but couldn't seem to find the words.

"We can't just leave him here. Now, let's get going." Shen got onto the turtle's back carefully, stepping ever so softly onto the carpet of algae, and set Chang down in the center of the great shell. Reluctantly, Lao began to step onto the turtle's shell, craning one leg over to it, and then the other, all the while Shen guided him over and made sure he didn't fall into the water.

Once Lao was safely on, Shen went to the head of the turtle and lightly patted onto it with his hand. The turtle then began to swim, keeping its glowing eyes above the surface of the water, paddling graciously with its flippers. Along the underside of its flippers and its shell, there were dozens of gemstones of all sorts of colors embedded into it. Lao became curious of the gleaming dots under the water that caught the sunlight, and he reached his hand into the water.

"Hey!" Shen said in a deep tone. "Don't touch its underside, it's quite disrespectful." Shen softly pulled Lao's hand out of the water where it came to rest in his lap as he sat.

"I'm sorry. I just haven't seen one of these before. What exactly is it, Shen?" Lao excused himself and looked up to Shen.

"He is a Baobei. In fact, he's one of the last of his kind."

"What happened?"

"Well, it's a very tragic story. There were once many of them in these waters. But, they were hunted for the gemstones on their undersides. I wasn't around to see most of them, but I knew where a family of them had lived when I was a child, right around here in fact. I suppose I just got lucky with this one." He patted the turtle on its shell softly and then went over to its head, still poking out of the water.

"Is that why you gave him that rock?"

"Yes. Baobei love receiving gifts, especially more gems." Shen smiled softly and began to pet the turtle's head once more, and a little smile of sorts came across the creature's beak. Shen then looked to Chang, completely knocked out, in a slumber that not even a thunderclap could rouse. There was still the sinking feeling in his chest, and he couldn't quite place what it was, but he paid little attention to it. There were more important matters at hand.

The Baobei moved at great speeds, yet swam smoothly enough for its passengers to remain in comfort. Chang of course stayed unconscious, not stirred by the bobbing turtle or the crashing waves. Lao played with a little rock in his hands that he'd put into his pocket before they got onto the Baobei. Shen, deep in thought, rooted through his bag to find his scarf.

He pushed a few small leather pouches out of the way and then came upon it, drying out slightly, but still sopping wet. He looked for a moment at the insignia on the fabric, the rodent creature with scales on it, now fading with the seawater. The green was now looking more like gray, and the creature itself seemed almost foreign. He wrapped it around his neck and made sure to cover up the skin of his neck.

Lao's eyes began to become heavy, his heartbeat slowing a bit, and his mind going blanker and blanker. The feeling of the waves around him and the soft bobbing of the Baobei through the waters made him tired. If not for the abrupt stop, Lao would have fallen asleep right on the shell, on the soft bed of carpet-like algae.

"We're here." Shen said. He picked Chang up and slung him over his back, his chin resting against Shen's shoulder, face in the fabric of his scarf.

They found themselves in a pond of sorts fed in from the sea with shores of darkened sand. Beyond the shore, there was a deep forest of green trees, light dwindling around and leaking through the canopy of leaves, illuminating the creatures roaming it. There were little flightless birds of muted browns and yellows bouncing around on the ground through the grass. And there were deer with curled antlers, too, like ram's horns, and they would run into the trunks of thinner trees with them and shake nuts from the branches and onto the ground below.

Shen noticed this and then began looking through the bag at his hip. He pulled from it a medium sized leather pouch, empty and baggy, and then walked into the forest with Chang on his back. Lao trailed behind, and once he made it to the shore, he looked back at the Baobei. Its eyes, though empty and glowing, showed some kind of emotion. This feeling sank into Lao, and he smiled at the creature, then waved goodbye. The Baobei brought one of its front flippers to its beak and pecked at something on it, then turned its gaze to Lao. Quickly, it spat a small gemstone out at Lao, who put up his hands to catch it.

"Thank you!" He shouted and smiled even wider. The Baobei clapped its flippers against the water with a great splash, and then dove under the water, its whiskers glinting with a glittery golden dust as it departed. Lao looked down at his hands, at the gemstone, coated in seawater, with that earthy and salty smell lingering, and noticed its shine. It was a beautiful green gemstone, laden with bands of darker and lighter green color within its smooth surface.

"Lao! Come on! We have to get moving!" Shen shouted. He was a ways into the forest, still within Lao's sight, bent over and fiddling with something on the ground. Chang was placed sitting up against a nearby tree, a paperbark, with delicate and soft peeling wood.

Lao ran up to his companion, pocketing the gemstone into his brown fabric pants. When he got to where Shen was, he tilted his head in confusion. "Shen, what are you doing?" He asked bluntly. Shen was rooting through the fallen leaves and tall grass underneath large dark wood trees, looking for something Lao figured.

"I'm searching for tree nuts. Walnuts, banli nuts, that sort of thing."

"Don't you already have some in your bag?"

"Yes, but we can always use more. Whether we eat them or sell them, they're good to have." Shen seemed like a crazy man, wild green eyes and unkempt, dark brown stubble along his jaw and upper lip, searching through the ground for nuts. "Aha!" He exclaimed. "Here's a whole bunch!" He'd found a small stash, hidden in a carved hole in the ground, covered by leaves and twigs. As he took handfuls of the nuts, putting them into the pouch, he felt a sudden *clonk* on the top of his head. "Ow!"

He looked up, and his eyes met with the culprit. In the trees, in a high up branch, there was a little gray rodent, tossing pebbles down at him. It had beady black eyes and big ears disproportionate to its head, and a bushy tail that wrapped around its body. It tossed another pebble, this one rugged and not at all smooth, making contact with Shen's head again. "Hey!"

Lao started to giggle, which shortly turned into a hearty laugh as Shen closed up the pouch of nuts, put it back into his bag, and shuffled over to Chang. "This is not funny, Lao!" Shen said, ducking more oncoming pebbles tossed by the furry fiend.

"I think it is!" He laughed even more now, walking over to where Shen had Chang, still unconscious in his deep slumber.

"Come on! I only took a few nuts! All this over some stupid nuts!" Shen looked even more crazy now, waving his arms and crouching as he made his way to Chang and Lao, shouting at the little rodent in the trees. Finally, the pebbles stopped raining down on top of him, the rodent scurrying off to its nest in the trees. Shen sat down, next to Chang, and placed his hand onto his own chest, breathing heavier after the ordeal.

Shen took the cover off of his bag at his hip and pulled from it a withered piece of paper. As he looked down at it, he noticed that most of the area of the map was faded, the colors and the ink smudged, blurring, wet from the seawater the bag had went through. Thankfully, the island of Shuijiao, which they were currently on, was relatively untouched by the water, save for its southwestern shore. They were now in a forest at the southeast shore, and the main town was in the center of the island, according to the map.

"Let's go, Lao. We should make it to town before full nightfall if we start walking now." Shen put the map back into the bag and it tore slightly. He picked Chang up and slung him over his back once more, making a mental note to himself to try and buy a new map in town.

The two started for the town, named Wenyong, after an ancient myth about the island. It was said that Wenyong, a great being from the oceans, rose from the seafoam and brought the island to the surface, so that humans could live on it. All fable, of course, but the tale had always delighted Shen as a child. Shen was silent, and Lao too, looking around at the creatures and the trees, admiring the different colors of the flowers throughout the leaves and the grass.

There was one creature that caught Lao's eye in particular. He had only seen it for a brief moment, but it seemed somewhat familiar to him. It was rodent-like, certainly mammalian, and yet it had scales all along its body. Everywhere but its belly had sharp scales along it, a brownish color like the rest of its body. On its head, thin snout on the front, there was a white line of scales down the forehead. Lao wanted to get a closer look, but the creature scurried off before he could.

Soon enough they were at Wenyong, and night had just fallen on the island. The town was relatively loud, rumbling with voices. Green and pale yellow lanterns along strings were strung above, connected from building to building, and shone with a warm glow that was ever so inviting. The buildings were made almost exclusively from light colored wood, with some having bamboo roofs and others wood. There were people going down the street of dirt, some in groups, some alone, and some even bringing wagons with them, filled to the brim with crates.

"Here we are." Shen said to himself. He began to look around, trying to catch a glimpse of a guard to flag down and help Chang. Suddenly, a glimmer of light reflected off dull bronze armor caught his attention, and his heart leapt with joy. "Sir! Sir!" He called out, running to the guard, who was standing at the edge of the street with a sword in his hand. Lao ran at Shen's side, not having trouble keeping up at all. "Sir, this man has been hurt! Me and my little brother found him by the shore. He told us to get him to the barracks!" Shen acted as panicked as he could, and this panic was felt by the guard too.

"O-of course! Come on," the guard said, putting his sword into its holster and slinging one of Chang's arms over his shoulders, Shen putting the other arm over his shoulders. They began walking away from the street and the town, but not for long, as they came upon the stone building in the forest. It was cracking and grown with vines, but it held strong, for what Shen could tell was many years.

"Is he going to be okay?"

"We'll have to tell the captain. She'll be able to help him." The guard said. The green feathers scarce on his helmet were caked in a layer of dirt, and yet the color of them shone bright to Shen and Lao, who was watching carefully as the two brought Chang to the building. The guard knocked with a clenched fist against the wooden door, and after a few seconds, it opened inward.

Out from it came a beastly sight. A woman, darkened tan skin, laden with scars along her muscular arms and on her cheek, burly and large in size. She had a bandage wrapped around her left ear and part of her head, blood staining it, and her hazel eyes pierced into Shen's eyes. There were green markings painted along her neck, and her bulky chest was locked in a thick bronze mail, the rings shining in the torchlight at the side of the door. "What happened?"

"I don't know. My little brother and I found him at the shore, bleeding and mumbling. He told me to bring him here."

"Did he tell you his name?" The way she talked was stoic, serious, and yet it had a twinge of feeling to it. It was clear to Shen, and even Lao somewhat, that she wanted to help.

"I believe he said his name was Chang. Yes! Chang Wen, he told me." Something changed briefly in the woman's eye, and she instantly reached her hands to him.

"Here, set him down on the wall." She took it upon herself to pick him up off Shen and the guard's shoulders, putting him down against the stone. She knelt down to him, putting a hand to his chest. She could feel his breathing, faint, but still present. "Wei! Go get the herbs! They're in my bag! Go, now!" She shouted at the guard, who scrambled with his footing and then ran into the building.

"Ma'am, thank you."

"Please, there's no need. He's my responsibility anyhow, the knucklehead."

"If you don't mind me asking, what's your name?" Lao asked, piping up and tapping his foot on the ground.

The woman began tearing off Chang's shirt and bandages that Shen had put on, cutting away the fabric with a little bronze dagger. "My name is Captain Lian Shu. I'm the standing officer of this island." She ran her fingers over the wounded soldier's skin and scanned the gash at his side. "The cut isn't deep enough to kill him, he'll live." She said happily, smiling. "But, we will need to put the herbs on to keep infection at bay."

The guard from before returned, black hair upon his head where the helmet once stood, and he had a worried look painted across his face. "Captain Shu, there are no more herbs," he said gravely.

"What?! How is that possible?"

"Corporal Yuhan's squad was ambushed by a group of Vasai soldiers. We've got too many wounded to tend to. There won't be enough herbs for him."

"No!" She shouted.

"I have some herbs. It's not much, but it might help him until you can get more," Shen said, pulling a leather pouch packed tightly with green leaves and little white flowers. He handed it over to the Captain.

"Thank you, sir. Really, thank you."

"It's my pleasure, really. I'd hate to see a young man die like that. Now, if you'll excuse me, my little brother and I have to get to the market." Shen turned to walk away, Lao walking beside him, when the Captain spoke up.

"If you would like, I can send an escort to help you there. The forest can get awfully scary at night." Sweat dripped down her forehead as she mashed up the herbs in her hand after inspecting them.

"That won't be necessary. Thank you for the offer, though."

"If you ever need anything, don't hesitate to find me," Captain Shu said, now putting the side of her fist to her chest in a salute. Shen did the same, and Lao joined too, awkwardly saluting the Captain. She smiled and Shen and Lao began walking back through the trees until they reached the town's street once more. The initial bustle they encountered before had died down, though there were still a few more people walking up and down the dirt road, along with a single wagon parked by one of the market stalls.

The noise had died down too, becoming mere murmurs that filled the ears of Shen and Lao as they began to walk down the road. Lao's eyes drifted off, looking in on each of the stalls around him. There was one stocked with weapons, helmed by a burly looking man with a bald head, braided black beard, and darkened tan skin that was covered in black markings at his arms. There was one filled with all sorts of fish, some with bright red scales, some with dull silver scales, some looked odd with bulging eyeballs or wing-like fins, all being tended to by a frail little old man who spoke with a firm voice to his patrons.

There was one in particular that caught Lao's eye completely. This stall was relatively small, in a little dark corner free from the reach of the lantern light. What light there was in the stall came from a candle on its counter, and this light, from a small frame, bounced off the various gold things that were collected in the confines of the stall. This particular stall caught Lao's attention so much so, that he departed from Shen's side and walked to it, curious as ever. While he did this, Shen made his way to a stall stocked full of spices in little clay pots and herbs hanging from wooden drying racks.

    At Lao's stall, there seemed to be no one there, empty, the flame of the candle on the counter swaying with a light breeze. Its wax was white, pale, and melting down the side of it. The stall was filled with golden things. There were golden teapots encrusted with jewels on the handles, golden helmets with smudges of dirt on their surfaces and engraved designs on their sides, and golden necklaces strung with wooden beads and medallions with strange symbols Lao didn't recognize. But what really held his gaze, was the golden sword hung on the post to the right next to the counter. It was fairly plain, not entirely golden, the blade being made from a shimmering bronze. The handle, however, was pure gold, wrapped in leather with a jade gemstone at the bottom of the handle. Lao reached out to touch it, a thievish thought in his mind, fingers outstretched, when a sudden noise jolted him.

    "Hello? Who's there?" A voice croaked out from the darkness at the back of the stall. Out from it, into the light, came an old woman. Her face was riddled with wrinkles, dotted with little moles, and her nose was quite large on her face. Pale green, murky eyes darted around, a tiny pair of pitch black pupils within them now fixated onto Lao. "Speak up, boy, who are you?"

    "My name is Lao," he said quietly.

    "Hm?" She asked again, and put a large golden horn to her ear, tilting the opening toward him. He looked at her with a raised bushy eyebrow, and he scratched at the shaved part of his hair.

    "My name is Lao, ma'am." He said louder, and retracted his arm back, away from the sword. The old woman jumped back a bit, startled by the loudness, and then looked toward the sword. With a limp, she walked over to it and brought it down with a shriveled, gnarled hand. Then, she set it down on the counter with a *thud*.

"I saw you were looking at this piece. I assume you wish to buy it, and not just stare at it like an idiot, right?" She brought the listening horn over to Lao again, and the light of the candle danced off of its golden surface.

"Y-yes, ma'am. But, um, I don't really have any money."

"No money?" She shouted, bringing the horn down and looking at him. "Well, what do you have then? You seem like a nice boy. I'd be willing to trade with you if you have anything good."

Lao thought for a few moments, patting down the pockets of his tunic, and then patted over the ones of his pants. Suddenly, he felt something, small and smooth in one. He reached his slender fingers into the pocket and felt the little gemstone that the Baobei had given him. Quickly, he pulled it out and placed it down onto the counter with a little click against the wood. Light from the candle's flame shone against it, and the green colors were scattered around the stall, bouncing off the surfaces of all the golden things hanging up and on the counter.

"I have this," Lao muttered.

"What?" The old woman brought the horn back up to her ear again.

"I have this!" He shouted.

She jumped once more, and then her eyes went to the stone. "Hey! No need to yell, kid." Lao rolled his eyes at her, though away from her gaze.

Lowering the horn from her ear and setting it down on the wooden countertop, she brought forth a tiny looking glass from her pocket, and then picked up the stone from the counter. She brought the glass to her eye and raised the stone to the glass, looking at it all around, moving it around with her fingers and staring from every angle. "This is a beautiful stone! Where by chance did you get such a fine rock?"

"If I told you, you wouldn't believe me."

The old woman lowered her looking glass, placed the little stone back onto the countertop, and looked to Lao with a raised eyebrow and a hand on her hip. "Try me." Lao giggled a bit, and then put his hands into his pockets.

"Well, um, I found it, washed up on the shore. Yeah, it was just sitting there." Lao had his head tilted down, and he muttered the words, though just loud enough for the old woman to hear him, albeit through her listening horn.

"You're serious?"

"Yes, ma'am. I did say you wouldn't believe me, didn't I?"

"Fair enough, kid." The old woman hobbled back over to the stone and held it up. "I'll give you the sword and I'll even throw in the scabbard," she said and gestured to the leather scabbard that was stowed away near the sword itself, "on one condition."

"What's that, ma'am?" Lao was giddy now, almost bouncing up and down with excitement.

"Not only do I get the stone, but you have to tell me how you *actually* got it as well." She smirked, showing off yellowing teeth. Her long eyelashes batted with her words and she stood there with an unflinching smile for a bit until Lao spoke up.

"Seems like a fair trade to me," Lao said, smiling. "Come close," Lao said, almost whispering.

"What?" The old woman shouted again, and Lao rolled his eyes. When she raised the listening horn to her ear, he got extra close and cupped his hands to his mouth before speaking.

"A Baobei gave it to me." He stepped back and smiled. The old woman looked puzzled for a moment, and then smiled to herself, eyes closed. Carefully, she took the sword in one of her hands and then went to the shelf to grab the scabbard. When she returned, she picked the sword up and then slid its blade into the scabbard, which had a convenient carrying strap that Lao slung over his shoulder where the scabbard would rest upon his back. "Thank you, ma'am," he said, smiling and nodding, brown eyes bright and shining in the candle's light. The old woman simply nodded and then slipped back into the shadows of the stall.

"Lao! Lao, where are you!" Lao could hear Shen's voice, not too far away, and bolted to follow it.

"Here, Shen!" He shouted, finding his companion quickly just around the corner.

"What's that?" Shen asked, and pointed to the sword.

"Just a little something I bought."

"With what money?"

"That is life's biggest secret, my friend." Lao brought his voice down low and raspy like a wise old hermit, and stroked an invisible beard at his chin with his fingers. He took the strap from his shoulder and held it out in his hands in front of Shen. Shen smiled, and bowed jokingly, taking the sword into his hands.

"Thank you, kind sir." He quipped. Shen pulled the sword from its place, and began admiring it. He ran his fingers across the handle, feeling the smooth leather and then felt the little individual gemstones pressed into the crossbar. He ran his fingers across the blade, his green eyes scanning over the finely folded bronze, and then sliced the tip of his finger a bit. "Ow." He muttered, and looked at the droplets of blood bubbling up onto his skin.

"You okay?" Lao asked.

"Yes, just a little cut is all." Shen slid the sword back into the holster and placed the strap onto his shoulder, the scabbard slapping softly against his back. "Now, we should be getting to the inn down the road. It's nighttime, and we'll need rest for tomorrow."

"What's tomorrow?"

"Tomorrow we leave for Lujing by ship. We'll have to get plenty of sleep to outsmart the dockmaster." Shen smirked and winked at Lao. There was still a burning thought in the back of Shen's mind, a thought as to how Lao had actually acquired the sword. But, that was not the most important thing on his mind. So, the two simply walked, in silence.

They walked down the road and while Lao's eyes were bright and wide and looking down the road, Shen's were drifting off elsewhere. First, they went to the bag at his side, and he rooted through it until he came upon the coin pouch that he kept. With his fingers, he pulled the handful of little silver coins and counted them, dropping them one by one into the pouch. It took a while, but in all, he counted out forty-five coins, each of them with an engraving of a tea flower on one side and a one on the other.

Then, his eyes went to a sight in one of the houses the two had passed by. He saw a family, just a young man and his wife, setting a bowl of soup down in the middle of the wooden table, and their little boy digging a spoon into it. It was normal, jovial, warm lights of a lantern brightening up the living room. Yet, there was a warmth that pulsed through Shen's chest, and then it dissipated into a colder feeling.

Shen brought his eyes to the road, and then stopped as they reached the inn at the street corner. The building had large, brown triangle-arched roofs, and a yellow awning down one side above the door. Its green wooden walls were dull and welcoming, and the lanterns hung up outside were painted with designs of flowers and little birds. In one of the windows, light shrouded by bamboo blinds inside, Shen could see the shadow of a man, hunched over and looking toward the front door. 'He must be expecting someone,' Shen thought.

    He went to the door, Lao following close behind, and reached for the doorknob, bronze and dirt-stained. He twisted, and pushed it in, then felt an immediate hit on his head coupled with a mighty *clang* sound. Dropping to his knees, Shen rubbed at the spot where he'd been hit with his hand, and the stinging pain set in. As he looked over, he noticed the innkeeper, crouched in fear, a tin frying pan held clenched firmly in his shaking hands.

    "Oh dear!" He said, and scrambled to help Shen up. "Are you okay?"

    "Yes, I'm quite alright, just a bit dazed is all." Shen lied right through his teeth, for he was in a great deal of pain in actuality.

    "Please, forgive me, sir. I-I've just been so paranoid lately. Vasai soldiers have been all up and down my neck! They think I'm housing Mystics!"

    "Why would they be thinking that?" Lao asked.

    "They say they've been tracking some on the run for days now. I doubt they're on this island, though. They're probably already on the mainland by now."

    "Why do you say that?" Shen asked now, walking over to a chair and sitting down. The innkeeper closed the front door and walked to the front counter, putting the pan down on top of it.

    "No real reason, I just think they're looking in the wrong place. If anything, I'm pretty sure they're just using my inn to get close to the Batung barracks. Anyway, what can I do for you two?" The innkeeper was small and frail-looking, with darkened tan skin. He was balding, with wiry wisps of hair on the sides of his head and a pair of tiny glasses on the bridge of his nose.

"We just need a room for the night. We'll pay."

"For the night, it'll be fifteen Yin. And, I'll throw in a free meal tonight and tomorrow morning before you leave. Consider it an extra apology for the pan."

"That's very kind of you." Shen said. He flipped open the flap of the bag at his side and reached for the coin pouch, pulling it out and opening it. He pulled from it fifteen little silver coins. "Here you are."

"Thank you, sir." The innkeeper took the coins into the palm of his hand and stuffed them into his pocket, a warm smile across his face with dimples forming at the corners of his mouth. He grasped the pan and moved to the stove, a simple bed filled with coals and a metal grate over it. Placing the pan on top of the grill, he reached for a peculiar little device next to the stove. It was mostly made of metal, and had a handle which the innkeeper grabbed onto. At its tip, it had a little piece of flint which would move with a squeeze of the handle. The innkeeper held the tip near the coals, put his face up near it, and squeezed the handle, simultaneously blowing a bit of air at the spark.

Up the flames went within the coals at the stove, and then quickly fell down, burning steadily. The innkeeper brought out a pitcher of water and poured it into the pan, then took a handful of brown rice grains from a cup near the stove. Then, he took a crate from the floor and opened it, finding two filets of chicken among the filled crate of ice. He put the lid back on and pushed the crate of ice back under the counter by the sink, and began to cut up the chicken. Once it was cut into small pieces, he placed the chicken in with the rice in the pan, stirring it periodically and dripping in some brown sauce as the fires rose.

After everything had been cooked thoroughly, the innkeeper sprinkled the dish with herbs and green vegetables, and portioned it out into two bowls for his guests. He then took the crate back out and dumped some of the ice onto the embers and the coals, quenching them. "Dinner is served," he smiled, bringing the bowls over to Shen and Lao, who sat calmly at the table in the lobby.

"Thank you." Shen said, picking up the wooden fork.

"Thank you, sir!" Lao said chipperly, beginning to scarf the food into his mouth.

"Lao, slow down! It's hot!"

"I don't care, Shen, I'm hungry!" He let some food go down his throat and the heat got to him, burning at his throat slightly. "Ow!"

"I told you."

"Oh hush." Lao said, putting the fork down and crossing his arms. Shen and Lao now took smaller bites, each bringing their forks of food up to their lips and blowing air softly onto them before eating. In a while they both finished, and were promptly full of warm food.

"Thank you. Now, will you show us to our room?"

"Yes please, and thank you. The food was wonderful," Lao said.

"Certainly." The innkeeper led them up a flight of stairs, wooden and creaking, but sturdy nonetheless. At the top, on the second floor, the highest floor, there were only three rooms, and Shen and Lao's was the one at the far back. He led them to the door and opened it, giving them a small golden key. "Here you are, sir. I expect you'll return it to me in the morning?"

"Of course, thank you." Shen said, and then led Lao into the room, closing and locking it behind him as the innkeeper fled back down the stairs. The two sat on their beds, small and draped with furry blankets. Lao took his tunic off, placing it over the back of a chair near the door, and felt his bandage with his hand.

"Shen?" Lao asked, lying down in the bed, the blanket on the floor next to it.

"Yes, Lao?" Shen answered, beginning to tuck Lao into the bed, putting the blanket over him.

"Something's been on my mind for a while."

"What's that?"

"Back on Yedao, when you asked why I run, you said you do it because you have a motive."

"Yes."

"Well, what is it?" His brown eyes twinkled in the candlelight from the nearby table, wide and jewel-like. Shen thought to himself for a moment, and then when he finished putting the blanket over him, he sat down in a chair he'd pulled next to Lao's bed.

"You really want to know?"

"Yeah!" He said giddily.

"Alright, well, it's sort of a story," Shen began, and looked away from the boy as he spoke. "When I was a boy, I was separated from my mother and younger brother."

"You actually have a brother?"

"Yes. Him and my mother were Vasai Mystics. They could control the waters and the ocean. My father and I, however, were Batung Mystics. So, when they came for us, we were separated." Lao nodded along as he talked, and his smile he once wore was now fading as he grew more tired. "I was taken to a camp on the Batung mainland with my father, while my mother and brother were taken to Vasai."

"But didn't they-?"

"Yes. They disposed of most Mystics in those camps. But, I have heard from a friend that he's still alive. He's still out there. He's on a small island in Vasai, if my friend tells the truth. So, that's why I'm running. I'm running to something, to my brother." Shen finished, and looked over to Lao, who was now in a deep sleep, turned over on his side. Shen smiled, and brought the blanket up to Lao's shoulders, then laid down on his own bed.

    He stared up at the ceiling, watching a shadow dance in the candlelight. Soon he too fell into a slumber, blanket wrapped at his feet. From the darkness came a light, and then the light turned into an image. Shen saw his brother, young with tanned skin like his own, just a child. He was knelt down, kicking and screaming as two men in silver armor gripped at his arms. Around him, pillars of water whipped and smacked at the soldiers. Then, one of them reached for his sword, and pulled it, smacking Shen's brother in the head with the butt of the hilt. The young boy was dragged into a darkness, a pit, black shadow arms pulling him in.

    Suddenly, Shen woke up, cold sweat on his forehead and candlelight dim, only an ember clinging to the wick's tip. He fell off the bed, legs wrapped in the blanket still, and hit the ground with a soft *thud*. Shen pulled the blanket from his legs and tossed it onto the bed, and looked to Lao in his bed. He was so silent, sleeping heavily, and Shen smiled. Walking to the door, he made sure to lock it behind him as he walked out, placing the little golden key into his pocket.

    He made his way to a nearby pond, guided only by the light of the moon. There it sat, calm and still, a perfect reflection of the gibbous moon captured within the pond. Around it there stood little trees, and there were rocks peeking through the surface of the water. In the pond, gently swimming, there were a group of little fish, silver and white in the moonlight flickering off their scales. Shen sat at the edge of the pond, floating a rock through his hands and then lightly into the water, then looked up. The stars were shining bright, and the night sky was untouched by a single cloud. Shen got no sleep that night, but rather rested his eyes as he sat by the pond.

Runaway

In the morning, Lao woke to the smell of tea, steam rising from the pot and drifting to his nostrils. "Hello, who's there?" He rubbed at his eyelids with the backs of his hands.

"It's me, Lao. Now come on, get up, we've got a long trip ahead of us." Shen's voice spoke. Shen was just finishing up making the tea, placing the kettle onto the counter and putting out the little flames in the bed of coals. He had dark bags under his eyes, and wore a slight smile across his face, as his eyelids drooped down a bit.

Lao swung his feet over the side of his bed and sat up. Feeling a bit light-headed, he dropped back down and laid there, shutting his eyes. Soon, he felt a stinging sensation and a *thump* against his forehead. "Ow! What was that for?" Lao sat up again, rubbing the spot on his forehead, red barely showing through his dark tan skin.

"I said get up, didn't I?"

"Yeah. But you don't have to hit me with a rock."

"It was only a pebble, luckily. Anyway, it won't happen again… probably. Now get up!" Shen walked over to Lao's bedside and set down a cup of hot tea down on the table next to it. "Drink. I put some herbs in it. And don't worry, they don't taste awful this time." Shen returned to the counter, pouring out tea into another cup for himself.

Lao got up out of the bed, feeling the cold morning air against his bare skin, and took the teacup into his hands, then sat back down. He looked down at the cup, into the liquid, seeing nothing but a light honey color and a few specks of dark green settled at the bottom. The tea smelled of mint, jasmine, and a hint of sugar, all crawling up and into Lao's nostrils through the steam. Bringing it up to his lips, he took a sip, and felt the warmth pool into his stomach and the taste fill his mouth.

"Good?"

Lao took a break from drinking for a moment. "Very," he said, returning to the drink. Shen looked to him, smiling, and then put his bag around his waist which he'd picked up from the table.

"Good. We have to go soon, so finish up quick." Lao nodded his head, still sipping, while Shen readied himself. He dusted off dirt and squeezed out what little water there was from his scarf, then wrapped it around his neck, just below his chin. From the leather bag at his hip he pulled a fresh map he'd bought at the market stall, more or less the same as the previous one, though with more embellished edges with designs of flowers and vines. It still covered the same area, that being the territories of Batung, and a cut off portion of Ogon to the right of the mainland, the largest mass of land there was on the paper.

He looked to the second largest land mass, about a third of the size of the mainland and to its far left, and read the word 'Lujing' scrawled onto it in black ink. That was their destination, and it would be a fairly short trip, almost the same distance they'd already traveled to get to Shuijiao. The hardest part though, would be getting past the dockmaster and onto the ship, inconspicuously.

Lao finished up his tea and set the cup down onto the table, standing now. There was an ache in his shoulder, where the wound and the bandage lay. "Shen? Shouldn't you change my bandaging?"

"I did last night, while you were asleep." Shen said, stuffing the map back into his bag.

"Really?"

"Yes. You're a pretty heavy sleeper."

"I guess so," Lao muttered. He walked over to the tunic at the back of the chair and grabbed it in his hands. The fabric had dried out and was soft again, still clutching onto the smell of the water, just barely. He put it over his head and pushed his arms through the sleeves, feeling the soft fabric glide across his skin, then tightened the strings at the front and checked to make sure the hood was still attached behind his neck. Sure enough, it was still there. "Let's go!" Lao shouted chipperly.

The two walked out, making sure not to leave a single thing, and Shen even grabbed a pair of wooden bowls and wooden forks and stuffed them into his bag, making a mental note to himself to get a bigger bag, or even a second one, if they got the chance. With a lock of the door, the two descended the stairs and Shen handed over the little golden key to the innkeeper.

"Hope you enjoyed your stay, boys."

"Yes, sir, it was quite nice!" Lao said smiling.

"Well I'm glad to hear it, little one," the old innkeeper cooed. Shen simply stood, a hand on Lao's shoulder, smiling and nodding to the old man. "The docks should be just up the road, to the north, there should be a sign once you get up there. Take care now." With one more goodbye, and a wave, Shen and Lao started up the road.

"So, how are we going to get on the ship? Don't we need a ticket or something?"

"Not here. But, they do check if you're a Mystic if you're not on the list. And of course, we can't have that happening, right?"

"No. That would be really bad."

"Exactly."

"But, then how are we going to get past the guards, or the dockmaster?"

"I have an idea. Tell me, how good are you at pickpocketing?"

"Hmm, well, I haven't done it in a while, but I think I can manage it."

"Alright. Then listen close." Shen leaned in close and laid out the plan, telling all the details of both his part and Lao's. By the time he'd finished explaining, albeit with a bit of pausing in order to gather his thoughts, the two of them had reached the docks. "Okay, you know what to do," Shen muttered and was off, carefully walking into a crowd at a nearby building and slipping behind it.

Lao smiled, and walked ahead toward the dockmaster standing just before the dock leading to a large wooden ship. The ship was built strong, planks held firm by nails and metal brackets that dulled with weathering, and people were walking all through the little plaza by the docks, talking amongst themselves.

The dockmaster was a certainly burly man, dark tanned skin and a thick moustache along his upper lip, dark black on his face. His brown eyes peered at everyone, as his eyelids sat squinting. He held a little book in his hand, the papers weathered a bit, fading with age. Lao walked up to him, hands in his pockets, fingers running over the fabric inside them and fiddling with something in one. "Mister, have you seen my big brother? We're supposed to get on the ship and I can't find him." Lao's voice wavered, dipping down lower as if choking back tears.

"What's your name, little guy, and your brother's? I'll see if you're on the list." The dockmaster leaned fairly close to Lao, and he could just barely see crumbs of bread in his moustache as he smiled. Behind him, there stood a guard cloaked in bronze armor and a bronze helmet upon her head, with bright green feathers at the sides. From behind a building nearby, a rock came flying by and struck the soldier right in the side of the head, sounding a *clank* against her helmet.

"Hey! Over here!" A deep voice cried out from the area. "Come and get me!" The guard became angry and ran in the direction of the rock. The dockmaster turned around and looked for any sign of the perpetrator, hoping to catch a glimpse of them, putting the book into his pocket.

Quickly, Lao swiped the book from the dockmaster's pocket just as he ran toward the sound after the guard, and pulled the item from one of his pockets. It was a little piece of charcoal, blackened and smudging Lao's fingers. He turned the pages frantically and found two empty spaces, then hurriedly scrawled the names 'Shen Jin' and 'Lao Jin' on the paper, doing his best to try and match the handwriting of the other names. He then put the book into the waist hem at the back of his pants and the charcoal into his pocket again, then put his hands behind his back.

"Come on! You gonna catch me?" The voice seemed to come from everywhere. It sounded from behind one building and then from another, and all through the road. The guard was busy running through each of the buildings, and the dockmaster was running up and down the street in his search. "That the best you can do, moustache man?"

"Come out, now!"

"It doesn't work like that!" The voice was still coming from all around, and soon, the dockmaster walked back to the docks and the ship, after stopping two more guards and getting them in on the search. He looked out again, in the direction the rock was thrown, and heard no more voices.

"Sir?" Lao said, tapping the man's back.

"Yes?" The dockmaster turned to Lao and bent down toward him.

"You dropped your book, sir," Lao said, handing him the book from behind his back, wiping his eye with his other hand.

"Thank you, little guy," the dockmaster said with a smile, and took the book back into his hands. The first guard shortly returned, out of breath, beads of sweat gathering on her dark tan forehead, and the other two guards were in the same condition, standing behind her.

"Sir, there's no sign of him. He must've gotten away."

"A shame. But, there's no use in looking for him. We have business to do after all. I've gotta get this ship all packed up and on its way," the dockmaster declared.

"But sir, what if he's a Mystic?"

"Nonsense. Probably just some prankster trying to get his rocks off." The dockmaster stood for a moment, and then broke into a hefty laugh. The guard looked to him, a serious and unamused look on her face, and a red mark peeking from the side of her forehead. "Alright, not that funny. Anyway, son, what is your name?"

"Lao, sir. Lao Jin." Lao muttered.

"Lao! There you are!" Shen came running up behind, a bit out of breath himself, but held together fairly well. "Hello, sir. My name is Shen. I see you've found my little brother," he said to the dockmaster.

"Shen!" Lao wrapped Shen in a hug, burying his face into Shen's chest.

"I'm here, little guy. I just had to run and get my bag." Shen hugged back, a bit surprised, and patted the side of his bag.

"Hmm." The dockmaster brushed his fingers against his moustache and then opened up the little book. He flipped through the pages, skipping over the names that had been marked with charcoal lines through them and those free of marking. Soon, he came upon the two names, and put his finger to them. "Shen and Lao Jin, here you are! Go right ahead." The dockmaster stepped aside and gestured for the two to get to the ship, closing the book and pointing toward the dock with it in his hand.

"Thank you, sir." Shen began walking with Lao onto the dock up to the ship, before the dockmaster grabbed him lightly by the arm.

"Hey, keep an eye on your brother. I got a little sister at home, and I try to keep her out of trouble as best as I can. You keep him and yourself safe, Mr. Jin." He said sternly, yet had a subtle hint of kindness to his voice. Shen understood this, and nodded to the dockmaster, then ran his fingers through Lao's hair, ruffling it, then led him onto the ship.

Soon, the two of them settled into the bustle of the ship, and Lao began to notice some things. First, the passenger cabin of the ship, somewhere between the middle and the back of the ship, was relatively small. It was about the size of the lobby of the inn they'd stayed in the night before. The walls were lined with people, most about middle-age, but some were quite old, with little children in tow in some cases. Huddled in blankets and draped in cloth garb ranging in color from green to brown, they sat against the walls, with the space in the middle filled with piles of rations of berries and bread.

An old couple at the left wall was sitting calmly, when the woman with glasses against her face noticed Lao. "Young man, would you and your brother like to come sit with us? We have some space."

"And we don't bite, unless you tempt us," the other woman spoke, smiling and brushing a strand of dark gray hair from her green fading eyes.

"Song! Don't say that, you'll scare the boy." The woman with glasses on her wrinkled face nudged her partner in the side.

"Hey! I'm just kidding, Su. You know that." The other woman placed her head against the woman with the glasses's shoulder.

"Um, yes. I suppose that would be quite alright." Shen spoke, and walked Lao over to the two, keeping him close by. He noticed there was optimal space, and settled in quite nicely with their own mound of blankets. "Thank you, ma'ams."

"You're welcome. What are your names, if I may ask?"

"Shen Jin. And this is my brother, Lao." Shen placed an arm around the boy's shoulders and pulled him close to him.

"Hello," Lao muttered, a bit shy.

"Nothing to be scared of, little one. My name is Su, and this is Song." The woman with the glasses said softly, and reached out a calm and wrinkled hand to Lao and Shen. Lao shook it first, feeling the copper ring around her finger. Shen did the same, and then Song reached her hand out. Again, the two shook her hand, Lao first, and felt the copper ring around the finger closest to her pinky.

"So, what's taking you to Lujing?" Shen asked. Lao sat next to him, huddling close, chewing lightly on the inside of his cheek.

"Su and I are going back home from vacation. Shuijiao was quite beautiful."

"Especially this time of year," Su chimed in.

"I agree. My little brother and I were here to see family."

"Oh? Well that's nice. I hope you enjoyed yourselves." Song spoke.

"It was wonderful." Shen said softly. He pulled the pouch of tree nuts he'd gotten in the forest from his bag and pulled out a handful of them, popping one into his mouth. Chewing calmly, he held out his hand to the two women. "Care for some?"

"Oh no thank you, deary. My teeth aren't possibly strong enough anymore."

"Mine are," Song muttered, and grabbed three of them into her hand, the grainy surface of them brushing against her wrinkled palm.

"Help yourself," Shen smiled.

Soon, the ship was on its way, and Lao could feel the faint patter of water and waves under him along the bottom of the ship. Through the trip, Su and Song bickered a bit back and forth to each other, all while Shen was trying to sleep. At one point, while the two of them were arguing over which of them looked better for their age, a conversation both Lao and Shen wanted no part of, Lao interjected, changing the subject.

"Excuse me, but, do you know where I could go to get some air?" The boy spoke, leaning over Shen and looking toward the women.

"Yes, little one, if you go that way, you can go onto the deck," Song said, pointing a gnarled finger toward the back of the passenger cabin.

"I'll go with you, Lao." Shen said, standing up. He brought his hand down for the boy and helped him up, then led him out of the doorway and up the small steps onto the back deck. The view over the side of the ship was breathtaking, a brilliant sun shining its light against the rippling waves. Shen looked out, awestruck, and stood at the side of the ship, looking out on the waters as fish jumped out of them, silver scales glimmering in the light.

Lao, simply wanting to get some space from Su and Song, was looking around at the people on the deck. There was of course guards posted, swords held at their sides and bronze armor shining in the sunlight, feathers at the sides billowing ever so lightly in the breeze. Then, he noticed a woman, staring into her hands. Curious, Lao walked to her and spoke up.

"Excuse me, are you okay?"

"Hmm? Oh, yes. I'm just… I'm thinking."

"Oh. Why are you going to Lujing? I'm just a bit curious. I can go if I'm bothering you."

"No, you're quite fine, young man." The woman tucked the thing she held in her hands down into one of her pockets. Lao noticed this, but decided not to say anything, for fear of bothering her even further than he felt he already had. "I was sent away by my parents. They don't want me at home anymore." She began to get choked up, clutching the fabric of her shirt at her chest.

"Why's that? If you don't mind." Lao leaned up against the side of the ship, next to the woman, and was looking down at his feet as he tapped one of them against the wooden deck.

"I wanted to marry a boy… from Ogon. And when I told them about it, they were furious, and they put me on this ship to go stay with my aunt Yang in Lujing."

"Why couldn't you just stay there and marry the boy?" He was curious, naive, unsure of what the right thing to say would be, so he simply spoke his mind as best he could.

"I have no where else to go. Aunt Yang is the only one I can really turn to now."

"Can I tell you something, ma'am?"

"Sure," the woman said, and wiped a few tears brewing in the corners of her brown eyes.

"When I was about ten, I ran away from my parents. They were awful to me. They would yell at me and throw things at me, and one day I just couldn't take it anymore. So I hid in a wagon and rode all the way to the docks, where I got on a ship and went to Yedao." In between certain words, Lao would get a bit choked up, pause, and then continue on through his story.

"That's awful!"

"Yes, and even worse, I had no one on Yedao. I was alone on the streets. But now, I'm here, on my way to Lujing with my big brother!" He seemed to cheer up in an instant, the thought of his new friend, Shen, in his mind.

"That's nice. I hope your trip goes okay." She said, a soft smile upon her lips.

"You too, ma'am. I'm sure things will turn out alright." Lao gave a little smile and then scurried off to Shen, tapping him in the side.

"Yes, Lao?"

"Come on, let's go back to the cabin, I wanna get some sleep."

"Alright," Shen spoke. The two filed down back into the stairs and found that Song had fallen asleep, pressed firmly next to Su, who was biting at a piece of bread she held in her hands. "Ah, hello again, ma'am. Everything alright?"

"Quite, deary. She tuckered herself out from all that bickering. She'll be out like a rock for a while," Su giggled, biting off another piece of the bread. Shen and Lao sat back in their places, untouched since they'd gotten up in the first place. Lao wrapped a few of the blankets around himself and quickly drifted off into a light snooze while Shen and Su talked amongst themselves.

"Tell me, Su, where are you and Song from exactly?"

"Oh, well, we come from a little old town in Lujing. It's a nice place. Though, not much to do there, so you can understand our trip to Shuijiao, eh?"

"Of course."

"What about you, young one? Where are you from?"

"Well, ma'am, if it had a name, I'd certainly tell you. But, it's a small island, I can tell you that much. And it's north of the mainland, closed off from everything else."

"Are you going back there?"

"No, ma'am. I'm afraid not. Though, if I could, I certainly would." The two sat in silence for awhile, until the sunlight peeking through portholes shifted into a pale moonlight which illuminated very little in the cramped passenger cabin. Soon, Lao woke from his sleep and found that Shen was the only other person awake besides himself. Su had fallen asleep earlier, and was calmly breathing while her eyelids fluttered with unknown dreams. "Lao, is everything alright?"

"Yeah. I just had kind of a bad dream."

"Would you like to tell me about it?" Shen was calm, concerned, rubbing Lao's arm gently with his hand to try and calm his nerves. Lao shook his head softly. "Alright. Well, if you want, you can lay your back up against my side and I'll keep you company while we wait for the ship to stop." Silently still, Lao nodded his head and then shifted himself, putting his back up against Shen's side, as he'd said, while Shen draped an arm around the boy, keeping him close.

"Thank you, Shen."

"You're welcome, Lao. Now get some sleep okay?" Lao nodded and then calmly nodded off until his eyes shut and his eyelids began fluttering with better dreams. Shen soon fell asleep too, into a sleep that was unaroused by neither wave nor nightmare.

In the morning, Shen, now well-rested, awoke with a yawn and looked to Lao. He found that the boy was now gone, missing. Even more strange, everyone else was gone too, only blankets and bread crumbs left behind. "Shen!" Lao's voice called, which was followed by the sound of footsteps coming down the stairs from the deck.

"Lao. What's going on?"

"We're here. We're at Lujing. Come on!" Lao hurriedly pulled on Shen's arm, leading him out of the ship and onto the docks nearby, the blanket once wrapped around his body fallen to the middle of the floor in the passenger cabin.

"Alright! Alright!" Shen said through chuckles, being dragged along by the boy. The rest of the passengers were gathered onto the docks, and guards were posted nearby, looking through the crowd. Shen's heart dropped slightly, and then he quickly started pulling Lao into the crowd, pushing person after person out of the way to get past the guards.

They made it out of the group, through everyone, and past all the guards, while Lao remained silent, putting the pieces together in his head as he saw some of the guards examining some of the passengers' necks. As they continued down the docks, Lao looked back and saw the young woman from the deck. She was looking again at something in her hands, but she was smiling this time, some tears staining the dark tan skin of her cheeks. She looked up and noticed him, smiled again, and then waved to him, a small golden necklace in her palm, the chain wrapped around a few of her fingers. Shen led Lao down the docks, until they arrived just outside of them, and onto a dirt road.

Saddle Up

Going on down the road, Shen began to look the map up and down, running his finger along the paper carefully. It seemed as though the distance they would have to travel got farther and farther, especially if they continued on walking as they were. Shen noticed a small, unnamed port town nearby, and decided they'd stop there. He thought perhaps they could get a better way of moving along, something better than walking all the way in bare feet in Shen's case, or sandals in Lao's. The town was a ways away to be sure, made even more grueling on foot, but it was a more tolerable journey than walking all the way across Lujing.

Throughout the whole trek, Lao couldn't stop complaining about the pain in his feet. Shen was silent for a while, looking toward Lao each time he would speak, until the nagging finally got to him. "Lao, what is the matter?"

"It's so far. And my feet hurt!"

"Just a little bit longer, Lao. My feet hurt too, you know. I mean, I'm not even wearing shoes at all." Shen winced each time the bottoms of his feet, bruised and scratched, met with a jagged section of gravel or a protruding rock.

"Do you have any stories you can tell me?" Lao asked, lagging a little bit behind on the path.

"Would you like to know how I first learned to use my powers?" Shen looked to Lao, now next to him, and smiled.

"Yeah!" The little boy ran up next to Shen, the pain in his feet seemingly vanishing. His eyes were wide and his mouth was open in a little grin, showing off his teeth. Shen flicked his wrist upward and a little rock floated up to it, and as he rotated his hand a bit, the rock began to circle around it.

"When I was a little boy, very little in fact, my father started to teach me how to move rocks. We started simple, just some pebbles in the garden. But, I couldn't for the life of me figure out how to move them, without using my hands of course."

"So what'd you do?"

"Well, my father sat me down in front of the gravel in the garden by the flowers, and he said to me: 'look at the rocks,' and of course, I looked at them, as strange as it seemed. I stared at them with all the might I could manage. So, after a few minutes of staring at the rocks, my father said: 'now aim your palm at one of them,' and I did." While Shen talked, Lao looked toward him with awe, little twinkles in his brown eyes. "And after a few minutes of that, he told me: 'now feel the rock, feel each bit of earth in it and feel it with your being.' Now, I didn't know what that meant, but even still, I did it."

"Then what happened?" Lao chimed in.

"I focused incredibly hard, and I could feel the rock in myself. I didn't feel it in my head or deep in my chest, but I could feel it there, very faintly, in all of me. And once I felt it, I moved it, and I brought it toward me too quickly and it smacked me right in the face." Shen chuckled a bit and then heard Lao giggling right next to him. There was a big smile on both of their faces, and Shen could feel a warmth in his chest he hadn't felt in a long while.

As they walked on, Shen still held the rock, floating around his hand, and now added two more to it, all rotating around in the air around his hand. He could feel their weight in his body and all through him as they moved about. Soon, they could both see the town nearby, the sun raining down light onto the fields surrounding it. Suddenly, the rocks dropped, clattering onto the gravel on the ground. A single guard nearby the path into town was looking off, not noticing the two of them walking, his bronze armor shining in the sunlight that hit it. They got closer, and the guard finally noticed the two of them, and then placed his hand on the hilt of his sword at his side. "Who are you?" He shouted.

"Please, sir, we mean you no harm," Shen pleaded. Him and Lao walked up to the guard, slowly and calmly, their hands at their sides. "We just want to go into town."

"Who are you?" The guard said again. He was squinting, and the helmet on his head had its usual green feathers dusted with dirt.

"My name is Shen, and this is my brother Lao."

"Hi." Lao muttered.

"That's all I needed to know. I usually know everyone that comes into town, we get a lot of regulars, but, when I saw you two, I didn't recognize your faces. Thought you might've been bandits, but you two don't look like bandits to me. All's good." He smiled warmly, which put Shen's nerves at ease. "But I will have to take that sword of yours, just for the time being. It will be placed in the armory where you can pick it back up when you leave. Just say your name to the man at the counter and he'll give it right back to you." The guard spoke with such a cadence and speed, that Shen could barely keep up with the words that he said.

Shen took the strap from off his shoulder and held the sword in the scabbard in his hands, then gave it up to the guard. The guard grabbed it in one hand and then placed the side of his fist to his chest in a salute with the other and smiled. "Safe travels."

"The same to you," Shen said. He saluted back at the guard and Lao, who had been looking up at Shen, looked to the guard and saluted to him as well, albeit a bit awkwardly. The two then continued on into the town, not through any gates, but along the path offshooting from where the guard was posted. The town was fluttering with life. People danced around in the square, and little children dangled their feet down and swung them as they sat atop barrels. There were little stub-horned dogs with thick wooly coats prancing around as well, barking and playing amongst each other.

    One of the little dogs ran up to Lao and ran all through his legs under him, brushing its coat against his trousers. It had little horns atop its head right in front of its floppy little ears, the horns reflecting some sunlight with their peach color and metallic sheen. Its coat was a beige color, and its eyes were a bright pale blue, a deep contrast to the black pupil that watched from the center of the eyes. Tiny legs with dainty feet tapped against the stone ground as it ran all around Lao, who giggled as he watched the creature.

    "Hi, little guy," Lao said crouching down. He ran his fingers through the dog's fur on its head, and felt the smooth material of its tiny horns. The dog barked a yapping bark, short and high-pitched, its tail flailing behind it.

    "Lao, we should see if we can find the stables. I think they're that way," Shen said. He pointed to an arrow-esque sign near one of the buildings, and on it there was a picture of a bird's head, big and bulky, burned into the wood with fire, pointing down one of the dirt paths in the town.

    "Alright," he said to Shen, "I gotta go, little guy. But I'll try to see you before I go!" Lao chirped, and the little dog bolted off toward a gathering of little kids, all much smaller and younger than Lao.

    The two continued on their walk, now on the path the sign had designated, and the pain in Lao's feet had returned. He didn't say anything, however, as his mind was too preoccupied with the things his eyes saw as they followed the path of the sign. The buildings were all made of strong bamboo, all held together in planks with thatch fiber ties, and the windows were of a fairly clear paper. People went in and out of buildings periodically. There were stores that people went into with coin pouches in their hands and came out of soon after with golden or copper trinkets or with bags of ice and meat or vegetables, depending on the store.

  Running over, Lao entered into one of the stores with Shen close by his side. The door swung open and the bamboo *clicked* against the inside wall. Lao and Shen entered and the door closed behind them, sunlight shining in through paper windows. The little boy's eyes were darting all around, scanning the walls, which were lined with all sorts of landscape paintings and jewelry of fine gold and silver. "Ah, customers! Welcome!" The young man at the front counter shouted, and smiled widely at the two. His skin was a dark tan and he had a thin moustache above his lips"Anything you're looking for in particular?"

  "No, sir, we're just looking," Shen said, walking over to Lao, who was walking all along the walls in search of something interesting.

  He saw necklaces with tiny gemstones placed into the pendants and bracelets of tightly smithed bronze, embellished with all sorts of designs. The paintings were of Batung's brilliant green fields of swaying grass against backdrops of blue skies and mountains. Some he could tell were even imported from elsewhere, like the one of beautiful palm trees in the sand overlooking the vast turquoise waters of Vasai. But none of these paintings really caught his eye as much as a little copper ring in a corner did. "How much is this?" Lao asked loudly, picking it up into his hands and looking all around it, seeing markings etched into the metal, then taking it to the counter.

  "Well, I'm not too sure. In fact, I don't think I remember this piece at all," the shopkeeper said.

"Do you have a price in mind? Anything at all? I'm sure we can pay in some way," Shen began. He started to open his bag up, undoing the flap and reaching his hand in, as the young shopkeeper stopped him.

"I don't suppose that will be necessary."

"You mean you're keeping it?" Lao asked disappointedly, drooping his head and his eyes down toward the floor.

"No, my boy! You are," he chirped, and handed the ring to the boy.

"But, why?" Lao, curious as he was, asked.

"Well, you found it. And I would suppose since I had no knowledge of it to begin with, that makes it yours! Also, it is much too small to fit my finger, and it looks to be the perfect fit for yours."

Lao put it onto his ring finger, and smiled widely to himself as it seemed to fit just right onto it. "Thank you! Thank you, sir!" Lao jumped up and down with excitement, and Shen closed up his bag, looking to Lao with a smile.

"You are quite welcome," the shopkeeper said with a warm smile, and patted the boy on the head.

"We should be going now, Lao." Shen said, leading the boy to the door.

"Okay!"

"Thank you very much, sir," Shen said to the shopkeeper.

"You are so very welcome!" The shopkeeper said chipperly, and waved goodbye as the door closed and the two of them were back onto the dirt road.

As they by an alley in between two buildings, Lao saw something that made his heart sink a little bit. There was an old man, withered with wrinkles upon his face, wrapped in blankets and sleeping on the ground in a corner. The blankets were riddled with holes, and some had little black bugs crawling all over the fabric. Standing above the old man, keeping him in the corner, was a man with big bulky shoulders and a dagger in his hand. The blade glinted in the little bit of light that shone down from the sky into the alley. His head was clean-shaven, with bruises all along the skin. Lao stopped dead in his tracks at the entrance to the alley, and Shen noticed this after walking a few more steps, then stopped himself.

"Lao, what is it?"

"That man. He's going to hurt that old man," Lao muttered.

Shen walked back to Lao, and watched with him as the man twirled the dagger in his hand. Just then, Lao ran forward at the man, and bumped into his back. "Lao!" Shen shouted, running after the boy.

"Hey! Don't hurt him!" Lao was smaller than the man, but still thought he could stand a chance, even as the man turned around to face him. Upon his dark-tan face, there was a deep scar down his right eye which blinded it, turning it pale and clouded. He wore a face of anger and huffed heavy breaths as he stared down at the boy before him.

"What did you just say?"

"You heard me!" Lao felt a surge of confidence rush through him, as if he was unstoppable.

"Lao, stop!" Shen grabbed at Lao's wrist and pulled him back behind him. "Sir, please. He didn't mean any foul-business to you. I promise."

"Don't get in my way," the man said, and then turned back to the old man cowering in the corner.

"You can't do that!" Lao broke free of Shen's grip and ran around him back to the man, then placed a firm punch on the man's back. The man straightened his back and slowly turned his head back around to Lao.

"Did you just do what I think you did?" The man was becoming frustrated, a firm grasp on his dagger tightening evermore now.

"That's right!"

"Lao, stop, now," Shen said in a stern tone.

"You should listen to him. You wouldn't want to get hurt would you?" The man turned fully around to Lao and brushed his finger against the metal of the dagger's blade, bright and bronze. Instinctively, Shen moved his arm back for the sword, perhaps for intimidation, only to find it was of course gone from its place, residing in the armory elsewhere in the town.

"That's enough." It was as if Shen had changed completely in a split second, his tone dropping down to a more serious one, and his eyes staring knives into the man. Shen thought for a bit, just staring at the man in front of him, scanning over every little detail. The scar was old and fading, but still all present on his face, a grim reminder of a blade that Shen could tell the man never forgot the feeling of. After a few more moments of thought, Shen came up with an idea. "How about a deal?"

"I'm listening," the man put his dagger into the holster at his side, a tiny brown leather one with a strap that hung around his waist. He put on a little smile, which was off-putting considering the number of cracked and yellow teeth in his mouth.

"A fight. No weapons and no killing. The last man left standing wins," Shen said as seriously as possible, "if I win, you let the old man and us go, and you leave this town."

"And if I win?" The man was intrigued, a thin black eyebrow raised at Shen.

"If you win, you do whatever you want to that old man and I will give you all the money in my bag." Shen pulled out the little coin pouch after opening the bag's leather flap, and shook it around in his hand, the silver coins inside jangling and clinking against each other. For a few moments, the man scratched at the skin of his chin and looked at the pouch.

"Fine. But we fight right here, and right now," the man said low, "and the kid stays away." The man's head swiveled to the boy standing next to Shen.

"Alright," Shen turned to Lao, "Lao, get out of here. Wait for me right outside the alley. I shouldn't be too long," Shen spoke in a low whisper, kneeling down to Lao's level. "You need to go, though. Please."

"Shen, I can't."

"You have to. I'll be fine, I promise," Shen said, and gave a smile to Lao. Lao didn't smile back, scared, the thought of what might happen to his friend lurking in every part of his mind. But all the same, he nodded and walked off behind Shen out of the alley, then sat down on the ground against the wall next to the alley's entrance.

Shen was left, standing in the alley, the man staring him down with a glint in his eye and a smile on his mouth. He began unbuckling the waist strap that had the scabbard which held the dagger at his side, and tossed it to the side onto the ground. "You know, man, you got some real nerve. You know that?"

"This? This isn't nerve. This is probably more stupidity than nerve," Shen said. He was free of weapons, not a blade or even a stick in sight. He took his bag into his hands and placed it softly along the wall of the alley, right up against the bamboo planks of the building next to them.

"Couldn't have put it better myself. Now, we gonna do this?" The man readied himself, crouching his legs and taking an offensive stance with his fists raised up at the ready. Shen simply stood still, looking him up and down, getting a good fix on him. He saw the weight shift from foot to foot through each leg as the man bounced in his position and prepared to fight. Shen took his own stance, a rather awkward one, with his feet firmly planted the same way as the man, in a general fighting position, though with one hand behind his back. The other hand was held up in a clenched fist, ready to strike.

"Your move," Shen mumbled.

The man lunged toward Shen and threw a lazy punch, which Shen ducked under and swooped next to the man. In a quick motion, he flicked a rock toward his hand from behind him and using his powers placed it up against the front of his fist along the fingers. Swiftly, Shen swung his own punch at the man and struck him in the back just below his neck. Each muscle in his skin could be felt all forming around the rugged rock with the punch.

Shen jumped back a bit, getting into the corner and discarding the rock from before. As the man gathered his wits, Shen brought up another rock and placed it right in the same place as before, all away from the man's sight, thankfully. The man huffed a mighty breath and lunged forward again at Shen, but ducked a bit this time. A firm hit was laid into Shen's stomach, and he could feel the air escape his lips from his lungs as it landed. Dazed, he managed to hold onto the rock with his powers, and swung his fist down to place a strike against the back of the man's head.

The man doubled back and huffed again, then placed a hand at the back of his head. Bringing his fingers to his face, he could clearly see a bit of blood dripping, red and warm. He wore a face of pure anger, and the usual huffing he once did was now a rage-fueled puffing that increased as he dashed forward toward Shen. Shen's eyes widened and he just barely brought another rock from the ground behind him before the man tackled him to the ground. One of the man's hands was wrapped tightly around Shen's throat, gripping and groping as he squeezed the airway shut from the outside. The other hand was preoccupied with punching Shen across the face as hard as his weary state could muster.

Shen's face became red and strained, veins popping from his forehead, and blood began slowly dripping from his nostril. His arm was outstretched as he lay on the ground. He looked toward the gravel on the ground, the rocks and pebbles, and he began to focus. He focused hard with his hand clenched in a fist, and he felt for the rocks and brought them to the surface of his fist. The rocks all gathered, forming a layer of the jagged pebbles all along his fist. As more and more air was squeezed out of him from his throat, Shen put all the force he had into one swing, punching the man square in the side of the jaw, and down he went.

Sprawled out, unconscious, bleeding and bruised, the man lay on top of Shen with his legs bent haphazardly. As he laid breathing heavily, Shen shed the rocks from the skin of his fist and stayed breathing for a moment, taking in all the air that could be had. After a few moments of regaining his breath, Shen pushed the man off of him and sat him up against the wall of the alley after dragging him. He then walked over to the old man in the blankets and shook him, rousing him from his sleep.

"Sir. Sir, you need to get up," Shen muttered.

"Hmm?"

"Come on," Shen said, and stood the man up, putting his arm across his shoulders and starting to walk, "I'm going to get you out of here."

"Sun," the old man mumbled and walked with Shen, his head hung low and his eyes toward the ground.

"Yes. Yes, sir, the sun is very bright this time of day." Shen shook a bit of pain from his hand for a moment, but it shortly returned.

"Leaf," the old man pleaded. "Cold… Flower…" The old man was muttering to himself, mumbling as he stared down at the ground.

Finally, Shen had gotten the old man to the outside of the alley, and Lao ran to his side. "Shen! You did it!" He shouted with a smile.

"Yes, Lao."

"You're bleeding!"

Shen brought his fingers to his upper lip and felt a cooling liquid, then waved it in front of his eyes. It was indeed blood, the red staining his fingertips. There were bruises all along his head and his face, and they stung every once in awhile. "So I am."

"Are you gonna be okay, Shen?"

"Of course, Lao. I can handle a street fight enough," Shen said as he tilted his head to Lao, smirking.

"Is he okay?" Lao noticed the man was still mumbling to himself and became a little worried, as well as somewhat scared of the strange old man muttering nonsense to him.

"Yes. I'm sure he's fine. He's just a bit out of it is all. I'm sure." Shen himself didn't understand what was wrong with the old man, but knew all too well that he had to say something to Lao, or he would never stop asking. "We have to get him somewhere safe, away from that man."

Shen looked all around. There was a building with men of burly stature and wiry beards tending to hot metal at the anvil, pounding at it with hammers. Next to that, he saw a sort of stall where a shady looking man in a robe was selling fish that could be smelled all the way from where Shen and Lao stood. Further down, he saw a local apothecary with a wood-burned sign of a mortar and pestle above the door and various green herb leaves and flowers were hanging against the outside by the paper windows. Without a second thought, he shuffled the old man and Lao over to it and opened the door.

Inside, watering a small plant in a wooden pot, there was an older looking man, slouched over with his little metal watering can. The shop smelled of wonderful scents like lavender and sage, and there were beautiful green lanterns hanging from the ceiling with willow and blossom trees painted on in delicate strokes. "Be right there," the man said, and put on a warm smile. His back was bent, and his belly big and rounded, which gave him the appearance of an old moss-tortoise, made more evident by the frilly sort of green robe he wore.

"Sir. We need your assistance, right now." Shen set the old man from the alley down in a nearby wooden chair, blankets still clinging to his scrawny frame. His eyes were wide open, showing brown irises with beady black pupils.

He kept mumbling those words, over and over again. "Sun… Leaf… Cold… Flower…" He whispered it softly to himself. It was almost chilling to Shen's ears, and certainly to Lao's.

"Oh my! Mr. Yimu!" The man placed his watering can down next to the wooden pot with a *clink* against the bamboo floor, and quickly shuffled over to the old man in the seat. "What is it, sir? Is everything okay? Was Zi Tai getting on you again?" The man muttered, rubbing his hand on one of the old man's shoulders slipping from the blanket.

"Sun… Leaf…" The old man simply kept repeating those words. "Cold… Flower…" It seemed even the man who knew him couldn't decipher the meaning of the words, nor why he spoke them in such a specific order. Neither Shen nor Lao could figure out why he kept on repeating it, why they were the only words that could come from his cracked lips.

"Excuse me. I don't mean to interrupt, but who might I ask is Zi Tai?" Shen interjected, and fiddled with his hands a bit in waiting, feeling the bruises start to form against his skin and within his muscle.

"He's a nasty man, always coming in and harassing me for more shangyin. He even shakes down poor old Mr. Yimu here for it!" The man went into the back of the store for a moment, and shortly returned with a small stone cup of water. He walked back to Mr. Yimu, still mumbling in his spot in the chair, and put the rim of the cup to his lips. "Drink. Drink."

"Shangyin?" Lao questioned.

"Yes, Lao. It's a plant. It can help with very severe pain when combined with other herbs."

"But it is very potent and dangerous on its own," the man interrupted. "Zi Tai only wants the pure plant from Mr. Yimu and I so he can peddle it to more of those thug types outside of town. I can't believe they'd be so cruel as to hurt a poor old man like Mr. Yimu."

"You won't have to worry about Zi Tai any longer in this town, sir. For now, we must leave. Take care of him for me, will you?" Shen said as he began walking out of the door, Lao walking with him in tow, as the man stood up.

"Would you like me to help with those wounds of yours?" The man asked, but the two of them were already out of the door and back on the dirt path toward the stables. They walked on, and soon they came upon the burned wood sign of the bird's head just above a larger bamboo building. With a little push of the door, it swung open and inside was lit by a few candles and a single green lantern in the center of the ceiling above them. The room was quite short, Shen having to duck slightly in order to keep his head from bumping into the lantern as they entered into the room.

Behind the counter, there seemed to be no one, and nothing, save for a little metal wind chime hanging by the side of the counter. Lao, curious as he was, reached over and poked at the wind chime. Each of the several metal rods of various lengths jangled against each other for a few moments before dissipating into a soft hum that hung in the air. "Just a second!" A feminine voice called from a nearby closed door, a simple one of a lightweight bamboo that would simply swing open in place.

Soon, the voice returned and was accompanied by a face. Bright green eyes shone within the head of a shorter girl, about middle-aged, who had sweat all along her dark tan skin which she wiped from her face with her arm. Her black hair was brought up into a messy bundle which had a mess of brown and gray fuzzy feathers hanging on all over. She ruffled a hand through her hair and adjusted the dark green bandana that was wrapped around her forehead, then the thin fabric farming robe she wore loosely upon her chest with the sleeves pulled up. "Phew! He is a handful, I will tell you that," she said, "now, what can I do for you boys?"

"We're looking for suitable mounts for our journey. I assume we have the right place?" Shen asked.

"You assume correctly, sir!" The girl placed the side of her fist against her chest and smiled widely. "The name's Xue Yimu, at your service!"

"Shen Jin," he said saluting back. "And this is my little brother, Lao." Lao smiled at the girl and saluted to her, and then brought his hand back down to his side, smiling a bit at her.

"Well, it's very nice to meet the two of you. Would you like to see the birds?" She asked.

"Yes please," Shen said. Lao simply nodded and followed behind Shen as the three of them walked through the swinging door Xue had entered from. Xue was leading them into the stables themselves, a facility which looked like just another part of the main building from the outside.

The floor was covered in all sorts of straw and leaves, dry and dead from being cut down and placed there. A smell of waste lingered in the air and nipped at Shen and Lao's nostrils, which Xue just shrugged off as if it was nothing. Sunlight from outside shone in through slits in the walls like windows, though with empty frames so both the light and air could come into the stables. Lao looked around, pinching his nose to avoid the harsh smell, and noticed a few empty stable stalls until they reached the back end.

There, standing with its back turned, staring at the wall, was a large dimian bird. It was a majestic-looking beast, standing up on huge stocky legs riddled with dulling yellow scales the same color as its beak. Its feathers were puffy and ruffled a bit, and every once in awhile it would shake off a fly from its body that had nipped it. It had a thick body and little wings held close to its sides, and a long neck that craned up until it ended at its head, with feathers above its eyes flared up like eyebrows. Turning slowly, it began to tap on the ground a bit, until it revealed its face. Staring back at Shen, Lao, and Xue, were big orbs of yellow with tiny little black pupils in the center. The creature shuddered a bit to itself, and then belted out a loud *squawk* at Shen.

Taken aback, Shen couldn't help but giggle at the sight of the bird. "This is Ping. He's the handful I mentioned earlier," Xue said. The bird let out another *squawk*, this time in Xue's direction. The once majestic creature was now akin to a bumbling idiot, beady little pupils always staring ahead at the wall behind them. Every now and then, Ping would duck his neck down and sniff at Shen's head, then let out more *squawk* sounds before snapping back to staring at the wall. "He's a bit," she paused for a moment, "special. But he's a complete sweetheart," Xue said. She reached her hand up to the bird's head and begun to scratch softly at the feathers, while Ping leaned his head into her palm.

"He has a beautiful coat," Shen said, holding in a bit of a chuckle. His feathers, while indeed ruffled, were quite soft to the touch as Shen and Lao ran their palms along his back, feeling it as soft as cotton fabric. Lao stopped petting abruptly as his eyes were caught by a new sight in the stall across from Ping's.

There was another dimian, smaller, clearly a juvenile, sitting down with its head nestled into its body feathers. This one's feathers were a deep grayish brown, and one particular patch at the center of its forehead was colored a pale white. As Lao stepped closer to it, it brought its head up and fluttered its eyelids open, showing big black pupils with yellow around their rims. Suddenly, it stood up and backed up into the darkness of the back corner of the stall away from Lao, letting out low chirps as it crouched.

"Qiu! That's no way to treat a new friend," Xue said, and turned to the bird, walking over to the stall while Shen was busy patting Ping's head. The bird became less reluctant, stepping toward Lao for a moment, until the boy brought his foot forward, when the bird jumped back into the dark corner, chirping softly to itself again. "Sweety, can you do me a favor?" Xue knelt down in front of Lao, who nodded his head. "I need you to hold out your hand for her. She needs to get your scent, alright?" Lao nodded and Xue walked back behind him to where Shen was, grabbing a saddle hanging from the bamboo beam next to Ping's stall.

Lao brought his arm out, holding it above the stall door, with his palm open. Once more, the bird stepped toward him, moving her head ever so slightly as she neared closer. Lao made no sudden moves, and the bird continued on her path toward the boy. Qiu gradually came into the light, and her eyes seemed warm and comforting, her yellow beak shining in the light of the sun coming in from one of the windows. She brought her head down toward Lao and began sniffing at his palm. The boy could feel each breath of air go into her nostrils to then be pushed out back against his skin. Abruptly, Qiu pecked slightly at his hand, which made him pull his arm back swiftly. Qiu brought her head up and tilted it to the side, her eyelids blinking a bit.

"There you go! Good girl!" Xue finished helping Shen onto the back of Ping's saddle and walked back over to Lao, bringing her hand up to pet at Qiu's head.

"Wait, she's okay with me?"
"Of course!"

"Then, then why did she just try to bite me?" Lao stammered.

"She's just gotta get used to you. She wasn't trying to hurt you, she's just curious," Xue assured him with a smile, which served to put his nerves at rest a little bit. Xue scratched at her hair for a second and then retreated to the back of one of the stalls.

"Where are you going?" Lao asked.

"Getting you a saddle, little guy. Hang on, I'll just be one second." Xue rifled through piles of discarded leather with mounds of straw placed on top of it all. There were pieces of the leather, made from the hide of ram-horn deer, with little divots in the surface and with metal rivets deeply pressed into the leather. Finally, she came upon a smaller saddle, long discarded from when she used to race as a child.

"Thank you, ma'am," Lao said with a smile.

"No problem! Now, you'll need to put it on her if you want her to trust you. Okay?" Xue handed the saddle over by the straps into Lao's awaiting hands. Lao became slightly frightened, wondering whether or not the dimian would try to bite him again, or kick at him with her sturdy legs. But all the same, he pushed the door to the stable open and entered, the saddle held firm in his hands.

Qiu let out small, curious chirps as the boy got closer, and her eyes darted down to the saddle. Quickly, she dropped down to the ground, nestling her legs up into her belly slightly as she crouched low. "What's she doing?" Lao asked.

"She's coming down to your level. Now, put it on her, slowly and carefully," Xue cautioned.

Lao grasped at the heavy saddle in his hands, and calmly walked up to Qiu. He brushed a hand against the feathers atop her head, and sat the saddle ever so gently onto her back. The bird flinched a bit, a few feathers near her eyes twitching slightly, until she relaxed and brought her head up. Opening her eyes, Qiu snapped her beak a bit and let out a low chirp, then lifted her left leg up, bent, held close to her chest. "What's she doing now?" Lao asked, still a bit uncertain of the dimian.

"You see those straps on the sides?" Xue asked, and pointed to the leather straps dangling down either side of the saddle near Qiu's wings. Lao nodded. "Those go around her wings and her legs, like a harness. Go on. She trusts you enough now."

"Are you sure?"

"Of course."

"You'll be fine, Lao," Shen interjected, riding slowly close to where Xue stood. He was sat atop the saddle on Ping's back, smiling as he bobbed with each step the dimian took forward. Ping turned his head sharply, looking toward Lao with his big bulging yellow eyes and beady little black pupils, and let out a soft *squawk*. "She can't be any more unmanageable than Ping here," Shen said as he patted a hand against the dimian's side.

Lao worked up his nerve, and slowly, he grabbed hold of the left strap and brought it carefully over and around Qiu's leg. It was pulled through, and her wing with it, which she fluttered around softly, comfortable in its place. The strap rested softly in the feathers of her belly and she snapped her beak again in a bit of joy. Lao took the other strap into his hand and carefully did the same thing as he did before, putting her right leg through it. Again, the dimian fluttered its wing after it was pulled through the saddle harness strap. "Well done, Lao!" Xue shouted.

Lao stepped to Qiu's side and started to climb onto her back, onto the saddle. Suddenly, the dimian crouched down again, bending her legs up against her chest again. "Thank you, Qiu," Lao muttered, and calmly pet the bird along the back of her neck. He climbed on fully now and gripped at the holds on the front of the saddle, located just below Qiu's neck. Qiu stood up, and wobbled a bit as she found her balance. She brought her head down and preened at the feathers on the base of her neck near her breast. "It's very wobbly up here," Lao said, keeping his rear firmly planted in the seat of the saddle, holding on tightly to its holds.

"You'll get used to it," Xue said.

"Thank you very much, ma'am," Shen said, "how much do we owe you?"

Before Xue could answer, the sound of the wind chimes from the front desk rang through the stables, and Ping began to stamp on the floor with one of his feet. "I'm in the stables! Come on back!" Xue shouted. Pushing open the door into the stables, the person entered and Shen and Lao both looked toward him. It was the old man from the alley. "Dad!" Xue said, and ran to the old man covered in blankets, hobbling over to them.

"Sun… Leaf…" The old man looked up into Xue's eyes and peeked through squinting eyes.

"Dad. How many times have I told you? No more shangyin. No more! The stuff is destroying you!"

"Ma'am," Shen interrupted, "is your father okay?"

"I'm afraid not, sir. He's been sick for a long while. And I've told that apothecary to stop giving him shangyin time and time again! It's no good for him." Xue helped her withered father into a chair by the stable door and began to rub at his shoulders. "Dad, no more shangyin. Please."

The old man looked up to her and whispered. "Sun…"

"Xue. This may seem out of nowhere, but, do you by any chance know a man by the name of Zi Tai?" Shen asked, bringing Ping over to her.

"I hate even hearing that name. My father has almost been killed by that man too many times! I've had it!"

"You won't have to worry about him coming around anymore. I took care of him," Shen said. He rubbed at his hands, bruised and cut up, and smiled toward Xue.

"You killed him?" Xue asked, taken aback.

"No no no, he's alive. Beaten, but alive. I can assure you, though, he won't be coming back to this town ever again."

"Thank you. Thank you so much, sir. Please, if there's anything I can do-"

"Just, please let me know how much for the birds." Shen smiled.

"Free! Completely free!" Xue shouted.

"Nonsense," Shen said as he flipped open the flap of his bag. He reached in and pulled out the little coin pouch, feeling the soft leather against the skin of his palm. He unlaced the string and opened it up, then put his fingers inside and seized ten little silver coins. "Ten Yin. Please," he said, and held out the coins to her in his palm.

"That's more than enough for you, sir. Thank you." Xue got up and led the two of them, mounted on their dimians, to the large back door of the stables. She pushed it open and large amounts of sunlight flooded in. "Here you are. Safe travels to the two of you," she said chipperly.

"One more thing, ma'am. If I may ask, where can we go to get some more coin? We're quite low, and we'll be needing more soon." Shen said as he brought Ping out of the door somewhat, turning the bird to see Xue.

"Let me see your map, I know a place I can mark on there for you," Xue said. Shen placed the coin pouch, filled with twenty little silver coins, back into the open bag, and then pulled out the rolled map parchment. Xue unrolled it and took a small piece of charcoal from her pocket, then traced it along the paper, placing a small dot marking on the parchment, a ways north of where they were. "It's a place called Senhong Alley. Go there at night, and try to find a man named Tian Lo. He should be holing up in a dark corner. Ask him to play a game of Chengshi with you. I know all of this sounds quite shady, but it's your best bet if you want some quick coin."

"Thank you, Xue. Come on Lao, we should get going if we want to get there near nightfall."

"Thank you, ma'am," Lao said. Qiu made a little chirp and stamped against the dirt ground.

"Awe, it's okay, sweetie. Lao's gonna take good care of you, okay?" Xue said warmly. The dimian quickly calmed itself, as if understanding the words Xue spoke. Shen and Lao left, waving goodbyes to Xue and her father, who sat in the chair and smiled at them as their birds walked down the dirt road toward the town exit where the armory was located.

Know Your Opponent

       Shen and Lao, firmly planted on their dimians, made their way to the armory quickly and entered through the doorway after tying Ping and Qiu to posts outside. Inside, there was a man stood at the counter, fiddling with a knife in his fingers, sitting lax in a small and frail chair with one leg crossed over the other. He ran the tip of his finger over the blade and looked deeply into the reflection of the silver metal. Suddenly, Shen tapped his foot onto the ground and cleared his throat loudly. The man sliced the tip of his finger slightly as he jolted from his seat and came crashing to the floor. The chair below him had crumbled under the weight of his movement, and he pulled himself together after a few moments and stood up with his back straightened before Shen.

    "Yes, sir! What can I do for you?" He said loudly, his finger wrapped in the cloth of his tunic.

    "Are you okay?" Shen asked, raising a thin eyebrow.

    "Yes. Of course," the man behind the counter brought his finger from his tunic, and a big red splotch of blood was stained into the fabric. Along the tip of his finger, there were little beads of blood forming and then dripping down the side of his finger.

    "Your finger is bleeding." Lao pointed out.

    The man looked to his finger and could feel pulsing bits of pain from its tip "So it is," he said. He wrapped his finger once more in the fabric of his tunic, this time on the other side, and put on an awkward smile. "So, what brings you to the armory?"

    "We're here to pick up a sword that's been left with you," Shen said, "my name is Shen."

The man went into the back room and the sound of many metallic objects clattering to the ground could be heard, followed by a pained 'ow.' A short time later, the man emerged and brought with him the sword, sheathed in its leather scabbard with the strap dangling down by his arm. The man wore a crooked smile on his face as he set the sword down on the counter and rubbed at a fresh bruise on his forehead.

"Thank you, sir," Shen said. He grabbed the sword from the counter and tore off the tag reading his name on it, placing it down on the table. Then, he placed the strap around his arm and his neck, the scabbard coming to his back with a little bounce.

"Don't mention it. You two have a safe trip." The man brought his hand down from the bruise on his forehead and saluted to the two of them, and they graciously returned the gesture, Lao finally getting it right.

As they walked out of the building and back to their birds, Shen pulled the sword from the holster and spun it around in his hand. Not a single blemish, scratch, or dirt mark could be seen. The blade shone brightly in the light of the sun. Abruptly, Ping let out a loud *squawk* and snapped his beak toward the blade.

"Ping! Calm down!" He moved the sword's blade away from the bird quickly and put a hand against the bird's forehead. However, Ping continued trying to snap at him with his beak, trying to get at the sword in his other hand. His beady little pupils were fixed onto the shine of the blade as he *squawked* and snapped his beak.

"He really wants the sword," Lao said with a chuckle, climbing on top of the saddle on top of Qiu as she knelt down to his level. As she stood back up with Lao on her back, Qiu let out a low chirp, which Ping darted his head toward.

"No kidding." Shen placed the sword back into the scabbard and patted Ping's back. The bird knelt down with his legs bent and uttered another low *squawk* as Shen climbed on top of him, grabbing at the handles of the saddle firmly. The both of them pet the feathers on the back of their birds' necks and soon they were off down the road.

After about half the trip toward Senhong Alley, a long and mundane journey in all fairness, the dimians started to become tired, Ping especially, and the evening was just breaking. Shen patted on the side of his bird's head and the bird let out a loud *squawk* which served to rouse Qiu, who was walking next to them with Lao sat atop her back. Her legs became wobbly as her feet made contact with the dirt path below. "Lao, we should stop for a while," Shen said. His eyes scanned across the landscape and he could see a billowing stack of smoke come from behind a hill of emerald grass.

"Alright, Shen," the boy said, "how's that sound, Qiu?" Lao brought his head up and around to look at the bird's face. Qiu let out a little chirp and tapped her foot onto the ground. "Alright, let's go then."

They continued on, and Ping began to become less snappy. He was certainly more quiet now as they neared closer and closer to the source of the smoke. All of them were fairly quiet, save for a few passing chirps from Qiu as they passed by small rodents burrowing through the ground or rooting through the grass in search of field bugs. Lao observed this carefully, his eyes to the side in the fields, looking at the flowers and the patches of tall grass.

He rather enjoyed watching as a little field mouse pounced onto a particular bit of grass, only to be bombarded with a swarm of tiny bugs, beating at the creature's fur with little wings. The flowers were beautiful during this time of year as well. There were some in brilliant yellow shades that the field bugs would nibble on, gathered in great packs in the cup created by the petals.

The purplish white flowers that dotted the field scarcely were prime targets for the field mice to pull down to drink at the dew left over from morning.

    Before they knew it, they'd found the source of the smoke, and were each delighted to find it was a small village. The smoke was coming from one of the smaller huts by the stream at the back of the village, puffing out from a hole in the thatch roof and climbing up into the sky where it thinned into nothing once it got high enough. People in the village were quite divided. There were older people, who were busy tending to the little farm fields of soybeans, and younger kids, who occupied themselves in other ways. The children of the village chased each other around in fun little games they played, and laughed and giggled as they did so.

    There was one person unlike the others in the village, though, who caught Shen's eye. He looked to be about teenaged, and sat at the base of a tree with his eyes toward the ground. Black hair was hanging across his forehead below his wide-brimmed farmer's hat, shielding his dark tan skin from the sweltering sun. The tree he sat under wore no leaves, pale and dead and beaten by the sun's heat, with limbs outstretched where little birds would perch. There was a long stalk of grass he held in between his teeth, suckling at it out of lack for something better to do with his time, his mouth shaped into a pout to echo this fact.

    Shen moved Ping in the boy's direction and Lao followed with Qiu, until they were just before him. "Excuse me, do you know where we can get some water? And maybe some food for our birds?" Shen asked, clearing his throat once again.

    "Ask one of the elders. I'm busy," the boy snapped.

    "Doing what?" Lao asked, his head tilted.

    "Lao, don't prod, it's impolite."

"Waiting. I'm on lookout for the soldiers."

"Soldiers?" Lao asked, his head still tilted in the usual inquisitive manner.

"All the adults of the village joined up with the military years ago, when I was a kid."

"But aren't you *still* a kid?" Lao asked.

"No! I mean, I'm a teenager. I'm sixteen. But, that's besides the point, I'm waiting for them to come back. My mom sent me a letter that they were coming. They're going to come back, I know it. Soon." He seemed unsure of himself, and yet said it in such a way that Shen could almost picture all the soldiers making their way into the village, clad in shining bronze armor glinting in the sunlight.

"That's wonderful," Shen said, "now, again, do you know where we can get some food and water?" The teenage boy pointed to the hut with the smoke billowing out of the top, his face shrouded still by the shadow of the farming hat.

"There. Old man Yu lives there. Tell him Nai sent you," the boy said, and without using his fingers, shifted the stalk of grass over to the other side of his mouth.

"Thank you, young man." Shen patted the back of Ping's neck and the bird lurched forward, bound for the hut at the back of the village. Lao and Qiu followed too, and the dimian carrying the boy chirped lightly as they began to walk through the dirt path of the village.

The village was cloaked in a kind of thin smoky air at eye level which contrasted the sunlight above. There were scattered fires by some of the huts, built up with gathered bamboo and logs and nursed by some of the elderly that weren't tending to the farm land with long tools. Crops were dull green and dusted with dark brown dirt, soaked with fresh water from underground irrigation systems crafted out of heavy stalks of bamboo. Farmers looked up briefly from their crops and smiled at the two on the backs of the dimians, wrinkled faces hidden under the shade of their hats. They waved at them and then quickly returned to the crops, digging through the soil and every once in awhile kneeling down to pick at one of their leaves.

    The two of them made it to the hut and noticed that there was not a post in sight for them to tie their birds to. Shen thought for a moment, thinking up a solution to this, and then figured a plan of sorts. "Lao, could you please go in and get Mr. Yu? I'll stay out here and watch Qiu for you." Lao nodded and then tapped at Qiu's neck. The bird then crouched down low, and the boy jumped down onto the ground.

    As he entered into the hut, Qiu stayed sat against the ground, her legs bent up into her breast, her neck craned back and her beak preening at the feathers of her little wings. Shen pet at Ping's feathers and the bird let out low chirping sounds as he did so. Qiu waited patiently, her big eyes darting every now and then to bugs that would buzz around her head. After a few more moments of waiting, Lao exited the front doorway of the hut, followed shortly by an old man with a long graying beard and a bald head.

    "I'm back," Lao said, climbing back on top of Qiu, who happily chirped as she stood back up from her sitting position.

    "Ah! Mr. Yu! Thank you so very much for taking the time."

    "You're welcome, young man," the old man spoke low and walked with a thin bamboo cane in one hand. "Now, what supplies do you need exactly?"

    "We just need a bit of water and perhaps some food for the birds here," Shen said, and brushed his hand down the feathers on the back of Ping's neck. "We'll pay."

"No need, sir. We've got plenty, and even if it were not the case, any friend of my grandson Nai deserves proper supplies." Mr. Yu retreated back into the confines of the hut while the two waiting outside sat atop their dimians, the birds crouching down to the ground to sit and rest their weary legs. Shen got up off of Ping as he sat, and stood next to the bird in waiting for Mr. Yu. Lao did the same, while Qiu nestled her head into the feathers of her neck. The old man emerged once again, carrying with him a small waterskin and a few apples in a sack. "Here you are, boys. I assume this will be enough."

Shen set the waterskin down on top of Ping's saddle, then untied and reached into the sack. He pulled from it two apples, then tied it back up, tossing one of the apples to Lao, who caught it awkwardly in his hands. Ping began to sniff at the apple held in Shen's hand, craning his neck over and sniffing wildly at the fruit. Suddenly, the bird tilted its head to the side and snatched up the apple with its beak, throwing its head back as it chomped down on the apple and then choked down the pieces.

Lao, after letting out a fair little laugh at the strange bird, held out the apple held in his hand to Qiu. The dimian, curious with her head tilted, brought her head down to to it and began to sniff. Once again, Lao could feel the air breezing past the skin of his palm as the bird inhaled and exhaled. There was a twitch of the brow feathers above her eyes, and then she pecked at it. A little chunk came off and into her mouth, and she swallowed it down joyfully. She came back down for more, taking an even bigger bite this time. A few times she did this, until there was nothing more than a core left over. "Good girl," Lao said, tossing it to the side and placing a hand on the back of Qiu's head to caress her feathers.

"Thank you very much sir, we greatly appreciate it."

"It's no trouble, really." Suddenly, a great noise filled the air and mingled with the smoke which held above the hut. It was a horn, a long, droning note which rang with a sound similar to an animal's cry. Both Shen and Lao stood with confusion upon their faces. Yet, Old man Yu bore an ecstatic look. "They're home! My son!" He quickly scurried off, his bamboo cane clicking furiously against the dirt path.

Shen quickly got on Ping's saddle, the waterskin resting firmly between his thighs, and took hold of the saddle's handles. He tied the light sack of apples to the strap of his bag with a thick string he had, where it rested right up against the bag. Lao got up onto Qiu's saddle, and the bird calmly chirped as she turned around toward the path ahead. They walked down, Shen leading, with Lao close behind, until they reached the dead tree near the center of the village. Though, it was different now. Nai, the boy from earlier, was nowhere to be seen, missing entirely from the withered trunk of the tree.

Old man Yu was also not to be seen, but not for long, however. From behind one of the larger huts at the entrance to the village, there came a large grouping of people. Most of them were the regular citizens the two of them had seen upon entering and walking through. But, there were a few clad in dulling and scratched bronze armor, unshining. Men and women alike walked in the cluster along the dirt path, a clamor rising amongst them, until they made it to the area around the tree.

Shen could see families reuniting. He could tell that the worn faces with heavy eyes of men and women were those which were as once spry and young as they'd been when they left. Elders laughed and cried as their children were returned to them. It had been so long. "You're home, and without a scratch on you!" Shen heard from one of the old men. In his arms, wrapped in embrace, there was a man, his black hair draped down his neck as his helmet laid useless on the ground. Still, neither him nor Lao could spot Nai. Not even Mr. Yu could be seen, or the sound of his walking stick be heard tapping against the ground.

There was another voice speaking now, a worn and bruised man, one of the soldiers. "We lost the island. Vasai has it now. I'm… I'm just glad to be home," he said solemnly. Shen thought back to where he'd began on his journey, staying on the island of Yedao where he'd later find Lao. To its southwest, there was a smaller island, called Lucao, which had been having territory disputes between Batung and Vasai for many years. No longer, as it would appear.

After minutes of watching as families joined and shuffled back to their huts, there were only three left behind. Mr. Yu and Nai were standing by the tree, their arms collectively wrapped around a woman. Her armor was heavily scratched, and her arms were wrapped in an assortment of bandages, all stained with a fading red. She held her face in Mr. Yu's neck, and from where they were, Shen could hear the faint sound of sobbing. All three of them stood there, dust kicked up in a breeze at their feet, crying to each other.

Lao could feel a heat bubbling up inside his chest, and he began walking Qiu over to them, quietly and calmly. Once he'd gotten there, he waited a while until they had let go of each other. "Hello, young man," the woman said breathily, sniffling and wiping tears from the top of her cheeks.

"Hello."

"Young man, I'm terribly sorry. But, now is perhaps not the best time," Mr. Yu spoke softly, his wrinkling cheeks painted a red upon the dark tan and caked in tears.

"Here. It may not be much, but please take it." Lao let go of the saddle's holds for a moment and took the copper ring from off his finger and handed it to the old man. "It's for the apples and the water." Lao smiled and took hold of the handles again.

"I can't possibly accept this, young man."

"If you won't, then she can have it," Lao said, smiling widely, and gestured toward the woman in the armor with a nod. Mr. Yu pondered for a moment, looking down on the ring, and then smiled to himself. He then handed it over to the woman, passing it off into her calloused hands.

"For me? But, my fingers are too big for it," she said, a small smile on her lips.

"You can put it on a little chain and wear it as a necklace!" Lao said chipperly. "Now, I've gotta go. It was nice meeting you, Mr. Yu!" He left before the woman could even introduce herself, and as he walked Qiu back to Shen, the three of them all waved softly toward the boy. Shen had simply been watching the whole time from his distance, smiling to himself.

"That was very nice of you," he said softly.

"Well, she was sad. I couldn't just leave her be like that. And besides, I didn't need the ring anyway," Lao said, and then started walking Qiu toward the entrance they came into the village from. Shen smiled once more to himself, and then followed after the boy, quickly getting in front of him again and leading the way.

The road was long indeed, but the path was not riddled with harrowing tasks or dangerous creatures, as Lao thought it might. It was a peaceful ride. Qiu chirped softly as they passed slow under canopies of trees, and Ping was a bit quiet throughout. Though, when they encountered an animal, whether it be a forest bird or a tree rodent, Ping would belt out a wild *squawk* that would frighten the creature. When he did this, Shen laughed it off and Lao too, giggling to themselves as they moved along.

The landscape of Lujing was beautiful to them. As they saw it, the tall trees in the forests and the bright emerald grass of the plains, their hearts were filled with a sense of adventure. The greens were everywhere, and they kept them going when things got tiresome. Every now and then, Lao would find a rock poking from under the sole of his foot, kicked up by one of the birds. He'd shake it here and there and eventually the little pebble would free itself from his sandal. It would hurt at first, but then the boy would look to the side of the path again, and he'd see the sun dipping lower and lower toward the hills.

Soon, night was upon them. The two could just see a huge forest ahead, the size unlike the ones that came before. The trees were tall and buildings of brick and bamboo were weaved throughout their trunks. Light from lanterns hung up and strung through the forest shone with a warm glow that was deeply encased in the darkness of the leaves and the sky. The forest was directly connected at the right by what looked like a city. The buildings there were tall and strong, built of brick and wood, held by the great pillars of bamboo that grew in the forest next to it. Lanterns extended to the city, and Shen decided to stop there, turning Ping toward it on the path.

"Where are we going?" Lao asked.

"If the mark Xue put on the map is right, we can find Senhong Alley there," Shen answered, pointing a finger toward the city. So, after all the traveling that they'd done from the village, the birds would have to put up with more still until they could reach Senhong and have a proper sit down. By the time they arrived in the little city, the sun had found its bed in the confines of the hills, and the stars took their place. A canvas of brilliant white lights twinkled in the sky against the black of the night sky.

The city was quiet, and only a few people gathered in the dirt streets. Most was silent, no sound besides hushed talking and the clicking of Ping and

Qiu's feet against the dirt and gravel. People swiveled their heads in confusion as the dimians walked the streets. Lao figured it was because they were new to the area, having never been there before. Shen thought the same, and neither of the two actually said anything out loud on the topic.

    They passed under shoddy signs for smiths and for general shops, and even one for golden trinkets, as Shen could tell from the ring of gold engraved into the wood hanging against the building. But, as they walked, they found an offshoot of the road through the city. It veered right, and wormed its way through through the buildings and led into the forest. Above it, posted on one of the buildings, there stood a tiny sign reading: 'Senhong Alley.'

    "This is it."

    "Are you sure we should go, Shen? I don't like the look of it," Lao said warily. Noises came from the corridor made by the buildings. There were noises of talking, like loud whispers that crawled out into his ears. And there was a kind of music, too. It was nothing more than a hum, and a subtle drum beating in rhythm, but it was noticeable all the same. The humming was like a singing, a music that sounded ancient and chilling.

    "We have to get more money, Lao. I know it's intimidating. But, just stay close to me and you'll be okay." Shen smiled to the boy as they passed into the offshoot path. "Okay?"

    "Okay," Lao said, smiling with his head tilted down some.

    They passed through, and as they did, the music began to get louder and louder. The voices became louder too, and yet Lao still could not figure out what they were saying. The first thing to come into view for the two were the lanterns. Strung all along the buildings were bright glowing lanterns in green and orange and yellow, and some even had designs of birds or flowers painted onto them. The lanterns were followed by people, all walking through the bustling paths through buildings. Sounds of people talking grew and grew, climbing up into the air as the words left their lips.

There were some people sat on the sides of the buildings in chairs at tables, and they were playing games among themselves. Some had tiles of ceramic shaped like stars and flowers, and they were trading them back and forth, while others had cups that they'd rapidly move around after placing something under one of them. "Chengshi!" One of the people shouted from a table in a dark corner of the street. He sat alone, and had an eye scar on his left eye which caused its blindness. "Come and play Chengshi, the game of honesty!" He shouted again.

Shen reluctantly brought Ping over, while Lao and Qiu followed very close behind. When the two of them arrived at the table, there was a convenient wooden post by one of the buildings. Shen got down from Ping's back, and the bird shook its body around, letting free a feather or two to float down to the ground. He tied up the dimian and Lao did the same for Qiu, getting down from her and tying a rope around the post and then one of the loops on the saddle. The two birds were obedient, and calmly sat down in the darkness with their heads up at attention. Though, every now and then, Qiu's eyelids fluttered with tiredness.

"Ah! A player! How do you do?" The man at the table shouted, a fist to his chest in salute.

"Yes. Hello," Shen said, a salute shot in return. Lao was sitting up against the building next to Qiu, while the bird gently nudged his leg so that he'd pet at the feathers of her head. "Would your name be Tian Lo, by any chance?"

"Why yes it is! How did you know?" He shouted, a broad smile on his face. "Wait, did Xue send you?" Tian asked, leaning forward with his scarred, blind eye squinting.

"Yes?" Shen answered, sounding more like a question than an answer, as it had been intended to be.

"Well why didn't you say so! She's a good friend. Great kid, too," Tian said calmly, leaning back into his seat. "I talk to her through messenger lizard all the time," Tian said as he pulled something out from inside his shirt. He seized it, and then held it in his palm. It was a little lizard, brown in color with black striped scales, raised up to give them a rather sharp appearance. The little creature had big blue eyes, and suddenly, a little fly landed on one of them. Its tongue snapped out and slapped its eye, pulling the little fly back into its mouth. "His name is Xiyi."

"Right," Shen said awkwardly.

"So, what brings you? Oh, you want to play a round of Chengshi, right?" Tian said, getting excited and putting the lizard back into the inside pocket of his shirt. He pulled a stack of wooden coins from under the table and placed them onto the table.

"Yes. But, I'm afraid I don't know how to play."

"That's alright! I'll teach you." Tian said. "To start, how much money do you have on you?" Any previous humility or generosity that was gleaned from Tian was wiped away as he leaned forward over the table and rubbed his fingers together greedily.

Shen pulled the hide pouch of coins from out of the bag at his side and dropped it atop the wooden table. "20 Yin. All there." He leaned back and smiled, especially once he noticed a devilish grin creep onto Tian's face. "Now, how do I play?" He asked, half-serious, half-playing dumb.

"Well," he started, "to start, I'll be taking those," he said as he grabbed the pouch of coins. He then reached a hand into his shirt pocket and pulled the lizard back out. "No, not you, Xiyi. Can you grab the chips and the cards for me, little buddy?" He said, bringing his face close to the lizard. The little creature tilted its head for a moment, then crawled into the pocket of Tian's shirt, and came back out with a stack of wooden coins and a deck of cards. "There we go!"

"Excuse me? When do you explain how the game works?" Shen asked.

"I'm getting to that!" Tian protested as he placed the lizard back into the pocket of his tunic and placed the chips and cards onto the table. "Now, each of these wooden chips," he said holding one up, "are worth two Yin. Ergo, you paid twenty, you get ten in return." He slid ten of the wooden chips across the table to Shen.

"Thank you."

"My pleasure. Now, with those chips you place bets on a card that I draw," Tian said, and pulled one of the cards from the top of the deck. "You will guess a number, place a bet, and I will say either 'higher, lower, or correct.' You can either guess a different number, or stick with your answer." Tian smiled and leaned back in his chair. "If you're correct, your bet will be matched by me and your original will be given back. So, you get double what you bet. If you win, that is. If not, your bet will be taken. Simple, right?"

"Sounds like it. Mind if I try a round?"

"Of course."

Shen slid forward one of the wooden chips, which had images of leaves and flowers engraved into them, across the table to Tian. "I think the card is four." Tian thought for a moment, then lifted up the card. He looked to Shen, and his left eye, the blind and scarred one, began subtly twitching in one of its corners.

"Higher," he spoke, a smile still on his face and the twitch still in his eye.

"In that case, I think I'll change my answer to five," Shen said, testing something that was gnawing at the back of his mind. Tian slowly lifted the card, facing him, and then turned it around toward Shen. He could clearly read the number four written in finely stroked ink on the card.

"Looks like you were right the first time. Care for another round?" Tian slid the chip to his side, into his larger pile of wooden chips.

"Sure!" Shen slid another wooden chip across the table and smiled, looking to Tian's face. Tian pulled another card and placed it face down onto the table. "Hmm, I'm going to guess eight." Tian flipped its edge up so that only he could see the number, and then put it back down. His left eye began twitching again, and it remained as he said his answer.

"Correct."

"Then I'll stick with it!" Shen smiled, giddy as almost a child would be, fabricated of course. Tian lifted up the card and turned it once again toward Shen, and the two written on it was clearly seen by Shen in the dim light of the lanterns near them. "Well that's a shame!"

"Another round?" Tian said, sliding the chip into his pile.

"Well I can't stop now! I haven't won yet!" Shen did the same thing once again, sliding a chip across the table and betting on the card that Tian had drawn, face down on the table. "Five." Shen guessed.

Once again, Tian lifted the card so he and only he could read the number, and then he looked to Shen. His eye again began twitching, a soft jitter at the corner of his left eye. The cloudiness was certainly off-putting, and through the fog, Shen could almost make out the outline of his now useless pupil. "Higher." The twitch remained, and Shen pondered for a moment.

"I'll keep my answer."

"Sorry" Tian said. He showed Shen the card and it read a black one on its front. He took the wooden chip again, a big smile across his face, and added it to his growing pile. "Another?"

"You know it!" Shen said, having it firm in his mind that he'd had Tian figured out. He put down seven chips and put them forward. "I'm all in." He then looked as Tian pulled a card and put it down. "One." Shen guessed.

Tian lifted the card a bit and looked at it, and as he went to speak, Shen noticed that the twitch in his eye had vanished. "Correct." He said.

"I'll keep my answer." Shen said. Tian showed Shen the card, this time turning it over on the table instead of holding it up, and sure enough, the number one was written in black ink on the card. "Yes! I did it!"

"Well done." Tian said, passing over seven of his own chips to Shen.

After this, Shen had figured out that whenever Tian had lied, his left eye would begin to twitch. He used this to his advantage each consecutive round, earning a total of forty-two wooden chips. Tian was fed up, and as Shen could tell this, he cashed out and collected 84 Yin from Tian, who had been keeping a stash of the coins under his seat in a heavy bag. "Thank you very much, Tian. I'll use this for a good cause, you can be sure of it."

"Whatever," he snapped.

"Send Xue my regards!" Shen packed the 84 Yin, eighty-four little silver coins, into a larger empty hide pouch he kept in his bag that had once held the tree nuts from Shuijiao. The two of them climbed back onto their dimian birds, and with a wave goodbye to Tian, they were off to the city next to the forest, going through the alley as the sound of the music picked up again and subsequently died out.

"How'd you do that?" Lao asked.

"Do what?"

"Beat him so bad. You were doing awful when you started, but then out of nowhere you beat the pants off him! How?"

"Well Lao, you should always know your opponent." Shen looked to Lao, smiled, and winked.

"What do you mean?"

"If I told you exactly what I did, it'd ruin the secret," Shen protested.

"Alright," Lao sighed, changing the subject, "where to next?" Lao asked, smiling as he rode on and pet Qiu. He ran his fingers through and against the soft brown feathers on the side of her neck. The bird chirped quietly as he did so.

"Judging by the map, we will need to cross the Bridge of Kunan. I'll ask about it in town after we settle in and sleep. Sound okay?" Lao nodded and smiled more. "Good. Then let's go." The two made their way to an inn, paid 10 Yin from their pouch, and slept for the night, bound for the Bridge of Kunan in the morning.

The Path Less Traveled

In the morning, the two awoke with fresh faces and the light of the sun in their eyes. Shen was asleep on a cot near the corner of the room, the sun only slightly reaching him from a side window of the inn room they occupied. Lao, however, was sprawled out on the floor, soft cloth blankets wrapped haphazardly around his legs, with the sunlight directly hitting his face from the paper window. The boy groaned and turned, facing away from the window and toward a wall. "Too bright," he grumbled.

Shen sat up, and with a yawn he stretched his arms out. He placed one arm in front of his face to shield his eyes from the light. "Lao, are you awake?"

"No," the boy answered, muffled and snappy as his face rested in the blankets.

"Come on, get up. We have to make it to the bridge before the evening."

"Why? Can't we just sleep some more and go later?"

"I will explain on the way. That is, if you get up now."

"Why should I?"

"I've got stories to tell you," Shen said, now up and about. He smirked and walked over to the counter where his tunic and his bag rested. Stroking the stubble on his jaw and upper lip with his fingers, he grasped at the tunic and pulled it over his bare body. The cloth glided over his tan skin as he put his arms through their holes. He tied the front strings and then grabbed the bag, tying its leather strap around his waist, letting the bag rest at his hips.

He looked over and saw Lao up off the floor, his blanket folded at his feet and his own tunic worn neatly on his skinny little frame. "Let's go then!" Lao said. Shen reached into the bag and pulled his scarf out, still a bit worn and faded from the waters between Yedao and Shuijiao, which they had traveled over not too long ago. He wrapped it around his neck and the little insignia of the scaly rodent could be seen only slightly, tucked in fabric right by his collarbone.

    The two stopped by the front desk where the innkeeper, a sweet little old lady with tired eyes and dark tan skin stood. She waved and smiled warmly as the two of them left out the front door. Shen and Lao stopped by the inn's stables, a few posts where Ping and Qiu were tied up, and made sure they each ate an apple before they left for the streets. People were already out in the streets, though it was still morning. There were whole families gathered at carts at the front of stores which sold all sorts of foods. Some were selling general things for travelers and merchants, like salted meats or fresh vegetables like soybeans harvested from nearby farms. But, others were more exotic. These carts sold cooked flowers, drizzled in honey sauces, and fried field mice and hopper bugs which were dusted in spices. Curious, Lao tugged on Shen's tunic. "Yes?"

    "Can I get a fried bug?"

    "Don't you think it'd be gross?" Shen questioned.

    "Might be. I just want to try it!"

    Shen nodded and they made their way over to the cart. The man running it had burned hands, knots of skin which were free of any hairs that grabbed at the sticks which the food was skewered through. He smiled as they approached, and then greeted Shen with a salute once they arrived. "How do you do, sir? Care for some treats?"

    "Quite well, thank you. One fried hopper bug for my brother here, please" Shen said, opening the flap of his bag to find the coin pouch after saluting to the man.

"No need to pay! These ones are so easy to catch, I figured I'd just give them out!" The man, with his burned hands, his calloused fingers, grabbed one of the sticks with the fairly large bugs stuck at the top. The bug was hefty, its legs thin compared to its bulky body. He handed it to the boy, who gladly took it.

Lao looked on it with a bewildered look. He brought it up to the side of his mouth, and with his teeth, he nibbled a tiny piece of the bug. There was a tremendous crunch. The innards and the shell of the bug filled into his mouth, and their strange taste, coupled with the potent spices, made for a rather interesting experience. "It tastes… weird."

"Most people say gross or nasty, and some even just throw it away. You are the first to call it 'weird' that I know of!" The man laughed.

"Lao, give me a taste," Shen said, and the boy handed over the stick with the bug atop it. The smell of the spices was strong, wafting their way into Shen's nostrils as he held the bug to his mouth. He took a fairly larger bite, though still a nibble, and stood chewing for a moment. The crunching was still loud, and Shen could feel one of the legs poking at the inside of his bottom lip.

"Not bad."

"Seriously?" Lao questioned with a raised eyebrow.

"Well, I've certainly eaten worse,"

"I don't even want to know," Lao said.

"Ha! Now I've heard it all! Well, I'll let you two be off. Have a good one!" The man said, turning back to his treats.

"Before we go, can I ask you about something?"

"Certainly. I know this town like the back of my hand, you know." The man said and turned back to Shen.

"Excellent. Well, we're making our way to the mainland, and would like to know about a particular path to get there."

"And that would be?"

"The Bridge of Kunan," Shen said in a questioning tone. The man thought for a moment, his hand rested on the bottom of his chin, and then turned again to Shen.

"Ah, yes! I remember now! That place has been around for hundreds of years. There's a man there that can help lead you across. It's rather dangerous to go it alone, and he's mighty friendly. His name is… oh, why can't I remember? Oh! I remember now! His name is Oba. Good man from what I've heard. Now, you best be on your way, Oba doesn't stick around near the nighttime."

"Thank you so much," Shen said, saluting at the man once again, a fist to his chest.

"My pleasure. Take care now!" He saluted back, and then turned around once more to his bugs and his mice, chewing on the fried skin of one of them. Shen and Lao left and made their way back to the birds. The smell of smoke lingered above them, as the fumes from fires burning in houses lifted up and up into the air above. As they approached, Ping began to become excited, stomping against the ground with his feet, *squawking* loudly with his beady pupils aimed at Shen. Qiu was less roused, sitting still on the ground with her legs bent up into her breast.

"Easy boy! Easy!" Shen said, and ran his hand along Ping's neck. He brushed at the dimian's feathers, feeling their softness, while the bird hummed a chirp low in his throat. Lao giggled a little to himself, and then climbed up onto Qiu's saddle as the bird stood up. Shen lightly patted Ping's head and the bird crouched down, his big legs tucked up into his bulky chest. He climbed onto the saddle and bounced lightly as the bird stood up and clicked its beak, ready to head out.

They left shortly, once they had drank a good bit of water from the waterskin. Though the days were getting colder, and they had no need of water to cool them down, they both knew it would be important to keep hydrated on their journey. The birds needed the water too, as they had the harder task of the four of them. They would be the ones walking over huge distances, with little to no stopping in between destinations. It wasn't as if they could outright complain as Shen and Lao could, but that did not keep them from voicing their disdain in the ways they could.

When the path got particularly rocky, and less soft dirt or grass was there to cushion his feet, Ping would become feisty. He would shake his head around and around, wobbling Shen in the saddle's seat, until he would pull him to more softer ground next to the path. These little fits of unease would be accompanied by his signature loud *squawk*, which always served to give Lao a good laugh. And, though he was essentially the butt of the joke, Shen even got a laugh out of it once or twice.

On the path, Lao wondered what this Bridge of Kunan was like. Was it filled with horrid creatures, who would want nothing more than to rid the two of them of their lives? Were there bandits and thieves waiting to steal away all the things they carried with them? Or, perhaps it was a nice place. Was it beautiful, a sight to behold by only the eyes, as words would not do it justice? Were the shores below it coursing with brilliant rocks that held the waves in their grasp as they crashed back and forth from the sea?

Shen had no such thoughts, but that's not to say his mind was entirely blank. He had heard stories of the Bridge of Kunan. When he was a child, his mother, a fine woman with her pale tan skin and flowing black hair, would tell him the story of the bridge. She told him that long ago, in the time before any of the Mystics had even lived, there was a warrior named Kunan Zhanshi. He fought against evil spirits who had threatened his village, and even the whole of the Batung mainland. Through his fight, Kunan experienced many hardships. One of these was his trek across the bridge which would later bear his name. Of course, these were simply tales, and Shen knew that Kunan Zhanshi was most likely a simple soldier, held up to such high esteem by locals. Nevertheless, the bridge was indeed treacherous.

From more recent stories he'd overheard from merchants and traders in taverns on Yedao, he knew the bridge was a force to be reckoned with. It was said to have planks of rotting and thin wood, held up only by string made from animal sinew. The merchant tales always told of strange things being seen all throughout the mist which surrounded the bridge. Some of their stories even had men being dragged into the fog, never to be seen again. But, like most stories Shen was told, they were probably just that, stories, which shouldn't immediately be taken for the truth.

Soon they had begun to near it, the entrance to the bridge, and Shen began to see the falsity in the merchants' tales. For one, the bridge itself was not made of rickety wood planks and sinew string, but hefty stone bricks all stacked together. The entrance was a magnificent arch with pedestals at the sides which held statues of formidable-looking spirits, down on all fours with their fanged mouths open in a roar. Then, Shen noticed something, an old man, hunched over, huddled into a corner and tending to a pot of something with steam rising up from its depths. There were torches, unlit, sat up against one side of the arch by one of the statues, and the old man grabbed at one of them to stir whatever was resting inside the pot.

The old man briefly looked up from his pot, and then brought his head back down and continued stirring. Shen walked up, Ping softly clicking his beak toward the old man, and Lao followed atop Qiu. As she let out a chirp, the old man looked up and smiled a bit. "Hello, travelers. I'm Oba. Care for some stew?" He lifted something from the pot, a wooden spoon, and took a tiny sip from it.

"Not at the moment. But, thank you for the gesture," Shen said cordially. He begun a salute, his fist near his chest, before Oba had stopped him.

"No need! No need! Not sure if you can tell, but I'm not from around here. There's really no need for the Batung salute."

"You're from Vasai, aren't you?"

"Well now, what gave it away?" He pointed up to his eyes, which were a muted gray color. "Most people say the eyes. You won't find anyone, Batung or Ogon, with eyes like these."

"Your skin, and your looks; you look a bit like my grandfather on my mother's side. She was from Vasai."

"Was?"

Shen thought for a moment. "Um, yes. I haven't seen her in such a long time now, since I left home."

"I assume you're on your way back?"

"You would assume correct."

"And who's the young one with you?" Oba pointed a crooked little pinky at Lao, who was calmly sitting atop Qiu. The bird was lightly preening at her feathers with her beak, clicking it every now and then.

"My younger brother, Lao."

"Hello," Lao said shyly, waving a hand at his side.

"Hello. You two are here to get across the bridge, yes?"

"That's right," Shen said, and got down from Ping's back. "If you'd be so kind, could you guide us?"

"Certainly." Oba smiled and grabbed at a waterskin, taking off the little metal cap. He took the pot into his hands by the handles, and carefully poured the broth into the waterskin. As it filled up, and his hands rested on the leather surface, Oba could feel the warmth of the stew against his skin. He took the cap and placed it back on, like a cork, and slung the waterskin's strap over his shoulder. "That should do it." He reached over and grabbed one of the torches into his hand, then pressed its tip into the fire beneath the pot. It lit softly, the flames jumping onto its surface, and then Oba kicked some dirt onto the hot coals. "I'll let it put itself out, I should be back soon enough," he said as he smiled.

They began walking and as soon as they stepped foot along the bricks, Shen realized a truth to the merchants' tales. The area all around was misty, covered in a thick fog, one which they hadn't noticed on their way onto the bridge. It was so dense that none of them could see a thing right in front of their faces. They all huddled close together, but not so close to let the torch set fire to their clothing. Though, at times, Shen could feel the heat of the flames of it nipping at the stubble on his jaw. "Oba, have you heard the story of this bridge?"

"Of course. The great Kunan Zhanshi is a great legend, you know."

"He is? I've never even heard of him" Lao said.

"Well then, young one, why don't I tell you the story?" Oba cooed, and smiled warmly at the boy.

"Yes please!"

"Hmm, where to begin... Oh yes! I know. Now, long ago, in the time before the Mystics, when the gods still reigned, there was a simple man. He came from a lonely little farming village on the outskirts of the mainland. Now, this man, he had no name. His mother, his father, they did not give him one. They thought that the boy should live up to his name, and make it himself. And so the boy lived on and on, until his mother and his father both passed. At that point, he was only referred to by his last name, Zhanshi." Oba took a moment to pause, his mouth becoming dry and his lips cracking and chapped.

"Are you okay?" Lao asked.

"Yes, young one, just a bit parched is all."

"We have water if you need it," Shen said, reaching for the waterskin on Ping's back, who was walking at his side.

"No need. I can continue." As Oba continued on with his story, the fog seemed to clear a bit, and Shen and Lao could see sharp, jagged rocks coming into view around them. "A man now, Zhanshi's village soon became the target of evil spirits. The creatures were huge, big hairy beasts with mouths of teeth like daggers and eyes of piercing yellow. After they attacked more and more of the village's soybean crop, Zhanshi grew tired, and decided to challenge the spirits. He met them here, on this very bridge, and they fought. Zhanshi fought valiantly, and vanquished all but one of the spirits, but at a cost. He was carried back to the village, bleeding, and upon his deathbed, the villagers dubbed him Kunan. Kunan Zhanshi, the suffering warrior."

"That was very well-said, Oba."

"Thank you," the old man said.

"Another, another!" Lao jumped up.

"Please, Lao, we can't bother him too much. Let his throat rest," Shen said as he felt his scarf droop down a bit on the back of his neck.

They walked on without many other words, snaking through along the brick bridge. Soon, more of the jagged rocks came into view, and the sound of the waves crashing into them could be heard underneath. Shadowy shapes wormed around in the mist, whipping back and forth. Shen looked all around, seeing all the rocks, and once he grew tired of that, he examined Oba. He seemed content, quiet, and yet, there was something off about him. His neck was exposed partially, as part of his robe was drooping down on the back of his neck. It took him a moment to see, but as the torch's flame swayed more and more over it, he could see it. There was a light blue spot, a part of his skin, right on the back of his neck.

"Oba, how far until we reach the mainland?" Shen asked, warier now.

"Not too far, I imagine."

Out of nowhere, one of the shapes slowly emerged from the mist, and lashed around at Shen and Lao's feet. It was almost clear, though with little specks of dirt lodged in it. It whipped around at their legs, smacking into the bridge and exploding into water. Shen looked to Lao, who was walking beside Qiu, and shouted to him. "Lao! Get to me, now!" The boy ran over, leading Qiu with him. But, another shape came from the mist, a water tentacle of sorts, and it wrapped itself around one of Qiu's legs.

"Qiu!" Lao screamed. The dimian let out a shrieking chirp, and kicked at the water with her other leg. It was no use, though, as a second water tentacle came from the mist like the first, and wrapped itself around her other leg. "Qiu! No!" Lao tried to run to her, his arms outstretched, but Shen was holding him back, his arms around the boy in a tightly locked hold.

"No, Lao!" As the water tentacles pulled and pulled, they dragged the bird into the mist, off the bridge and down into the water and the rocks below. A shrill call could be heard going down, and then stopped. Shen looked over at Oba, who stood still, one hand holding the torch up, and the other at his side.

The other hand was moving back and forth, side to side, whipping around at the wrist. "You!"

He turned around, looking over his shoulder, as another water tentacle drifted to him and pressed against the flames of the torch. The fog crawled in around them, and visibility was almost nonexistent. All that could be heard was the crashing of the waves against the rocks, and the faint sound of footsteps against brick. "Where are you?" Shen shouted. He reached into his bag and pulled out a medium-sized rock, and held it in the palm of his hand. From next to them, a water tentacle rose up and whipped at them. Quickly, Shen moved the rock, and guided it into the water, smashing against it with a splash. He then brought it back to him, back into the palm of his hand.

"Why? Why are you doing this?"

"I knew what you were. I saw the mark. How could I be mistaken by one of my own kind?" Oba's voice came, cutting through the mist.

"Answer me!"

"You can't know about me. You can't know, you can't go and tell them. Do you know what they did to me? To my family? Everyone always finds out. I can't have that!" Another water tentacle arose, and grabbed at Lao's ankle. Shen quickly threw the rock into the water, severing it, letting it splash to the brick. He had no way of telling where Oba was. He only had his voice to go off. "You will not leave here alive!" Shen put his arms out, extended at his sides, and he felt every little rock, every pebble, and he brought them to him. They all formed around his hands, and all over his arms.

"Lao, get down."

"But-"

"Now!" The boy quickly crouched down onto the ground, his arms instinctively draped over his head. Shen raised his arms in front of him, his hands open and facing outward, coated in rocks, and he fired them all out in a wave in front of him. Most of them simply cut through the fog. But, a few of them clattered against rocks, and a very small number hit the target. Once he heard Oba shout out in pain, he lunged forward a bit and moved his hand to the wall of jagged rock to the right of the bridge. He felt around with his senses, and grabbed onto a chunk of the rock, moving his arm toward the bridge, taking a sharp pillar of rock with it, without ever actually touching it, as the nature of his senses was.

"You won't best me!" Oba jumped forward over the pillar, and came into view through the fog. He brought his hands up and water moved with them. Then, he dropped his arms down, and the water whips fell and crashed upon the bridge, cutting it and letting the bricks burst around. Feeling the shock from the bridge under his feet, Shen brought a few more rocks to him against his hands, then turned to dodge as another burst of water flew at him. As he spun, he crouched down and launched two of the little rocks at Oba's legs, hitting him in the knees. "Ah!"

"Lao, stay behind me with Ping!" Lao ran around to Shen's back, and found Ping. Ping was knelt down on the bridge, his legs tucked up into his chest, his head hung low. He was chirping low, clicking his beak, and his eyes were closed.

"Ok!" Lao shouted.

"You think you can protect him? I thought I could protect people too. I thought I could protect my family! I thought, and I thought wrong!" Oba brought another tentacle of water up from the side of the bridge, and lashed it toward Shen's feet. Shen let the water strike him, and he tripped, as the force of it beat against his ankles. But, as he lied on the brick of the bridge, cracked and rough, he felt for another chunk of the rock wall to the right of them, and then moved it into the bridge. The bridge split at the brick, cutting a deep crack along the center. Oba lost his footing, and fell backward onto his rear.

"I know I can protect him!" Shen brought another rock to him and then launched it at Oba once the old man had gotten up. The rock smacked him in the stomach, and he doubled over as it did. Shen latched onto another chunk of rock and broke it off from the wall with his senses, and then waited, his hand controlling the rock held behind his back. When Oba readied another water tentacle, and right as it was about to strike at Shen again, he ducked and moved the rock into Oba's side. It crashed into him and knocked him to the ground. Quickly, Shen grabbed onto another section of the rock wall, with both arms outstretched, and brought it quickly to Oba, encasing him in the rock and pulling him back to the wall.

"No! No! You can't!" He squirmed. Shen walked Lao over, with Ping close behind, scared and chirping as he clicked his beak. They looked on as the mist began to clear, revealing the old man, beads of sweat dripping down his face. "You! How did you… How?" He shouted. His eyes were wide, his mouth jagged and wicked in its form, and his hair was unkempt.

"What kind of sick man would kill an innocent dimian, would try to kill a child?" Shen shouted.

"You… you can't leave here! You can't tell them! I… I won't let them take me!" He shouted into the sky, and both his hands, held firmly at his sides, flicked upwards, as two blades of water slashed at the rock holding him. They gave, bursting in puffs of rock, dust, and pebbles, and he crashed down onto the rocks. He was still stuck, but now, the rock holding him was freed from the rest of the wall, and he was now falling down into the water. It struck the jagged rocks a few times, and he could be heard shouting as he fell, before everything went silent. The fog crawled out, and left as the other end of the gate could be seen. Shen sat down, falling to his rear, and let his legs stretch out in front of him.

"Shen?" Lao asked.

"Yes?"

"Qiu's dead, isn't she?" The boy had tears in his eyes, and sat up against Ping. The soft feathers of the dimian were somewhat comforting. But, not comforting enough to ease the oncoming grief.

"Yes. She's gone now, Lao."

"Do you really think so?"

Shen leaned over and took Lao into his arms, letting the boy's head rest on his shoulder. "I'm afraid so, Lao. But, it's okay."

"It is?" Lao said, his tears building and building in the corners of his eyes, stinging with warmth.

"Of course. She fought very hard to buy us enough time. If not for her, we probably wouldn't be standing here. She let us get to him, by letting herself go."

"But, she's gone. She's really gone," Lao cried, tears falling down his cheeks, his face nestled in Shen's shoulder.

"She's only gone if you let her go."

"Hmm?" Lao looked up, and with a hand, he wiped away a tear or two from his eyes.

"Yes! If you keep her in your mind," Shen said, and poked a finger onto Lao's forehead, "and in your heart," then poked the same finger to the boy's chest, "then she'll live forever."

"I... I miss her, Shen..."

"I know, buddy. But, she'll always be with us. Okay?" Lao wiped away more tears from his cheeks, which stung a bit, and nodded his head. More tears inevitably gathered in his eyes, but he was a little better now. "Alright. Let's keep moving. We all need to rest, and make camp when we get to the mainland. Okay?" Lao nodded again. Shen walked over and climbed onto Ping's saddle, then let a hand down to Lao, pulling him up onto the saddle too, letting the boy sit behind him. They walked on, and the brick could be seen wearing down from their fight. It was a solemn reminder, and it would stay there for as long as people continued to cross the Bridge of Kunan.

As they walked on, Ping grew tired, Lao stayed silent, and Shen thought about the stories that he had heard merchants tell. He remembered the tales of giant monsters, reaching through the fog and pulling men back into it. Images flashed through his mind of Qiu, how Oba made the water wrap around her legs, and how it pulled her into the depths of the mist. It was almost identical to the way the merchants described watching their men get dragged by beasts. And then it clicked. It was Oba. It was Oba pulling those men to their deaths all those times before. Perhaps they weren't all just stories.

Once they walked under the exit gate and through the path on the mainland, Shen moved his hands up at his sides, flicking his wrists. Lao looked back, and he saw the two statues of the spirits that stood at the entrance burst into pieces. The path was not dirt or gravel, but paved stone. It was welcome. The area around was beautiful, with tall grass and flowers that bloomed spectacularly bright colors against the emerald landscape. They gained distance quickly as the sun began to drift into slumber behind the rolling hills, and soon they came upon a mighty forest. "Welcome to the mainland," Shen said.

It was full of tall trees, and countless clearings that would be perfect for camp. So, Shen steered Ping into the forest, and once they had made it a significant way inside, he stopped Ping and hopped off the saddle. The night time had come upon them, a deep darkness creeping up into the sky as dots of light shone through the blanket of dark. Moonlight crawled upon the ground through the clearing in the trees and onto the ground. Lao got down from Ping, once the bird had crouched down, and walked over to a tree. Ping looked down at the ground, his beak clicking softly, and his chirping low and humming.

  Lao sat against the tree, his legs bent in front of him, his face rested on his knees in his arms laid atop them. Shen reached into his bag and grabbed at a few things, the sleeping rolls, the fire starter, and the waterskin. He laid them all out, got the fire going, and then crept into his sleeping roll, letting its warmth wash over him. It had been a long day, and he was thankful that him and Lao made it alive. The thought and the grief of losing Qiu was still heavy on him, and heavier on Lao, and these thoughts stayed up in his mind as he drifted off into sleep.

Rest and Recovery

      Shen awoke early in the morning from a nightmare. It had snuck up on him in the night, like a skulking spirit come to haunt him. He saw the faces of his mother and his father, his brother too, and watched in horror as they faded into nothing. His hands reached out and swiped at where they were, but they could feel nothing. Then, he was back on the mainland, back on Batung, back in the camp where he had been put those twelve years ago. Before he could leave and burst through the bamboo gates, he woke up to the sound of tree birds and the smell of dirt.

      The sun was up, just enough to cut through the treeline and land in his eyes. Lao was sound asleep, curled up inside his sleeping roll. He held his eyes closed firmly with the skin between them scrunching up. Every once in awhile, he would toss and turn in his slumber, and then settle back into place. Shen let the boy sleep, and walked over to the center of their little camp, to the fire.

      It was built with sticks all set up in a cone, and there was a circle of rocks that Shen had collected lining the outside. At least, that's what it had been. Now, the fire stood almost completely put out, only a few embers remaining. The sticks had all been burnt, and other manner of brush that had been stuffed in by Lao was now just ash. Shen grabbed for the firestarter, which he'd stuffed into his leather bag the night before, and brought it down to the embers. He set it upon one of the rocks, then left for the trees for a moment. When he came back, his arms were full of short sticks of average thickness, and a few large seedlings which dropped from the trees above.

      He knelt down and tossed a few of the even shorter sticks down into the embers. Then, he set up the remaining sticks in the same cone-like pattern as he had before. He clutched the firestarter in his hand again and put it just above the shorter sticks on the embers, and with a mighty click of the device and a blow of air from his mouth, Shen watched as the fire went up, encompassing the sticks and starting to burn away at their bark. He sat back and put his still bare feet up to the side of the fire, letting the warmth wash over his skin. The feeling climbed up from the dirt-dusted soles of his feet, through his legs, and shot through his chest. He breathed a sigh of relief as he began to hear Lao shuffling again in his cloth sleeping roll.

"Morning, Lao," Shen said, getting up and walking over to his bag.

"Morning." The young boy said, now sitting up and out of the warmth of his sleeping roll.

"Did you sleep alright? I know the ground isn't too comfortable."

"Yes. But, I kept having this really bad dream."

"Would you like to tell me?"

"I saw Qiu again. I miss her."

Shen stopped what he was doing, putting the things he'd pulled from his bag back in, and walked over to Lao. He sat down, legs crossed as Lao had, and looked to him. "That's alright. I'd be a bit worried if you weren't feeling sad about it."

"Yeah," Lao chuckled softly for a brief moment.

"It's okay," Shen said. He placed a palm to Lao's back and rubbed at his back to comfort him. For a while, they just sat and watched the fire. Sometimes, when the fire died down too much, Shen would get up and go over to it, blowing on the embers and putting the tree seeds into it. Lao would watch as the little seeds burst into flames. He'd note the smell too, like sap, and it would tickle his nostrils until chills crawled down his spine. After he did this, Shen would walk over and sit right back next to Lao.

This went on for a while, and neither of the two of them had any complaints about it. It was quite soothing, and though he still thought about her, Lao had more happy thoughts about Qiu than sad ones now. As Lao's stomach began to grumble and groan, he put a hand to it. "I haven't eaten much. I'm so hungry," he complained.

"I was just going to get up and leave for food."

"What are you gonna get? It's not like there's much."

"I saw some ram-horn deer on the way in here. I'm sure I can find one of them," Shen said with a smile. He went over to where his bag was and rifled through the contents, freeing the sword and its scabbard from the other clutter inside. With a light toss of it, he put the strap around his shoulder and slung it onto his back. "I should be back soon."

"You're leaving me alone?"

"You can handle yourself, right?"

Lao thought for a second, and then patted the scars on the back of his shoulder. "Yeah, I'll manage," he said smiling.

"Good," Shen chuckled. With a friendly nod to Lao, and even a salute to him, Shen walked off into the trees. They seemed to get larger the further he went in. It was as if they were hulking behemoths, watching over the creatures and Shen as they walked underneath. The leaves shielded the ground from most of the sunlight shining down, and what little there was illuminated the bugs that skittered across the dirt.

As he walked, he began to take notice of something along the dirt. He saw hoof tracks embedded into the ground. They seemed to follow the general path of where the sun was shining down, under where the canopy of leaves was scarce. He crouched down and placed two of his fingers into the tracks to tell how deep they were. They seemed fairly shallow, at least more shallow than what he'd consider deep, and so he figured the ram-horns had been in a hurry. The creatures must've been running at a fair pace, making their bodies lighter, as to not make such deep dents in the dirt.

While he chased after the tracks on the ground, he started to recall memories from his childhood. When he was young, around Lao's age, maybe younger at about twelve years old, he had escaped from the Mystic camp he'd been put in. He remembered what his father had told him, about how to use his abilities and how to hunt and how to simply survive. The man knew that they would one day escape the camp, and have to fend for themselves. Sadly, he couldn't have anticipated his departure from the world himself. But, as his young son walked on, he carried on the legacy of the Jin family name.

Though, the name was less important now. In fact, it was rather smeared with dirt and dust, as young Shen's face was. He remembered having to crawl along the ground, pick up bugs and bite into them for nutrients, all while hiding from guards that were searching for him. Once he got a safe distance away from them, young Shen hid from them in a cave by a pond. Food was still scarce, and he had almost no muscle to speak of. His body was cadaverous and skeletal, a sunken in image of what the boy before was.

In time, he learned to catch fish with his abilities. At first, though, he could not cook them. He would later learn that from a friend in the capital city. But, for the time being, he ate the fish raw, every little scale and bone. He would bite into it and tear at the flesh and muscle until blood stained his teeth. In a moment, all these memories that had filled his head left, all swept away by a single sound. It was a low and gruff *eeeegh*. It startled him a bit, and his head swiveled in its direction.

Lying there, up against a tree, was a ram-horn deer. Though, unlucky for the both of them, the thing was horribly mangled. Its eyes were poked out, bleeding from the sockets. There was a huge three pronged gash along its chest, leaking more blood and a few entrails. Its sounds were guttural, blood-curdling even, and deeply immiserating. Shen knew that it'd be normal to look away, but he had seen worse things than this, than nature. Before he could walk over to it and possibly free it of suffering, another noise alerted him.

    It was quieter than the ram-horn's sound, and yet all the more chilling. A gentle scratching of wood rang in his ears, seemingly coming from right above him. He looked up, but he saw nothing. Spinning around, looking at every single tree trunk, he still could not find it. It would find him. When he brought his head back down, a thunderous flapping sounded above him, and as he brought his eyes to it, he saw a monstrous hookbeak careening down toward him, talons at the ready. Its eyes, beady and menacing, stared down at him. An adult, it was much larger than the one Lao had encountered, about the size of the ram-horn's whole torso.

    In a swift motion he moved to the side, avoiding it just barely, and reached for one of the rocks he kept in his bag. He rifled through and through, but could not find a single one. He must've used them all in the fight with Oba. Cursing himself in his mind, Shen leapt to one of the trees as the talons came down once again. The creature landed on the ground, and hunched over, its beak like a fishing hook glistening in the sunlight. It snapped and shrieked softly, walking over slowly. Shen chose not to run. He moved around, avoiding the path of the monster, and searched tirelessly for any kind of rock, either a few small ones or one fairly large one.

    As he scrambled for anything, the hookbeak lunged forward at him, furiously flapping its wings. It shrieked and squawked chillingly at him, and clicked its beak, all while staring him dead in the face. Its long, thin tail whipped around wildly as it neared him. Shen dodged it frantically and then his bare foot came upon something on the ground. He looked down, and to his relief, it was a firm and fair-sized rock. He lifted it into the air, flicking his wrist up slightly, and then turned to face the hookbeak.

It jumped right up and went for him. Shen just barely escaped the clutches of its talons, and used his sense to throw the rock into its back with a flick of his wrist. It squawked loudly as it crashed to the ground. In a puff of dirt dust rising from the ground, the hookbeak fell. But, afterward, it crawled right back up and lunged at Shen again. He quickly avoided it, ducking under its path, and got to a tree. In a moment, he reached his hand to the side and felt around with his senses for any sort of rock again. As the hookbeak came back, fast and menacing with its beady little black eyes and ruffled feathers, Shen used his other hand to raise a wall of dirt from the ground.

The hookbeak struck right into the dirt, and its wings folded along its back slightly. It was a dumb creature, monstrous and vicious, but dumb all the same. It shook its head and freed the dirt particles from its feathers. While it was occupied, Shen had sensed more rocks, and pulled them to his hands, forming a sort of spike with them on his palm. The hookbeak was busy pecking at the dirt wall, unsure of it, when Shen brought it down with his other hand. It took a moment to adjust to the change, looked to Shen, and then leapt into the air. Shen smirked, and swiftly sent the rocks into the creature's neck. The rocks struck it in the center of its little neck, and an audible snap could be heard,

It fell to the ground, limp, and with a heavy breath, Shen walked to it. Looking around for a quick moment, he searched for a stick of proper size, and then promptly found one. Once he'd done this and brought the stick over to the bird's carcass, he got busy plucking it. He wrapped his fingers tightly around the feathers in clumps and pulled. All of them gave way with a sort of tearing sound, which was almost nauseating to hear, had Shen not been familiar with it.

Once the thing was properly de-feathered, he pulled his sword from its scabbard while his other hand held the bird's carcass, now bare and smoothish.

He took the sword in his hands, and carefully placed the blade's edge to the bottom of the dead hookbeak's neck. He sliced, and sawed, and the rest of the neck and the head fell to the ground, blood trailing after it. Then, he moved to the legs, sawing the things off with vigor. They fell too, but Shen did not scrap them as he had with the head, and instead, he sawed off the talons individually, saving them in a small pouch in a pocket of his tunic. He figured he would take them to either keep or sell to an apothecary to be used in medicinal remedies.

Next, he took the blade and pointed it on the rear of the bird's carcass, shoving the blade into the skin. He then sawed a circle out of the bottom and emptied the body of the entrails. They all fell to the dirt with a *splat*, with blood pooling out. He held it up there for awhile, waiting for the blood to drain. Eventually it did, and once it did, Shen picked the stick up off the ground and put it through the carcass, in through the rear hole he'd cut and out through the hole made by severing the neck and the head.

He carried it by holding the ends of the stick, one in each hand, and began to walk back to the camp. With a look to the now completely dead ramhorn deer, he thought to himself, and decided he would let it be, since he wouldn't want to disturb it in death, and since he already had enough to cook for both him and Lao. He had a sense for where things were, like mental notes, and he found his way back to the camp, to the fire and to Lao, with ease. The boy jumped from his sitting position once Shen came into view. "You're back!" His face quickly changed, a bushy black eyebrow rising as he rubbed the shaved portion of his hair, the fuzz on the back of his neck. "What's that?"

"Food." Shen smiled.

"I thought you were going to get deer. That definitely doesn't **look** like a deer."

"It's a hookbeak."

"You can eat those?"

"You can eat any animal."

"But, hookbeaks? They're dirty and creepy, right?"

"Yes, that may be, but they aren't half bad in terms of taste," Shen said, and walked over to the fire. Lao had kept it going well, sticks placed in burnt over and over as the flames climbed up. Shen set up a spit with two tall sticks on either end of the fire, then propping the stick with the bird's body along the two standing ones. "You should at least give it a taste. You've eaten worse."

Lao thought back to the bug he had eaten the day before, how it crunched and filled his mouth with a sour kind of taste. "You've got a point," he said, his face formed in minor disgust.

Over the next hour or so, Shen continued to spin the cooking carcass every once in awhile atop the fire. While he did so, Lao would put sticks and brush into the fire. Sometimes, when Lao would mix in seedlings from the trees or leaves, the flames climbed especially high as the plants bursted into fire on the ground of ash and sticks. It was a peaceful time. Neither of the two spoke, and the sounds of the forest, the birds chirping and the bugs whizzing past, was enough sound for them at the time. Even Ping stayed quiet, instead choosing to sleep with his head nestled into his chest, his neck craned downward.

Once the food was cooked, it gave off a fantastic smell. Roasted meat was a commodity to the both of them. Shen picked it up off the spit, letting the two sticks standing on the side fall as they loosened from the dirt. He brought it over to the bag, and pulled a tiny piece of white meat from it. Tossing it into his mouth, his taste buds watered. It was food, something scarce in his days, and it made his heart jump. He pulled a few pouches of something from his bag, then proceeded to take pinches of what it was out and dust it over the meat of the bird. Green herb dust coated most of the meat evenly, and the smell of herbs was delightful when mixed with that of the meat itself. He brought it over to Lao and the boy could smell it too, and smiled.

"Eat up," Shen said. The two of them took turns, taking the stick in their hand, using the other to pry off a piece of meat and eat it, then passing it off to the other one of them. It was tender, juicy, better than anything Lao had ever tasted. After a while, Shen gave Lao the stick and let him eat to his heart's content.

"You don't want any more?"

"Not right now. Plus, I need to go and feed Ping," Shen said, walking over to his bag.

"Can't he eat some of the meat?"

"No, Lao. It'll make him sick if he eats any of it."

"Oh. Okay," Lao said, and returned to the meat, taking off pieces and chewing on them, letting the taste flood into his mouth.

Shen reached his bag, and carefully reached a hand in to grasp the sack of apples he had been given. Once he had them out, he set them down next to him. He then reached back in and pulled the waterskin out, fairly full, about halfway. He took the cap off and gently poured water over the blade of his sword, after he'd pulled it out of its scabbard. The blood and the dirt washed away easily, sliding off as his hand lightly glided over its surface. Then, after it was free of dirt and blood, Shen wiped away and dried the water from it with a cloth he kept in the bag. He put the sword back, sliding the blade into the scabbard with ease.

Shen grasped an apple in his hand and closed off the sack once more. He walked over to where Ping sat, still and resting his eyes. His beak clicked ever so gently as he breathed heavily in his sleep, and his feathers fluffed up every once in awhile. Shen patted him on the head, and the dimian's eyes fluttered open, big yellow orbs with tiny black pupils staring back at him. "Hey, buddy, you hungry?" Shen said smiling. The bird looked into his eyes for a moment, his neck craned up and his head held up, and was silent. For a moment, that is, before he let loose a loud *squawk* that rattled the sticks around his body.

Ping brought his head down and began nipping at the apple in Shen's palm, then simply resorted to choking the whole thing down. He finished it and looked back to Shen with his big, dumb eyes, and then nudged his forehead into Shen's chest. "Good boy, Ping. Good boy," Shen said, giggling a bit to himself. He carefully pet the bird along its head and neck feathers, soft and delicate with their brownish color.

Throughout the rest of the day, the two of them took turns keeping watch, while the one of them not on watch would get some rest. Shen had laid out the rules before he took first watch. "When I'm on watch, you get some sleep. And, when you're on watch, you listen and look out for anything. If you see anything, wake me up, shake me as hard as you can to do it. Can you handle that?" Shen had said. Thankfully, for both of them, Lao wouldn't have to wake Shen up for any reason.

They each managed to get several hours of sleep, until the night rolled around, when they had their fill of sleep. The fire was still going, aided by the sticks tossed in by whoever was on watch at the time. Ping was fast asleep, not having to worry about whether or not he was on watch, and rested gently and quietly. As the darkness held itself up in the sky, and the abundant sunlight was swapped for the scarce moonlight, Shen was on watch. He sat in front of the fire, poking at it with a thick, long stick. "Shen?" He heard Lao say, who had turned over to face him in his sleeping roll.

"Yes, Lao?"

"Can I ask you about something?"

"Of course."

"What's that mark on your neck?" Lao said.

Shen rubbed at the back of his neck, and the green circle on his tan skin felt like nothing more than regular skin, as that's what it was. "This? This is the mark of the Mystic."

"Mark of the Mystic?"

"That's a more dramatic name for it, but yes."

"So, Mystics have it?"

"That's right, every single one of them."

"Why is yours green? Are they all like that?"

"Because my abilities come from Batung. If I were of Vasai, for instance, the mark would be blue, and I would be able to control the waters. Like my mother and my brother," Shen explained.

"And like that man on the bridge?" Lao said quietly.

"Yes. Like that man on the bridge, too." The two went quiet for a while, and the air was filled with the sounds of the crackling fire, sticks bursting at the bark with flames. Lao rolled back over in his sleeping roll, while Shen stayed awake. He was scared of going back to sleep. He was afraid that he'd have another nightmare, and have to face his parents again, and especially his brother.

His brother was in his mind at almost all times. Shen would often keep his brother's face in his head, fearful that he would forget it. This wasn't the case, but Shen couldn't help but worry that he would forget his last family in the world. The night crawled up more into the sky, and soon the whole of the canopy above them was black, unable to be seen. Though, sometimes a rogue ember would drift up into the air, and illuminate a leaf or some for but a moment, before fading away into the wind.

    Soon, it became Shen's turn to take watch. But, he did not want to disturb Lao's sleep. He needed it much more than himself, and Shen had already gotten more than enough sleep. With a heavy breath, he walked over to his bag and pulled a few berries out from a pouch. Sitting by the fire, still, he chewed on them, waiting for the time to pass. When he'd finished the berries, he went back to the bag and grabbed the map. Looking over it, he found that there was a nearby town. It was labelled, in very small writing: "Zhaoyin." He rolled the map back up walked back over, then tucked it into the bag. Sat next to the fire for the remainder of the night, he decided the two of them would leave for Zhaoyin in the the morning, since they were in need of supplies. As the fire went down more and more, Shen stared into the embers, his brother's face coming across his mind.

Old Wounds

      Another morning now, Lao awoke with the sun shining right in his eyes. Shen had gotten perhaps an hour or two of rest. But, his main concern was with the map and the distance it would take them to get to the next town. He held the parchment in his hands, and sat up against Ping's side, who was still fast asleep, his sides rising and falling as his lungs took in air and expelled it out. The town Shen saw, Zhaoyin, was fairly close. Though, it would certainly prove a grueling walk, considering the mental weights each of them carried. Shen rolled up the map and tucked it into his bag, which was tied around his waist and at his side again, just as Lao was waking up.

      "Shen?" He called out, rubbing his eyes.

      "Yes, Lao?"

      "Is it morning?"

      "Closer to afternoon than morning, but yes, still morning."

      Lao sat up now, his legs crossed. He sat next to his sleeping roll in a patch of grass. "Are we leaving?"

      "Very soon. We need to get some more supplies, we're running a bit low."

      "Alright." Lao stretched his back and reached his arms up into the air, belting out a hefty yawn. "Where are we going now?"

      "A nearby town. Only a little ways away. Zhaoyin, it's called." At that, Lao became quiet, and some color drained from his dark tan face. His eyes went wider, and the flecks of gray in the brown were alighted by the sun. He averted his gaze for a moment, and then brought his head back to Shen, his eyes narrowing back to normal. "Is something wrong?"

"No!" Lao protested. "The name sounds kind of familiar to me, that's all," he said, smiling lightly.

"Oh, alright then. Well, roll up your sleeping roll. We should be heading out soon so we can explore the town while the sun is still up," Shen joked.

"Heh, yeah," Lao commented. He spun around now, sat up on his knees, and rolled up the cloth sleeping roll tightly. With a thin leather string, which he tightly wrapped around the cloth of the roll, he secured it and tossed it to Shen. Shen caught it with both arms and carefully stuffed it on the inside of the bag at his side. He did the same with his sleeping roll, and tucked it on the inside of the bag, adjacent to Lao's, nudged away from the other contents of the bag.

Shen reached his hand in and grasped an apple, the second to last one in the sack he had stuffed into the bag. He brought it, resting calmly in his palm, to Ping's nose. The bird sniffed and sniffed, still seemingly asleep, and then his eyes shot open, little beady black pupils staring down the apple in Shen's hand. In a flash, the apple was seized by his beak and gobbled down, less time taken chewing and more time taken choking it all down. Ping darted his head around for a moment, and then looked to Shen. He was quiet, pondering, at least until he stared Shen in the face and let out a loud *squawk* that rattled the man's ears.

"You're welcome, buddy," Shen laughed. He reached his hand up and pet at the feather's of Ping's forehead and top of his head. Shen walked over to the fire and stomped at it with his bare feet, crushing down the embers and breaking the burnt sticks up into gray ash that picked up and fluttered in the wind.

The two of them checked around the site for a little while, searching to make sure they would not leave anything before they left. When they had found they had packed everything, Shen patted onto Ping's side and climbed on the sitting dimian. Lao approached too, and climbed on behind Shen, holding onto the saddle's holds as Ping stood up. They left with a little wave goodbye to where the fire used to blaze and a smile. The road ahead would be long, but it was nothing they couldn't handle, especially after the boat trip with Chang, of which Lao still had fearful memories.

Dirt was the path which they had traveled to get to their little campsite, and it would be the same path that they'd take to get to Zhaoyin. Things were quiet as Ping walked with his scaly feet audibly tapping against the ground. The area around them was some of the same. Grass waved around in the breeze as bugs scurried under their shadows. Birds skulked above the bugs, waiting for a perfect chance to swoop down and scoop up a beak full of them, or at least one or two. The sky was cloudless, wonderful, and the sun was stretching up and out of the hills in the east.

Soon, they came upon a sign, which firmly read Zhaoyin in black and carved into the wood. It was in the shape of an arrow at the top of a wooden post, and it pointed ahead on the path. There was another sign on the post, one below which read Yi-Weng. It was shaped like an arrow as well, and pointed to the right along an offshoot of the main path. Shen stopped Ping for a moment and looked the signs up and down. He pondered for a moment, and then carried on, pulling Ping forward and walking him onward through the straight path.

As they walked on and on, the area around them began to change slightly. There was still the luscious grass and the brilliantly colored flowers, which was a beautiful sight, but there were new things to see now. Amidst the flowers all in reds and yellows, some even light purples that danced in the breeze, there were little streams of water that flowed in from a river nearby. The two of them on Ping's back could hear the sound of the rushing water behind a grove of trees. Lao could even see little silver fish swimming around in the streams that gathered into pools in the ground.

Soon they reached the front gates, and the happy aura of what they'd walked through began to leave them. The gates, wooden and worn, were all scratched up on the posts on each side of the path leading into town. There was a sign along the top of the gate, which bore the name Zhaoyin along it. Though, that was scratched up as well. Lao shuddered in his seat and let go of one of the holds, using his hand to scratch incessantly at the back of his neck. "My, this place looks out of shape, huh? Wouldn't you say so, Lao?"

"Hmm? Oh, yeah." He said, a bit caught off guard. They entered and began to walk throughout the town, along the stone-laden path running through the buildings. The buildings were largely made of bamboo, and framed with wood like most other places they'd been. Though, here, the color of them was fading, worn, and dull. They were not as bright as the buildings on Yedao or Lujing, or even as the little huts of the village.

As they walked on, Shen began to notice that people were scarce. Sure, there were a few tending to shops and some buying things, sliding coins of Yin across wooden countertops, but most of the street of stones was empty. Lao was not worried about this, however, and had his own worries in mind. In his head, things came back to him. He looked around by the buildings and spotted a sealed wooden crate. Suddenly, memories began coming back to him, flooding into his mind as images flashed by.

He remembered, albeit vaguely, storming out of the door of his home, slamming it and cracking the wooden hinges. There was a steady shouting behind him, but it was muffled, and he couldn't make out what they were saying. He just started running. He ran and he ran into the night, amidst rain and cold, and he made it to a forest. In a big fallen tree, hollowed out in decay, he slept for the night, shivering in the bitter winds that drifted in. The next morning, he ran again, fueled by something animal inside him, until he made it all the way to the docks on the western edge of the mainland.

There, he found a large wooden ship. Merchants joked and laughed as Lao waited patiently behind a few crates. The overwhelming scent of fish climbed up into his nostrils. Once the merchants had finished their drinks, they began to get dumb, careless, allowing Lao the perfect opportunity. He ran, light-footed in his young age of ten, onto the ship. The crewmembers were busy on the main deck, singing sea songs as the boat took off into the harbor, bound for Yedao, where they would deliver the rest of their fish from Vasai in return for boxes of soybean seeds.

As the men drank even more and giggled amongst themselves, telling story after story about their adventures on the water, Lao snuck down to the bottom of the ship. There, the ship held all of its cargo. Lao had thought he experienced the worst of the fish smell. He was sadly mistaken, as the smell drifted up from crates and back into his nostrils. He had to keep from breathing from his mouth, for fear of tasting the putrid smell.

The boat sailed into the night, under the watchful stars and the moon, until it arrived in Yedao's main port, though small, in the morning. Lao had fallen deep into sleep. The men of the ship, however, were wide awake. They went down into the cargo hold, and began moving the crates. Lao, snoring, was awoken by one of them. "Hey!" He shouted. Lao scrambled, knocking over one of the crates, which fell and hit the man in the side. "Come back here!" The man shouted toward the boy, just as he ran up the steps of the ship and jumped off into the water below.

"Lao?" Shen asked. Lao was pulled from the recesses of his mind.
"Huh? What?"

"You're shaking. Is something wrong?" Shen asked as he stopped Ping. They stood to the side of the stone road.

"I'm... I'm scared Shen."

"Scared? Why?"

"I don't like this place... I don't like it," Lao muttered. He was shaking still, his fingers trembling as they gripped at the saddle's holds.

"Lao, it's okay. I'm here. We're not going to be here for long, alright?"

"Okay. You promise?"

"I promise. We're just going to get food for Ping and some water. That's all, okay?"

"Okay." Shen turned around in his seat and ran a hand through Lao's hair, and for a moment, he smiled. But, when Shen turned back around, the smile faded from Lao's face back into an expression of worry.

The two walked on, Ping carrying them with a bit of stride in his steps, until they reached a general shop. A man stood outside it, leaning up against the wall with his head down and his arms locked together. "Excuse me, but, could we get water and food here by any chance?" Shen asked.

The man brought his head up and smiled a bit. "Of course."

"Do you run this shop," Shen asked.

"Me? No, Zhan runs the store. He's inside. My name's Hao, his assistant. Pleased to meet you," the man said, looking up to Shen on Ping's back. He put his fist to his chest in salute and smiled more to him.

"The same to you, Hao." Shen smiled and returned the gesture.

"I'd be happy to take care of your dimian for you while you're inside."

"That would be wonderful, thank you," Shen said, hopping down from Ping's back. Lao jumped off too, aided by Shen, who held onto the boy's arm as he climbed down. Ping shook his torso and a few feathers came off, fluttering down to the ground. The bird looked to Hao, tilted his head, and then let out a loud *squawk*.

"Haha! Quite a noisy one isn't he?"

"I still haven't gotten used to it," Shen said giggling. Lao stood next to him, smiling, chuckling a little to himself. The two of them walked into the shop, swinging open the wooden door, as Ping let out a few chirps while Hao pet at the feathers along his back. The inside of the shop was quaint, with little candles in holders along the walls, alighting the room. The flames of the candles were the only light in fact, as there were no windows in sight. The front counter was manned by a sturdy looking man with a scraggly black beard and dark tan skin.

"Morning. What brings you here?" The man boomed.

"Would you happen to have water and some apples? Or any kind of food I can give to a dimian?" Shen asked. Lao was looking around on the walls, which were lined with shelves that held all sorts of things. There were some with basics, like water jugs or bags of spice. But, some had odd things, like copper tea kettles or wooden gauntlets with chipping surfaces.

"Indeed I do. Hang on one moment, I'll need to go out back and get to the tap for the water. There should be apples in a sack in the corner over there," he said pointing, then grabbed at something from the floor. He opened a door behind him, not seen before, and sunlight poured in until it shut behind him.

Shen went over to where the man pointed and grasped the sack of apples, slightly bigger than the empty sack he had stuffed in his bag. He opened up the flap of his bag and seized the old sack, filling it with around sixteen or so apples. Then, he walked the sack back over to the corner and set it back down, putting the old sack, now filled, up onto the counter. The man was still gone, and the two of them could just barely hear the sound of the water flowing and hitting the ground outside. In a moment, there was a sound behind them, and the front door swung open, letting light in just before it closed.

Shen and Lao both figured it was Hao, perhaps checking up on the two of them or just seeing what Zhan was doing. But, it wasn't Hao. Shen turned around, and the face of the man before him was foreign, completely new to him. However, when Lao turned around, his heart sunk deep into the pit of his stomach, and his body began to tremble. He began backing up, right into the counter, knocking the apples over and spilling them out onto the countertop. "Lao, what's the matter?"

"Lao? Lao!" The man before them's face became enraged, and as he lunged forward, Lao turned and jumped over the counter. He ran to the back door, and swung it open, not caring to shut it behind him as he ran all the way to the front gate of the town. "You come back here, Lao! Now!" The man shouted out the door from the counter.

"You have no right to yell at him like that. Who do you think you are?" Shen protested, getting in front of the man.

"Jiang Han. I'm his father. I have every right to yell at that boy, now get out of my way," he said, pushing Shen out of the way and jogging in the direction Lao had run off to. Shen followed quickly, getting on Ping's back and thanking Hao for taking care of the dimian as he did so. While Jiang trailed after Lao, Shen was shadowing close behind.

Away from the shop, Lao was still running, and as he did, all through the stone road, he suddenly stopped. He stood in front of a house that was all too familiar to him. The wooden hinges were busted, cracking more and more and chipping while the door itself stood crooked in them. Windows were broken, the paper of them ripped. Lao stood and simply stared at it. He remembered all the things that happened in that house, all the punched in walls and broken floorboards from stomping. Even the yelling bounced around in his head with a residual echo that haunted him.

Tears began welling, a heat building up, in the corners of his eyes. But, just as he was about to cry, he was grabbed at the arm by a firm hand. "You're back. Finally. How dare you run away from me like that! I'm gonna teach you never to do that again."

"Get off of me!" Lao shouted. He tugged at Jiang's grip, shaking around and trying to get free.

"You are my son and you will listen to me!"

"I don't want to be! I never wanted to be!" Lao tugged and tugged until he was shoved by his father. He hit the ground, and stumbled back on the grass. Jiang walked up, his hands balled in fists, as Shen came up behind him.

"Back away from him. Now."

"You don't tell me what to do. I raised this boy, and I'll do whatever I want with him."

Shen grabbed something from his bag, sticking his hand in under the flap, and then he flicked his wrist forward with his palm open. A little rock struck the side of Jiang's head, and he shouted in pain at the impact. "Get away. I won't say it again." Lao ran over to Shen and got behind Ping, scared.

"What would your mother think? Huh? You think she'd like how you're treating me?"

"Mom is gone!" Lao shouted, tears flowing from his eyes and down his cheeks.

"You watch your mouth," Jiang said. As he stepped forward, Shen put his arm to his sword's handle and gripped it, then scowled in the man's direction. His dark brown eyes went wide, and then narrowed in a grim look. "Fine. Go. But don't you ever come back. You hear me?" Lao stood silently, looking around Ping to his father. "I said go!" Ping lowered himself and Lao quickly climbed on. The dimian stood up and Shen led him to the front gate. As Lao looked back, he saw his father slam the door behind him and heard a loud yell from the home.

"Shen... I'm scared."

"It's okay, Lao. It's okay, I promise. You won't ever have to see him again."

"But, what about the food? And the water?"

"We'll go to the next town over. It's not too far, and I don't like this place anyway."

"Okay."

"If you'll let me, I can keep you around. I wouldn't want you back out on the streets again."

"Really?" Lao asked, brushing a few tears from his eyes.

"Of course. We've come this far, it may be a bit strange if we didn't stick together now, wouldn't it?"

Lao smiled a bit, still tearing up. "Yeah. I guess so."

"Would you like to hear a story? Maybe it can help us get through the journey."

"Yes please."

"Alright," Shen said, and began looking around, thinking of what he would say. He looked to the trees, to the birds fluttering through them. There were more animals out now, the birds of course, and some ram-horn deer grazing on the emerald grass. "Ah, here's a funny story." He said as Lao settled into his seat behind Shen. "It was much before you were born, on the day my little brother was born. I remember it like it was yesterday. My mother had just brought him into the world, and my father was giving him a bath. I didn't care too much for having a baby brother. He was loud and wouldn't stop crying unless he was sleeping, which was rare. But, when I walked into the room to see him, he moved the water from the bucket and splashed me with it."

"He did?" Lao giggled, wiping the stained and dried tears from his cheeks.

"Oh yes. And I got so mad that day. I remember my father laughing so hard he knocked over the bucket and my brother falling out. The water and the soap got everywhere."

"Haha! Really?"

"Yes! I should remember, I was the one who had to clean up all of the water and finish giving him a bath." Shen smiled and laughed a bit, and then he went silent.

"Shen?"

"Yes, Lao?"

"Do you miss your brother?"

Shen thought for a moment. "Every day and every night." He dropped his head down and reached a hand out to pet at Ping's neck feathers, to which the dimian chirped softly.

"It's okay. We're gonna find him."

"Yes. Yes we are, Lao." They walked on, and as they did, they both smiled. When they reached a fork in the dirt path, Shen noticed the post with the signs again, and grabbed a rock from his bag. He held it in his hand, and then launched it forward, breaking the sign which read Zhaoyin, and then brought the rock back into his hand. Stuffing it back into the bag, he pulled Ping toward the path's offshoot, bound toward Yi-Weng.

Ping walked steadily on, not faltering in the slightest, motivated by bugs that would fly past his eyes that he'd snatch up in his beak and choke down with a hearty *squawk*. As they came closer and closer to Yi-Weng, Shen began to take notice of something. The animals that were once abundant on and around the path became scarce. There would occasionally be a field mouse or two that'd scurry across the path from one patch of grass to the other, but other than that, there was not much. Soon, they reached a treeline, and just beyond it was the town.

    The dimian stepped in, and then he heard a sound. It was a low rustling, a moving of leaves or bushes, and it made him stop in his tracks. All was quiet for but a few moments. That is, right before they jumped out from behind the bushes and the trees. Ping leaped to the side, just as two hookbeaks lunged toward his feet. "Woah, boy! Easy!" Shen said, and then noticed the birds. His mind quickly shifted into survival mode. "Lao, look for a rock! Hurry!"

    Lao swiveled his head around frantically as the birds on the ground neared closer to the dimian under them. One of them was an adult, a female, from the looks of the yellow feather markings around its eyes. Its long and thin ratty tail whipped behind it as it lunged again at Ping's legs. While it did so, the other one, just a juvenile, jumped a bit off the ground and scratched at Ping's leg, placing a mark in the scales. Ping screeched in pain and kicked his leg, knocking the juvenile hookbeak into a nearby tree. It got up and shook off the impact, then began to circle around the dimian from a safe distance while its mother attacked.

    Shen looked around too, and could not find a rock. But, Lao had better luck. "Shen, there!" He shouted and pointed to one of the trees in the little treeline they were in. There, a few medium-sized rocks lay toppled over one another. Shen narrowed his eyes a moment and then put his arm out. He flicked his wrist up, and a pillar of dirt collided with the underbelly of the adult hookbeak, knocking it into the air. Then, Shen whipped his other arm around, moving the rock in a circle through the air, where it would stop in front of the bird and launch forward.

The hookbeak was struck in the chest, and knocked all the way into a bush by a tree. With a few pattering footsteps the juvenile made its way to its mother and found her, lying lifeless. It let out a loud call, a shrieking and howling *raaaaaaaaaiii*, which rang in Shen and Lao's ears. Soon, the sound dissipated, and the air was left silent. The juvenile sulked off into the trees, and Shen and Lao smiled. At least, until the air began to fill with sound. It was an immense fluttering that came from all around them. It came from the trees and from the bushes, even the air above them was filled with the sound.

Surrounded by the shroud of trees, it took only a moment for them all to come crashing down through the leaves. An entire swarm of hookbeaks came bursting through the treeline, all with sharp beaks poised and ready to strike. "We're getting out of here! Now!" Shen shouted. He patted the side of Ping's neck hard and the dimian took off, running frantically toward the town past the treeline. The hookbeaks, angry and hungry, followed close behind, using their strong talons on their scaled toes to grip the trees and swing forward. Ping let out a few *squawks* as he ran faster and faster to the town.

As one of them, one bent on flying into the two of them, got closer and closer to Lao, the boy brought his hand back. In a stroke of what he considered pure luck, he struck at the bird with his fist, hitting it square in the forehead. It shook off the blow, but lagged behind more now. "Shen! I punched one!" He said frantically.

"You what?"

"I punched one!"

"How did you manage that?"

"I don't know, but I don't think I can do it again! We have to get to town."

"Alright, I have an idea, but you'll have to hold on tight!" Shen shouted, and Lao proceeded to grip onto the saddle holds even tighter than he already was. Shen stood up, balancing his feet on the saddle as Ping ran faster and faster. He reached his arms forward, and lifted a ramp of dirt from the ground. Ping took the cue, and ran even faster up the ramp, and then took off out of the treeline and into a field just ahead of the town. As the hookbeaks gripped onto the trees, dumbfounded, Shen turned and flicked his hands upward, causing the dirt ramp to explode into a flurry of dirt and pebbles.

"Woo! We did it!" Lao shouted, smiling to himself.

"Yes, we did." Shen took a heavy breath, and then sat back down in the saddle as Ping slowed down back to a walk. The bird walked on, a bit wobbly now. "You did good, buddy. Good job!" Shen said smiling as he patted the side of Ping's neck softly. The dimian let out a hearty and happy *squawk*. They walked on, and soon, they made it into the town of Yi-Weng, much more welcoming and bright than the last. The gates were painted yellow and pristine, with not a single scratch on them, and there was the sound of wind chimes as they walked under the gate and into town.

A Soldier's Story

  As they entered, they were greeted with a sight unlike any they had seen in their previous travels. In the center of the town, not too far from the gate, there stood a great fountain, water falling out at one end and into the pool collecting below. Lilies atop pads floated along the water as silver and bronze fish of all sizes swam under them. Lao marveled at them, getting down off Ping, walking up to the fountain, and smiling down into the water. Shen stayed on top of Ping and brought the dimian closer to the fountain.
  He looked around and noticed that the town was in fact much more lively than the one before. People walked all throughout the dirt path that ran through the town, carrying sacks of what Shen had assumed was produce or other goods. Some walked in and out of shops with wooden signs at the front detailing what was to be sold inside. There were buildings which housed animals for people to purchase and raise, in hopes of getting the meat and other goods from them. There was even a tea shop, whose sign was shaped into a big tea cup, wooden and scrawled with black words. Shen took a mental note of this building as best he could, and walked Ping onward, with Lao slowly trailing right behind on foot.
  They continued down the neatly laid dirt path toward a general store. Shen wasn't sure where he would find such a place, and he certainly couldn't find a sign for one on the buildings they'd already gone near. He called Lao over, and the boy ran back to Ping and climbed atop the saddle once again. With a pat to his side, Ping was off in a slow trot down the path toward the back of the town. As they passed through, people waved and smiled, and some even spoke salutations to them. Shen looked around more and more, his green eyes

scanning all over, and yet he still could not find what he was looking for. Lao looked too, but he instead was looking for a person.

There was a man walking down one of the paths, toward a building with a sign reading 'fresh herbs and spices.' Lao looked to him and shouted. "Excuse me, sir?"

The man walked over with a bag on his back, bouncing as he stepped toward Ping and the two atop him. "Yes? How can I help you?"

Lao looked to Shen and he smiled. "Could you point us in the direction of the general store please? We need to get some water and apples for our dimian here," Shen explained. He reached his hand down and pet at the feathers on the side of Ping's neck.

"Certainly, I'm heading there now, actually. Just follow me, if you would." The man adjusted the strap of his bag and began to walk. Shen brought Ping alongside him, tugging at the handles of the saddle as the bird stepped onward. They walked for just a few moments, and then the man spoke up. "Where are you two from?" He asked.

Lao spoke first, softly and calmly. "Zhaoyin."

"Ah, nearby, right?" Lao nodded to him in response. "Yeah, I've been by there before. Never really liked that place. It always seemed shady and scary to me, kinda rough and tough."

"Yeah. That's why I left," Lao said.

"Good on you. You're strong for doing that so young. I applaud your sense of freedom."

"Thank you," Lao said.

"And what about you?"

Shen spoke next. "Oh, you wouldn't know it."

"I've been many places, friend. Try me."

"It doesn't have a name, actually. It's a small island off the northern coast of Batung. I don't really think anyone lives there anymore, and it's been too long since I've been there myself."

"Fellow travelers! Oh, this place really is great. I'm really going to miss this town when I leave. Well, here we are," he said, and Shen and Lao looked ahead of them to find the building. As he brought Ping to a stop, he looked and saw its welcoming atmosphere. Yellow and green paint was splashed in brilliant patterns all across the front of the building on the wood.

"You're leaving? Where are you going from here?" Lao asked.

"Wherever the wind takes me, young man. I'm a nomad, a man without a home."

"I can respect that," Shen added.

"Anyway, enough chitchat, shall we," the man said, and they all walked to the front of the building. Shen looked to the building and found a wooden pole, about waist-height tall, with a rope tied to it. He grabbed it into his hand, pulling Ping by the saddle with the other, and tied him by the saddle and neck to the pole. Once secured, the dimian pecked at the rope, cooing softly.

"Aw, I know, buddy. It's just for a little bit, I promise." Shen said. The bird looked to him, blinked its eyelids over its giant yellow eyes and beady pupils, and then let out a great *squawk*. "That's the spirit, buddy," Shen said with a straight face, patting Ping on the head. They entered slowly, first Lao, leading with joy in his stride. Shen and the man entered next, one right behind the other, and the door shut behind them.

"Welcome! I'll be right with you," a voice called out from behind the bamboo counter. There was a soft shuffling sound, and then the sound of metal clattering to the wooden floor, followed by a disgruntled *oof* from the person behind the counter.

"Everything alright back there?" Shen asked, beginning to look around at the shelves. Most everything on the shelves and the tables lining the walls was some sort of food item. There were vegetables sitting in piles of straw and leaves, and hunks of meat wrapped in cloth sitting in buckets of ice nearer to the counter.

"All good! Just dropped a few pans is all," the voice said. The voice soon had a face, as the person behind the counter stood up and dusted off their brown cloth tunic. "Hello. I am Xu Wing, and this is my store."

"Kinda small," Lao said.

"Yes, well, it's got all the necessities, young man. Doesn't need to be that big for that, now does it?"

The boy shook his head and smiled a little. "I guess not," he said.

"You wouldn't happen to have apples and a bit of water would you?" Shen spoke up, his eyes trailing to the man they were with. He had left Shen's side, wandering around the store and picking up random objects.

"As a matter of fact I do. Apples are over by the tea leaves to your left, and I'll grab the water bucket. It's still fresh and cold, lucky for you." The shopkeeper knelt down and picked a bucket from the floor, a wooden one, which had a handle and a channel at the front for pouring water out in a steady stream. Shen placed the waterskin onto the countertop as he'd gotten it from out of his bag, and then walked to the left of the shop to retrieve the aforementioned apples. He found a basket, a large one with a great wide mouth, which was filled to the brim and then some with ripe apples. Next to it, he'd spotted a pile of cloth bags, fairly medium sized, about the same size as Shen's side bag, if not a little smaller.

He held the cloth bag in one hand, and with the other hand he grasped apple after apple, until the bag was filled just enough to be tied off at the opening. All in all, there sat twenty apples inside the bag. It was enough, a good amount that Ping could survive on for a while before buying more. Shen looked back to the pile of bags, and close by it, there sat a smaller pile of thin rope strands. Slightly frayed, Shen grabbed one of them and took it with him as he walked back to the counter, where the shopkeeper stood, full waterskin in hand held at the neck. "Get everything you need?" He said.

"Should have," Shen answered.

"Let me figure out how much you'll be spending. This will only take a moment," the shopkeeper said, and then reached a hand into the bag. Feeling around for a while, he then pulled his hand back out and grabbed the strand of rope, wrapping it around the top of the bag and tying it off tightly. "Twenty apples and a waterskin," he said to himself. "That'll be 14 Yin, please," the shopkeeper said, a smile across his face.

"Certainly," Shen said. He reached into his bag and pulled the coin pouch from it. Then, he proceeded to pull 14 little silver coins from the pouch and he placed them all onto the counter, then put the pouch back into the bag on his side.

The shopkeeper looked at them for a moment, seemingly counting each coin out in his head, before speaking up once again. "Thank you! You're all good to go," he said with a smile, scraping the coins into his hand.

"Thank you so much," Shen said. He grabbed the bag of apples from off the table and handed the waterskin to Lao. Shen looked to the shopkeeper, and with his free arm, he placed his fist to his chest in a salute. The shopkeeper returned the gesture, and Lao even put forth a salute of his own. With a smile, the two of them turned and began walking toward the door. As they reached the threshold of the doorway, the man they had come in with stopped them, a few herbs held in a cloth in his hand.

"Leaving so soon?" He asked.

"We should get going. Might as well explore the place a bit more before we up and leave, hm?"

"Ah. Well, it was surely nice meeting you two. If you could, stop by Xiang Chun's tea shop. It's by the front gates. Best tea in the mainland if that's your pleasure," he said, a big smile on his face.

Shen thought and in an instant, he remembered the shop they had passed by on the way to the general store. He remembered the big sign, the one of the big wooden tea cup. "I'll be sure to run by," Shen said adjusting the scarf around his neck.

"Make sure to enjoy yourself, and safe travels!" The man said, biting into one of the herb leaves he had gotten.

The two of them waved to the man, and pushed the wooden door open, walking out into the town once more. Ping was sat lying next to the pole he was tied to, his legs tucked up under him. With the sound of the door opening and closing his head shot up and he stood quickly. He let out a gracious *squawk*, and began happily tapping his feet on the ground, one after the other, until they both reached him. "I missed you too, buddy," Shen said softly. He reached into the bag of apples after untying it, and pulled one from inside. Ping's beady little pupils were fixated on the yellowish-red fruit, and his head moved when Shen's hand did. Shen tossed it lightly up into the air, and Ping snatched it in the blink of an eye, gulping it down after only chewing once.

"One of these days, he's going to choke," Lao giggled.

"I certainly hope not," Shen said, "he's our ride." Just then, Ping lightly pecked at Shen's side with his beak. "Hey!" Lao laughed, while Shen scowled at the dimian. "No biting!" Lao kept laughing, and Shen built up a chuckle or two from the whole ordeal.

They were now back on the dirt path through the town, with Ping walking at their side instead of carrying the two of them. Shen held one of the harness straps of Ping's saddle in his hand, walking him along the path. People walked by and waved, a few with dimians of their own, which put a nice warm feeling in their hearts as they waved back with smiles on their faces. Beautiful green grass like the kind in the fields of the mainland lined the sides of buildings, sprinkled with all manner of little flowers below the taller grass. The sun was up above, shining warm light down on the bare backs of their necks. The back of Lao's neck and head in particular was affected greatly, on the account that he had the hair there shaved. Around his ears there would come a burning sensation, but it was fleeting, and something that Lao had already gotten used to from living out on the streets in the sweltering sun.

    Once they arrived at the tea shop, both of them took notice of the fact that nowhere on the building were there any windows. No empty frames or even ones filled in by translucent paper. As they walked in however, and the door shut behind them, the lack of windows was truly apparent. The only light that could be gleaned from inside came from lanterns strung up at the ceiling and candles upon the tables. The lanterns were lit on their insides by a flame, shining their colors of yellow, orange, and green upon the walls of the building. Candles were melted slightly at their tops by tiny flames dancing in their own heat, thin smoke rising up and out of the roof through little slits on the ceiling at the back of the building. They walked in, and were promptly greeted at the door by a nice older man.

    "Hello! Welcome to my shop! My name is Xiang Chun. Please, make yourself comfortable," he said. Upon his chin there stood a mighty black beard, and atop his head was little more than a few wisps of black hair. His skin was dark tan, like most citizens of Batung, freckled with moles along the right side of his neck.

"Thank you very much," Shen said.

"There should be a table with two chairs for the both of you back in that corner," Xiang said pointing into one of the back corners. "I'll be right with you." He smiled to the two of them and then rushed off to another end of the room.

Shen looked to Lao and smile. "Are you gonna get anything?" He asked the boy, beginning to walk across the room.

"Is there anything else but tea?"

"You don't like tea?"

"I've never actually had it," he said.

Shen's eyes went wide, and he had to keep himself from speaking too loudly, lest he might disrupt the other patrons of the shop. "What? You've never had tea? Well, that won't take much to change, now will it?"

"I guess not," Lao said, giggling a little and smiling to himself.

As they walked into the more middle part of the room, Shen looked toward the back right corner, the one adjacent to where him and Lao were going. There was a figure sat in a chair in the back section of the table, facing outward at the other patrons. They were shrouded in darkness, with only a single candle placed on the table, not putting forth enough light to illuminate them. Just as Shen turned his head, he heard a voice. "Hey, scarf." It was softer, with a twinge of force to it, lying under the surface. He reached a hand up to his neck, taking the faded green fabric of his scarf into his fingers. Looking around, he couldn't find anyone clearly calling out. "Yes, you. Over here," with the last words, it became apparent that it was the figure at the back right corner table who was speaking.

Careful not to draw too much attention to himself, Shen grabbed Lao lightly by the wrist and brought him over, walking to the table in question. Lo and behold, sat around the table, were two other wooden chairs, set facing the figure on the other side of the tabletop. "You mean me?" Shen asked.

"Sit down. I don't mean to make you uncomfortable, in a cushy tea shop of all places." They were still in the shadows, their features unknown to both Shen and Lao. The two of them warily took their seats across from the figure.

"Who are you?" Lao asked.

"And why have you called me over?" Shen asked. He was both curious and nervous, his heart beating a tiny bit faster than it normally would, yet he asked firmly.

"Relax, I mean no harm. I know what you are, you know, and vaguely, **who** you are." As Shen and Lao listened closer, they could tell that it was a woman behind the voice, though muffled as it was. "Don't worry, your secret's safe with me."

"Know what? What exactly do you think you know about me? Who do you think I am?" Shen asked, persistent in figuring out who this mysterious woman was.

"I can't speak here. You'll risk people finding out, and we wouldn't want that, now would we?"

"Is that a threat?" With each moment passing, Shen noticed more things about the woman. She was leaning forward a bit, and he was overwhelmed with details about her. Her skin was a light tan, a familiar shade that Shen knew well as the Vasai skin tone. The glint of the candle's flame lit a good view of her eyes, which were a light hazel color flecked with gray. A more glaring detail, which somewhat intimidated the both of them, was the mask she wore on her face, covering her jaw, chin, mouth, and nose. It was wooden, painted in light blue at the mouth region and white at the area by the bridge of her nose. Upon it, in black, there was a partial face painted on in lines. A big nose hung above a wide, open, smiling mouth of a spirit, flashing white fangs among regular flat teeth.

"No. I don't mean it to seem that way. We can talk elsewhere, at a different time. Please, meet me at the fountain at sundown, it'll be safe to talk there." She spoke and Shen could see her black hair, tied up at the top in a bun and fixed with twigs, bounce the light of the candle flame off it slightly.

"How do I know I can trust you?"

"You don't know. But please, I ask you, please trust me on this one. I am not your enemy." She leaned back in her chair, and just like that, her image was gone, taken by the darkness and the shadows once again. Shen got up from his seat and Lao followed suit, standing and beginning to walk toward the table they'd intended to get to.

"Who was she?" Lao asked, wide eyed as he sat down across from Shen at the table.

"I don't know," Shen said quietly. He thought to himself for a moment about what he was to do.

"Hello again! Sorry about the wait, one of the customers was giving me some trouble with their order. What can I get for you?" Xiang was over and standing before them in no time at all. With a chipper look on his face and a brilliant smile he stood and waited for the two of them to answer.

"Just a simple green tea, please," Shen said. He looked to Lao, waiting for his response.

"The same, please," Lao said with a bashful tone laced into his voice.

"Alright! Would you like any food with that? I can get you some sweet buns, if you'd like, or some deer jerky, both freshly made if I may add."

"Some sweet buns would be nice, yes. Lao, would you like some?"

"Can I share them with you?"

"Of course," Shen said with a smile.

"Okay. I'll be right back with the tea and buns. Sit tight," Xiang said, and he was off again through the shop like a rogue gust of wind. The two sat for a while in quiet. Every now and then, though, Shen would make a comment on the decor of the building.

"Having no windows doesn't really do much for the place, hm? It sure makes everything more ominous than one would expect from a friendly tea shop."

"It's definitely spooky in here," Lao added.

"The lanterns are pretty, though, aren't they?" He looked up and around at all the lanterns. The greens and yellows and oranges shined in the air, and their lights hit the walls around them dimly. It was both eerie and warming, welcoming even.

"They are." Lao said.

From another side of the room came Xiang again, with a mess of things in his possession. He had the teapot in the grip of his left hand, with two cups balancing awkwardly up his forearm. In his right hand, held atop his palm, was the plate of steaming hot sweet buns, golden brown on the top of them glistening with butter in the lantern light. "Do you need some help, Mr. Chun?" Shen asked.

"Oh I've done this so many times it may as well be breathing!" He moved his arms around gently as he accounted for the balancing of the things in his hands. Quickly, he set down the teapot, full and with a wisp of steam drifting up and out of a tiny hole in the lid. Next, he rolled the teacups from down his arm and into his hand, placing them down in rapid succession that neither Shen nor Lao could keep up with. Then, a lot less flashy this time, Xiang placed down the plate of sweet buns onto the table, his hand retreating back and showing off a warm red mark on his palm from the heat of the plate. "There we go! You know, there's only been one time I've messed that up," he began trailing off, his eyes looking elsewhere, fixed as though he were staring at something far far away, "never again," he said solemnly. "Well! Eat and drink up while they're still hot!" He said it chipperly and quickly, then dashed off to the front door as another patron entered.

    The two of them took to the tea and buns slowly, pacing themselves. That is, until they had actually tasted one of the sweet buns. Their taste was unlike anything they'd ever had. So much flavor poured from them into their mouths that after the first bun, the two of them couldn't help but grab as many as they could carry in the palms of their hands. "Hey, no fair! You've got bigger hands," Lao said.

    "You took more of them!" Shen said in return, almost childish in his tone. Soon, the buns were all gone, and they were left with the tea. The smell was wafting into their nostrils and was sweet. Shen reached over and grabbed the teapot, his other hand grasping one of the plain ceramic cups that were left on the table. His voice was calmer now, less whiny than it was before. "Would you like me to pour it for you?" Shen asked.

    "Yes please," Lao said, waiting slouched back in his chair, fairly full from the sweet buns he'd devoured. Shen tipped the teapot over slightly, and the clear brown liquid poured in a steady stream, billowing into the cup as the steam and the smell rose further into the air. The smell began to make Lao somewhat tired, or at the very least, made his already set tiredness increase. It was soothing, welcoming. Once he was done pouring, Shen took the cup by his fingers and placed it in front of Lao. "Thank you." As he began to sip, the taste flooded his mouth. The little hairs on his arms tingled and the heat of the tea drifted down into his stomach. He let forth a sigh of enjoyment, and soon was finished with a cup. Then, he was done with another cup, while Shen had only just finished his first.

By the time the sun was beginning to set, Shen and Lao had gone through two whole pots of tea. Xiang came by, and as Lao looked around, he noticed that almost everyone had cleared out while they were busy. There were only a few stragglers, pairs of friends or couples that stayed to eat or drink some tea. "All done?"

"I believe we are," Shen said. Lao stayed quiet as his eyes began to drift into exhaustion, a light smile on his lips. As he began reaching into his bag for his coin pouch, Shen was stopped by Xiang's hand, resting on his shoulder.

"No need to pay, sir. Someone's already paid for your things, had a mask on. Friend of yours?"

Shen thought for a moment and then spoke up, softly and calmly. "Yes. I'll have to remember to thank her for that. Thank you for letting me know," he said. He backed his chair up and stood, dusting off the bun crumbs from his tunic. "Lao," Shen said loudly.

Lao jolted awake from his daze. "Hm? I'm up, I'm up," he said, standing up and pushing his chair in.

"You have a good one, now. Safe travels," Xiang said, a fist to his chest in salute. Shen returned it, as did Lao, sleepy as he was, and then they were out of the door and toward the fountain at the center of the town.

Around the base of the fountain, on the ground, there sat a few lanterns. The light emanating from them illuminated the scales of the fish in the water, bouncing it all around in the water. In the little light that there was from the lanterns and the sun, the woman from the tea shop could be seen. She stood leant up against a building wall near the fountain. "Didn't think you'd show," she said, muffled again as it was spoken from behind her mask.

"I thought it only fair, since you paid for our things back there."

"No big deal. I'm a friend, remember?"

"Who are you?" Shen asked, and then moved closer toward her.

The woman removed the mask, dropping it down and letting it rest by her collarbone, the leather strap tightening it to her face loosening as it fell. Her face was brought into the light, clear as day to Shen, who was paying utmost attention. "My name is Reina. Reina Yamato, if you want a more formal answer." Her pale hazel eyes glinted in the light, a light which also served to show the two little dark blue lines, painted horizontally onto the bridge of her nose. A light tan hue composed her skin, and it almost reminded Shen of his own mother.

"My name is Shen-"

"Jin," she interrupted, "I know."

Shen walked even closer, right up to the woman, and became confused. "How do you know that? Answer me."

"Relax. Please. I don't want to cause a scene. Friend, not enemy, remember?" Lao watched on, hiding partially behind Shen. "I recognized the symbol on your scarf, the crest. The Jin family crest, right?"

"You're still not answering how you know it."

"I was getting to that." She said, getting a bit frustrated with the man before her. "If you couldn't already tell, I'm not from around here. I was stationed here years ago. That crest was on the top of my list to look out for when I was still a Vasai soldier. I never asked why. I learned never to ask my superiors why we did anything."

"You're with the Vasai army?" Shen said, getting loud.

"Was! I *was* with the Vasai army. I left years ago, and went into hiding."

"Why?" Lao piped up, stepping out from behind Shen.

"Because I regret everything I did when I was there. Everything."

"Why? Why are you even telling me this? Why are you here?" Shen asked plainly.

"Because what I did was abhorrent. I came here, to Batung, because I thought I could help those in need, help people like yourself. Mystics. Because I need to pay for what I've done, and I haven't fully done that yet. Though, I suppose I've already started." Reina leaned forward, bringing her body into the light, and her right side came into view. She was without a right arm, a burned and scarred stub poking out of the rusting silver armor she wore, severed near the shoulder. It was unmoving, a grim reminder of her own past mistakes.

"How did that happen?" Lao asked, curious and solemn in his voice.

"Lao! Don't just ask things like that, it's rude!"

"No. It's fine. I need to say. If I ignore it, I'll never truly pay for it, will I?"

"Are you sure?" Shen asked, the anger in voice dying down, replaced with consolation.

"Yes. I need to let people know what I've done. It was my third time in the field, and I was so young. I was stationed in Ogon by my commanding officer in order to take care of any straggling Mystics that had escaped capture. I'd already killed two of them before this incident, the parents. We had been tracking another of them down for weeks, their young boy, until we finally found him. We had him cornered, and I could see the horror in his eyes. His whole body shook with fright. All we had to do was take him to the camps. That's it." Her voice wavered and her eyes began to water. "I lunged at him, and fire bursted from his hands. Like instinct, my arm went up to shield me, and since I was wearing metal armor, it burned the whole of my arm."

She paused. Her eyes continued burning with a poignant sensation, and tears dripped ever so softly from the corners of her eyes. "Take your time, please," Shen said.

Waiting a few more moments, she spoke again to finish her story. "All the muscles in my arm were burned, and I couldn't even move it. They couldn't get the armor off my arm, and they had to cut it off. So I... I laid there, screaming in pain while the other soldiers killed the boy. I… I didn't want him to die. I understand why he attacked me. I was the enemy, not him. I was the monster." Reina was sobbing now, tears streaming down her cheeks and stinging her skin as they did so.

"It's okay. Truly. There are others that wouldn't think the way you do, about Mystics like me." Shen reached his arm out and placed a hand onto her left shoulder. He gently squeezed it, and Reina's tears began to dissipate.

"Thank you. What I did can never be forgotten." She said, sniffling, her eyes quickly drying.

"The important thing is that you acknowledge it and are willing to make things right." Shen said, bringing his arm back.

"Yes, and on that subject, I need to tell you why it's so important that I've found you. My mission for the last few years has been to help those in need. Maybe then I can better my life, redeem myself. I overheard you by the general store. You're travelers right?"

"That's right."

"Let me join you. Whatever you or anyone we meet might need, I will try to help. Please." Reina pleaded, her fingers rubbing across the wood of the mask around her neck.

Shen thought, and Lao too, though one met their answer faster than the other. "I think you should," Lao said.

Shen looked to the boy. Like back on Yedao when he'd asked about his abilities, Shen noticed a gleam in Lao's eyes. It was all together mischievous, naive, and inspired. It was a look that Shen would grow to enjoy, even envy, in time. "Okay. You may join us. But, I need to tell you a few things before we leave town."

"Excellent! I have a camp just outside of town, and some extra tents actually." Reina seemed more chipper than before, happy even, with a soft smile across her face.

"Alright, let's go then." On the way out of the town, Shen explained their journey. He explained why they were traveling, spoke of Shen's younger brother and of the island he supposedly was staying on. It was simple: make it to Sukoshi Island and find him.

He did not let it show, but Shen was still wary of Reina. It was not a distrust, however, nor full on trust. Rather, he held a neutral trust of her. He hoped in excess in his mind that she was truly good, that she would be able to redeem her own actions of the past. But, that was yet to be seen, and they had a long journey still ahead of them in the morning.

Rumors

      The day had begun, and already Shen was at odds in his own mind as to where they would go next. There were multiple towns in the vicinity, within at least walking distance. He thought to himself what they might need, and nothing really came to mind, save for some herbs. Looking over the map again and again, he narrowed it down to two options. The first was a medium sized town by the name of Wan-Jeong, near a flowing river that led a long and winding path next to the capital. The other was a smaller town, right by a large forest. Next to it, scrawled in black ink, was the name Lu Min.

      He looked to Reina, who was stuffing a few things in her bag, rolling up her own cloth sleeping roll, and spoke. "Reina, how well do you know this area?"

      She looked up from her things. "Moderately enough. What do you need to know?"

      "Well, we have two choices of where to go next," Shen started, and handed over the map, "Wan-Jeong and Lu Min. Either way, we want to eventually reach the capital. Those names bring anything up?"

      "Hmm," she said, thinking for a moment. "Wan-Jeong is right near the Shui River, which goes all across the country. If we go there, we'll more than likely have to take the river to get to the capital."

      "What's wrong with that?" Shen asked.

      "Soldiers are patrolling the rivers. They've found Mystics hiding on the banks before and are stopping anyone they find traveling the waters. You don't want that to happen."

      "No," he trailed off.

"I've only ever heard of Lu Min forest, not the town, and even then, I've only heard the name from a few traders in the capital. If traders are talking about it, it must be fairly harmless."

"I suppose that settles it," Shen said.

Reina handed Shen the map back and scratched at the back of her head. Her hair was let down, the sticks that once held her bun up were out and laid on the floor. Now that the sun was shining, Shen was able to see more of her. He saw the regular silver armor she wore on her chest, fitting her form perfect enough to allow her optimal movement. Along with it, however, there were plates of the silver armor embellished with designs fixed upon the sides her thighs. They looked like the scales of a fish, in that they were stacked atop one another. Reina reached down and grasped the twigs, placing them back in her hair, holding up the bun the black locks were fixed into.

Another thing that truly caught Shen's eyes was what she had upon the small of her back. At the area where her waist met her back, on the armor, there was a loop of hide leather which housed a small sword, its handle facing her left side. It dangled about lightly as she moved, even though it was held firm to her person. "You didn't mention the sword," Shen said defensively, bundling his hand together in a fist.

"I had forgotten about it, honestly. I mean you no harm whatsoever. Friend, remember?"

"Right. Of course." Shen said, and the atmosphere sort of drained itself of sound. That is, until Lao awoke.

"Ow!" The boy cried from his tent.

"Lao? What is it?" Shen said, rushing over to where Lao was.

He got up, rubbing his back near his shoulder blade with his hand, his face molded into a pained cringe. "I slept on a rock, right on my scar!"

"Let me see."

The boy removed his tunic, dropping it to the ground, and turned his back to Shen. The wound was healed, for the most part, no dry blood or anything like that. However, there was a firm bruise in the center of the three scars. "It's nothing bad, Lao. Just a bruise."

"How'd you get that?" Reina asked, creeping up behind Shen with all her stuff packed and secured to her back.

"Hookbeak." Lao said.

"Nasty things. And the worst part, they're everywhere."

"Yes. You have everything?" Shen said, tightening his grip on his own side bag and the tent Reina had given him, strapped to his back.

"Yeah."

"Do I have to pack up my tent and stuff?" Lao asked.

"Yes, you've gotta pull your own weight."

"Aw man!" Lao said, picking up his cloth tunic and sliding it back onto his body.

After everything had been packed up, the tents and the sleeping rolls, the bags of food which were secured to Ping's saddle, they all began moving toward Lu Min. Shen and Lao were sat atop Ping, who was content after having eaten a fresh apple. Reina, though, was on foot, walking next to the dimian and her two companions. "Are you sure you're okay with walking, Reina? I don't have to be up here you know," Shen said.

"It's fine, Shen. Really. It's not that big of a deal." The two of them had fussed with each other over who would be walking even before they left. Shen had wanted to walk. He was content with walking, to feel the soft ground or the firm dirt under his bare feet. But, Reina insisted that it was her that walked. She didn't want to burden him, to put a block in the trust she was gradually building.

Lao was indifferent, instead taking care not to fall asleep and fall off of Ping's saddle.

"Everything alright back there, Lao?" Shen asked.

The boy jerked a bit in his seat on the saddle, his eyes adjusting to the light from the sun flooding toward them. "Hmm?"

"You got sleep last night, right?" Reina interjected.

"Not as much as I wanted."

"Something keep you up?"

"Qiu." Lao said it plainly, and things went silent.

Shen turned his back a bit and looked to the boy. "I know, Lao. It's alright. You don't have to tell her if you don't want to."

"I'm missing something, aren't I? Qiu? Who's that?" Reina added.

"We had another dimian with us. We… lost her, a while back." Lao said. Even though he had not explicitly said what had happened, Reina could tell by his voice. She knew in her mind that Qiu had died. She knew what loss looked like, and she could see it festering in his bright eyes.

"That's awful."

"Yes," Shen said. Lao simply nodded, his stomach in knots and his mind dazed.

The rest of their trip was uneventful. Every once in awhile they would see some brilliantly colored bug hop from the tall grass onto the path or a little rodent scurry around, leaving waves in the blades of grass. Lao took to napping, resting his head on Shen's back while he directed Ping where to go. Reina, however, was on the lookout. Her eyes were constantly darting back and forth as noises alerted her attention. They were always nothing, of course, but Shen began to get worried. Sometimes he would ask her what she was doing, or if she'd seen or heard something, and everytime he would get the same answer: "nothing."

     They arrived around the afternoon time, and in Shen's mind, he figured there'd be many people moving about. It was lunch time after all, and farmers would usually be going out to fields to tend to their soybean crop, then make it home for food. But, there was no one. It seemed as though the whole world was empty, as empty as this little town was. Everything was quiet. It was a kind of quiet that could make even the slightest breath sound like the loudest sound imaginable. Soon, the silence was broken however, as a door slightly creaked open nearby.

     "What is it? What… What do you want?" They stuttered frantically.

     "Is this Lu Min?" Reina spoke up, stepping forward toward the house.

     "Yes. Why have you come here?" They spoke again, still hiding behind the door.

     "We only want to stop for a meal. That's all. We'll be gone by nightfall, we promise."

     "Alright. Please, come inside. Quickly." The person said, and then the door swung open wider, the person behind it gone.

     "Are you sure about this?" Shen asked.

     "We don't really have much of a choice, do we?" Reina replied.

     They all began walking toward the house, Lao still in a slight sleep, soon to be roused. The house was fairly normal, bamboo walls and wooden roofing, with minor chips and cracks in the material, though it still looked sturdy. Ping knelt down, tucking his legs into his breast, and Shen hopped down off of him. He reached for the apple bag, grabbed one of the fruits, and tossed it to the dimian, who happily gobbled it down. Shen reached his hand out and shook Lao. "What? What is it?"

"We're here. Come on, you want food right?" At the mention of food, Lao jumped off the bird's back, kicking off with one of his feet. Unhappy with being kicked, Ping reached his neck out and pecked the boy lightly in the side.

"Hey!"

"Haha, come on, Lao. We should go, Reina's already inside."

"Hrmph. Fine." Lao pouted. The both of them entered into the house, after tying Ping to one of the posts outside of course, and looked around. There were windows, which let in sunlight from outside. But, there were also lanterns, only a few of them having flames alight inside them to bring a warmer atmosphere to the room.

"Guys. Over here," Reina said. She sat at a little table with three chairs, over in a corner of the little entry room of the house they were in. Shen and Lao walked over and took their seats. Both of them noted silently the discomfort of the chairs. They were wooden, no cushions or anything, and it seemed as though the both of them were splintering at their backs. Before they had time to question about it, the owner of the house emerged from the kitchen at the back.

"Please. Forgive me. We're always welcoming of travelers. But, unfortunately, this is all I have to give you." He was an old man, shriveled and thin, his dark tan skin riddled with moles upon the arms. In his hands, he slowly set down three little bowls of soybean soup. "If not for them, we might have some fresh meat to cook up for you folks."

"Them?" Lao asked.

"The Faceless," the old man said. His hands went up to his face, clutching at his cheeks with his calloused fingers, worn from probable years of farmwork. "The forest, they're from the forest. Evil spirits. They… They get you to talk, and when you do, you become one of them!" He fumbled with the spoons in his hands, dropping them to the table with a great clatter. "Sorry.

Sorry, I should collect myself," the old man muttered. He calmed himself, and then began to talk again. "None of our people have come back from the forest, and those that are left of us won't go in to hunt for game."

"We can help you!" Lao piped up, sipping at his soup, the bowl nestled in his hands.

"Lao, please, we can't afford to make too many stops." Shen said.

"But, those people."

"You know, we're going to have to go through that forest eventually if we're getting to the capital," Reina added.

"We can go around the forest," Shen pleaded. "I want nothing more than to help people, but I don't think we have the time or energy to do so right now."

"It's not that bad, Shen. Please. We can help these people, really. It would take us even longer to go around the forest."

"Please, Shen," Lao said, a quiver building in his bottom lip.

"There may be a reward in it for you. A more filling meal for one, and we have necklaces from the capital we've received for marriages. Beautiful silver, truly," the old man said. It appeared as though he was shaking, his fingers trembling with their gnarled and cracked look, wrinkles etched into the dark tan skin.

"Alright. Alright. But, we go on one condition."

"Anything," Reina said.

"Yeah, anything!" Lao added.

"We leave from the forest by nightfall. No excuses. I won't have us getting lost and stuck in that forest, alright?"

"Okay, that's fine by me," Reina replied.

"Me too," Lao said, smiling.

"I must warn you folks of something before you leave. The Faceless, they will do anything to make you try and talk. Don't. If you do, your soul shall be taken and your body will become like them, destined to doom others to the same fate. Please. Take the utmost care," the old man said, his voice wavering, his eyes worried and frantic.

"Of course. We'll leave once we finish eating." Shen said, and a feeling grew in his stomach. It was one of worry, especially when he looked to Lao, hopeful as he slurped at his soup bowl. He calmly sipped at his own bowl of soup until it was nearly gone, not wanting to drink it all as the taste was less than satisfying. Reina had finished hers, placing down the bowl calmly as she wiped her lips with the sleeve of the tunic she wore under her armor. Lao had finished hers much quicker than the other two, slapping his bowl down and rising from his chair with a wide smile.

"Come on! Let's go!" Lao shouted, tugging on the fabric of Shen's tunic, trying to get him up and standing.

"Alright, I'm coming. Hang on," Shen said, chuckling a bit as he stood up and pushed in his chair.

"You shouldn't be so adamant, young one. Be wary of the spirits. I've never seen anything like them before," the old man said.

"We'll take care. Thank you, sir," Reina said, standing up and walking over to Shen and Lao, standing beside them.

"Thank you again for helping us. There is another part of this village, on the other side of the forest. I will send a message to my sister there. They will be waiting there for you once you've finished with the Faceless." The old man said, walking to the back of the kitchen, grabbing something, then returning. It was a little cage, and inside, there sat a little messenger lizard like the one from Senhong Alley, though this one was much greener. However, it still bore the same look, sharp raised scales and big blue eyes. "Go. Before the night comes. And remember to be careful. When you find them, don't talk." They were out the door with a salute and more pleasantries, and back on the path going through the village, headed this time for the other side.

The path was straight, with little to no curves as they walked it. Ping had no troubles, and was content with carrying the both of Shen and Lao on his back, and even with being dragged along by Reina, clutching onto a rope tied to one of the holds of his saddle. Lao was more awake than ever, his eyes as bright and wide as the smile on his mouth. Shen was quiet. He looked forward with a plain expression on his face, his hands gripping the front of the saddle as Ping moved forward and forward. Inside, he was worried of course. He had not encountered a spirit before, and especially not one as formidable as the old man had made the Faceless out to be.

They soon approached the forest, and immediately, the darkness of it overwhelmed them. The trees were tall and thick at their trunks. Leaves of the darkest green shrouded most any sunlight that could be shone from above, and as such, the ground under them was darkened and difficult to discern. Even so, every once in a while, the three of them could see some bright little lights appear in the forest, just through the treeline.

"What's that?" Lao said.

"I see it too," Reina added.

"Do you think it might be other people?" Lao asked.

"I don't know. But, I suppose we'll find out soon enough." Shen brought Ping forward and they all walked into the forest, in the midst of where Lao had seen one of the lights. They walked further in, and already they could tell it would be hard to navigate. Shen had the map of course, and Reina had hers, but it didn't show any kind of path through the forest itself. It merely showed the forest as splotches of green on the parchment.

  Soon, Lao noticed another light, but this time, he saw its source. It was a little creature, glowing. Big circular red eyes gleamed on its round face, just above a little glistening black beak. It glowed in a light bluish-green light, and tall pointed ears on its head twitched as it looked to Lao. "Hey!" Lao shouted, and instinctively he ran toward the creature, back behind a tree.

  "Lao, no!" Shen said, pulling Ping toward where Lao had run.

  "I'll go after him," Reina said dropping the rope she had in her hand, and she began to fast walk toward the boy.

  Lao followed the little creature, its fluffy-looking coat bouncing with its tiny footfalls zooming through the underbrush of the forest. "Wait!" The boy said. He ran and ran until it darted to the side, and he'd finally lost sight of it. The problem was, however, that he'd also lost sight of Shen and Reina too.

  Reina looked around her, and found that she was now in an outcropping in the trees, surrounded by a circle of them, and her worn silver boots rested on rocky dirt. Lao was nowhere to be seen. In fact, Reina figured the boy was actually not close to her position at all. On top of that, she could no longer hear Ping's heavy footsteps, nor Shen's shouts for Lao. As she looked around, she could only find a large rock in front of her some steps away, alight with the little sunlight that came from the hole in the canopy of leaves above her. In a few moments, Reina began to hear the *snap* of a branch breaking underfoot ahead of her.

  Shen had wandered too, and he found himself in an outcropping similar to where Reina was. Though, instead of being just dirt and a single rock, his was filled with a small pond, some tall grass, and a few bigger rocks. Shen hopped off of Ping and tied the rope to one of the trees around him. He walked forward, and inside the pond's waters, he noticed nothing. Neither fish nor little water plants waved inside the shallow depths of the pond before him. As his head swiveled around, he found nothing around him. Though his eyes saw nothing, his ears could pick up something. From the bushes or the trees, Shen heard a rustling, and as he did, he brought his arm back behind him, his hand gripping the handle of the bronze sword.

The Spirits of Lu Min Forest

Elsewhere, in her section of the forest, Reina too heard a noise. The noise quickly revealed its source, though, as a figure emerged from the trees and made its slow way to the rock before her. The sight was off-putting to say the least. It was a large figure, almost muscular in its stature, and it was completely black apart from where its face would be. There, it wore a sort of mask of cream white with little pointed ears on the sides. Even more so than its appearance, its position was also unnerving. Its big arms were bent, hands placed firmly upon where its eyes would be, had it had any. The fingers were bent, and as it crouched atop the rock in front of her, the walking shadow moved its head around in some sort of silent agony.

In a moment, Reina moved her hand to the handle of her sword at the small of her back. But, as she stared down the spirit before her, she brought her hand down and her arm back to her side. As she looked at it, its skin began to look like it was moving. The darkness of it was like a thick fog that crawled along the surface of its arms, legs, and torso. Despite it, Reina simply kept staring, and even took a seat upon the dirt as she did, just looking intently to the spirit. She'd have kept this up, this little game of sitting and staring, had the thing not started making sound. Its head turned toward her, hands still on its eyes, and she could hear a voice. "Corporal. What do you think you're doing?" It said, deep and human-like.

Far away from where she was, Lao kept looking all around. He couldn't find a trace of either of them. The grass under his feet was moist with dew from the morning, still almost fresh, no sunlight to burn it up. Around him was a darkness, though once in a while the trees would sway in such a way from the breeze that light would come through for but a second. Lao couldn't see the creature from before either, nor hear the little pattering of its feet through leaves and branches on the forest floor. He stood, still looking around, until more of the lights came into view around him.

They were from the creatures, their little rounded faces peering back at him with red glowing eyes. Almost as soon as they had appeared, though, they were gone again, melding back into the darkness of the forest trees leaving little sparks of their bluish-green glow. From their place in the darkness, there came a new figure. It hobbled out of the darkness, with a body even blacker and darker than the shadows which it emerged from. Upon the front of its head was a similar white mask to the spirit by Reina, though this one's was more thin and rigid, with each little wood grain visible from where Lao was stood. It came out with its hands on where its ears would be, the sides of its head, gnarled little fingers gripping at nothing.

Its head seemed to dart around, looking at nothing, until its mask fixed itself to Lao's position. Seemingly, it was staring right at him. Even with no eyes, it was still as though it was staring right into him. Lao felt his heart drop, his hands began to shake, and his forehead started to drip sweat slowly down from his skin. His breath faltered as he stared intently at it. And, worse still, his legs came out from under him, dropping him to the ground as the spirit began wailing and jumping around in place. It was a horrible sound, a shrieking *waaaaaaagh* that pierced the air around him. He wanted to scream out for help, for Shen, Reina, anyone, but he knew in his mind that he couldn't.

In another part of the forest, Shen couldn't even hear the sounds made by the Faceless near Lao. He couldn't even begin to think where Lao and Reina might be, nor hope to know where that was. The only thing before him were the rocks and the pond. It would almost be peaceful, if not for the slowly approaching spirit from the trees. Into the light it came. Its skin was black and dark like it had been for the two before it. The mask upon the front of its head was small, matching the size of its head, and even the rest of its form. It seemed almost childlike in its stature, small and scrawny. In a quick motion, it lunged forward to the pile of rocks on the other side of the pond. After a quicker motion, it crossed its legs and sat atop the pile of rocks, placing one of its hands firmly around its own throat, the other covering the area of the mask where its mouth would've been.

    Shen brought his hand away from the handle of his sword, unfazed by the spirit. If anything, he was sort of amused by it and its strange look. The amusement would have continued, were it not for the light which shimmered in the pond before him. His eye was caught, and as he brought his head down to look into the water, he could feel his legs weakening. There, right in the center of the pond, there was the image of his mother's face. He sat down with his legs crossed, having a hard time processing what was before him. It was clear as day, as if it were his own face staring back at him, but it was hers. There right in front of him was her light tan skin, her black hair, the dark green eyes looking to him from the water.

    Away, Reina was still looking to the spirit before her, crouching down on the big rock. "What? Was it something I said?" The voice called. "You should know better than to look at your commanding officer like that." Reina had this look painted onto her face, a horrified scowl with her eyebrows furled.

    "You should've killed him yourself," another voice cried. But, it didn't come from a different place, and instead came right from the spirit in front of her again. It was another familiar voice, a soldier she had once known. But, he was long gone. The only thing that could've made the sound, the only other being in the vicinity, was the blank-masked spirit before her.

"He's right. Why did you hesitate? Hm? You could've easily killed the little stain. But you didn't, did you?" The voice from before was back, deeper and more bassy than it had been earlier. "You're a coward you know. The king would've had your head, too. But you ran."

"You ran," the other voice said.

"You ran," another one said, a female voice, gruff and scratchy.

"Why did you run?" The deep voice said, and the Faceless swiveled its head over to her position. It was like it could feel her wanting to scream, the sound bubbling up at the back of her throat. "Because you're a coward. And you can't even say it," the voice cried. Reina felt her nerves tense and tense, twinging at each little movement the spirit before her made.

"Coward," the other voice said.

"Rotten coward," the female voice returned.

"Why did you run? You abandoned us," another voice came now, a younger man's, still from that same place, the spirit before her. Reina stared the spirit down, her eyes shaking in their sockets, until she could calm herself. She slowed her breathing. Inhale, hold it, then exhale. She continued and continued until her nerves were calmed, and the spirit was nothing more than a figure crouching on a rock.

"You couldn't kill me? Why? Why didn't you kill me?" A new voice, a small, soft one, shattered across her mind. As the sound of it burrowed into her ears, seemingly from within her own head, the feelings from before came flooding back into her body, her heart dropping and thumping even more in her chest.

As the spirit before Lao continued to scream, the boy found himself shaking. Throughout his whole body there was a terror unlike any he'd felt before. He could feel each of his fingers shake while they gripped at the grass and the dirt beneath him. Try as he might, he couldn't get the sound of the thing out of his head. *Aaaaaiiiieeee*, it began to cry, jumping around with its little thin legs. It leaped from the ground to one of the trees near it, latching on with its feet, staring down the boy with its blank white mask. It moaned and wailed, clutching the sides of its head with bony fingers, its dark body almost blending in with the shadows of the trees' leaves.

      Lao wanted to scream too. He wanted to shout with every breath in his lungs 'stop!' But deep in his mind he knew he couldn't even if he did want to. The Faceless before him knew this. It preyed on his fear, his desperation to cry out. It searched the deep recesses of the boy's mind and found what he feared most. "You! You're the reason she's dead! You are nothing but a waste!" It shouted in a voice too familiar to the boy. It brought back a wave of memories, a burning sensation along with it, burrowing its way into the corners of his eyes. The spirit looked to Lao, and it noticed something. Lao was not crying. The boy, clenched fists, wiped away the growing tears from his face and stared the creature down as it screamed and screamed evermore into the forest air. It jumped to another tree, closer to Lao now, spindly legs gripping onto the trunk firmly.

      "Why won't you ever listen to me? You never listen, boy!" The voice came again, and it seemed like it came from everywhere at once. "Listen! Listen! Listen!" It screamed over and over, and the spirit jumped from the tree, crouching down on the ground just feet from Lao's face. But, nevertheless, the boy kept staring, no sign of faltering evident in his face. His eyes gleamed with a light of smugness, as he looked to the thing wailing before him.

      Meanwhile, Shen was battling his own demons. Upon the surface of the pond, there still sat the still image of his mother's face. But, soon, it began to grow smaller in the water. Smaller and smaller it became until it was all but gone. It was then that a gnawing feeling itched at the back of Shen's mind. Like nothing he'd ever felt before, he watched as a new image came upon the water, his father's face. It was anything but foreign to him. The scar upon his black and bushy brow, the short cut hair atop his head, the solemn green eyes staring back at him. Shen could make out almost every pore within the dark tan skin of his father's face in the water. Soon, though, it too began to shrink.

Shen wanted to smack at the water, to bring the pictures back, but he could not. He could only watch as they were disappearing from his view. As a new image began to move on the pond, Shen could hear what sounded like footsteps coming from all around him. There wasn't anything truly there, of course, but it sounded like it. That, coupled with the image of approaching soldiers surrounding him from the water, served to drive an almost forgotten primal fear into Shen's being. His heart thumped against the inside of his chest, his mind racing, until he thought and realized. This wasn't real at all.

It was as if something had suddenly clicked in all of them. As the Faceless crouching upon the rock in front of Reina spoke, within her own mind no less, she came to the same realization. "You couldn't kill me! You know you had to, but you didn't! Why? Why. Why. Why. Why. Why?" The voice was frantic, tiny and shrill as it bounced within the confines of her head. But, it couldn't get to her. Her nerves were calm, her face poised in a blank expression without any emotion. No tears nor warmth of any filled the corners of her eyes as she stared down the spirit.

Lao too knew what was happening. The spirit cried more and more, a mighty *aaaaaiiiieeegh* filling the air around the boy. No matter how much it screamed, Lao couldn't help but giggle in his own mind. It had no power over him. Scream as it might, any form of wild howl it could muster, it did nothing, like arrows snapping upon shining armor. He looked the thing in the mask, right where its eyes might be, and he let a smirk creep upon his face. The spirit, still screaming, suddenly stopped. In a single moment, its body fell into a cloud of black smog. Once the cloud had dissipated, there was the mask sat on the ground, and before him, where the spirit once stood, was a young woman.

Reina stared her spirit down, and even she could not help but crack a smile upon her lips. The thing ceased its talking, its shouting, both inside her head and out, and collapsed in a similar way to how Lao's did. The black fog puffed up into the air for a brief moment, and left behind a large man, muscular, gripping onto his arms as they glistened sweat off his dark tan skin. He looked down at his feet and his eyes met with the mask. In a swift motion, he brought his foot down, and the mask shattered apart under his wooden sandal. "Thank you," he said, looking to Reina as he adjusted the bow and quiver on his back.

Shen was different from the other two. When he was posed with his spirit, not wild and erratic, but calm and sitting upon rocks in front of a pond, he did not smile. He simply looked to the thing with peaceful eyes, and the spirit fell into the black smoke, drifting over the water of the pond and then rising into the air. Shen's head tilted up, his eyes on the smoke. When they came back down to the rocks across the pond, however, they were met with a child sat on the rocks. His eyes were worried, frightened even, his feet wrapped in little bandages stained with dirt. "Come on, little one, let's get you home," Shen said, and stood up.

Lao rushed to the woman's aid, running over to her side. "Everything okay? Are you hurt?"

"No, I'm quite fine, young man. Thank you. Thank you so much." She seemed alright enough, maybe a slight limp as she stepped forward to him, but nothing more than that.

"Where do you live? I can get you there," Lao asked,

"Lu Min, on the other side of this forest," she pointed in a certain direction, which seemed to be the way Lao, Shen, and Reina were headed. "How… How long have I been here?"

"Don't worry about that, please. Right now we need to get you out, okay?"

"Alright. Yes." She said, mild-mannered and timid in her stature. Walking in the direction she had pointed, Lao followed close behind her. He constantly looked around him, searching for a trace of Shen or Reina. His eyes kept wandering, and in some time they found something. Perched on a branch in a tree, there was one of those creatures. It glowed with its normal bluish-green tint, but there was something different about it. As its long ears twitched, Lao noticed its eyes were now completely black. Not a shiny kind of black, like a darkened metal, but a deep black that wore no shine in it. Nodding to himself, he looked away, almost frightened as to what the little things were exactly.

Reina was already beginning to approach the other side of the forest, where the man she'd found was also from. They crunched through the branches on the ground and the pebbles embedded in dirt, nearing closer and closer the edge of the treeline. "Did you see any ram-horns on your way in here?"

"Not that I can remember, no," Reina answered earnestly.

"Wait," he said quickly, kneeling down upon the ground on one knee.

"What is it?"

"Quiet. I hear one," he said. Reina could hear no such thing. But, this was only temporary, as there was soon a soft little group of footsteps getting closer and closer to where they were. In a few moments, a ram-horn deer came from the shadows of the trees, head bent down to feed on grass that happened to grow on the forest floor. Slowly, the man reached his hand back and grasped his bow in one hand, using the other to acquire an arrow. With great speed, he snapped the arrow onto the string, pulled it back, and watched the arrow shoot into the skull of the creature before him.

It dropped immediately, falling to the ground with a soft *thud* upon the dirt. He walked over and put his bow around his shoulder again. Reaching down, he grabbed the legs of the fresh kill and draped it over his neck and shoulders. "You want any help carrying that?" Reina asked.

"It's my job to kill the thing, might as well carry it too, right?" The man said, and looked to the woman next to him with a smile before heading back onto their path to the town on the other side of the forest.

Elsewhere, Shen climbed atop Ping's saddle as the child before him stood anxiously. "What's the matter?" Shen asked the boy.

"Does… Does he bite?" He asked, pointing to the dimian, who was content with pecking along the surface of the tree he was near.

"Of course not! Ping here is the friendliest dimian you'll meet," Shen smiled, patting the side of Ping's thick neck, feeling the softness of his feathers. The bird instinctively crouched down, allowing enough height for the child to climb on. "Unless you have anything shiny," Shen said with a little smirk. The child giggled to himself and climbed on top of the saddle behind Shen, a smile upon his little dark tan face. They walked, following a newly seen bright light that shone upon a certain path in the ground. Lao and Reina saw it too as they walked.

"So, where are you from?" The man said to Reina, adjusting his grip on the ram-horn carcass upon his shoulders.

"Not sure if you can tell, but not here. I was born in Vasai. I moved here, a few years ago, seemed nicer here."

"I figured as much. I recognized the armor and the mask," he said. Reina reached her hand up to the mask around her neck, feeling the grain of the wood, each smooth edge of the teeth in the face. "Don't worry, I just wanted to see if you were honest. You passed, if that wasn't clear enough," the man said, and laughed to himself. Reina chuckled too, albeit a touch awkwardly. She wondered if he'd want to know how she'd lost her arm. After all, plenty of people had asked her on her travels about it. But, he never did ask. He simply kept a calm silence about him as they walked the bright path further and further out of the forest.

    Shen made it to the edge of the forest, and he could see the village in full view, much larger than the one before it. Waiting at the entrance to it, there stood a man. "Shao!" He cried.

    "Dad!" The little boy shouted, and jumped off the dimian, rushing toward the town where the man was with his arms open wide. Shen smiled to himself and began looking around. From the treeline at his sides, he noticed more people coming from the shadows. There were men and women, even a child, all looking dazed in their faces as they strode toward the town ahead of them. Soon, though, there was a familiar face.

    "Reina! Over here!" Shen cried, bringing Ping over to where the woman had exited the forest.

    "Shen!" She shouted, walking over to him.

    "Where's Lao?" He asked.

    "I don't know, I thought he was with you."

    "I figured he'd be with you, since you went after him first."

    "No."

    "Hey! Shen! Reina!" A familiar voice called out from behind them. Within the forest, alight by the bright path on the ground, there was Lao, jumping up and down with the woman at his side, the both of them smiling. The boy ran up to Shen and wrapped his arms around his stomach once he'd gotten off Ping. "I finally found you."

"That's right, I'm here."

"Did we do it?" The boy asked, letting go and backing up. The woman he was with continued on toward the town, following the small group of people that also came from the forest.

"I think so, Lao," Shen said. The three of them smiled to one another, and turned back toward the town, walking along with the rest of the people, a great relief resting in their chests.

Onward

They arrived to the town and instantly, they noticed a sheer difference to the one they'd come from. The atmosphere was much brighter, with children laughing and playing around amongst each other, sunlight shining down upon the ground. Flowers were brighter and the grass too, all of it vibrant and full of life. "This place is wonderful," Lao said, smiling.

"It hasn't been like this in a long while. But, everyone is returning now," an old woman said, walking up behind them, with a walking stick in her palm. "Was it you," she asked, pointing her finger at the three of them, "was it you that vanquished those spirits?" Her face was wrinkled, dark tan skin like leather upon her face.

"I believe so, ma'am."

"Splendid! My brother sent for me. He told me three heroes were coming to free us of the curse. You three, you're heroes."

"We're no heroes," Reina said, her weight shifted to one leg as she stood, her hand on her hip.

"Nonsense! He told me all about you three. The stoic man," she said, looking to Shen, "the scrappy young one," then to Lao, "and the armored warrior woman," and finally, to Reina. "Come, come, we have food! Liu has brought ram-horn!" She went around to the back of them, pushing them forward into the village with her walking stick, smiling widely.

They reached a bigger building than the others in the village, made from thick bamboo that softly creaked as the wind blew by. Windows were cut out on the front and the sides, and inside there could be seen brilliant yellow lanterns, all of them unlit. "What is this place?" Lao asked, curious.

"We use it for all sorts of things, dear. But, lately we've been using it for dining and town meetings. Please, go on in." She urged the three of them again with her walking stick, poking them each in the small of the back to get them forward. They entered, and were greeted with many people. Most of them had come from out of the forest, but some were completely new faces. There were women with their children, men standing caringly at their sides. Candles were lit with flame atop long wooden tables, plates of lettuce and fruits piled upon them. A particular smell filled the air, too, one which served to pique the interest of the three of them.

"Ma'am, if I may ask, what's that smell?" Reina asked.

"Oh, Liu and his wife Xian are cooking the ram-horn into a roast," the old woman said, taking a seat at one of the tables. Like something had went off in their brains, the three of them rushed to sit down at a table near the woman, ready with their backs straight.

"I'm so hungry!" Lao said, a hand pressed onto his stomach.

"Me too," Reina said chewing lazily on a piece of lettuce.

"Why don't you have some fruit, Lao?" Shen said, reaching for a little handful of berries in front of him on a plate.

"I'm saving up for the meat. You can't beat meat!"

"Yeah. This dimian food is nothing compared to a nice, warm, tender roast." Reina said as her mouth began to water, a hint of drool forming at the corners of her mouth.

"It's certainly nothing special. But, it's nutrients right?" Shen said, expecting an agreement. Instead, the smell returned, and it was more potent than ever. After much waiting there came from a door at the back of the room, the large man Reina had found, carrying an enormous platter with him, balanced in his hands. Atop it, there sat the biggest hunk of meat any of them had ever seen, darkened edges and glazed over surface. Each fiber of the meat could be seen as Liu set the platter down on the table before the three of them.

"To our traveling heroes!" The old woman stood up and shouted, a fist to her chest in salute. Everyone around them did the same, holding their fists firm and close to their chests. "You may eat first if you-" the poor woman would've finished what she was saying, had it not been for the three of them.

"Gimme!" Lao shouted, practically climbing over the table, reaching for the big silver serving fork stuck into the meat.

"Ladies first, kid!" Reina said, pushing Lao's face out of the way with her arm.

"No shoving! Calm yourselves, and let me at it!" Shen said, grabbing a smaller fork from the side of the platter. Each of them grabbed a sizeable portion of the meat, a good chunk of it, and yet there was still more left to be had. Reina was eating first, sticking her fork into her chunk and eating it without cutting it into bits. "Reina, do you need a hand?" Shen asked.

Reina turned slowly, her mouth and chin dripping in sweet honey glaze from the meat, and her brows formed into a scowl. "Is that some sort of joke?" She muttered, a mouth full of food shifted into one of her cheeks.

Biting into one of the pieces he'd cut, Shen thought for a moment. When the realization finally hit him, he looked to her right shoulder, the burned area where an arm used to he. He dropped his fork onto the plate he'd been given. "I am so sorry. I didn't mean it like that. You know what I meant, anyway." He said.

"Uh-huh, sure."

"I'm serious!" He protested, picking his fork up from the plate.

"Will you two just be quiet and eat!" The old woman piped up from her table. The villagers were lined up in front of them, grabbing little bits of the meat and piling it onto their plates, then retreating back to their tables. Some were children, who were quite delighted with the banter the two before them were having. Some even giggled as the two bickered between themselves. Lao, unlike the others, was not keen on talking. He devoured the food before him, and it was only a matter of minutes until it was all gone from his plate.

They'd all finished their food across a period of minutes, maybe an hour, and then there was a period of rest. Lao had fallen into a pleasant nap almost seconds after he'd finished all his food, and other children in the room did the same, taking naps along the walls of the hall. Shen and Reina sat and rested their eyes, while most of the other attendants took their short leave to tend to fields of crops toward the back end of the village. The old woman walked over to Shen, took a seat next to him, and poked him in the side with her walking stick. "Hm? Yes?" Shen asked, lifting his eyelids open.

"I would like to thank you again. There will be more thanks, at the necklace ceremony in a few minutes, but I would like to thank you personally."

"Please ma'am, there's no need for that."

"You are much too humble. You helped all those people, this whole village and the one on the other side of the forest."

"I wasn't initially going to. But, those two helped convince me," Shen said, and gestured his hand to his two companions, leaning their backs against each other in their seats, eyes resting closed.

"You have a good heart. I know you do. And them as well, of course. Please, don't be so hard on yourself, you did the right thing after all," she said with a smile, the corners of her eyes crinkling as she did. She got up from her seat and began walking to a back wall, where there was a raised platform on the floor under lit lanterns.

"I never caught your name, ma'am."

"Quan." She said, and walked off as Shen rested his eyes closed once again.

Later on, the three of them received their silver necklaces. They were simple, but the meaning behind them was so much more poignant than the look of the jewelry. The ceremony involved everyone in the village. They had all gathered before the platforms, where the three heroes stood, and watched as Quan set the necklaces around their necks. Afterward, Shen explained that they had to move on, and they were all showered with goodbyes from the people of the village. Liu and his wife, the woman Lao had freed from the forest, gave big hugs to the three of them. The child, Shao, that Shen had freed, walked up to him and gave a big smile and a salute to the man. He shot a firm salute back, and he couldn't help but let a smile creep upon his face.

"From here, it should be a straight shot to the capital if you go north. Follow the road," Quan said.

"Of course. We'll keep our eyes on the path," Shen said. Reina was busy fixing the saddlebags upon Ping's saddle. The dimian let out a loud *squawk* and pecked at Shen, grabbing the necklace from his neck and breaking the chain of it. He held it in his beak, letting the chain dangle from his mouth. "Ping! Give that back!" Shen cried. As he reached his hand to try and grab it from the bird, Ping moved his head away again and again, keeping it away from Shen. "Come on!"

"Haha! Quite the trickster isn't he," Reina said, petting the feathers on the side of Ping's neck.

"You have no idea," Lao said with a sigh.

Shen proceeded to keep reaching, keep trying to get at the necklace clutched in the dimian's beak. "Will you just give it back!" He shouted, and Ping poked him in the side with his beak. "Ow! Hey! What was that for?" Shen said, and Ping let out a low and soft *squawk*. "Fine. You can keep it, for now. But I want it back later!" He said pointing a finger at Ping, and the bird sat down, allowing them to get on. "Hop on, Reina. You too, Lao."

"You're walking?" Reina asked, walking to the side of the dimian.

"It's only fair right? You walked here, and I rode. So now, I walk to the capital and you ride. Fair."

"I guess so."

"Come on, get on, we better get moving if we want to reach it before nightfall," Shen said, urging Reina to get onto the saddle.

"Yes! The man is right! You need to get going, now!" Quan said, and with her walking stick, she poked them all. Reina hopped on and Lao behind her, sitting just a tiny bit apart from each other on the saddle. Shen grabbed the bit of rope tied to the saddle and tugged on it, while Ping stood back up, almost smiling with the necklace fixed between his beak.

"Thank you for everything, Quan. And everyone else. Thank you all!" Shen shouted, and began waving goodbye. The people of the town of Lu Min all waved goodbye, and some gave salutes, while a few simply smiled. They were off again, walking down the dirt road, bound for the capital. Quite a bit into their journey, Shen tapped the side of Reina's leg, on the calf where there was little to no armor. "Reina, do you have your map handy?" He tapped his side, on the leather bag whose strap was tied around his waist. "I've got mine, but I wonder if yours has the roads more accurately drawn out."

"Well, I can certainly check." She said, and reached for the bag at her side, lifting the little leather flap of it. Suddenly, Shen tugged at the rope on the saddle, and Ping stopped. "What? What is it?" Reina said, and her eyes drifted from her bag to the area in front of them. Much farther ahead of them in the road, there stood a whole group of people. Most of them were taller, and from what the three of them could tell, they all had ragged clothes on. Some had ripped pants, tied with string at the middle of their shins, and some had tunics with sleeves torn from them.

"Should we go talk to them? Maybe they know the way to the capital," Lao said.

"No. They're bandits," Reina said.

"But, how do you know?"

"Look at their sides. Weapons," Shen said, pointing ahead down the road. Lao looked ahead, and as he squinted his eyes, he saw that most of the people standing in the road carried swords or hatchets at their sides.

"Are we going to fight?" Reina said, bringing her arm back and gripping the hilt of her sword lightly.

"No. There's too many of them for us. There's only three of us and about ten of them. We keep moving toward the northeast. Let's go," Shen said, and turned in the direction diverting from the road, tugging on the rope. They walked even further, taking care not to let their gaze drift to the bandits behind them. In the air, there hung an incredibly faint smell. Smoke. Only Shen could smell it, and in that, he could only get subtle hints of it as the breeze shifted.

They soon came upon a grouping of trees, toward the north, where they would need to head to get to the capital. Shen stepped forward and put his hand up. Reina tugged on the holds of the saddle and Ping stopped, while Lao looked on, wondering what was happening. Shen looked around on the ground until his eyes came upon a rock. He flicked his wrist, and the rock leapt from the ground and shot into the little forest. Afterward, there was simply silence. Then after a few more seconds, there came people walking out from the shadows of the forest.

They were dressed like the ones before, and there were only about four of them. "We can take them," Reina said.

"No, we shouldn't."

"Why not? There's only four of them."

"Four that you can see right now. Who knows how many are hidden away in there. They could easily ambush us, especially with the cover of the shadows."

"So what do we do?"

"We keep moving northeast. There should be a mountain range that way that cuts toward the capital in the north. Come on, let's get going," Shen said, and as the three of them continued on their trek to the mountains, Lao looked back to the little forest. He saw the bandits, all peeking from inside the trees. Once they'd realized the boy was looking at them, they flashed their sword blades into the sunlight and then dipped back into the shadows.

Reina was a bit fidgety in her seat, jerking and twitching, trying to get comfortable in the saddle seat. There was something gnawing at the back of her mind. She couldn't quite place what it was, though, so she could only sit and move around as she tried to fight with her subconscious. Perhaps it was a nagging desire to go the first path, down the road to the north, which the bandits had blocked off. They were almost like a cornered animal in that regard. 'But, it was only a minor setback,' she thought. "Everything alright, Reina?" Lao asked, tapping the woman on the shoulder of the missing arm.

"Hm? Oh, yes. I'm just a bit uncomfortable in this seat is all. It doesn't really have a lot of cushion, does it," she said.

"You get used to it," Shen piped up.

"Speak for yourself, Shen. My butt has been aching for this whole trip," Lao whined.

They walked even further, until they came upon another living roadblock. It was only two men this time, both of them clad in tunics missing sleeves and ragged pants with ripped ankles. Both had swords held in their hands at their sides which looked to be stolen from a soldier from what Shen could tell. "There's only two. I can take them Shen," Reina said, gearing to hop off the uncomfortable seat of the saddle.

"Fine. But make it quick, we need to get moving," he said. The woman hopped off the saddle with a little bit of glee in her chest. She loved the thrill of fighting, the adrenaline pumping through her as she swung her sword. The one thing she dreaded, though, was taking a life. She wasn't against it, quite the contrary in fact, but the sheer thought of ending someone else's life was still heavy on her. Of course, she'd done it many times before as a part of the military. But, that didn't mean she enjoyed it. 'It was a necessary evil,' she'd like to think.

She walked up slowly to the two of them, and one of them wore a smirk on his face. "Ha, you're quite the rebel. You've only got one arm." He said, and brought one of his hands up to scratch at his stubbled chin.

"How do you expect to take on the both of us?" The other one said, tugging on the bandana wrapped around his neck.

"I only need the one to take you two down." Reina said, bringing the mask up to her face. She brought her hand to the back of her head and made sure the leather strap of the mask was tight against her face. Once it was secure, Reina brought her hand back to the back of her waist and tightly gripped the sword handle in her fingers. With one swift motion it was pulled from its holding place and at her front. She looked menacing, the face of the mask flashing its sharp white fangs and the blues of the paint on the wood were contrasted by the green fields poised behind her.

"I'll take that mask of yours when I kill you," the bandit with the bandana said.

"It's not wise to trash talk the one wearing armor," she said, and lunged forward with her sword ready to swing. The bandit with the stubbled chin held his sword up and was prepared to swing downward at the oncoming Reina. But, instead of charging headfirst into the bandit, she shifted her footing just before getting to him, and rather moved toward the side. She brought her arm back, and sliced at the small of the bandits back, placing a sizeable gash upon his clothing and through the skin. The other one, the one with the bandana, moved to the woman before him and quickly slashed toward her thigh. There was a loud *clank* sound as the metal of the blade clashed against the metal of the armor she wore. "Bad move."

She lunged to the side and jabbed the blade of her sword into the left calf of the bandit with the bandana. He shouted and swung his sword wildly as the pain jolted up his body. Unfortunately, he managed to land a slight cut upon Reina's left shoulder, on an area where there was little armor to protect her. As she grunted in muffled pain, she pulled the blade from out of the man's leg and stood at his side, stabbing him through the chest.

"Brother!" The other bandit screamed, and ran forward to Reina, shaking the pain off of him. Reina quickly pulled the sword from the bandit's chest and raised it to block the oncoming strike. She felt the push the man gave as he came down with his sword. He kept pushing the blades together, unable to break the woman's guard. Soon, his arms began to become weaker, and as they did Reina dipped under his blade and ran her sword through him.

He let out a strained choke sound as the blood pooled on the metal of Reina's blade. She could feel each breath leave his body, his chest falling as the air escaped his lips. Soon, though, he went limp, and Reina pulled the blade from his chest. She wiped most of the blood from the blade of her sword, just as a noise nipped at her ears. It came from nearby, and as she looked around Reina could see more bandits approaching from the tall grass around them.

They had been in hiding, lying upon the ground in waiting. Now it was there time to enter the fray. "Shen! Lao! We have to go! Now!" She began running back to them as her mask fell down to her neck off her face, and swiftly hopped onto Ping's saddle.

"Keep going forward! I can just barely see the mountains from here," Shen shouted.

"Kid, I'm sorry you had to see that. Right now we have to go, okay?" Reina said.

"Yes. Let's go!"

Shen started running forward, and Ping kept a good pace toward the mountains ahead. The bandits watched, gathering on their sides, looking on as the three moved ever forward. As Shen looked back, he noticed one of the men smirking, his sword stabbed into the ground at his feet. They continued on, and soon the mountains were just before them. But, there was something else that stood before them, too.

Upon the side of the mountain, there sat a huge network of wooden structures built into the side. And, even worse, more bandits began coming out of the little wooden shacks built on the platforms. All of them were clad in the same clothes as the ones on the road. They had led the three into a trap. Shen looked on with a scowl, his hand moving back to the sword upon his back. "What do we do? We're surrounded," Reina said.

"We fight our way through," Shen said, pulling the bronze sword on his back from its scabbard. He looked toward the bandits before them, eyeing up the swords and hatchets they held in their hands. Lao was frightened, his legs growing weaker as he watched the men come from the wooden shacks on the mountainside. "Keep close to me, Lao," Shen said, and the three readied themselves to fight.

Fight the Way Out

      "What should I do, Shen?" Lao asked, almost shaking in his seat on the saddle.
      "Don't fight. Come, hop off and stay with me," Shen said, reaching a hand up to aid Lao in getting down. The boy lifted off with his hands and grabbed Shen's wrist, jumping down as his feet hit the dirt ground.
      "But, what about Ping?"
      "I'll tie him up to one of the trees around here near the bushes. He'll be fine, kid," Reina said.
      Memories floated to the front of his mind, memories of Qiu and the bridge of Kunan. He remembered the sound she made as she was dragged from the stone. "Are you sure? Do you promise?" He pleaded.
      "I promise." Reina grabbed onto the rope of Ping's saddle and walked the dimian over to one of the lighter colored trees nearby. Slowly, she wrapped the rope around it and tied the knot as tight as she could make it.
      "Stay here, boy. We'll come back for you," Shen said, and twisted the sword in his hand a bit, getting his wrist used to the weight of it. Ping stomped his foot onto the ground and then sat with his legs bent up into his chest, clutching down onto the silver necklace in his beak. "Let's go. Stay close to me, Lao, and don't try to fight them."
      "Okay, Shen."
      "You want me to lead?" Reina asked, stepping toward the wooden ladder that led to the beginning platforms on the mountainside.
      "Yes. Lao and I will follow you up. Go, now." He said, and the woman before him began running. She held the sword in her hand at her side, its weight

being little more than a minor annoyance as she ran with it. The muscles of her bicep and forearm were more than enough to carry the weapon. But, that didn't mean it didn't irritate her somewhat as she moved. When she came to the ladder, she reached her arm up, still holding the sword, and hooked it onto one of the rungs. "Do you need me to help you up?"

"No! I've got it." She said, grunting as the pain in the wound in her shoulder began to ache. Carefully, she hoisted herself up and placed her foot on the bottommost rung of the ladder. The wood creaked as she began to climb, steadily hooking her arm onto the rungs and pulling up her whole body, including the heavy silver armor that encompassed most of her form. "Come on. Let's go," she said once she was all the way up on the platform.

From behind her, she could hear rapidly approaching footsteps from the other end of the platform. She turned her head back and her eyes met with one of the bandits, a hatchet in his hand, poised to attack as he charged to her. As the man lunged forward at her, swinging downward with his sword, Reina dodged toward the side of him, bringing her sword onto the head of the hatchet as the bandit swung down. The blade of the sword hooked onto the steel head and with a single swing away from her, Reina launched the weapon over the side of the platform. "You-" the bandit tried to get out, but was quickly interrupted by the blade of the woman's sword piercing through his side.

She left the blade inside his body for a few seconds, before she pulled it from him and kicked his limp body over the side of the platform to the ground below. Reina brought her head up and looked to the ladder she'd climbed up. Shen and Lao had just made it up and were now staring at her. "Let's keep moving." She said, a twinge of something somber in her tone.

"Right. Lao, keep to me." Shen said, shaking a feeling that held in his mind. The three continued, going up a grouping of stairs leading to another platform where two more bandits stood.

"You won't make it out of here alive," one of them said, a scar upon his brow and a hatchet gripped in his hand.

"Yeah. We're gonna be cleaning up blood from these planks for days after we're done with you," the other said, hunched over and scrawny in his figure. He held a dagger, loosely gripped within his fingers.

"You better be careful not to eat those words," Reina said. "I'll take the skinny one. You get the one with the hatchet. Got it?"

"Got it," Shen said, looking around for rocks, his eyes resting on the side of the mountain the structure was built out from.

"Alright. Go!" Reina shouted and ran around the left side of the platform, toward the bandit with the scar on his eyebrow. While she did so, Shen clenched his fist and pumped it away from the right of the platform, where the mountainside was. A large chunk of the rock in the mountain formed into a pillar and struck the man right in the side, knocking him right over the edge of the platform on the other side. Shen, in a split second, lifted a big chunk of dirt from the ground below, just barely breaking the man's fall.

"Mystic scum!" The scrawny bandit shrieked, his dagger held lazily at his side.

"Don't drop your guard," Reina said, and sliced the bandit straight across the chest. Blood burst from the wound, a gaping gash left upon his skin as he fell to the wooden platform, writhing in pain. "Let's keep moving," Reina said. She wasn't sure whether or not the wound she'd given him was fatal. But, then again, she didn't have the time to care about such things. They continued up another ladder, Shen helping this time, hoisting Reina up with his hands. The jump was much more than she had bargained for, as she landed on the next platform and rolled forward.

"Hey! You won't make it past me!" The bandit in front of her shouted, raising his large hatchet to strike at her.

"Wanna bet?" Reina muttered.

"No. I've got this one. Protect Lao," Shen said, jumping over the crouched Reina and looking to the mountainside again. He moved his hand, pointed to an area of the mountains and broke off a few bits of the rock. Then, he jolted his arm and hand in the bandit's direction, sending the rocks flying into his chest. He doubled over and dropped the hatchet in his hand, instead clutching his stomach in pain. Shen walked up to the man and brought one of the smaller rocks to his knuckles as he made a fist. He placed a firm punch on the back of the bandit's head, knocking him out. "I'll lead now," Shen said, climbing the stairs which led to another platform, one which branched off into two other paths of wood.

The three continued, Lao hiding behind Reina, keeping up with the woman as they ran ever forward. More bandits were gathering toward them, swords at the ready. They were quickly dispatched however, as Shen brought more rocks from the mountainside. He launched them forward all at once. Most of them reached their target, the bandits' foreheads. However, two of them missed, and instead flew behind the men. "Having trouble aiming, dirtskin?" One of them said, and jumped forward at Shen.

He quickly moved out of the way, but the blade of the man's sword knicked Shen in the side, producing a small cut in his skin. Shen shouted as the pain struck him, but he soon shook it off. He swung his own sword, hitting the bandit in the leg, causing him to let out a rugged shout. Shen brought one of the rocks to his fist again, and turned, punching the man in the back of the head, sending him to the ground. The other bandit, a tiny and younger looking man, came from behind Shen with a little hatchet in his hand. He swung it down and the head stuck just barely into Shen's shoulder. "Agh!"

    The bandit let go of the hatchet and took a step back, a horrified look in his eyes. But, that quickly faded, as he wore a scowl on his face and placed a strong kick on Shen's lower back. Reina ran forward and ran the young man through with her sword, hearing the choking sounds as he tried to take in air. After just moments, she pulled the blade from out of him and kicked him over the edge. Shen reached his free hand back and pulled the hatchet from his skin. It was freed easily, but the pain it released as he did it was unnerving.

    "Shen!" Lao shouted, running to his side.

    "Lao. I'm alright, I'm alright."

    "Are you sure? That looks like a nasty one," Reina said.

    "Trust me, I've had worse," he said, a sort of smile on his face. "Let's keep moving. We need to make it to the capital before night."

    "Right. You hang back with Lao, I'll lead." Reina said. Shen simply nodded.

    "Are you sure you're okay, Shen?" Lao asked again.

    "Yes. Yes, Lao. I'm fine," Shen said chuckling a bit.

    "Come on!" Reina said, running forward toward the rightmost platform. They would've stuck together, had it not been for the bandits again. Two of them had jumped down from a higher platform, kicking Reina over to the left platform. She clattered to the floor, preoccupied by one of the bandits that kicked her, while the other one went after Shen and Lao. "Shen!" She cried. The man before her was huge, like a big boulder with muscles that barely fit in the tunic he wore. There were scars all along his arms from blades long broken, and in his hands he held a long hatchet with a bulky and sharp steel head.

"You're not going anywhere little lady," he said, his deep and gruff voice complimenting his rugged look.

"Who you callin' little?" Reina said, getting up and gritting her teeth.

Meanwhile, on the right platform, Shen and Lao were running from the other bandit that had kicked Reina. He was hot on their heels, a sword held in his hands as his feet pounded on the wood. Shen picked Lao up quickly and placed him on the ladder once they'd gotten to it. The boy quickly climbed up and fell onto the floor of the platform above, while Shen turned to the bandit behind. He brought his arm back and slid the sword back into its scabbard. 'I can do this without weapons,' he thought, and moved another chunk of the mountainside, bringing it out in a long pillar which blocked off the bandit from the path to the ladder.

"You can't hide forever!" The bandit said.

"I don't need to hide," Shen said, punching just in front of the pillar, launching pieces of the rock pillar into the man ahead of him. One rock hit him in the chest, knocking him back, and then another. Soon, the bandit was struck seven times, both in the chest and the stomach, knocking him all the way back over the edge of the platform.

"Shen!" Lao shouted down from the above platform.

"I'm coming, Lao. Hang on," he replied, climbing up the ladder as the scabbard tapped against his back. He climbed up onto the platform where Lao was and the two continued toward the top of the structure. Shen looked over to the left, and his eyes met with Reina, who was still facing up against the bandit on her platform.

"I am Shan."

"Why tell me your name? Hm?" Reina said, pacing around the large man, twirling her sword in her hand by twisting her wrist.

"I believe it wise to know the name of the one who'll end your life," he said. Shan swung his hatchet down at Reina, who jumped out of the way, the head of the hatchet embedding itself into the wood.

"In that case, my name's Reina," she smirked, and swung her sword at him. But, he moved out of the way, pulling the hatchet from the wood platform and smacking her in the chest with the back end of his the weapon. Reina was sent to the floor, her sword clattering on the wood at her side.

"Reina, hm? Quite the arrogant one, aren't you?" He said, and swung the hatchet downward again. Reina quickly jumped up and landed her feet onto the long handle of the hatchet. She brought her leg up and kicked Shan across the face, then jumped backward toward her sword on the floor of the platform, gripping it in her hand. "Urgh. Good hit. But you won't get another one so soon," he said.

"Don't be so sure," she said, lunging to his side and slicing him across the thigh. Shan dropped to his knee, clutching the hatchet in his hands much firmer now.

"You're a good fighter," he said clenching his teeth. He pulled his wits together, his muscles aching as blood pumped through his veins. The gash in his thigh was leaking blood faster and faster, a stain forming, dripping from the cloth of his pants. "I need to tell you something. If you live through this, and you very well may, you need to go over the mountain."

"What? Over the mountain?" She kept her distance from him, pacing around as to keep his eyes moving.

"That's the only way to get to the capital. From the looks of you and your companions, you're travelers. I'd venture to guess that's where you're getting to." He swung his hatchet forward, which Reina dodged, and then swung again, getting the head embedded into the wooden platform again. The woman came up behind him and jabbed him in the shoulder, quickly pulling the blade out of his body once she did. "Yagh!" He grunted, breathing heavily, as Reina placed a kick to his jaw, barely fazing him. More weighty breaths escaped his lips. "You're going to kill me, aren't you?" He asked, on his knee once again.

Reina looked to him, still a distance away, and dropped the blade of her sword down toward the floor. "I'll let you die here," she said. She looked him in the eyes, tiring and drooping with each pump of blood that escaped his body.

"Perhaps in another life, we might've been allies," Shan said, becoming delusional in his fatigued state.

"Perhaps. But I already have my allies," she said, looking over to the higher up platforms where Shen and Lao stood. "Shen! How is everything going up there?" She shouted, beginning to run up to where they were.

On their platform, up against the mountainside, Shen and Lao were busy in their own fight. Arrows pierced the ground around them from up on the mountain. There was a patch of grass where a man stood, thin with his face shrouded in a thick cloak with a hood. Shen continuously raised chunks of the rocky mountain to block the arrows, letting them strike into their surface and snap. Lao hid behind him, scared, but also with a sense of bravery. He wanted to be able to fight, to help out, to swing a sword and take down the man shooting arrows at them from the mountaintop. But, he couldn't, and instead was to be content with hiding behind Shen, who turned toward the woman below. "Could use a little help!" He said, and just then an arrow pierced through his thigh, blood dripping from the arrowhead. "Gah!" He yelped, grabbing at his thigh with his hands, the rocks protecting him and Lao falling from out of the air.

"Shen!" Reina shouted, just barely getting to the platform where Lao and Shen were stood.

"Reina! Please, help!" Lao screamed, lying down behind the pile of rocks in front of him and Shen. The man on the mountain was busy coming down through a path which cut through the mountaintop and led to the platform they were on.

"Is he okay? Is everything alright?" Reina pleaded, standing in front of the two of them, her back facing the man coming down from the mountain.

"Reina, I'm… I'm fine. Relax," Shen said, his face becoming paler than the tan it regularly was.

"Shen. Shen, stay with me," she said. A million thoughts raced through her mind. She couldn't help him right now, they were actively being pursued by the man from the mountain. Even if they weren't under attack, none of them had the herbs or the bandages to help him at hand, they were all in the saddlebags with Ping. The veins in his neck began to darken, and immediately she knew that the arrow he was hit with was poisoned.

"Is he okay? What is it?" Lao said, tears welling up at the bottoms of his eyes.

"He's alright, kid. We have to help him, but he's going to be okay," she said. She reached her hand down to his thigh and quickly snapped the head off the arrow. Afterward, she pulled the back end of the arrow out of the skin, and it cleanly came out, a bit of blood spurting from the hole in his leg.

"You won't be helping anyone," the bandit said, his bow along his shoulder by the quiver, his hands occupied with a sword. Its steel glimmered in the sun that was just barely coming down behind the mountains. He ran forward and swung, but the blade was met in turn with Reina's.

"I disagree," she said with gritted teeth. She held her blade against his for mere moments, until the muscles in her single arm began to falter, at which point she stepped back just a bit and kicked him in the shins. The heavy boot she wore placed a sizeable bruise on his leg which took form almost immediately. He backed up and then came back once again, swinging his sword horizontally, aiming at her right side without the arm. She moved her body to the side and lunged away from the blow, bringing her sword along with her, pointing it toward the bandit.

"You're a good fighter."

"Funny, that's what your friend Shan said before I stabbed him," Reina said. She could see the man's expression quickly shift. Before, he was cunning with a devilish smile across his lips. But now, his face was nothing short of horrored.

"You killed him?"

"No, I couldn't kill him. He was too nice of a man. But, I will admit that I didn't make the effort to save him. Which is a lot more than I can say for you!" She ran forward and ran him through with her sword. There was no protest, no objection, no attempt to block the blow. He simply stood and watched as his own blood steadily dripped down and coated the steel of her blade.

"You…"

"I know," she whispered. "I'm a monster. I'm truly sorry for doing this. But, I have to… I have to protect them," her voice was calm and soothing, almost haunting. The man with the bow was slightly comforted by the sentiment, and he dropped his sword upon the wooden platform floor as the last shreds of his strength drifted off into nothing. "Please forgive me," she said, pulling the blade from out of his chest, his body falling to the floor. There was a lurking sense of regret in her mind, for what she had said to him before. 'I didn't mean it. I just said it to break his concentration further,' she thought, but how much of it was true she couldn't tell.

"Reina," Shen muttered in a raspy breath.

"Shen! You're okay!" Lao shouted.

"Shen, we have to get you out of here. We have to keep moving, okay?" Reina said, putting her sword away and picking up the weakening Shen. The veins along his neck were much darker, an almost blackish purple color. She looked around, Shen's arm draped over her shoulders, and noticed the huge wooden stairs that descended from the back end of the platform they were on. "Kid, let's go. We need to get going on the path and fast," she said, jogging with Shen, his legs only moving slightly as his muscles could barely move.

"Right," Lao said, following close behind.

They came down the stairs as fast as they could, Lao almost tripping as his little feet got the better of him. Shen let out strained breaths as each little step came under his bare feet, scuffed up, even cut from gravel and splinters that had brushed past them. Soon they reached the bottom and walked all the way to Ping. Reina set Shen down up against the tree and took out her sword. She quickly slashed down and severed the rope right by the knot, letting it hit the ground.

"Can you get onto the saddle by yourself?" Reina asked, putting the sword back in its holding place at the back of her waist.

"I can… hurgh… I can try," he said, bending his knees to try and stand, but the strength was just simply not there.

"Alright, that's an easy 'no.' Let's try something." Reina walked up to him and got to her knees. Ping stood up and watched as Reina did so, watching as she put her arm out to hold her up. "Now climb onto my back, wrap your arms around my neck. I'll lift you. If Ping crouches, I can get you onto the saddle."

"You'll hurt yourself," he said, coughing.

"If that's what it takes to get you some help, then that's what it'll be. Now quit arguing and let's go." Shen did as she said, and through a couple heavy breaths Reina stood up and lifted him off the ground. "Hey, hey, easy on the throat."

"Sorry. My muscles… they're starting to tense up," Shen said. He could feel the chilly metal of her armor upon the skin of his arms.

"Alright. Ping, crouch down, buddy." She said, and the bird quickly did so, tucking his legs up into his chest again. Lao watched on as Reina placed the weakened Shen onto the saddle. "Kid, get on. I'll lead you two through the path. We're going to have to run." She said, standing in front of the bird as Lao climbed onto the bird. Shen managed to sit up, and grabbed hold of the saddle holds with the energy that stayed in his arms and hands.

"Where are we going?" Lao asked, wiping some forming tears from his eyes. "Are… Are we going to help him?"

"Yes, Lao. We're gonna go across the mountain path and get some help. There's bound to be people on the way. Now, you ready?" She asked, and prepared herself to run.

"Yes." Lao said, and grabbed hold of the back holds of the saddle, ready for the dimian under him to start bolting through.

Back to Health

The path they took was much more rugged than they had anticipated. All manner of rocks scattered the surface of the dirt, and they irritated the feet of Reina and Ping as they now jogged, tired from the run up the mountain's starting path. "Have you seen anyone, kid?" Reina said, tired, sipping from the waterskin she'd grabbed from one of Ping's saddlebags.

"Uh huh. That's why I didn't tell you about it before now. I just figured I'd keep that information from you, for fun."

"Haha, very funny. So you haven't seen anyone?"

"No, Reina, I haven't seen anyone."

"You know, I could certainly do without the sass," she said, turning to him as she put the waterskin back, fixing it to a leather string on one of the bags.

"Right, right, sorry." They kept on, and Reina's feet ached as they stomped more and more on the rough ground. Through the leather bottoms of her boots, she could feel the individual grooves of the rocks, the gravel and the dirt, as she stepped with each jogging stride. Shen was looking worse and worse now, his face almost as pale as an Ogon native, and his veins were ever blackening. Thankfully, though, as they were coming upon a stretch of forest, Lao noticed a small hut just on the edge of it. "Reina! Look!" He said.

As he pointed, Reina could see smoke billowing from a hole in the thatch roof, a chimney of sorts squared out of wooden logs at the top. They kept on, much faster now as they were driven by a sense of hope. Soon the hut came into better view, and they noticed a man sitting in a chair at the side of the door. "Oh my! Travelers," he said. He practically jumped from his chair, running into the hut.

"Hey! Wait!" Lao shouted.

"Please! Our friend, he's injured, we need to get him some help," Reina said as she reached the front door. She stamped her foot in front of the door and pounded against the wooden door a few times with her fist. There was no answer.

"Please!" Lao shouted, hopping off of Ping, who had crouched down to help aid them in retrieving Shen.

The old man came from out of the door, swinging it open inwardly, and as his eyes met with Shen, his eyes widened. "Oh! I'm terribly sorry! Come, come, get him inside," he said, shuffling swiftly to get inside the hut, going toward the back wall where there sat the light of a candle. Night was quickly approaching, and so the lights from the candles inside the hut were the only thing to aid their eyes once the darkness arrived. Reina hurriedly lifted Shen onto her back again, but this time, his arms didn't grip her neck. After all, he couldn't move a muscle. He was stiff as she carried him into the hut, laying him down onto a cot, as directed by the old man. "How long has it been?" He asked looking at Shen's shoulder wound.

"Um, he's been hit in the thigh," Reina said, pointing with her finger. Lao came in from outside, after having tied Ping up to a tree at the front of the hut.

"Right!" The old man proclaimed, lifting a finger up, and then diverting his attention to Shen's thigh, seeing how the blood was much thicker than it usually would have been. "He's been poisoned."

"What?" Lao said, and tears came back to nip at the corners of his eyes.

"Don't worry, young one, please. You came just in time. A few seconds, though, and your friend here would've been a goner."

"Are you serious?" Reina said.

"Nah. You'd be fine even if you waited until the morning," the old man said with a chuckle as he fiddled with a mortar and pestle, smashing down little green herbs into a fine paste.

"Don't joke like that!" Reina said, fighting back the urge to smack the old man in the shoulder or the back of the head.

"Looks like someone doesn't like a good joke," the old man said, raising his eyebrows at Lao.

The boy couldn't help but crack a little smile. The smile would soon fade, though, as he noticed the old man rubbing the paste from the little bowl onto Shen's wound. "What are you doing to him?" Lao asked as he wiped away some tears from his cheek.

"Treating him."

"And that'll stop the poison?" Reina asked.

"Not entirely. It will only fight off the effects of the poison until I can administer a cure."

"Cure?"

"That's where you come in, actually!" He said, one of his eyes twitching, his wrinkled brow jittery on his face. "I need you to go into the forest and retrieve a red plant." He scurried off to the back of the hut again, and came back with a little piece of parchment. "It looks like this. Scarlet aloe. I've run out of it, and we don't have time to run to the capital to buy it, so you're stuck with finding it."

"Wait, why can't you get it?" Reina said.

"Because I need to stay here and help your friend recover. I'll patch him up with bandages and everything, and keep fighting the poison off. Consider this little mission payment for my services," he said, a grin on his lips.

"Payment?"

"Hey, I don't make very much being a recluse in a hut, you know. I can't just be giving out my services for free," he snapped, heading back to the back of the hut and getting a roll of bandage cloth. "Now get going," he shouted to them, "the quicker you get it, the quicker you can get back on the road," he said. With that, Reina tucked the little drawing into one of the smaller pockets on her side bag, and the two of them were out of the hut and into the forest.

While they were off, almost quite a bit into the forest, the old man was tending to Shen's wounds. Once the paste was amply applied to the hole in his thigh, he took to bandaging the wounds on Shen's shoulder and side. The old man brushed the fabric of Shen's scarf away from the wound and his hand reached up to grip the old man's wrist. "What's going on? Who are you? Where am I?"

"Be calm. Please. If you don't relax, you'll accelerate the effects of the poison."

"Poison? From the arrow?"

"That's what did it? I figured you had just been playing around with the wrong plants," the old man said, laughing, wrapping the bandage cloth on the gash in Shen's skin. "Could you do me a favor and grab the little bowl over there, on that table," he said. He pointed right next to Shen's arm, where a little wooden bowl rested on a table.

Shen did so, and the muscles in his arm were gradually loosening their tension. He grasped it and brought it back, setting it down on his stomach. "What is it? Some kind of medicine to help fight off the poison?"

The old man reached a hand into the bowl and pulled out a little chunk of something brown with little specks of gray upon it. He put it to his cracked lips, and his yellowing teeth nibbled at it. "Haha, no, it's rodent jerky. Blasted little things are the only creatures that I can manage to catch in my old age," he said with a smile, and chewed harder and harder on the piece of meat.

"That came from a rodent?"

"They get pretty big around here. Almost as big as a hookbeak, which believe me, we get plenty of too." The old man put down the piece of jerky and went to Shen's side, taking the bandage cloth. "Make sure you don't move the muscles in your side too much, you could very well let your bandages fall off."

"You know, you have quite the sharp wit for your age," Shen said, wincing as the cloth of the bandage stuck onto the little slash wound in his skin, stuck on by a combination of herb paste and drying blood.

"Witty, senile, it's all the same at my sort of age. And speaking on sharp, you're not very so, hm?" He smiled, picking the jerky back up and taking a much bigger bite now.

"How do you mean?" Shen managed to sit up, dangling his legs over the side of the cot. His muscles were much more relaxed, but with each pump of blood there came a little twinge of pain in his thigh.

"You don't even recognize your own people," he said, his mouth half-full with chewed jerky.

Shen looked to the man, his dark tan skin, the bald head with little moles and wrinkles upon it. "You're from Batung. Not very uncommon considering we're in the mainland, wouldn't you think?" He ran his fingers through his black and straightened, slick back hair, feeling the sweat that had gathered within the strands of it.

"Not very sharp indeed." The old man said with a click of his teeth. Shen brought his hand down to itch at his neck, and he found that his scarf had fallen off, bundled in a heap on the floor. He scratched the back of his neck, and though it didn't produce any kind of warmth, it was as if Shen could feel the green mark on the skin of the back of his neck. "Exactly, my friend." The old man smiled, and took a seat by a window, awaiting the return of Reina and Lao.

    The two of them had been out in the thick of the forest for quite a bit. Sunlight was fast depleting, and Reina's feet were growing more and more tired as they walked on. "Any sign of the plant?" Lao asked.

    "Nothing. Maybe the old man's just sending us on a hunt for nothing."

    "I don't think he'd be that cruel."

    "Not cruel. But, crazy? It's entirely possible," Reina said, cracking a little smile as her feet stepped over a rather rugged pebble.

    "You're just mad that he joked about Shen."

    "I am not!" Reina protested. "Well, I am, but because he shouldn't be joking at all."

    "I know, I know," Lao said.

    There was a sort of uncomfortable silence settling in the air in between their bouts of banter, one which could only be permeated by speaking. This Reina knew, and so she sought to fill the quiet with some noise. "Lao. I'm sorry you had to see all of that. I just want you to know that I was only doing it to protect all of us. You, me, and Shen, we have to do things to survive, right?"

    "Reina, it's okay."

    The woman was taken aback by this, her hazel eyes glinting with a little light leaking through the canopy above. "What?"

    "It's okay. You had to, right? It was either us or them. I've seen death, you know, it's not a new thing to me." He said it with an almost plain voice, and yet there was a little hint of sadness dancing about his voice.

    "Are you alright?"

    "Yeah. I'm fine. I'm still kind of recovering from all of that. I can stand seeing death, but that doesn't mean it isn't still hard to watch."

"I get that. How old are you, anyway?"

"Thirteen."

"You're serious? I figured you as younger than that. You're so… short."

"I am not that short!" Lao shrieked, his short and slightly curly hair bouncing as he whipped his head to her. He was indeed short, about two-thirds of Reina's height, which was the same as Shen's. He kicked a rock on the ground, and it flew into a bush, pushing away the blades of grass as it moved. As it did, though, Lao could see a little speck of bright red past the grass, growing up against a tree. "There!" He said, and started jogging over to it.

"You found it?" Reina asked. She walked over to the tree just as a muffled sound began to fill her ears, seemingly coming from above. While Lao was knelt on the ground, gripping the roots of the plant under soft dirt, Reina listened closely. From above, a shadow descended, and it quickly tried to attack Reina. It was a hookbeak, talons poised. Fortunately, Reina's armor was more than enough to stop the sharp claws on its feet, but Lao was not as lucky to be wearing such armor. He swiftly pulled the plant from the ground and ran behind the tree.

"Reina! You have to kill it!" He cried, clutching the little plant close to his chest.

"Well of course I have to kill it! But that's easier said than done, now isn't it?" She snapped, pulling the sword from behind her at her waist, holding it up as the creature looked her down. Its beady little black eyes were menacing, a true compliment to the mangey head they were staring from. Black talons crawled along the floor, letting the thing bob and sway around as it inched ever closer to her. "These things are creepy."

"Creepy and dangerous. Be careful."

"I know! I'm trying to get a good shot at it," she said, moving her head around, looking for an opening where she could slice at or even stab the thing. It lunged forward, and with a swift kick, was sent into a neighboring tree. Smacking into the trunk with a *thud*, the hookbeak hissed under its breath, readying its talons for another attack. "I'm gonna try something stupid."

"You're what?"

"Just hear me out," she said.

"What did you say the first time?" Lao questioned.

"Just watch!" Once the hookbeak jumped at her again, she brought her arm up and let it claw at the armor on her forearm. The talons scratched at the silver in vain, and Reina threw the creature down onto the ground. She then brought her foot down upon one of its wings, pinning it down, even breaking the bones inside as the bird shrieked. With a thrust of her blade, she stabbed the hookbeak through the head, killing it instantly.

"There might be more of them. We can't lead them back to Shen and that man. What do we do?" Lao said frantically, running to Reina while he carried the plant in one of his hands.

"I've got an idea. I haven't used this in many years, but it might work," she said as she pulled the blade from out of the creature. She put her sword back into its place on her back, bringing her hand up to her mouth. With two of her fingers placed at her lips just before her teeth, Reina blew air with her mouth poised narrowly, and a wicked sound filled the air. It was like a whistle, and it was just barely audible, like the shrieking cry of a boiling kettle. Lao immediately covered his ears with his hands, irritated by the sound. Almost out of nowhere, the sound of wings flapping echoed through the air, and seemed to scatter out in all directions away from them. "Yes! It worked!"

"What was that?" Lao asked, uncovering his ears.

"An old trick the military taught me. It's a warning call that sounds like a dying hookbeak. It freaks them out so much they can't help but run away. But, I've never had to actually use it until now, though."

"So you didn't know if it'd work?"

"Not a clue," she said, squinting her eyes as she smiled at him. "I'm something of a gambler, I suppose."

"Do you think we should head back now?"

Reina looked to the sky, which was gathering a thick film of darkness, night encroaching on them every second. "Yeah. Let's hurry and get back to Shen and that crazy old man."

"He's not crazy," Lao said, and the two began running back the way they came.

Shen, whose muscles were beginning to grow more and more tense with the poison's effects, was laid down, chewing on a mint leaf lazily tucked to the side of his mouth. He looked over to the old man sat in his chair, and who was steadily dozing off with his head tilted down. "Sir," he called. The old man stayed quiet, his chest rising and falling with each sleeping breath. "Sir!" He called again, and this time, the old man practically jumped out of his seat.

"Hm? What? What is it? Who's there? Military? Bandits? What? What?" He shouted frantically and darted his head around, eyebrow twitching again, a bead of sweat resting on his wrinkled forehead. "Oh, right, it's just you."

"I think you need to put some more medicine on my wound. It's getting… hard, to move my muscles, again." Shen strained himself, trying to lift his arm up, but only managing to rotate his wrist at a slow pace.

"Right you are. I'd almost forgotten about that. Silly me, right?" The old man grabbed his little wooden bowl of green herb paste. He stuck his finger into it while walking over to Shen, scraping some onto his fingertips. "Your friends should be back any minute now. At least, I hope they should. They've been gone a good while." Shen didn't answer back, the pain of his clenched muscles a bit much for him to deal with at the moment. "Right, medicine. I'll stop talking." He undid the bandaging and tossed the cloth aside, some dried up blood coming into the candlelight. The open wound stared the old man in the face, looking healthy, not infected in the slightest. There were bits of the dried herb paste around it, smudged along Shen's tan skin.

The old man put on more of the paste, and after a few moments, Shen began to get the movement of his muscles back. He rotated his ankles and his wrists much faster now, and carefully dangled his legs back over the side of the cot after a few minutes. The old man sat in his chair against the wall of the hut with a watchful eye on his patient. "May I ask you something?" Shen asked.

"Go on," he said.

"Why stay here? You could travel around like me and still avoid capture, but you don't. Why?" Shen reached down and grasped his scarf, setting it to the side of his pillow, soft cloth woven and stuffed with waterfowl feathers.

"Oh, now that's easy for a younger man like you to say. I'm much too old to be running around like that. I prefer to stay in one place. I'm a hermit in a forest hut, not some fugitive on a mission." He said it sort of snappy, but Shen could hear a warmth in his words. "My time is coming to an end here, whether I like it or not."

"I can respect that," Shen said, a slight twinge in his muscles shooting through his arm and then fading.

"You on the other hand, are much younger than I. You've got your whole life ahead of you. I don't blame you in the slightest for wanting to see the world through the traveler's eyes."

Just then, Lao and Reina came through the door, the light of the candles rushing out for a brief moment as the door was open, before being stopped by its closing once again. The night was upon them, the sounds of little bugs in the grass echoing throughout the air. "We're here," Reina said.

"Well I can see that," the old man said with a smirk, which brought about a smile from Shen.

"And we've got the plant," Lao said, butting into the conversation from behind Reina. He looked to Shen, sat up, and his nerves were eased. A brilliant feeling of relief washed over him. It was as if a million rocks' weight had been lifted from his chest, and he practically ran over to Shen's side once the ease had set in. "Shen! You're okay!" He cried, wrapping Shen's body in a hug.

"Alright, Lao, alright," he chuckled, "you're squeezing a bit tightly."

"Oh! I'm sorry," Lao said pulling away.

"Young man," the old man said, putting a hand on Lao's shoulder.

"Hm?"

"The plant?" He held out his hand, fingers cupped, palm open and waiting.

Lao looked down at his own hands and noticed the red aloe which had been sitting in his grasp for some time now. "Oh, right! I forgot," Lao said with a giggle. He handed the plant over, and the old man retired over to a little table in the corner. There were wooden bowls, mortar and pestles, little vials with corks in them, all stacked in strewn piles atop the table.

"What are you doing? Shouldn't you be giving him the plant?" Reina asked.

"Well I've got to make the medicine first. I can't just give him it and expect him to eat the thing," the old man spoke. He placed the little plant into one of the mortars he'd grabbed, then crushed it down into a fine powder-like substance with the pestle. Reaching over to one of the many vials, he took one with a little clear liquid inside it, one which contained tiny brown particles dancing around inside. He poured the liquid in and thoroughly mixed the substance with the plant powder, creating a new vibrant red liquid that shone with an almost metallic quality.

He brought the bowl over to Shen and put its rim up to his lips. "Drink," he said. Shen took it into his hands and poured it down into his throat, where it came down and rested in the emptiness of his stomach. "It won't fix it immediately, but it will fight off the poison's effects until it completely heals you. For the night, you'll need to sleep. You're all welcome to stay in here until the morning."

"Thank you very much," Reina said.

"Thank you!" Lao said, smiling widely.

"Now, I don't have anymore cots, so you will have to sleep on the floor. I have blankets, though."

"That won't be necessary. We have sleeping rolls we can use, and we're used to sleeping on the dirt ground, so a wooden floor is actually a plus for us." Reina sat down, her legs crossed, and took the cloth sleeping roll tied underneath her side bag. She unrolled it and Lao followed her lead, grabbing his own sleeping roll over by Shen's bag, unrolling it near Reina's. Lao climbed into his sleeping roll after taking off his wooden sandals, and Reina simply laid atop hers. The two of them went to sleep quickly, after the old man had dozed off himself. Shen was the last to fall asleep, staring at the thatch ceiling above him for quite awhile until he finally fell asleep.

In the morning, when the sun was still just barely waking from its own slumber, Reina awoke. She looked around and found that Lao and the old man were still both fast asleep. The old man was even snoring, as she'd noticed.

Shen, though, was not to be seen. Reina jumped to her feet and her first instinct poised her to burst out of the door and look outside for him. "You're up," Shen said. He was standing beside the door of the hut, up and about, his skin returned to its regular tan color.

Reina softly closed the door and began talking low like Shen, as to not wake the two sleeping inside. "You're alright. How do you feel?" She asked with a soft smile.

"Better. I never thought I'd ever take being able to move for granted," he chuckled. "I'm certainly glad I can move now, though."

"Yeah," Reina trailed off. "Shen, I think we need to talk."

"What about?"

"Those bandits. I… I killed them. In front of Lao, no less. I mean, he's just a kid; thirteen years old."

"Yes. But, he is a lot stronger than he looks. He's seen things I wouldn't wish on anyone."

"So he's said, but either way, it's an awful sight to see, no matter how many times you see it." She kicked a pebble across the ground, her hazel eyes pointed toward the horizon where the sun was just coming up. "I might add that you didn't seem too keen on killing them yourself. If I remember, actually, you made every effort *not* to kill them."

"I saw no reason to. There was no real need for me to kill them."

"What about to protect us? To protect Lao?"

"There were other ways. Incapacitation. I didn't need to kill them like I would an animal, for food or hide. I saw no personal reason to take their lives."

"I want you to know that I felt it necessary-"

"Reina, I know. You saw no other way to get out of that situation than killing them. It was the right thing for you. I won't fault you for that, ever. I can only ask that you take care when you kill. Please, try to know the real weight of the life that you take."

"Of course. Always. Thank you, Shen." The two of them stood outside the hut, watching as the sun climbed from behind the hills and trees. Birds flew in great flocks across the sky with their noises muted by the morning air. The sky was almost cloudless, the brilliant eye of the shining sun bearing down on them from afar. Green grass swayed in the wind that blew across the landscape, which could be felt on the skin of Shen and Reina, chilly, nipping at the little hairs on their arms. "You know, Batung may be beautiful, but I can't help but miss Vasai just a bit."

"You miss it?"

"Not everything about it. But, it certainly was nice. The beaches, the blue waves, the palms on the shoreline."

"We'll have to go through the Vasai mainland to get to Sukoshi Island. Once we find my brother, maybe you can stay in Vasai?"

"I'm not sure. I miss it, yes, but I'm not sure if I want to live in the place that made me become a monster, even if it *is* my home."

"It's certainly a difficult decision. Best not to think about it too much right now," he said, and just then, the door opened up from next to them. Out walked Lao, who had his sleeping roll bundled up and tucked underneath his arm at his side. "Morning, Lao. Did you sleep alright?"

"Like a rock."

"Good, we should get heading out. Reina, pack your things up, and Lao will help you."

"Aw, do I have to?"

"Shen, what about the old man? Shouldn't we let him know we're leaving?" Reina said, placing her hand to her hip.

"I think we should take care not to wake him. The man values his sleep, so I say we let him sleep." Shen went over to Ping and pet the bird upon his head. The dimian rose, and let out low sounds as he awoke, the little silver necklace no longer dangling from his beak, instead lying on the ground. He reached into one of the saddlebags and pulled out an apple. Ping's eyes went wide, the little black pupils fixated on the fruit in Shen's hand, which was quickly gobbled down before his eyes.

Reina and Lao went inside, and found that the old man was indeed still sleeping, snoring even still, shaking the wooden floor and rattling some of the herb vials placed on a table near him. Lao chuckled a bit to himself, just as Reina was rolling up her sleeping roll. After the task was done, she brought her hand up to scratch her collar, and her fingertips were met with the necklace around her neck. In a split second decision, she took the necklace off, carefully with her one hand, and brought it over to the old man. Softly, she put it atop the table next to him, and then walked back to her sleeping roll.

"You have everything packed up, kid?"

"Yep! You?"

"Seems like it," Reina said, and the two of them exited the hut, taking care to close the door with little to no noise. Shen was waiting for them, sitting atop Ping's saddle, a hand resting on the leather bag at his side. "Ready to go then?"

"I'm all ready. And you two?" Shen said as he patted the side of his bag.

"Of course," Reina said.

"Mhm!" Lao said, nodding his head. The boy then climbed atop the saddle and sat behind Shen, given that Ping crouched down to help Lao.

"Alright then, all we need to do is follow the path and look for any signs pointing to the capital. Sound like a plan?" The both of them nodded. "Perfect."

With a parting salute to the hut, and by extent the old man, they turned and began walking toward the capital once again, a warm sense of hope in their hearts as the sunlight stared them down.

In the Capital

  As they walked further and further toward their destination, they began to grow weary. Dirt and pebbles underfoot served to ache their feet even more than they were already feeling. The sun was steadily falling down by the hills, inching ever closer to the evening time. Soon, though, they came upon a sound, or rather Shen did. He listened close and could hear the rushing sound of a stream, coupled with the sight of a patch of forest on their path. "Hold up," Shen said, stopping.
  "What is it?" Reina, who was now sat atop Ping with Lao behind her, asked.
  "Water. I think we have to cross it."
  "Well, what are we waiting for? Let's go," she said, and started walking Ping forward once again.
  "Hang on. I think this might be a chance to get some hunting done," Shen said.
  "What makes you think that?" Lao piped up from behind Reina, who had now stopped Ping again.
  "Think about it. A forest, a nearby source of freshwater, ample grass for grazing."
  "It's perfect for ram-horns," Reina said, almost completing Shen's thought.
  "Exactly," Shen said, and the three of them continued on to the forest ahead.
  The trees and grass swayed in the wind which blew from the east, leaves floating about as they were taken by the breeze. Birds were more scarce now

than they had been in the morning, hiding among the branches, even inside little holes that formed on the trunks of the trees. But, their sounds of chirping could still be heard if one were listening with a keen ear. Lao, with nothing truly better to do, saw to it to listen. He listened for the sounds of the rodent-catchers, bigger birds with bulky feet to grab mice that scurried on the forest floor. Their calls were harsher than most others in the mess of the air.

He listened too for the calls of the bright colored seed birds, ones with little puffball bodies that gathered in great numbers high up in the trees to scout for seed clusters in the branches. Their green and brown hue blended well with the surroundings, so it was quite rare for someone to see one of them, even more so because of their miniscule size. Were it not for Reina's interruption, Lao would've stayed in his head, musing of the creatures that inhabited the forest they were now just in front of. "So, what do you plan on doing? It's not like you have a bow, and you certainly can't chase the things with your sword," she said.

"Trust me on this," Shen said walking into the forest and turning toward the direction of the stream which ran through it, "you two wait out here for me."

"Are you sure about this? You've just now recovered, and you want to go and hunt right afterward?" Reina said, her face poised in a sort of worried look. Her eyes were piercing, her eyebrows raised, and her hand fidgeting with the mask which was at the back of her neck, the strap turned to the front.

"I'll be alright, Reina. I'll yell for you if anything goes wrong, alright?"

"I think that sounds alright," Lao said.

"Okay. Just make sure you don't do anything stupid, alright?" Reina said.

"I can certainly try," Shen joked, and he continued on into the forest with his hands free, his fingers wiggling as he savored the ability to move the muscles in his hand. The wind was not as present on the inside of the forest.

Granted, the trees swayed, and the leaves fell, drifting like feathers to the dirt, but Shen could not feel the chill of the wind that had greeted him so early in the morning. His bare feet were strong on their soles, almost like rock, and the skin of the tops of his feet were lightly dusted with the dirt he kicked up with his steps.

    Soon he reached the edge of the stream inside the forest, and almost immediately rested his eyes upon a creature at the water. Like he had predicted, it was a ram-horn. But, unlike what he had thought, the creature was not as large as he had anticipated. It was juvenile, still wearing the curled horns upon its head, but its size as a whole was quite small compared to those that he'd seen before. Shen readied himself nonetheless, lifting a few rocks from the ground near him. He clicked them against each other in the air, chipping away at their surface, letting little pieces fall to the ground below. The ram-horn took notice of this only slightly, bringing its head up from the stream and looking back. Quickly, Shen threw the rocks into the creature's head and neck, which instantly pierced through and dropped the deer to the ground.

    "Thank you," he whispered to the animal, who was far gone from the world, lifeless. He took the sword from its scabbard on his back and took to skinning the animal, severing its head, and retrieving the horns from its head. He knew the ivory horns were a good resource, one which could be sold in markets for high prices to be ground up and used in medicines. He put the horns, completely dry of blood, into his bag and then pulled a cloth from the bag. After washing them in the stream, Shen handled the meat filets he'd gotten from the body of the deer, placed them into the cloth, and wrapped them up tightly to be put back into the bag. It seemed as though he was running out of space, and he would quickly need another bag, which could probably be bought from the Doshi market in the capital.

Shen tapped the side of his bag with his palm and came back to the path he'd walked before. Something came unto him suddenly, like a wave of devilishness that he felt he simply had to unleash on his unaware companions. A grin grew across his face, and he readied his throat to belt out a shout. "Help! Reina! Lao!" He screamed into the air, and afterward, he began to laugh.

"Shen?" Reina shouted, and she began to worry. She and Lao bolted toward the sound of his cry, Ping being taken behind them by the rope which Reina held in her hand. They ran all through the trees, pushing branches out of the way, crunching twigs and leaves underfoot. Once they'd gotten there, Reina had her sword pulled out, gripped tightly in her hand with the rope tied to Ping's saddle hanging down to the ground next to her. "What is it? Are you hurt? What-" she stopped, noticing what it was that was before her.

"Haha! You should see the look on your face," Shen said, sitting on his butt with his legs crossed, giggling to himself. "Ha! You, you look so worried!"

"Shen!" She shouted, red in the face. "Don't do that!"

"Haha! You're so red," he said, and pointed to her face.

"It's not funny!"

"I think it's kinda funny," Lao said, chuckling a little.

Reina turned slowly to the boy standing beside her, who had now picked up the rope on Ping's saddle. "Run." She said, and Lao's eyes went wide. She began to chase after Shen and Lao, and by extent Ping too, as they ran around the forest and the stream.

"I'm sorry!" Shen shouted, and then tripped over a stump, falling into the water. They all let out a good laugh, and Reina saw that she'd chased the two of them around enough. Wet, Shen took a while to dry off in the sunlight while Reina cleaned off the dried blood and dirt from the blade of her sword. After, they walked back to where the path was out of the forest and packed the meat

Shen had gotten into one of the saddlebags, making sure no more blood would leak from the filets. Once that was done, they departed from the forest and the stream, and continued their way to their destination with smiles on their faces, even Reina, who was content with Shen's punishment of sorts.

It was well into the afternoon when they approached the capital. As their eyes scanned ahead of them they could see, shining in the sunlight bearing down on them, tall buildings. They climbed into the air and were probably upwards of ten stories for the taller ones. The three of them approached the front of the city, where a tremendous bamboo gate stood. Along the top of the gate wall there stood soldiers in the same sort of armor as Chang had been, as Shen could tell. It was bronze, shining in the sunlight, and at the front of the helmets there were little bright green feathers. "Halt! State your business," one of the soldiers shouted, clutching a sword in his hand. Shen's heart sunk. 'What if they find me out? What will happen to Reina and Lao,' he thought frantically in his mind. "Well?"

"We simply want to shop in Doshi. We've got ivory to sell and things to buy," Reina butted in, her silver armor glinting a bit of sunlight from it as she climbed down from Ping's saddle.

The soldier above them atop the gate sheathed his sword back into the scabbard on the side of his thigh. He walked all the way down to one end of the gate, and proceeded to climb down a ladder on the outward side of the wall, down to the ground. Shen was beginning to get skittish. As the soldier walked over to the three of them and Ping, he thought of everything that might've happened if the mark on the back of his neck was found, how he'd be thrown back into a camp and probably killed. "Alright. All three of you, turn around, now."

The three turned their backs to the soldier, and Shen looked up to the top of the gate wall to see the soldiers lining up. Each of them wore their swords at their sides and their armor was sleek and smoothed. The soldier started with Lao, quickly looking at the dark tan skin on the back of his neck which had no hair to push away. Finding it clean, he moved on to Reina, again finding no such mark that would stir him to take them. Finally, the soldier got to Shen, and laid his hands on the scarf. "Sir, I'm going to need you to remove the scarf."

"Of course," Shen muttered. He unwrapped it, and his heart pounded faster and faster as his fingers gripped it. This was it. This would be the day that he would be taken back to one of those awful camps, put to work, or simply killed as soon as he arrived there. Not only that, but the same fate would befall his companions, or worse, he couldn't tell. The journey to find his brother would be cut so short, before even getting close. At least, that's what he thought, as the soldier ran his fingers across the tan skin of Shen's neck.

"Alright. You all are cleared to go. Please, enjoy yourself, and if you pass by the jewelry stall, tell the cute keeper there I said 'hi,' will you?" The soldier smiled at them as they all turned around, and cupped his hands around his mouth, looking to the top of the gate. "Wu! Open the gate!" He shouted up, and one of the soldiers at a far end of the top of the gate stowed away into a door. A few moments later, the large gate doors opened up outward before them, and Shen looked to them with a now fading nervousness. "You folks stay safe now," he said, and put the side of his fist to his chest in the usual salute.

"Of course," Reina said, and Shen wrapped the scarf back around his neck. The three entered, all on foot, Shen holding the rope tied to Ping's saddle as they walked down the stone path through the market city. People strolled all throughout the tall buildings, and the sound of clamor rose up and into the air as the three walked through. The buildings were painted a brilliant yellow that shone with the light of the afternoon sun upon them, with accents of red painted on their bamboo frames.

Shen thought to himself as his mind still recovered from what had just happened. He thought how the soldier could've possibly neglected the mark glaringly apparent on the back of his neck. His fingers reached up into the folds of his scarf, and he brushed their tips against where the mark was to be found. It was a subtle feeling, but as he felt it, Shen knew exactly what the oily substance was upon his skin. "That crazy old man," he said.

"What?" Lao asked.

"The one from the hut? What about him?" Reina said, her armor clinking softly as she walked on with the other two.

"He masked my mark. He must've put on some kind of dye paste to cover it up while he was treating me, and he did a perfect job of it, too," Shen said. He smiled wide, bringing his hand back down to his side. People around them were smiling too, all gathered at stalls that sold all manner of things. It was a lot like the market Shen and Lao had been to on Shuijiao, only much larger and brighter all around. There were red, green, and yellow streamers hung up on wires that stretched from building to building above them. Lanterns hung outside each stall, too, painted with pictures of birds or flowers that welcomed any who came to look upon them.

"That's a relief. I'd forgotten about that," Reina said, "but it might be best not to mention it so out in the open. We just got past the gate. Let's not get caught on our way into the capital, huh?"

"Right." Shen looked around and he began to notice that there were other dimians like Ping around. They were accompanied by people, and some even pulled carts filled with all manner of goods, produce or other sort of livestock. He noticed that one of the carts being pulled held a whole flock of chickens, their brown feathers rustling around as they moved within cages of wood, some of them coming off and fluttering down to the ground while the cart was pulled by a bright-eyed dimian.

Walking through, Lao noticed that there were many and many posters hung up on the buildings. Every once in awhile, there'd be one on a wall of a house or a stall, hung up by a thick nail. "Shen, what are those?" He tapped on Shen's side and he turned to the boy, his hand gripping the rope in his palm.

"What?"

"Those posters," Lao said, and pointed over to one of them, nailed to the side of what looked to be a house. Shen tugged on Ping's rope and began walking over to it, his curiosity as piqued as perhaps Lao's was. Reina and Lao followed close behind, Reina wondering in her own mind what it was Shen was doing, but following nonetheless. Shen grasped the parchment of the poster in his fingers, and as he read it his heart raced. It was a wanted poster of sorts, but it came direct from the Council of Batung, the ruling body in the country.

It had the official seal stamped in the corner, a small image of vibrant trees on either side of a downward facing triangle, a horizontal line through it the shape. Upon it there stood a drawing of a monstrous behemoth. It was like a badger, its mouth poised in a roaring look, long sword-like teeth poking downward. 'Zhi-Ming,' it said on it, along with a call to action: 'take on the beast anyone willing, and receive a 10,000 Yin reward and free passage to Ogon.' Shen's heart leapt at the thought. They could not actively go to Vasai, on the account of the ban on anyone coming in. But, if they could pass through Ogon, perhaps they could sneak through the smaller islands off of Vasai's eastern shore and get to Sukoshi Island by that way.

"We have a slight change of plans," Shen announced.

"What?" Reina asked. Shen handed over the parchment, tearing it from the wall and the nail, taking care not to rip the entire poster. Just as he did, Shen heard the door next to them creak open just a crack, but it was the least of his concerns. She read it over, and a small statement by the seal caught her eye. 'Supplies will be provided to the best of our ability. All who wish to take this challenge on must come before the Council and make their case. A hearing will be held on the morning after the half moon,' she read in her head. "Are you sure about this?"

"We don't have much of a choice. The only real way we can get into Vasai is through Ogon. This is the perfect opportunity to get travel."

"Zhi-Ming? I've heard much about him, from merchants and travelers."

"I know. I've heard about him, too, and I still think we stand a chance," Shen said.

"Who's Zhi-Ming?" Lao asked, his head tilted in confusion.

"A great beast, a spirit. He lives in the Daoyan Caverns on the eastern part of the mainland, and has been known to kill any travelers that might happen upon him."

"Sounds like fun to me," the boy said. In part, he was being truthful, an enthusiasm and excitement boiling in his chest. But, he was partly frightened too. While Shen and Reina passed the parchment back and forth amongst each other, he caught glimpses of the image. The thing's long teeth were menacing, and his gaping maw was not akin to any creature Lao had ever laid his eyes on.

"Lao," Shen said, "this won't be all fun. You have to be willing to risk your life. Please, if you are scared or don't want to do this, you need to tell me. There are other ways to get to Ogon. This isn't our only option."

"Shen, I want to do this. I'm not a scared little kid, you know," he said, a smirk forming across his lips.

"Well, I think that settles it," Shen said. "Reina, what do you think?"

"I'm alright with it just as long as you two don't get yourselves killed. The hearing is tomorrow morning. Where are we going to stay for the night?"

The door of the house they were stood in front of finally opened fully, and Shen's head swiveled over to it, meeting with the person who'd opened it. "Excuse me, but I couldn't help but overhear you three," she said. It was a small woman, dainty, with long flowing black hair that came down her back and rested between her shoulder blades.

"Oh, we're sorry, ma'am. We didn't mean to bother you."

"Not at all! You must be travelers, yes?" She clasped her hands together, her dark tan skin alight in the sun that shone from far down the stone path.

"That's right," Reina said.

"How wonderful! Please, if you need a place to stay, you can sleep here for the night."

"Are you sure? That's awful friendly of you to do for a group of strangers you've just come upon." Shen said.

"Well, I would like you to help me with one thing," as she said it, there was a clattering from behind her in the house. "Boys! Knock it off in there!" She screamed, and there was a tremendous pattering of footsteps. "Sorry. Children. I have my hands sort of full right now, and I can't make it to the market. If you could get me some fresh vegetables and meat, I'd be happy to let you stay the night here. I've got an extra room that you can all sleep in," she said it with a warm kindness that made Shen smile a bit to himself. It almost reminded him of his own mother.

"We'd be very grateful. What do you need us to buy?" Shen asked.

"Just some cabbage, soybeans, some broth, and a few filets of ram-horn meat. I'm making stew."

"We actually already have some meat," Reina said, and began rooting through the saddlebags on Ping's side. She pulled out the cloth-wrapped meat that Shen had gotten, and her fingers felt the cold bit of water and blood that had seeped into the fabric. It wasn't much, but it could certainly be felt by the skin of her fingertips as she handed it over to the woman. "I can help you with those boys if you need me to."

"You'd do that?"

"Why not? I have a little experience with children," Reina said. Shen wore a surprised expression, his eyes wide and his eyebrows raised. Lao too held this look, and both of them stood staring at their companion. "What? I used to look after my nephews when they were little," she said, her hand on her hip.

"Alright then, that settles it. Lao and I will head off to get the food. We'll be back soon," Shen said, and with a wave, he and Lao strode off into the market on foot, as Reina tied Ping up to a post outside the woman's home.

While they were off retrieving the things from a nearby cart and a stall, Reina and the woman were busy cleaning up the house inside. It was a wonderful abode as Reina observed. The table in the center of the room had a wonderful cloth draped over its wood surface, embroidered with images of local fauna, like little prairie birds or floral insects that might be found crawling upon the forest floor. Atop the cloth there stood a little wooden cage, empty with its hinged door open. Reina wondered for a moment what this cage might've housed, until the answer met her eyes, and her ears. "Lai! Put Mei back in her cage!" The woman shouted, toward her young son, a boy with short auburn hair and light tan skin, who was running around the table with a little yellow lizard gripped in his hands.

The creature was quite sharp looking, an array of scales poking out and toward its tail, like blades of grass that prickled the skin. "But mom! Dei is trying to take her from me!" The little boy said, and just then another boy came from down the stairs, taller and with longer hair.

"I am not!"

"Are too!"

"Both of you need to stop. How would you feel if you were all shaken up like that," Reina said sternly, and reached her hands out to the smaller boy before her. He carefully put the creature in her hands, and the lizard shook in her palms. Her big orange eyes blinked and darted around as she hoped with every fiber in her being that none of the boys would ever pick her up again. "Now, say you're sorry to her."

"I'm sorry," the little one, Lai, said.

"I'm sorry," Dei echoed.

"Good, now go and clean the mess you made upstairs," Reina said, a guess more than anything, but one which panned out, as the two boys bolted back up the stairs.

"Wow. That was so easy for you," the woman said, taking a seat at the table where the cage sat, letting forth a great sigh.

"It was nothing. Nothing I haven't dealt with, at least. Those boys remind me of my nephews, actually. How old are they?" Reina asked, putting the little lizard in her hands back into the cage, closing the tiny door behind it. She too settled into a chair, her leg muscles aching from the incredible amount of walking she'd been through in the last days.

"Dei is ten, and Lai is nine."

"Where's their father? If you don't mind me asking, of course, I don't mean to pry."

"Not at all. He was stationed here from Ogon before the boys were born. Maybe a year after I had Lai, he was sent back to Ogon and had to leave us."

"That's awful."

"I don't mind. I mean, yes it's hard raising these two troublemakers without him, but it's not like I don't talk with him. Mei here helps me send him letters and paintings of the boys on their birthdays. And, he sends me things back of course," she said, patting a hand on the top of the lizard's cage. The little creature turned and blinked with wide eyes at the hand that rested atop her cage.

"She swims all that distance?"

"Mhm! Comes back every time. You might mistake her for a fish if you weren't looking hard enough," the woman laughed. "I do miss him. And, seeing the boys, I can't help but remember him. They look just like their father," she began to trail off, but caught herself before she could get lost in thought. "But, enough about me I suppose, tell me about yourself. You mentioned your nephews?"

Reina had been lost in thought too, about what the woman before her might be feeling, before she snapped back into reality. "Hm? Oh, yes, well, I was maybe around sixteen when I first looked after them. My sister was eighteen and in the military, constantly on assignments and all. So, it was up to aunt Reina to look after the twins."

"Oh, twins? They must've been a handful."

"You have no idea. They were eight at the time, and they were obsessed with playing in the dirt. I might've had to wash them ten different times on any given day." Reina chuckled, and warm memories, images, came into her mind. The young boys standing side by side, wide smiles upon their faces.

"Have you talked to them recently?" The woman asked with a warm, soft voice.

Reina thought, and an image of the two boys came into her mind again. But, they were no longer young. They wore scowls upon their faces and were cloaked in shining silver armor, spears held in their hands at their sides. "The last time I talked to them, they were just going into the military."

"From the looks of that armor, I'd say it runs in the family."

"You could say that," she said with a chuckle, "yeah."

"I can't help but ask, and you'll have to forgive me, but, did you lose your arm while in the military?"

Reina thought to herself. It took all her power to keep her expression blank, to not show the somber feelings that bubbled up inside her chest. She couldn't outright say how she lost it. After all, how would the woman she'd just met think of her after learning of what she'd done? Mystics might've been 'scum,' but Reina was still a killer all the same. "I did, actually. You don't have to apologize for asking, you know. I was working guard detail at Fort Ashua on the eastern coast. There was a fire, and a beam fell on top of my arm. Crushed it bad."

"That's terrible!"

"It was certainly painful, yes. But, I'm still alive, and it left a pretty cool scar if I might say." Reina lifted the bit of cloth by her armor, the fabric which concealed the burn mark and skin of where her arm was severed from her body, and showed the woman.

"My, that is certainly heroic looking." Reina's heart dropped. She was no hero in her eyes. Her mind was filled with dark clouds, all billowing around with the thoughts of what she'd done. 'I'm not a hero. I'm a monster,' she thought. Were it not for the intrusion that followed these thoughts, Reina may have fallen deep into them.

"We're home!" Shen said, entering the door. Lao followed close behind, a large wooden basket filled with the fresh goods they were sent out to acquire. "We threw in some spices too. Thank you, really, for letting us stay in your home," Shen said, and shut the door behind them, once Lao had entered and set the basket atop the table.

"How was the market?" Reina said, shaking the thoughts from her mind.

"Busy! There were so many people, I thought I was gonna be swept up in them all," Lao said. He had a big smile on his face. It was enough to bring Reina's spirits up, and she found a great smile creeping upon her face.

"You almost did," Shen said.

"I know! And no thanks to you!"

"I was paying for the food! We can't just steal it," Shen protested.

"Boys!" Reina shouted.

"Yes?" Shen and Lao said in unison. Just then, Dei and Lai started rushing down from upstairs. They bolted and managed to trip over themselves, and they tumbled down the steps, coming to a crash in a heap at the bottom of the stairs.

"Not you, boys. Those- oh forget it," Reina said, a smile still upon her face, her palm placed on her forehead. She felt a laugh escape her mouth, and soon she was chuckling to herself.

"Dei, Lai, could you get the broth ready?" The woman stood up and began walking over to the kitchen nearby.

"Miss, you don't have to cook dinner," Shen said.

"What?"

"Please, you must be exhausted after dealing with those two's antics. We'll make dinner for you."

"Are you sure?"

"Oh yes, I'm quite a good cook."

"Says who?" Lao said.

"You've had my soup before!"

"I had it once."

"And you thought it was delicious."

"Will you two stop bickering and get to cooking?" Reina said sternly, a forming smirk on her face.

"Yes ma'am," they said together again, and stowed off to the kitchen.

"Forgetting something?" The woman said, walking over to her sons, who were standing by the bottom of the stairs now. Shen and Lao walked back over to the table, and with their heads down, grabbed the basket of things, taking them into the kitchen to cook.

The Council of Batung

After their dinner, which all of them thoroughly enjoyed, the three took to the spare room the woman had mentioned. It was quaint, small, but it was enough to fit the three of them. Lao even got a cot to sleep on, while Shen and Reina slept on the floor in their sleeping rolls. Despite this, though, they were content, and slept more than they had in the past days. Shen especially slept well, as no nightmares plagued his sleep. When they awoke in the morning, they felt refreshed, ready to take on the day ahead of them.

It was still dark when they left the home. The woman who took them in, who they came to know as Mina, was awake far earlier than the three of them had been. She had been sipping at tea when her three tenants came down the stairs, bags packed and ready. "Are you going to stay for tea? It's still warm," she'd said. The three declined, and instead hurried off to the Council building in the center of the city after Mina had assured them Ping would be safe at her home. People were scarce so early in the morning. That is, simple citizens, for the merchants and vendors were up and about, and seemingly had been since the night time. Produce was set up in wooden bins outside carts to be sold at fair prices, and the jewelry vendor was fast with her work, hanging necklaces from wooden pins on the supports of her stand.

"What do you think is going to happen?" Lao asked.

"I'm not sure. Maybe they'll take one look at us and deny us," Reina said.

"Let's hope not. Our journey will be much easier if we can take this on, you know," Shen said. He was determined. His brother occupied his thoughts on a constant basis, every waking moment filled with the image of his young brother's face, a face he hadn't seen in eighteen long years.

"Right. I know, Shen."

They had little clue as to where they were going, but the wooden signs upon posts were well enough to lead them in the right direction. It seemed as though they were on every corner. They pointed ahead down the stone road, 'Batung Council' written upon them in bold, black letters. Soon, they came upon the Council building, and almost immediately, they knew it was indeed their destination. It was huge. Not just tall, but bulky too. Painted a solid yellow, with accents of green around the bamboo framing, it was a monumental sight. Surprisingly enough, though, they didn't see so many people gathering as they had anticipated.

From the looks of the people there, it seemed as though they were just regular citizens, not up to take the challenge of slaying Zhi-Ming. Most of them were in cloth tunics and hide pants, no kind of armor could be seen on them, and absolutely none of them were carrying weapons of any kind. The doors were not yet open. They stood tall and strong, metal details lining the frame of the mighty wooden doors. Suddenly, though, as they arrived up to them, the doors pushed open to a wide room with the light of candles and lanterns shining from inside. For a moment, the doorway was empty. But soon, a figure walked out, a burly man of light tan skin with a head shaven, cut into patterns of Vasai origin.

"All who are here to see the Council, come and follow me inside. If you think you can handle it." His voice was not as the three had believed it would be. They all figured it to be booming and fierce. But instead, it was meek, much more nervous and strained than his appearance might've called for. All the same, Shen, Reina, and Lao stepped up to him. He nodded, and turned around, walking into the great building. As they entered, the architecture of the inner room became apparent to them as brilliant. Wooden pillars and panels bore engravings of mighty warriors. Under overhangs there sat many seats, cushioned with fabric and stuffed with the softest of wool presumably taken from the wooly cattle of Ogon, as most cushions of higher quality were.

The man led them in, and took a position in a group of maybe ten other men and women, all of varying stature. Most of them, though, were quite well-endowed with muscular physiques. It seemed as though, too, that the man who led Shen, Reina, and Lao in, was their leader. He stood, arms crossed, and looked forward. He looked toward the Council, the group which led the country whose soil all of them were standing upon. These men and women, old and wrinkling, who bore the dark tan hue of the Batung people, were the rulers of this country. "For those unacquainted, the Council shall now announce our names to you, in the name of transparency," the centermost Council member spoke, a man of dignified stature. He, like the others at his sides, wore bright yellow robes, but his were embroidered in white yarn with various images of flowers and vines. "I am Councilman Du, representing the Central Mainland," he said, standing up, and then sitting back down once his words left the sanctity of his mouth.

The man to his right stood up now, a smaller and thinner man with a thick black moustache upon his upper lip. "I am Councilman Chi, representing the Eastern Mainland."

To the left of Du, an old woman stood up. "I am Councilwoman Cheng, representing the Western Mainland." She took her seat once again, folding her hands atop one another on the council-desk in front of her.

To the right of Councilman Chi, another man stood up, who looked slightly younger than the aforementioned man. He had a cut along his right brow, and twitched his eye when he talked. "I am Councilman Jian, representing the island of Zhimai."

Once he had sat down, the member to the left of Cheng stood now, another woman, with wrinkles just barely stretching the surface of her neck and a mole above her left eyebrow. "I am Councilwoman Zhuang, representing the island of Lujing." As she sat down, Shen remembered him and Lao's time on the island she spoke of. He remembered the village, old man Yu and his grandson, and of Xue. The first meeting of Ping and Qiu crossed through his mind, and the preceding encounter in Senhong Alley. But, these fleeting images were just that, and were out and gone as the next Council member stood up.

The man at the far right of the council-desk stood up, and with a rugged voice, spoke loudly. "I am Councilman Dao, representing the Eastern Island Territories." He took his seat once again, and placed his hand to his mouth as he let out a hacking cough. Upon his left eye, there sat a leather patch, covering it, most likely hiding a deformity he would rather not be revealed to those standing before him.

The final Council member stood, a woman on the far left who wore a tight copper necklace that bore gemstones of green along its surface. "I am Councilwoman Kaishi, representing the Southern Island Territories," she said. She took her seat again, and Councilman Du in the center stood up.

"Now that the formalities have been dealt with, we can see to the issue at hand." He looked to the Vasai man and his group and then sat back down. "State your name for the Council," Councilman Du said.

"Mao Xinyi," the burly man with the pattern-shaved head said. His group shuffled around a bit, and some of them adjusted swords or knives they carried at their sides. Though his voice deceived it, he was a menacing man. At his back, fastened by a big leather strap, he carried a great trident, sharpened to a point that the finest of smiths dreamed of being able to master. The head of this weapon pointed over his shoulder as it was held diagonally to his back.

    The council talked amongst themselves for a moment, so hushed that they could not be heard by anyone else in attendance. Shen began to feel uncomfortable. It was a strange atmosphere, almost malevolent, like an eerie air that crawled up into his senses and stayed. He looked to his right, and his eyes met with another group. They were significantly smaller than Mao's group, consisting of only four people. Their leader was much different, too. She was small, almost frail, and from Ogon by the paleness of her skin and the blonde color of her hair, which was neatly fashioned into a braid at the back of her neck, as was the usual case of Ogon natives.

    "State your name for the Council," the man in the center of the Council said again.

    "Colden Egilhart," the woman with pale skin said. Her voice was much more booming than Mao's had been, and her blue, almost crystalline eyes imbued her words with an indomitable sense. She spoke with a force that filled up the room and bounced off the walls. There was a fur scarf of sorts, white, wrapped and tied around her arm by her shoulder. She wore big clothes too, lined with brownish fur, and boots made for stomping through heavy snow. She was thin though, her scrawny arms covered in black tattoos of claw marks and other designs poking through the short sleeves of her big vest. The man in the center of the Council talked with the others at the desk, before his eyes rested on Shen.

    "State your name for the Council," he said, his voice much louder and more commanding than it had somehow been before.

    "Shen Jin." Shen said, his heart pounding in his chest.

After some deliberation between the members of the Council, spoken in hushed tones, the center one spoke once again. "Very well. Mao Xinyi, please step forward. The Council will now ask you some questions pertaining to the task of killing Zhi-Ming. The rest of you, take seats behind you and you will be called for questioning when your time comes." He almost shooed them away, waving his hand toward the seats the three had passed on the way in. Mao and his group were fairly happy with themselves, grinning and chuckling as Colden and Shen's group shuffled off.

Unlike Mao, Colden and her group were fed up with the old man in the center of the council-desk. She wore a scowl on her face, and as she sat down, she huffed and scratched at the fur brushing up against the skin of her neck. "Bumbling idiot," Lao heard her say under her breath as they filed into the aisles close to the pillars which held the overhang. They all took their seats, Colden's group sitting far away from Shen's.

"A bit stuck up don't you think?" Reina whispered.

"They're the leaders of this country. You'd think they might have to be a little stuck up after so many years in those seats." Shen sat back, brushing his fingers against the stubble along his jaw.

"It all just seems a bit strange to me."

"You didn't have stuck up leaders in Vasai?"

"There's the King. But, he's a lot more lazy and less stuck up than the Council seems to be."

"Shh," Lao said in a whisper shout, "I'm trying to hear what they're saying."

After letting out a chuckle to himself at the expense of his young companion, Shen listened in on the Council and Mao along with Lao. It was quiet, but if they listened in close enough, the echo would allow them to hear what was being said all the way up where the Council stood. "I am a merchant by trade, and an adventurer by choice," Mao said, his voice still sounding like a sort of whine even from all the way back in the seats.

"And your group? They are merchants as well?" The old woman next to the centermost Council member, Councilwoman Cheng, said. From what the three could see, she wore giant golden earrings and had a black mole on the right above her lip. It was subtle, but even against her dark tan skin, the blemish could be seen from where they sat.

"They're from all sorts of backgrounds. We've got four merchants like myself, two blacksmiths, three mercenaries, and a lowly servant who worked for the King of Vasai," Mao said proudly, but his back slouched forward, and he somewhat shrunk in place as the Council members discussed quietly amongst themselves.

"What sort of servant might this individual have been? Please, have the person you speak of step forward," Councilman Dao said, scratching the skin of his cheek just under his eyepatch.

"Kumon, come here," Mao said, turning to his band of companions.

A small and frail man with light tan skin came forward out of the group, wringing his hands together, chattering his teeth to himself in nervousness. "I am Kumon, Kumon Mu," he muttered out of his cracked lips.

"What did you do for the King, Kumon Mu?" The far right Council member spoke loudly and clearly, letting the little man know exactly how serious the situation was to the Council.

The little man took a few moments to speak. He was jittery, and he furiously wrung his hands as he prepared to let the words flutter out of his lips. "I... I was nothing more than a servant to Miss Naizen, er, the princess. When the King was away for business, I looked after Sayomi," it was a slow speech, but he managed to stutter it out. At the mention of the girl's name, there came a slight twinge in Reina's face, which Shen picked up on. Though, more interested in the matters at hand, he neglected to mention it.

"Thank you," he said, and looked toward the center of the council-desk. "Councilman Du, you may proceed with your questioning."

"Thank you, Councilman Dao. Now, Mao Xinyi, why have you come to challenge Zhi-Ming? Fame? Fortune? Or do you just love the thrill of the fight?" Councilman Du, in the centermost seat, spoke clearly, and raised a bushy eyebrow. "In other words, what do you stand to gain from this endeavor?" He leaned back in his chair, while Shen leaned forward to listen in.

"Council, I want to kill the mighty Zhi-Ming to open up more routes for my business. I'm a simple man. As it stands now, the spirit has been killing traders that could be making business with me. I can't have that. How can I support my friends here, if I have no one I can trade with? That stupid spirit is going to kill all my customers if I don't stop him!" Mao became frustrated, stamping his foot on the ground and clenching his fist. He composed himself and looked to the Council once again. Of course, they were discussing, though it was a bit louder now than a whisper, and their discordant tones could now be heard by even Shen.

"Thank you. The Council will now take a few moments to discuss further. You may be seated in the back, you and your companions," center Councilman Du said. Shen listened even further as Mao shuffled into the seats closest to the big wooden entrance doors. They were much louder now in their speech, and Shen wondered if it was because they were no longer in the direct presence and earshot of one of the groups, it was just them after all.
"Councilman Chi, how do you think Mao Xinyi and his band will fair against

Zhi-Ming? They will be venturing into your jurisdiction after all," Councilwoman Cheng spoke, fiddling with the earrings she wore.

"Cheng, there is no need for the formal title, the groups have gone and cannot hear us. He seems like a strong candidate for the mission," Councilman Kaishi said.

"I think he seems cocky," Councilman Jian said, a twitch in his eye. He reached a wrinkled finger up to his brow and scratched at the scar, long faded, a pale reminder of whatever had happened to him.

"Cocky?" Councilman Du said.

"Yes. We've gotten a lot of them, and yet you still do not grasp how I mean when I say it. He is an arrogant fool to me." Councilman Jian leaned back in his seat, propping his head up with his arm, his elbow on the desk in front of him.

"And what's wrong with that? Shouldn't he get the chance to back his arrogance up with his actions?" Councilwoman Zhuang said, tossing back her deep gray hair, tying it up in a single bundle at the back of her head.

"If he manages to kill the beast, and that is a mighty if, he'll take a boat to Zhimai Island, my territory. He may be in your jurisdiction now, Du, and he'll roam into yours, Chi, if he takes this on. I'm not sure how you will act in your territory, but if he does something drastic or reckless in mine, he will face the greatest punishment I can administer upon him. I don't take kindly to his type," Councilman Jian muttered. His head was bare, bald, shiny beneath the lights of the candles and lanterns above them.

"Jian, you cannot just dismiss good help because you think they have a less than ideal personality," Councilwoman Kaishi said. The light from lanterns hanging above the council-desk reflecting off the metal of her copper necklace, catching little hints of the light and bouncing them off as she moved her head while she talked.

"I think he may pose more problems than he solves. That type of person is only ever out for themselves, and that is not the type of thing we need running around with Council supplies and especially funds," Councilman Jian said, rubbing two fingers against his forehead.

"I tend to agree with you, Jian, and especially so here," Councilwoman Cheng said.

"And why is that, Cheng?" Councilman Du said.

"Mao Xinyi is much more than a problem because of arrogance. Even more so, he seems to have quite direct connections with Vasai. We cannot stand to make arrangements with the people of the country actively vying for ownership of territory in our possession," Councilwoman Cheng said, her brows poised in a scowl, eyes sharpened in her expression. "Certainly not when they've already seized Lucao Island."

"Cheng, you cannot be so generalizing of them. They seem to be entirely disconnected from the King and his dealings. Perhaps they *are* just merchants trying to make some coin, can you fault them for such a motive?" Councilwoman Zhuang said.

"These notions will be taken into consideration," Councilman Du spoke quietly again, but Shen could still hear him, "for now, however, we must call Miss Egilhart to the Council for questioning." The Councilman looked to the seats, and he noticed Shen leaning forward. "Colden Egilhart, you may now come before the Council for questioning," he said it much louder now, and the woman with the pale skin and blonde hair took her group up to the front. She had a certain stride, a serpentine movement of her hips as she took each step forward, and a good head about her, poised up ahead of her and not down at her feet.

Once she arrived, Shen noticed something peculiar. The Council was speaking much much quieter now. In fact, they were speaking so low that Shen could no longer hear them. He could only sit and watch while the woman spoke with her hands at her hips to the Council. "What are they saying?" He asked in a whisper.

"I don't know, I can't hear them." Reina said.

"Do you think they're saying the same things as that Mao guy?" Lao asked. He leaned back comfortably in his seat, propping his feet up on the back of the seat in front of him.

"I'm not sure. She doesn't seem all that interested in business to me. She looks like some kind of hermit or something, maybe a warrior even," Reina said. They looked on, and saw that all of her group was decked in some sort of armor. While she didn't wear much, Colden herself wore shin and thigh armor, a dull iron with a dark gray color to it. The other three of her group wore heavy-looking iron chest and leg armor. Upon their groin areas there were heavy sets of chainmail, links clinking against one another whenever they would walk or even just shift their legs around. "Look at their weapons."

Shen and Lao both looked to their sides, and fastened by leather straps there were scabbards. The three she had with her all had swords, dark in color with hilts wrapped in black leather, but Colden's weapon looked to be a two-handed axe she had strapped to her back. It was menacing, crafted with Ogon patterns embellished into the iron head of the weapon. "They look like mercenaries," Shen said.

"Maybe they are," Reina muttered.

"Reina, I have some information you might want to know," Shen said.

"What's that?"

"I overheard the Council mention something about being opposed to Vasai. I'm not sure how we're going to explain your connection to the military without raising some suspicion."

"I've told you, I'm not with them anymore. I want nothing to do with them," she said it a bit irritated, her hand going up as she spoke.

"I know, and I believe you wholeheartedly, but they might not be so forgiving. Do you have a plan?" Shen said.

"I can figure something out to say. It won't be too hard to denounce the place I came from, especially after what they made me do."

"Don't be so sure in that," Shen said warily.

"Why?"

"You can't express your feelings on Mystics. If they even begin to think you sympathize with my kind, they might look into us further. We can't be found out."

"I know, I know. I'll figure something out. Come on, Shen, at least trust me a little bit." She joked, chuckling a bit as she spoke. The Council was taking great care not to announce the questions they were asking, though Shen had already heard a majority of them as asked to Mao earlier. But, unlike Mao before her, Colden was much more firm it seemed in her answers. Her stance had not changed once throughout the entire bout of questions. Where Mao would have shrunk, bowing to the mighty booming voices of the Council, Colden stood proud and took the brunt of whatever it is they were saying amongst their little whispers. She even twitched a grimace at the sound of Councilman Du's voice.

Of course, the Council and the woman they were questioning weren't always quiet. Councilman Dao especially was not one to stay quiet, his fierce cough echoing off the wooden walls of the building along with his voice. "Colden Egilhart, you hail from Ogon? What do you do there, or if you are no longer in said business, what *did* you do?" He spoke loud, and Shen could hear him now.

The pale woman pondered for a moment, as if searching for something in her mind to say, scratching at the back of her head, rooting her fingernails through the strands of light blonde hair. "As you know, Ogon does not have any formal government, nor does it have a military. But, I suppose if you have to place a title on my business, you could call it 'suppliant,' for the various noble families of the nine Ogon territories. Would you like the names of those families?" She spoke with a serpent's tongue, cunning. It wasn't outwardly apparent, as any cunning sort of person would have it, but if one were listening close enough, they could tell. And Shen could tell exactly how sly Colden was. Her voice danced with charisma, and waved about from her lips like the enchanting sound of a furred warbler's luring call to a field rodent.

"If you would," Councilman Chi said, his eye twitch visible even from so far away.

"The families I serve are the Aevir, Frigard, Verrmur, and Hrimhart families. That is all I can disclose, though, so you should not ask anymore of me." Though he could not see it, as Colden's back was turned to him, Shen could hear the smirk through the sound of her voice. "Those are the families I answer to in my dealings."

"Thank you. This will be noted," Councilman Du spoke, and he seemed to have some kind of plan of his own. All of the Council members seemed to have some sort of agenda on their minds, uniform amongst them all. "Now, why do you want to kill Zhi-Ming?" Shen and Lao, who was listening in now too, could not hear the woman's response. She spoke too soft for them to hear. "Very well said, Colden Egilhart. You may now take your seat while the Council discusses," Councilman Du said, and waved his hand to shoo Colden and her group back to their seats. They returned, and Shen's heart began to pump ever faster.

All the while they were talking, they would be waiting to call him and his two companions for questioning. He had faith in Reina's abilities. But, faith was not enough to dispel the lurking feeling of uncertainty. If even him himself was discovered as a Mystic, Lao and Reina would be taken with him, put into the same bouts of torture that he had endured those years ago. "What do you think they'll ask us?" Lao asked.

"Probably just a repeat of what they asked Mao and Colden. What do you think, Shen?" Reina said, and she looked to the man next to her. He was musing, but on his face there was painted a look of nervousness. His eyes were darting in place while fixed forward on the Council members at the desk so far ahead. There was an air about the room, one which cut through his senses, darkening his mind and his soul. "Shen?"

"Hm?" He shook his head and looked to his companion. As he looked upon her face, there came a soothing air that washed over his mind. This feeling might've lasted, were it not for the booming voice that came, shooting through the air of the room and landing amongst the seats they were sitting in.

"Shen Jin. You may now come before the Council for questioning," Councilman Du said loudly, with a twinge of aggressiveness laced in his voice.

Shen stood up and the two with him followed suit. The walk before them seemed to stretch on farther than any other distance they had trekked before, and it felt like time was slowing to a halt as they walked down the aisles of seats to the council-desk up front. "Reina, remember, don't give us away," he said.

"Shen, I know. Just trust me. I've got a plan, remember?" She let a smirk creep across her face, and adjusted the sword at the small of her back, feeling it slip uncomfortably a bit. It brought his nerves down slightly, but the looming threat that might befall them was always present. They arrived before them, and immediately, they felt the piercing eyes of the Council staring through them.

"So, your time has come now. Tell me, you, Vasai soldier, what brings you to our country? Don't think I neglected to notice that armor of yours," Councilwoman Cheng said. Her brown eyes were flaming with the lights of the candles sat atop the council-desk. As she spoke to Reina, somewhat angrily, her golden earrings bounced at the sides of her head.

"Members of the Batung Council. I know my appearance leaves a bit to be desired. I may look like an insurgent, yes, but I can assure you I'm not." She gestured to the stub on her right side, the burned skin showing through the flaps of fabric of the thin tunic under her armor. Such armor flickered with the light of the candles and the lanterns, putting forth an ominous glow that instilled her words with a sense of importance otherwise not gleaned. "I was made to do things that still haunt me to this day, and for it, I was given nothing. Instead a piece of myself was taken from me. I've come here to try and make up for what I did, and helping your country with Zhi-Ming might just help me do such a thing," she said proudly.

Her companions next to her were moved. Their senses were stirred up, a burning inspiration beating on the insides of their chests, which poised them to bring their heads up to the Council before them. Even the old leaders that sat before them seemed to be moved, with the exception of Councilman Jian, who was still in his lax composure. "Perhaps you truly do want to make up for your sins, if they should be fact, but that will only be seen in your actions,"

Councilman Du said. "Now, to address another cause for concern, I must ask *you*, Shen Jin, a question."

"Anything for the Council," he said, his hands clasped behind his back.

"Could you be related to the Jin family, specifically that of Bai Jin, and his son Kang?"

Shen wasn't sure how exactly the Council knew those names, the names of his grandfather and of his father respectively, but despite whatever way they might've known, he could not let it show that he knew them. "No more relation than in last name, I suppose. Those names are entirely foreign to me." He kept composed, and would not let any of the emotion he felt through memories overtake him.

"You do not seem to be of relation to them. The Jin family possessed brown eyes and dark skin. To my knowledge, neither Bai nor his son Kang ever had children with anyone, not of Batung anyway. Your story checks out. But, how will your words hold when our questioning begins?" Councilman Du said it with a harsher tone, but it was not rough, instead booming from his throat in a loud and smooth rhythm. Shen savored the thought of his family, and used every bit of his fortitude not to smirk at the thought that they didn't even know about his birth. But, another thought passed through his mind. 'Why did they know my family?' He thought. They weren't all that wealthy, and they certainly weren't any kind of important figures before the day Mystics started to be taken to the camps. For that matter, he wondered why Reina knew his family again.

He would have continued the endless thinking of possibilities as to how they knew his family, were it not for the voice of Councilman Chi breaking through the silence. "To start, those who undertake this task will be given supplies from my personal inventory. In order to see how much of and what you receive, we need to know what you have already," he said, running his fingers along his moustache.

"We have a dimian," Shen started, but was interrupted by Councilman Chi.

"And he is healthy? Where is he now?"

"He's in perfect health from what we can tell, and he's at a nearby house we stayed in for the night. We've come here just for this task, actually."

"And what else might you have, besides the dimian?"

"I have several medical supplies, herbs and bandages, and both of us have weapons." Shen gestured to the bronze sword in the scabbard at his back, and the Councilman before him began writing upon a piece of parchment, a long quill held in his hand. "Other than that, we currently have twenty-four Yin, as well."

"That is not a large amount. Do you not have work you can be paid for?"

"No. We are nomads, traveling the world."

"I suppose that is part of your personal reason for taking on this task?"

"Yes, Councilman. I wish to see the plains and mountains of Ogon for myself. And, with the passage I may gain from completing this task, I can do just that."

"And what about the little one?" Councilman Du said, interjecting himself into the conversation between the two of them. "What do you stand to gain from killing Zhi-Ming?" The boy had not anticipated he would be asked anything at all. Lao stood, a bit shocked, while the Council watched on and waited for his response. "Well? You do have a reason, right? A child like you might die taking on this sort of mission."

"I'm not a child!" He screeched. The chatter toward the seats from Mao and his group were silenced. "I want to prove that I'm not some scared little kid like I used to be. Plus, I wonder if there's any treasure that big spirit is guarding," Lao said, his attitude shifting, a devious little smile dancing upon his lips.

Councilman Chi shifted around in his seat, stroking the hairs of his thick moustache. "Just know, you won't be taking all the treasure, if you might find it." He smirked, and the boy before him smiled.

"Alright, Councilman Chi, do not patronize the boy. It is time for us to make our decision," Councilman Du said. He stood up, the sleeves of his yellow robes waving with the movement of his arm. "Please, take your seats and we will call everyone forward again when we have decided."

The three stood for a moment and then turned back, walking down the aisles of the seats. "That was it? I thought they'd ask a little more than that." Reina said. She brought her hand up and scratched at her bun of black hair, neutralizing an itch that had been building up since they walked up to the council-desk.

"Isn't it a good thing they didn't ask so many questions?" Lao asked.

"I'm not so sure. Asking so little might be because they've already counted us out of possibly taking the mission," Shen said.

"So, should we prepare for a new route to Sukoshi?" Reina added, just as they made it to their seats. They sat down and looked over to the other groups. Mao was actually dozing off, a thin piece of cloth draped over his face, rising and falling just slightly as he breathed in slumber. Colden, though, was attentive to the Council, leaned forward to maybe get a listen at what they were saying.

"Not so quickly," Shen said, "I don't know why, but I have a feeling we may be getting this mission."

"What makes you say that?" Lao asked, looking to him with his brown eyes.

"Call it a gut feeling," Shen said, a smile on his face.

"Speaking of gut, I'm hungry. You think Mina saved some of that stew in an icebox?" Reina said, rubbing her growling stomach.

"Now I'm hungry too. Did you have to talk about that stew, Reina?" Lao said. His stomach too began to garble a hungry tone, and he brought his hand down to meet it.

"Well it was good! I can barely get it off my mind," Reina said.

"Hush, I think they're about to say who gets the mission," Shen said.

The Council members were shuffling around, their yellow robes tossing around in their seats. Councilman Du brushed off a gray wispy hair from the white flower embroidered into his sleeve, which had probably fallen from Councilwoman Cheng's head next to him, and he stood up. "The Council now calls up Mao Xinyi, Colden Egilhart, and Shen Jin, as well as their respective companions. We have decided," he said. Everyone from their seats moved to the front of the big room and stood in front of the council-desk in anticipation.

"Say it, old man!" Colden shouted impatiently.

"Mind your tongue, girl," Councilman Jian spoke, his eye twitching under the scar on his brow.

The anticipation was crushing. Air's weight in the room pushed down all around Shen, Lao, and Reina. The sounds of the room, the echo of every last heavy breath that escaped their lips, was like an avalanche of senses, until Councilman Du spoke. "On behalf of the Council of Batung, I declare that Shen Jin and his two companions shall take on the task of slaying the spirit of Daoyan

Caverns, Zhi-Ming." He said it so surely, and yet the three stood before him were dumbfounded.

The Trek Begins

"What?" Colden screamed. "You have to be kidding me!"

"This is ridiculous! You'll ruin my whole business!" Mao shouted.

"Would you like to leave of your own accord, or be escorted by the guards? The choice belongs solely to the both of you," Councilwoman Cheng said, raising her finger toward them. There were no guards to be seen, and yet the two left on their own terms, storming out in a muted rage as they pulled open the great wooden doors and let them slam behind them. "Now, we can get on to business as usual."

"Shen Jin and company, congratulations on being selected. If you have any questions for the Council, please, make them known before your briefing," Councilman Chi said.

"Yes. I have two questions, actually," Shen said.

"Make them known. We would not want your voice to go unheard," he said again.

"To start, why us?"

"Well, there were a number of reasons that contributed to our choice of you three. But, the main idea we decided upon was your inclination to stray away from greed. Too many times before, we have been told that killing Zhi-Ming would bring individuals great wealth or great fame leading to said wealth. You three, though, seem to want to prove something of yourselves. And that, my friends, is greatly appreciated," Councilman Du spoke now, and there was a warm smile crawling upon his face.

"And as for my other question, why have you not dealt with this problem much earlier?"

"How do you mean?" Councilman Chi said, stroking at his moustache with calloused fingers.

"Well, you have countless soldiers roaming around. Why look for random citizens instead of sending in soldiers you can easily trust?"

The Council thought for a moment in silence, looking upon the three waiting for their answer. "Hm, that is certainly a complicated question to be answered. For one, a lot of our soldiers are reserve and haven't seen action since the Mystic cleansing of the year 500. And those that are not old and jaded like ourselves are in the southern islands and Zhimai working on construction of forts," Councilman Du said.

"Forts?"

"Yes. With the encroaching Vasai threat to our territories, we have been forced to build forts in case of any attack on our land. I'll ask that you don't pry too much. We cannot reveal much information to you, as it's classified," Councilman Jian said, his fierce twitching spiking in its movement as the words came out of his mouth.

"Now, have your questions been sufficiently answered?" Councilman Du asked, leaning forward on the council-desk upon his elbow.

"Yes, Council," Shen said.

"Excellent. On with the briefing. Councilwoman Kaishi, please retrieve the map and your little invention for them, will you?"

"Of course!" The little old woman with the copper necklace said, getting up from her seat and running behind into the darker recesses of the room. There was a bout of silence and then a great clatter at the darkness of the back of the room. "I'm alright! No worries everyone!" The woman came back with rolls of parchment, falling out of her hands as she made it back to the council-desk. "Darn things! Du, we need to invest in a cart for all of my work!" She said.

"Councilwoman Kaishi, please, you are being quite informal. This is supposed to be a formal briefing," Councilman Du said, fighting back a chuckle at the expense of his fellow Council member.

"Oh don't be so uptight, Du. I'm sure they have no problems with informalities," she said. "Do you?"

"I'm fine with it," Shen said.

"Not a problem to me," Reina said.

"No complaints here," Lao echoed.

"See? Now, can I get on with it?" Councilwoman Kaishi asked.

"Very well. Go on, Kaishi," Councilman Du said.

"That wasn't so hard was it," she said, and then spoke under her breath. "Snob," she said, and chuckled to herself. "Alright then! First, let me get you acquainted with the route you'll be taking." She placed a bunch of the parchments on the ground and rooted through them to find a map. It was old and worn, not used since perhaps before the genocide. "Here we go!"

"If I may interrupt, we already know the path to Daoyan," Shen said.

"Well then, that is certainly convenient, but I will leave this map with you just in case. It has the quickest path laid out for you to get to the caverns." She handed over the rolled up parchment, and Shen took it into his hands quickly. "Now! For my invention! I'm really proud of this one, and I think you are going to love it." She seized a small device from the pocket of her robe, and pulled it out to display for the three before her. The little thing was quite peculiar. It had a bowl-like appearance, and just barely fit the palm of the old woman holding it. Upon its rim there sat a glass panel covering the innards, a simple arrow made of a finely polished metal rock, along with tiny directional letters written in white paint.

"Councilwoman Kaishi, may I ask, what is this little thing?" Reina said, pointing to it with her finger.

"This? Only the greatest invention of our time! Well, until I invent something even better." She twisted it around in her palm, and the little arrow dangled in place, fixated in one direction though the rest of the device moved apart from it. "While I have yet to come up with a name for this magical device, I can describe just how it works. I have spent countless days studying the habits of this particular stone, which we excavated from a nearby mountain, and have concluded that it has an odd tendency to always point to the north! When doused with a special concoction of herbs, as I've done here, at least. Now you have no need to look to the sun for your direction," she said chipperly. Her face was ecstatic, blooming with a fascination only to be matched by Lao's wide eyes at the little device before him.

"And you're just giving this to us?" Shen asked.

"Why not? It may prove beneficial or even necessary to your journey to the Daoyan Caverns of the east. Best of luck on your travels!" She said, and quickly handed over the little device and a few more rolled up pieces of parchment, then she scurried off back to her seat. Once she arrived, she found her hair to be a bit tussled, and poised her lips to blow the stray strands from her brow, putting out a warm smile. Shen smiled back, struggling to carry the parchments held haphazardly in his arms.

"Thank you, Councilwoman Kaishi, for that," he paused for a moment, trailing off with the last word, "enlightening display of your supplies," Councilman Du said.

"Don't patronize me, Du," she jokingly snapped, and laid back in her chair with a lax smile playing about her lips.

"If you will, Councilman Chi, continue on with the briefing," Councilman Du continued on, shrugging off the remark.

"Of course. Now, I will make this as short as possible, in order for you and your companions to get any other necessary supplies you might need from the market," he said, and pulled something from the sleeve of his flowing yellow robe. "In this pouch, I have placed 100 Yin in coins, for you to purchase whatever you choose. Tomorrow morning at dawn, I will have an informant waiting for you at the eastern gate of the city. He will be clothed in similar robes to that which we wear now, so be adamant about that, and look out for him. With him, there will be a merchant's cart with about two week's worth of rations and produce."

"A cart?" Lao asked.

"Lao, please let him talk, it's rude to interrupt," Shen said.

"Please, there's no need for that, it's good for the boy to get involved in government and ask questions, you know. Too many young ones these days have no idea what we do here in the Council-" Councilman Chi said, before being cut off.

"Chi, you're going off on a tangent," Councilwoman Kaishi muttered, scratching at the thick copper necklace around her slightly wrinkled neck.

"Right. My apologies. As I was saying, about the cart, your dimian should be able to pull it just fine with the rig Councilwoman Kaishi devised and included. And, if the need should arise, you can use the cart's cover for shelter. Now, that should conclude the briefing for your supplies. Councilman Du will now give you a few parting words on the journey ahead of you. Best of luck," he said, and placed his fist to his chest in salute.

After salutes from Shen, Reina, and Lao, Councilman Du stood up, as Councilman Chi sat back into his seat with his robe billowing around him. "You three are about to take on a spirit that has long since been a nuisance in this great country of Batung. The journey will be rigorous, and the challenge even more so once you reach your destination. But, I believe you three will succeed. After, all, we would not have chosen you if we did not," he said, a smirk on his face. "After completion of the task, I ask that you will report to Zhimai for further processing. Look for the town of Taoyi on the island, and find where the Fort Taoyi construction is getting underway; our constituent handling your processing is overseeing the project. Now, I will ask, do any of you have any further questions for myself or the rest of the Council?"

"Yes, I have a question," Lao said. The boy stepped forward, and Councilman Du looked toward him with a kind eye. "Can we keep any treasure we find?" He said. The devious little smile came upon his lips again, and he almost giggled to himself as he let out the words.

"Councilman Chi, do you have any words on the subject?" Councilman Du asked, looking to his fellow Council member.

"Boy, if you can manage to stuff those tiny pockets of yours with Yin and treasure, you can surely keep it too," he said. "As long as it's not too much. Some of that does belong to the country and will be used for further construction on our forts," Councilman Chi finished his statement and stroked at his moustache again, feeling each strand of bristly black hair.

"Yes!" Lao shouted, and then regained his composure, putting forth a salute to the Councilman before him.

"Well then, if that will be all, I will let you be on your way. Watch yourself, be vigilant, and take care of one another," Councilman Du said it loud, and with a massive smile on his face. He stood in a salute, alongside his fellow Council members, who all did the same. The three all smiled, saluted back, and were out of the main door, one weight taken off of them and another placed on as the daunting task laid ahead of them. Through the streets they walked, and they soon came back upon Mina's home once again, to find the door was propped open.

"Ms. Mina?" Reina shouted in. There was no answer.

"Ms. Mina, are you in?" Shen called out. Still, no voice called back in reply to them. Suddenly, there was a great clamoring, and it sounded like the noise of heavy instruments falling and breaking wood somewhere inside the house. "Mina!" Shen shouted, and stormed into the home. The other two followed, Reina reaching down to grip the hilt of her sword and Lao looking around for perhaps a pan he could grab as an impromptu weapon.

But, their worries were soon calmed by the voices coming from upstairs. "It's mine! You can't just take it!" They heard, and recognized the voice as Dei's, Mina's older boy.

"Mom said I could have it!" Lai shouted next.

"Boys!" Reina shouted, and the commotion up the stairs stopped. All went silent.

"Is that her again?" Lai spoke.

"The lady from yesterday? I think it might be," Dei said.

"I can hear you, you know!" Reina shouted, and stomped a foot onto the bottommost step, feeling the wood creak underneath the sole of her boot.

"Dei! You spoke too loud!" Lai said, trying his best to whisper.

"What? You're the one who was being too loud!" Dei shouted without a care for who was listening downstairs.

"Boys!" Reina shouted again, and took another step, stomping onto the next stair.

The two of them came from out of hiding, clutching a framed picture in their hands. "Yes, ma'am?" They answered in unison

"Where is Mina? Where is your mother?" Reina asked.

"She went into the market, to the messenger lizard stalls," Dei answered. "I think she might've gotten a letter from dad."

"Do you know when she'll be back?" Shen asked, stepping forward toward the stairs. "We need to ask her something."

"She should be back before sundown. You can stay here until she gets back if you want!" Lai said, smiling wide, tugging the frame from his older brother.

"Hey! Mom said no inviting strangers into the house while she's gone," Dei said.

"These aren't strangers! They're mom's friends." Lai replied.

"You don't even know their names," the older brother spoke again, and grabbed the frame from his little brother.

"Neither do you, dirt-for-brains!" Lai said, snatching the item back from Dei.

"Hey!" Shen said sternly, and began walking up the stairs toward the boys. "What are you two doing? What's that in your hands?" He asked when he'd gotten to them, pointing at the frame Lai held in his little hands.

He handed it over, and encased in the frame, there sat a small painting. A man stared back from behind the decorative glass. Upon his face were marks, white paint in designs of the Ogon warriors, weaving around the shape of his bright blue eyes. His golden blond hair was wild, tamed only by a single braid at the back of his head that could be gleaned by the look of his hair. Skin of pale white was cloaked in hide armor lined with fur, and a great bear's skull was fashioned into a helmet along with wrought iron atop his head. "Is this your father?" Shen asked.

Silent, Lai simply nodded. "Yes," Dei muttered.

"Why are you fighting over him, then? Is he not the father of the both of you?"

"Yes, but, I wanted to keep the picture!" Lai said.

"You two are brothers. There is only one father for the both of you. Can you not learn to share him, between the two of you?" He knelt down to them, and handed the picture back between them, each of them using a hand to grab onto it. "Brothers shouldn't fight, especially not over the man who loves them both." He said it with a smile, and the two boys could feel their hearts warming up.

"Thank you, mister. I guess you can stay here until mom gets back," Dei said.

"Thank you very much, young man. And, one more thing," Shen said, leaning in close to the taller of the two little boys. "Be good to your little brother."

The boy nodded, and then scurried off to one of the rooms upstairs. "Come on, Lai! Let's play Qi!"

"Aw, but you always beat me!" Lai said.

"Then I guess you'll just have to get better. Now, come on!" Dei shouted, grabbed his brother by the wrist, and they left into their own little room near the spare one the three had inhabited the night previous.

"They all good?" Reina asked.

"Yeah, they seemed like they were angry about something," Lao added.

"They should be all fine. As for us, let's wait at the table for Mina to come back, shall we?" Shen said, walking down the steps and over to the table, pulling out a wooden chair and sitting down. He rested his back up against it, and his shoulders began to relax.

"You don't think she'll mind us just sitting in her house with her boys all alone in the house?" Reina asked, hesitantly taking a seat across from Shen. The chair she sat in seemed rickety, creaking, but perhaps it was just the hefty weight of her silver armor pushing down on the frail little chair legs.

"Yeah. It seems a little sketchy that we'd be here," Lao said. "It brings me back to my days squatting, though," Lao said, reminiscing. He remembered being shooed out of a home, waved off and back onto the streets after he'd been found hiding in the family's bamboo shed. "Good times," he joked, taking a seat next to Shen.

For a while afterward, they talked and talked, until the sun began to set on the horizon. It dipped beneath the great hills and slept amongst the trees which lined the landscape. Soon, the moon shined its light upon the capital. The market was all quiet, not even a single stall open for the night. Every torch and every candle was out, the wisps of smoke still hanging in the air and floating along the wind as they finally dissipated into the chill night air. Stars dotted all across the sky and swam around the black night and the moon that stared down the city. While the three of them were wrapped up in conversation, the door swung open and closed shut again, and Mina stood at the doorway.

"You three. What are you doing back here?" She said, slightly out of breath.

"We leave to take on Zhi-Ming in the morning. We need a place to stay," Lao spoke up.

"Oh! Well, you're certainly welcome to stay here for the night. I don't have any food for you, other than a few scraps of bread in the pantry. But, you can take the spare room again for the night." She looked around, walking over to the kitchen area, and she sat a piece of parchment down atop a wooden counter. "Where are Dei and Lai?"

"Sleeping. They crashed after a few rounds of Qi," Reina chuckled.

"They said you'd be back a lot sooner. What kept you out so long, Mina?" Shen asked.

Her face became flushed. She stepped back a bit, and grabbed for the parchment again, grasping it in her fingers. "Um, well, I suppose I should tell you, hm? I was meeting with him."

"Him?" Lao said.

"Heimel Fulnir, Dei and Lai's father," she said, and she brought her head low. It was as if it was something to be ashamed of. "I didn't want them to know. I know, I'm a horrible mother. How could I go and meet with their father without even telling them?"

"Why did you do it?" Shen asked.

"Hm?" Mina brought her head up, and blinked a bit, clutching the parchment in her frail hands, a bit of the ink rubbing off on her fingertips.

"There's a reason for everything, even if it's not the most obvious. I'm sure you had a good enough reason not to tell them." He said.

She let a small smile creep onto her lips, which faded once she opened her mouth to speak. "I was going to tell them. I swear. But, then he told me why he was visiting me so suddenly. He said he was being sent to Skurdur. He told me that Vasai forces were getting closer and closer to it."

"Vasai? But that's not possible. They haven't set foot on Ogon land since the genocide," Reina butted in, standing up from her seat.

"Yes, be that as it may, that's what he said. And worse still, he won't be able to write to me or the boys for a long while, at least for a half a year." She put the parchment in a pocket on the side of her dress. "How am I going to tell them?" Bringing her hands to her face, her skin was becoming paler, the emotion draining, and she panted in fear and nervousness.

"Mina, it's alright," Reina said. "I've experienced deployment. Everything will be alright, I'm sure of it, trust me." Part of her wanted to be right, but there was another part that almost didn't believe herself.

"You're sure?" Mina said, the color coming back into her dark tan cheeks.

"Yes. Now, you should be getting to bed. It is late after all," she said, and walked over to the woman, helping her up the stairs in her emotional state.

"Is she going to be okay?" Lao asked. The two women had retired to the upstairs, and since they didn't come back in quite a while, the two left at the table on the first floor had assumed they were both asleep, Mina in her bedroom and Reina in the spare room they would both soon inhabit along with her.

"I'm sure she'll be alright. It'll take some getting used to for her, and her sons, but they seem strong." Shen laid back in his chair, and heard the creaking sound of the backboard as his spine rested upon it. "How are you doing?"

"Me? Why do you want to know?" Lao asked.

"Well, it's been awhile since I got to talk with you like this. Things have been so chaotic lately, there's barely been time to breathe."

"Yeah," the boy said with a chuckle.

"Are you sure you were okay with what Reina did? With those bandits, I mean," he said.

"It was a little hard to watch, but, I've seen things like that before, living on the streets. People can get desperate, you know," Lao said.

"I understand that. You're very strong for your age."

"I'm not some little kid, Shen," he said.

"I know, I know. I just worry I suppose," he trailed off, and conspired in his mind to change the subject before the silence hung in the air for too long.

"We should be getting to bed. There's a long journey waiting for us in the morning, and we'll need to be up first thing at sunrise," Shen said.

"Yeah, don't remind me," Lao joked, resenting the very sight of sunlight that would negate his sleep. The two of them pushed in their chairs and made their way up the steps and into the spare room. There, Reina sat up against a wall, sleeping away as her chest rose and fell under her armor. It seemed as though she had not meant to fall asleep there, since her things, her bag and sword, were still fixed onto her. Quickly, the other two tucked into their sleeping rolls, felt the warmth of the cloth on their forms, and drifted off into slumber.

In the morning, Shen and Lao were awoken by Reina, shaking them awake. "Hey! Boys! Let's go!" She shouted, and was ready with her and their sleeping rolls rolled up neatly and tucked under her arm. They awoke, and looked to find they were on the floor, no cloth to support them.

"Ugh, a little more sleep maybe?" Lao muttered.

"No time, kid! We've gotta go, it's sunrise!" She said.

"What? Did we miss the informant?" Shen got up, and felt a cramping pain building in his side, which he'd thought came from sleeping on the wooden floor for two nights in a row.

"No, but we will if you two don't get up and get going!" She shouted, and started out the door. She soon found herself in the company of her companions, dashing behind her with their eyes widened. Practically jumping down the stairs to reach the bottom, Reina looked back up to find the two struggling to descend the steps. They were getting stuck up in the narrowness of the stairway, bumping up against each other in an attempt to fly down the stairs the fastest.

"Lao, stop pushing," Shen said, shaking his head, trying to get rid of the daze that was settling in.

"I'm not pushing! You're the one that's pushing!" The boy said, and finally got free of the jam. He bolted down the steps, and nearly tripped over his own foot, quickly jumping up despite it and standing straight.

"Wait for me!" Shen said, and flew down the steps. They creaked and rattled as his bare feet pushed them down, and one near the bottom even nearly broke under him. "Where's Mina?" Shen said. He'd slowed down, and had just an ample enough amount of time to look around and find the woman who had let them stay missing from view.

"She took Dei and Lai to go see their father. Now, let's go!" She said it hurriedly, and fled out of the door with a little salute goodbye to Mei, who was sound asleep in her little wooden cage on the table. Shen cracked a little smile, and he too gave the messenger lizard a salute. Lao, though, was dead set on zooming out the door with his two companions, that he simply ran right out without a second thought.

The three of them ran and ran, watching as the light of the sun grew and grew, stretching its gaze across the street. Stalls were opening, and the shiny wares they'd sell were glistening in the newfound light. Grass soaked up the warmth the sun gave as they grew a luscious green hue along the sides of the road. They approached the gate that had been described to them, and the doors were wide open, a figure with a covered cart standing by the big open door. "There you are," the man said, and turned. His robes were flowing, yellow, and trimmed in white cloth, much like those the Council themselves wore.

"Sorry about the wait, Mr. Hai. These two boneheads wouldn't get out of bed." Reina said. The two looked to each other in half bewilderment, the other half that of tiredness. "Did you get the bow, arrows, and glow rock I gave you the money for?" She said.

"Yes. But, it costed you just a bit more than you anticipated. You had no leftover cash from what you gave me. That glow rock is mighty expensive since the miners can't get into Daoyan anymore." He rifled through the cart, lifting the cloth covering its supplies, draped over a frame. Quickly, he pulled out a well-crafted wooden bow and a leather quiver with a good amount of arrows, along with a little object wrapped in a thin cloth. The cloth was just thin enough that there could be seen a light within it, glowing softly.

"Don't you worry, Mr. Hai. That's all gonna change once we kill that spirit." She said triumphantly, and the man before her put the things back inside the cart. The man soon left, and the two with Reina looked to her in a bit of shock.

"But, you, you already came here?" Lao said.

"You two wouldn't wake up, so I had to get here before the informant left. Mr. Hai was nice." She said, and walked over to the back of the cart, sitting on the stepping area near the back wheels.

"Where's Ping? Did we forget him," Shen shouted, to hear a loud *squawk* come from nearby him.

"Tugging the cart. Now come on, you two, let's get a move on, hm?" Reina said, and gestured for Lao to join her, sitting at the back of the cart. Shen walked to the front, and climbed onto the back of Ping's saddle, taking the reins that had been placed into the harness of the cart. He tugged on them once, and off Ping began to walk, letting out low noises as they slogged along the path out of the city, bound for the Caverns of Daoyan.

Obstacles

"Hey, Shen," Lao piped up. He'd been sitting amongst the produce boxed in wooden crates, leaning up against one of them with his sleeping roll at the small of his back. He chewed on the sleeve of the tunic that Shen had given him all the way back on Yedao. The cloth started to get soaked, a spot of saliva setting into it, and Lao recoiled as he realized what he was doing.

"Yes, Lao?" Shen said.

"I think some of the meat has gone bad," the boy said.

"Nonsense, these metal ice crates back here are meant to keep that from happening. And we haven't even opened them up, they couldn't be going bad in the slightest," Reina protested. She looked out from the back of the cover of the cart, looking to the road that was steadily retreating from them as they pressed forward on.

"Well something smells," he said.

"Maybe it's you," Reina said.

"I do not smell!" Lao lifted his arm up and took a sniff of his armpit. It was ripe. Sweat and dirt had since mingled, and the smell was settling in, creeping up into his nostrils. "Oh. Well, maybe just a little bit. But, what if it's you!" Lao pointed a finger at the woman next to him.

She lifted her arm as well, and sniffed. Like Lao, there was a pungent smell coming from her skin, bitter to the senses. She brought her hand over and pinched the cloth of her under-tunic, lifting it to smell herself even further. Indeed, as Lao had thought, she smelled too. "I do smell. Hey, Shen," she spoke up, and Shen stopped the cart.

"What is it?" He asked loudly.

"I think we need to stop to bathe, just for a little bit. We smell pretty awful back here. You know if there's any streams nearby?" She tapped her boot onto the wooden stepping platform by one of the back wheels.

Shen pulled the map from the bag on his side, and unfurled it. His eyes scanned the parchment, and rested on the area they were most likely to be near, using patches of trees as a landmark. "A while ahead there should be one stretching around some trees. Think you two can wait that long?"

"Whatever it'll take," Lao said, pinching his nose.

"Alright then. Sit tight, we'll be there in a little bit." Shen took Ping's reins again and directed him forward, walking forward once again, following the quickly narrowing path.

The sun crawled across the sky, and lit the entire world around them. It provided light for the grass and the flowers to bask in as they grew taller and livelier. It provided warmth to those animals that would sit at the edge of streams, drinking their water, and perhaps hunting if some prey might present itself. The stream they took to wrapped around the little forest on the map in a circular pattern, almost as if it was wrangling in the trees themselves. A few little field rodents scurried off as the wheels of the cart came to a stop just in front of the stream's edge. "Oh! Soap berries!" Lao shouted, and bolted out of the cart.

As he ran across the stream, stepping on rocks embedded in the ground under the water, Shen and Reina gathered at the streambed, looking to the boy in confusion. "What?" Reina said.

"Soap berries! These things are great," he said, standing under a bare tree which had little nuts clung to the branches that hung low. He took off his sandals and started climbing the tree and stopped once he had collected a sizeable number of the things from the branches, before he came back down and set them down on a rock. "They're just like the soaps the fancy herbalists sell. And, they're entirely free!"

"Lao, we have soap in one of the crates in the back. It's not a lot, but it's enough for the three of us." Reina said.

"No need for it! In fact, if we collect enough of these things, we can just sell that stuff. Now, look away, I'm gonna wash up first," he said. Shen and Reina obliged without a word and went into the cart, sitting in the back as they dropped the cover down. Lao undressed quick as ever and jumped into the stream, and found it was shallow enough for him to stand in with his shoulders sticking out of the water. He took one of the soap berries into his hands, and dipped it under the water. From its surface, it leaked bubbles and a pleasant aroma came from the little berry. He rubbed it against his skin, and the cleansing substance scrubbed away all the dirt and the sweat he had gathered, the pungent smell fading away into the water as he washed.

"Soap berries?" Reina asked, raising one of her eyebrows toward Shen.

"Don't look at me. I've never heard of them either. I'm as in the dark as you," Shen said, smiling a little to himself.

Lifting himself from the waters, Lao paddled over to the bank of the stream and grabbed for his clothes, odorous in their own right. He dunked them into the soapy water around him and took care to scrub out the smell from them as well. When he was all finished, he set them out onto a particularly sunny rock and let them dry for a moment. The sun was well up into the sky by now, and it only took a few minutes for the light and the heat to dry out his clothes entirely. Lao climbed out of the water and walked over to the rock, pulling the smooth cloth tunic over his head and pulling up his undergarments and his trousers, tying them tight with a string. "All good! You guys can look now," he said, and they came out from the back of the cart to see him standing with his hands rifling through his hair, "I saved both of you some soap berries, so you can wash up too."

"Lao, where did you find out about these soap berries? And," Reina stopped for a brief moment. She sniffed the air, and the pleasing aroma of the soap berries entered into her nostrils. It was flowery, pleasant to her nose. "Wow, is that the smell of them?"

"I learned it from some old lady when I lived on Yedao. Can't remember her name, but she taught me how to find them. They're pretty rare. You gotta look for the trees, the thin ones, and watch out for the maroon-colored nuts." Lao said it with more enthusiasm than Reina had heard before. But, Shen was fairly accustomed to this type of enthusiasm the young boy could muster.

"Alright then. So, Reina, do you want to go first?" Shen said.

"First? What, you scared of me?" She said, leaning on one of her legs, her hand on her hip.

"Well. I don't think you really want to get naked in front of me, considering how new we are to each other," Shen said, trying to stifle a bit of blush bubbling up in his cheeks.

"Oh, don't make it awkward. I won't be completely naked. I have wraps you know, and I'll even let you borrow some," she said, going into the back of the cart once again, dropping down the cloth covering to conceal herself. "If you're not too scared of seeing a woman half-naked that is," she shouted from the sanctity of the cart.

"You're scared?" Lao asked, raising his eyebrow.

"I'm not scared, Lao! I just didn't want to invade on her privacy. That's all," Shen stammered out.

"I think you're scared," Lao said, snickering.

"Why would I be scared?" He began taking his tunic off, tossing it onto a rock close to the streambed. The trousers clinging to his legs came off quickly, leaving behind the undergarments he'd been wearing for quite a while. There was a smell of his own emanating from his clothes as he tossed them to the rock, the fabric dipping slightly into the softly flowing water.

"Maybe you're scared she might punch you if you look at her the wrong way," he said, letting out a little giggle. Just then, Reina emerged from the cart, free of her armor, her black hair free, flowing down her back. There were so many scars etched across her light tan skin. They were pink, faded, long left to stay upon her after years and years of closing and opening. Her wraps were much like bandages, staining their white surface with blood from some of her cuts and marks she received from their fights with the bandits. The shape of her was muscular, though the more delicate accents of her frame were not lost to the burliness of her physique.

"So, by the looks of you, I don't think you're going to need these," Reina said, holding up a roll of the wraps she had put on her body.

"Reina!" Shen shouted, whipping his head around to meet her gaze. "I guess not. Don't you want to wash your clothes?" He said.

She climbed back into the cart for a brief moment before coming back out, a heap of cloth held in her hands. "Right. Almost forgot." Without skipping a beat, she walked over to the stream and set her clothes down upon a rock next to Shen's. She carefully stepped into the water and her skin shuddered a bit at the temperature, but slowly became acclimated to it. Soon she was completely submerged in the water. For a moment, she remained under the stream, until she resurfaced, tossing her hair back in a flurry of water droplets. "You going to wash up too, or are you still scared?" She joked, a smirk playing about her lips.

Shen took care getting into the water, feeling the tiny waves brush up against his ankles as he waded into the shallow parts of the stream. The flow of the water was almost therapeutic. He grabbed one of the soap berries from off a nearby rock Lao had set them down onto, and began rubbing it between his hands. To his pleasant surprise, they began emitting the sudsy bubbles that gave off the aroma he had smelled earlier.

Reina did the same, taking two of them in her hands and rubbing them against each other. She walked back over to the shallows, where Shen was busy lathering himself with the natural soap, and she did the same. The bubbles ran down her skin in droves. A sweet, flowery aroma filled the air and tickled her nostrils once again, putting a smile on her face. Once they had both finished, almost at the same time, they both entered back into the water. However, Reina did it a bit differently than Shen. She dove back into the water, creating a big splash, while Shen tried carefully walking back into the deeper parts of the stream.

"Hey! What was that for?" He said.

"Oh hush, you big baby. So uptight," she said, splashing him with water. "Loosen up a little."

"Ah!" Shen cried, jumping up.

"What?" Reina asked, swimming a bit closer to Shen. "I didn't splash you that much did I?"

Shen, who was busy wiping his dark hair from his forehead, had a wide-eyed look about him. "Something touched me!"

"Wow. You really are a big baby, aren't you?" She carefully paddled her legs over, trying her absolute best to keep above the water with only her one arm. "The big tough Mystic, scared by a little fish?"

"Fish? Oh, then why don't I show you how big and tough a Mystic I am," Shen said, a bit of confidence dancing in his voice. "Lao, this is a good chance for me to show you how a Batung Mystic like me goes fishing." He waved his hands around, keeping above the water, until his senses found a large rock under the water on the stream's floor. Around him, he found another rock, a sharp one, and brought it up off the ground. In one fluid motion, he raised the big rock out from under the water, popping a fish up with it into the air, and brought his other hand forward, throwing the sharper rock right into the side of the fish.

The creature flopped in the air at the strike, and then came down at the side of the stream with a *thud*. It was immobile, killed in one good hit by the rock Shen had thrown into it. It was fairly bright, not just silver in its color, but it gave off a rainbow sheen to it as well. "Show off," Reina said, sneering.

"Don't complain. I just got us dinner," Shen said, chuckling a little to himself, grabbing for his clothes on the rock. He grabbed Reina's too, tossing them to her. They both then proceeded to carefully scrub out the smells, the dirt, the sweat, the blood, everything that might've smelled unappealing, replacing it with the wonderful scent of the soap berries. Soon their clothes were washed, and they spent the rest of their time relaxing in the water, waiting for them to dry. Lao was relaxing in his own way. He had grabbed the fish, and placed it into the ice box they kept in the back of the cart. Once that was sealed, he came back out and joined his two companions, lying on the grass by the stream.

The clothes were dried quickly, and the two of them climbed out of the water to change back into them. Her hair still wet, Reina leaned to the side and attempted to wring the water from her black locks with her one hand. It wasn't as efficient as she'd hoped, though. "Shen, can you help me with this?" She asked, brushing off a bit of dirt from the surface of her cloth undershirt. Shen came over, just after slipping on his trousers, and looked at her confusedly.

"Help you with what?" He asked. Lao had woken up as the two were talking, sitting up upon the green grass, dusting off a few pieces of gravel that clung to the fabric of his trousers.

"My hair. It's still wet. I don't have enough grip with just the one hand, and I could use some help."

"You could say, you need a-" Lao started.

"Say 'hand,' and I'll use every bit of strength I have in this arm to punch you, kid," Reina joked, a smirk on her face, and the boy quickly stopped, walking over to the cart once again.

"No problem," Shen said, stifling a chuckle. He gripped the thick strands of hair Reina presented to him. Carefully, not pulling too hard, he wrung out the drops of water, that came dripping down and onto the ground below. They sank into the dirt, providing the grass below with sweetly scented nourishment. "Am I pulling too hard?"

Reina, who was beginning to become relaxed by the feeling of fingers lightly scratching by her head, spoke softly. "Nope. You're doing just fine," she said. Soon, Shen was done, and Reina's hair was dried out, free of water, for the most part. The sweet smell of the soap berries lingered in the air as Reina walked back to the cart and grabbed for her hair pins. She brought her hand up and bundled her hair together haphazardly atop her head, fixed in place with the twig-like hair pins she carried around with her.

"So anything more we need to do here?" Lao said, getting a bit impatient, eager to set off down the road closer and closer to their task.

"I've got nothing more to do," Reian said. She picked up her silver chestplate and brought it onto her chest, then fixed the specialized ties on the back, made so that even she could tie them. The armor was fastened and she moved onto her thigh armor, arm armor, and shin guards. These had the same ties as the chestplate, and so she had next to no problem fixing them to her body.

"We should be getting on with the journey. It's already the afternoon by the looks of the sun, and we wouldn't want to be caught on the roads at nightfall." Shen said. He had looked to the sky, and the clouds that dotted the blue served to accentuate the sun held almost directly above them in the sky. Seeing as the time would only go by faster and faster if they stayed any longer, they decided to keep on forward down the road.

As they went, the road seemed to waiver. Where it had once been strong, a dirt path with stones lining its sides, it had now turned to a passive assortment of gravel embedded into the ground. There were also breaks in the path. Whole areas of the path, wide enough to contain a few carts, became blotted out with grass and weeds. Soon, though, the three of them had discovered what it was that was causing these diversions from the usual. Reina, who was sat at the front of the cart atop Ping, pulled back on the reins of the dimian. "What's the hold up?" Shen asked from the back of the cart, muffled as his voice hit the cloth cover of the cart.

"You're going to want to see this for yourself," Reina said.

As he stepped out from the back of the cart, the light of the sun was nearly leaving, and only a reddish-purple hue filled the sky around him. He walked around to the front of the cart, and his eyes were met with a sight that served to make his heart sink a bit. Ahead of them there stood an immense crevice in the ground. He looked to its sides, and as far as he could see, it spanned for droves and droves in either direction. As he walked even closer to its edge, he noticed just how deep it was, and how wide apart its two edges were. "There's no bridge?" Shen asked.

"Not from what I can see. And worse, we don't have the daylight to check and see if there is one," Reina said, and hopped off of Ping's saddle. The dimian shook off a loose feather upon his brow, and blinked lazily. His beady little black pupils darted around as he tilted his head around in confusion.

"You think we should just make a camp for the night?" Shen asked.

"That's exactly what I had in mind," Reina replied.

"What's all the noise?" Lao asked with a yawn, coming out of the back of the cart. He came to the others, and his eyes too rested on the ravine that lay before them. "Woah! How are we gonna get across that?" Lao asked, rubbing at his tired eyes with the backs of his hands.

"Not sure, kid, but for now we're going to set up camp. Care to help?" Reina said.

"Awe man, but I'm still tired." Lao stretched out his arms, and he could feel the muscles pulling and loosening as he did so.

"The sooner we get everything set up, the sooner we can all get some sleep," Reina said.

"I'll get the sleeping rolls!" Lao scurried off to the cart and grabbed the three of their sleeping rolls, putting them out onto the soft grass nearer to the cart. While he got the rest of their sleeping things, pillows stuffed with waterfowl feathers, Shen and Reina gathered wood and rocks from a nearby patch of forest to make a fire that would warm them up once the temperatures dropped in the night time. After all, the sun was fast descending down into the hills, where it would sleep until the morning.

As soon as the two had set up the fire, the flames climbing up before them and its embers floating off into the wind, Lao had fallen right asleep. He couldn't even find the time to climb into his sleeping roll, and instead took to being sprawled out upon it, his pillow nestled softly in the crook of his neck.

Shen and Reina were still awake though, as the light of the moon illuminated them. The light of the fire also served to light up the area near them, and as they talked, its light flickered and danced along their skin, filling the night's dark hue with orange. "What do you think we should do?" Reina asked.

"I'm not sure," Shen replied.

"Maybe we should see if we can go around; that'd be the easiest way without risking too much," she proposed.

"No. We'd sacrifice too much of our time. There's no doubt in my mind that it was Zhi-Ming's rage that caused this."

"You think that spirit made this crevice? Even so far from the caverns?"

"It's certainly got me thinking. Things in Batung are starting to escalate. Vasai soldiers in our territory, the hookbeaks being such a big problem this far into the mainland. I've heard the stories about Zhi-Ming. Don't you think there might be some truth to the chaos his rage brings?"

"What makes you so certain he's like this now? After all this time," Reina questioned, tilting an eyebrow.

"When the Council spoke of the soldiers, I could tell they weren't exactly being the most truthful. I think they're sending civilians for the sole fact that we're expendable. With Zhi-Ming in such a fit of anger, they can't risk an incident wiping out any of their army," Shen said. He grabbed at his side, and his hand grasped the poking stick he had. With a light tap, he shifted a few of the logs in the fire with it and then returned it to his side.

"Be that as it may, we still need to find a way across if we want to take him down, don't we?" Reina said.

"Yes. And I have a plan for that."

"Care to share it with me?"

"I'll use my powers to get you across. It will take quite a bit of my strength, but I think I can hold up a bridge long enough for Ping and the cart to get across. After that, I'll launch Lao, you, and then myself across, and we can get on our way. How does that sound?" Shen said, and tossed another little log onto the slowly depleting fire. The flames grew as the log came into them, and the embers licked at the wood, burning its edges.

"You can't, can you? I mean, I don't know much about you Mystics and your abilities, but there's no possible way you can lift enough rock to support Ping *and* the cart, right?"

"Well, I've never tried it before. But, it's really the only option we've got. We can't afford to lose any precious time. Who knows what more Zhi-Ming's rage could cause?"

"That's if he is the one that's causing all of this. You have no real way of knowing that," Reina protested, tapping her boot against the ground in front of her, sitting on her rear with her knee bent close to her.

"We can't take the chance, Reina. The quicker we can kill Zhi-Ming, the better things will be for all of us. Do you trust me?" Shen said it in a sort of whisper yell, so as not to wake the sleeping Lao.

"Yes. I think I can trust you enough, but-"

"No 'but,' Reina. I need you to trust me on this. I trusted you back in the Council meeting. I need you to do the same for me. Can you do that?"

"Alright, Shen. Alright. But, you need to promise that one, you will make sure everything is safe, and two, you won't overwork yourself." Reina leaned in close to him, almost right in his face, and Shen could see the light of the embers flickering in her hazel eyes, even in the darkness of the night around them.

"I promise," he said firmly. Soon, the two of them had had enough of the night, and once the flame had died down they too settled in for slumber like their young companion next to them.

In the morning, when the sun was just up and above the horizon, Shen awoke. The flames had completely died out and left nothing but an ashen and burnt mess in a circle of rocks. He walked to Reina and lightly shook her until she too awoke, and then did the same for Lao. "Alright. It's time to get going," he said.

"What? But, how?" Lao questioned. He rolled up his sleeping roll and went to the back of the cart, tossing it into the cloth covering where it landed amongst a few sealed wooden crates.

"I'm first going to make a bridge for Ping to cross, and then I'll tell you what to do from there. Sound good?" He said, still a bit tired and weary from waking up.

"Alright." Lao too was still somewhat dazed, and rubbed at the back of his neck, getting a little cramp out of his muscles

"Shen, do you need me to do anything?" Reina said, coming back from putting her and Shen's sleeping rolls in the back of the cart with Lao's.

Shen walked to the edge of the ravine, and a few pebbles became dislodged, falling into the depths below. From what he could sense, the sides of the ravine were deeply rooted with layers upon layers of stone, the perfect material for him to create the bridge out of. "Everything should be alright, just be prepared if things go wrong." He put his hands up, fingers curled, and grabbed whole chunks of the rock, which began floating in flat disk-like formations toward their edge of the crevice. With little motions in his wrists, Shen brought the disks into a path from one edge of the ravine to the opposite.

Shen could feel his mind drifting. 'Maybe I should've waited until I was completely awake, gotten some food in me,' he thought. But, it was too late for that now. He could only use his powers now to hold up the giant disks of floating rock, thick in their size, and let Ping cross over them. "Okay, Reina, I need you to smack Ping." Shen said. His veins were bulging on his forehead, and sweat quickly began to trickle down his face and his back.

"You want me to what?" She answered.

"Smack him on the back once you have him facing the bridge. Just do it, please!" He shouted. The rock disks were almost as heavy to his senses as they would've been if he'd held them up with his bare hands. He praised everything, even the god Batung himself, that he was able to keep these up for so long. Reina walked Ping and the cart over to the start of the rock bridge on their side of the ravine, looking down into the depths, watching little chunks of the bridge chip off and descend into the pit. She brought her hand back, opened her palm, and laid a firm slap into the feather's on Ping's back, just under the saddle.

He took off, knowing almost exactly what to do, and his scaled feet pounded against the rock bridge. Suddenly, the rocks were becoming much harder to hold up for Shen. They seemed to be weighing down on his shoulders, and his fingers twitched violently as he tried to maintain his hold on the floating disks of rock. When Ping was about halfway, three of the disks closest to them fell into the ravine, unable to be supported any longer. "Shen!" Reina and Lao shouted.

"It's alright! I'm fine! Just, needed to get rid of some of the unnecessary weight," he said, and he felt a warm liquid drip down his top lip. As the taste of it settled on his tongue, he could tell it was from his nose, bleeding just a bit. He lifted the remaining rock disks with every bit of strength he had left to muster, and Ping made it all the way across the ravine. However, he slipped a bit on the last disk of the bridge, and so one of the smaller crates toward the very back of the cart slipped out and tumbled down into the crevice as Ping dashed to keep from falling.

"You're good Shen! You can drop it now," Lao pleaded, running over to him.

"Yes. Yes, I know," Shen muttered, and fell to his knees as he quickly let go of his grip on the disks, letting them collapse into the crevice, breaking as they collided with the walls of the ravine. From the other side, Ping let out a loud and worried *squawk*. "I know, buddy." He said it softly, his vision beginning to blur. "Alright, now to get us across," he said, standing up.

"Shen, you need to rest a bit. Please, drink some water," Reina said, pulling a small waterskin from her bag at her side.

"I have some berries. You should eat, too," Lao added. He reached into his pocket and grabbed a few little blue berries, the juices leaking a bit and staining the dark tan skin of his palm.

"Are these soap berries?" Shen joked as he grabbed them from the boy, a smile on his face, showing a bit of blood dotting his teeth which had dripped down from his nostrils. He took the waterskin Reina offered, unscrewing the decorative golden cap, sipping at the cold water on the inside of it. After he screwed the waterskin up again, he handed it back to Reina, and began chewing on the little berries Lao had given him.

The time passed by quickly, and the sun had now leapt right out of the hills on the horizon, just in time for the three of them to get going once again. Shen had rested up, his mind returning to a better state, and without a word he stood up. "You alright now?"

"Yes, Lao. Perfectly okay. Now, I need you to come here." He said.

"What is it?" The boy asked. In a split second, Shen flicked his wrist upward and a rock came out of the ground under each of Lao's feet, propelling him up and forward over the ravine. "Shen! What are you doing!" He screeched, flailing his arms in the air. With his other hand, Shen found the earth on the other side of the ravine where Lao would land, and softened it, turning it from a firm dirt into a dusty sand-like substance. Still screaming, Lao curled up as he braced for impact, and then was pleasantly surprised by the soft landing he endured.

"Shen! Are you insane?" Reina shouted, running over to him and grabbing his tunic by the collar. "You could've killed him!"

"Hey, Shen! That was awesome!" The boy shouted, a big smile upon his face.

"Seems alright to me," Shen said with a smirk.

"Did you know that was going to work?"

"Of course I did, Reina. I wouldn't have done it if I didn't know for sure it was going to work. Now, are you ready?" Shen said, readying his hands again.

"Ready for-" Shen wasted no time, and flicked his wrist upward again, more forceful with the motion, sending Reina forward into the air. She tucked her legs and arm close to her chest, and while she did, Shen increased the size of the puddle of soft dirt where Lao had landed. In seconds, she crashed into the soft dirt with little more than a light *thud*, and Lao laughed as she stood up. There was dirt clinging to the sweat in her hair, and she shook her head to get it off while he giggled to himself. Wasting no time, Shen did the same thing for himself, launching into the air and coming down next to Reina in the spot of soft dirt, feeling the cushion as his back landed into it.

"All good, everyone?" He asked with a smile.

"Yeah!" Lao said, quickly running off and climbing into the back of the cart.

"Shen?"

"Yes, Reina?" The woman laid a strong punch into his shoulder, a scowl painted onto her face. "Ow! What was that for?"

"If you're going to do that, ever again, give me a warning first!" She shouted. With a pout from Reina, and then a little chuckle as she began to relax herself, she climbed back into the back of the cart with Lao. Shen walked to Ping, pat him on the head, and hopped onto his saddle. He took the reins and looked to the map at his side. There was a little town he saw fairly close by in the direction they'd be traveling, and silently decided they'd stop there before night came. He tugged on the reins and they were off again down the path, looking back on the crevice they managed to cross.

The Nettle

The sun quickly fell away from them, descending further and further into the horizon. Creatures once content with the daytime and the sunlight now scurried off into the bushes, hiding from predators, animals ready to pounce under the covert gaze of the night sky. Little field rodents and bush birds jumped away as hookbeaks and larger lizards chased them around. The cart dragged along the road while the sunlight left the sky, and just before the sun fell completely down into the hills, the three came upon the town Shen had noted on his map. There was a sign out in the front, guarded by a soldier and a peculiar looking man. The sign read 'Qianma,' which Shen presumed was the name of the town. "Hello!" The little man at the sign said, waving his hands in the air.

"Hello there, may we enter the town?" Shen asked, stopping Ping and the cart once it reached the entrance of the town. There was a tall wooden archway like a gate that separated the town from the wilderness, which the path ran through and deep into the small town.

"Of course! We welcome any travelers! Please, we ask that you bring your dimian and your cart to Mr. Cui at the stables. If you look down the path, they should be to the left, right across from the tavern. You should stop in! The owner is a good friend of mine, very good friend, me and her go way back," he said, seeming to go on forever.

"Thank you, sir, we should get going now," Shen urged the man and hurried on into the town, the soldier standing guard at the sign, sword held calmly at his side.

"Right! Of course," the man said. He lifted his collar with a pinch and sniffed at his chest. "So eager to leave, is it my stench?" He asked himself, and the cart and Shen were gone from him.

Lao peeked his head out of the cover of the cart, just as a guard approached the back of it. "Halt! Stop the cart!" He shouted. Shen abruptly tugged on Ping's reins, stopping him dead in his tracks. "Sir, may I look through the cart?" Lao poked his head back into the cart and waited for a word from Shen, but no such word came. The cloth cover of the cart came parted to the side, and the guard stuck his head inside. Without any words, the soldier looked around, taking out his sword and poking around the crates and pots they'd been using for food, and then looked to the two in the cart. He eyed them up, and then brought himself back out of the cart. "Carry on," he said blankly and walked away.

"What was that all about?" Reina asked as the cart carried on, wheels clicking against rocks on the path as the cart went on through the town.

"No idea. But, take a look around." Shen said. Reina peeked her head out of the cart cover, barely lifting it, and she could see a majority of the town they'd already passed. Soldiers lined corners, standing guard with their hands at their swords on their waists. They seemed to be everywhere. There were a few filing in and out of a building, which Reina figured was some sort of makeshift barracks, and Lao noticed a few go into the tavern.

"They're everywhere," Lao said, hushed.

"Yeah," Reina added.

"What do you think they're here for?" He asked.

"Welcoming party?" Shen joked back at them. He hadn't the time to think on it too much, as they were stopped at the front of a large building, one story tall, which looked to be the stables. "Yes, sir? Can we help you?"

"Please, you'll need to leave your cart and your dimian here. Just tie him up by the front, if you're not going to be too long. But, if you're planning on staying longer, I'll gladly help you unhook him from that cart and keep him in the stables for the night." The man looked simple, plain, a regular cloth tunic of white upon his frame and a leather vest over top of it. His features were soft and muted, and his eyes were a little wiry inside his head. He appeared to be sleep-deprived, the whites of his eyes red, bloodshot in the look of them.

"What's the deal with all these soldiers?" Reina asked, getting out of the back of the cart. Lao exited as well, following after Reina, hopping down onto the dirt below the back of the cart.

"Protection. There's a terrible spirit in these parts, but that's all I can say, it may be watching us as we speak." Suddenly, the man became visibly paranoid. He began wringing his hands, grabbing for Ping's reins, unhooking the cart and wheeling it over and around to the back of the stables. Shen had gotten off of Ping's saddle and helped the man with the dimian, bringing him into one of the stable stalls which was cleaner and neater than the others.

"Spirit? What kind of spirit?" Lao asked, and his mind flashed with memories of the Faceless spirits they had encountered in Lu Min. But, his query went unanswered, as the little paranoid man finished up tying Ping and shuffled into the building with a slam of the door. "Well that was rude," the boy muttered.

"Yeah. And I don't think he's the only one like that," Reina added. As they looked around, they noticed the other people walking throughout the town. They were dressed in about the same manner, with the exception of the guards of course, and they shuffled around in the same sort of frantic state as the man at the stables. "Let's just get some food and a room at the tavern and call it a night, this place weirds me out."

"Agreed," Shen said.

The three of them walked across the path as a dimian-drawn cart passed by, empty of everything, the driver of which was staring intently at the road in front of him. Before them stood the tavern, a tall and old and rickety looking bamboo building with a rotting wood sign to the side of the front door. The black lettering was too faded to read other than the word 'Tavern.' They walked in, and the darkness of the room was nearly palpable. Candle flames and lanterns few and far between were the only real light in the room once the door shut behind them. No windows let in any sunlight, nor were there any other doors to be opened besides the one which the three of them had just come through.

As they entered and took a few steps forward, a hush fell over the entire tavern. People looked up from their drinks, setting their wooden cups down onto wood tables, and stared intently at the new faces illuminated only by the orange glow of the candlelight. While Shen and Reina walked on toward the front where the owner stood cleaning out a few wooden dishes, Lao could feel the pressure of all the eyes on them. A few of them were old, dark brown eyes glaring with furled brows. "Are you the owner?" Shen asked, sitting down next to Reina in one of the stools at the bar.

"Who's asking, and why?" She snapped.

"My name is Shen Jin. This is my companion, Reina Yamato. And-" Shen looked around for Lao, to find him a little closed off, his hands clasped together, standing nearby. "This is my little brother, Lao," he said, bringing Lao over to one of the stools, dragging him by the sleeve.

"Hi," the boy muttered out.

"And? That still doesn't tell me why you're here," the older woman snapped again, setting down a wooden bowl roughly.

Lao realized now that these people were not like the ones they had seen just moments ago outside. These people were tough, unflinching, perhaps not even fazed by the spirit the old man at the stable had mentioned. Not paying attention to Shen's conversation with the owner at the bar, his ears were turned to the conversation two men were having at a table near to him.

"I'm telling you, the Nettle has to be some sort of spirit. I've seen them before, I know how they act, lurking in the shadows," one of them went on, a brown leather patch over his eye. "I spent enough time on the sea to know a spirit when I see one."

"You've had too much to drink, Tao. The Nettle is nothing like any spirit I've seen. The spirits I've seen just mess around with people, maybe kill them by accident if they're unlucky, I've never heard of a spirit purposely killing merchants and raiding their carts." The other man had long flowing blond hair, and pale skin, with Ogon markings on his shoulders where his sleeves looked to be haphazardly cut off from his tunic.

"I'm telling you, Dertur! The Nettle is a spirit. Everyone in town knows it," the man with the dark tan skin and eye patch said in a sort of whispering shout.

His curiosity was incredibly piqued at this point, and the urge to speak up overwhelmed Lao, and so he spoke. "What's the Nettle?" The boy asked loudly, and the hushed conversations that had resumed throughout the tavern now all came to a halt. Everything was positively silent. The tension in the air could be sliced with a sword, and the pressure could be felt by the three of them sat at the bar.

"You want to know about the Nettle, boy?" The owner spoke, breaking the silence, setting down a wooden cup against the bar. As she poured some honey-colored liquid into it, handing it over to Reina, she spoke with a gravelly voice to the boy before her. "It's a spirit. Despite what certain merchants, or rather idiots, might say," she started, shooting a look to the man with eye patch nearby, "the Nettle is a spirit. There isn't much information, but stories have been popping up like crazy the last few days, from town to town, about merchants being killed and their things stolen. The method, though, is what really distinguishes the Nettle from any mercenary."

"How do you mean?" Reina interjected, sipping at the cup as she slid a Yin coin across the bar to her.

"The needles. They come from everywhere, and you won't know you're hit with them till the sickness sets in. That's all I know about it, though, from stories from a few survivors. And, little missy, you'd do not to interrupt me next time I'm talking, you hear?" She said, furrowing her brow, wrinkling the dark tan skin above her eyes.

"Sorry." Reina muttered, and finished off her drink, feeling a nice buzz settle into her mind.

Suddenly, a voice came from nearby, at one of the tables to the right of where Shen, Reina, and Lao sat at the bar. "Ha! You can't be serious. You actually believe those foolish stories?" A young man said, and he began to approach the bar. "You think it's some kind of spirit taking down the carts? Really? Nothing but Vasai mercenaries inciting chaos, I swear it."

"And who are you to say? Some kind of expert, are you?" The woman behind the bar said, tapping her palm down onto the bar counter a few times, to which one of the other patrons set a few coins of Yin down, and then proceeded to exit the tavern. As the door opened, only a little bit of light flooded in, moonlight and torchlight, as night had descended upon the town.

"The Nettle hasn't even come close to this town in the last few days," the man said.

"There've been sightings all over town. What do you think the guards are for? People have been seeing the spirit hitchhiking on carts from here to Ya-Min." Shen and Reina looked to each other with an affirming look, while Lao's attention was to the woman on the other side of the bar, looking to the skeptical man before her with a scowl.

"Nonsense! All nonsense! You've always been the superstitious one, haven't you? I'll prove the Nettle isn't real and it certainly isn't attacking the carts you hear about." The man said, and took from his pocket a hefty little leather coin pouch. "I'll wager on it."

"Ha! You'd do that? This feels like it could pay your tab two times over, Wang. How do you even intend to prove yourself, anyway?" The woman laughed and held the little bag up in her hands, and felt its weight, then sat it back down against the bar countertop.

"In fact, my cousin's bringing in her cart tonight. She's bringing a shipment of meat and spices all the way from Zhimai for the guards. She'll be passing through any minute now, stopping just outside the east entrance to the town. When the sun comes up in the morning, and shows how nothing's happened to her, you have to pay off my tab." The man had a smirk creep across his face, and he held his coin pouch firm in his grip.

"You can't put your cousin in danger like that," Shen interjected.

"And who are you to question me and my family? Huh? Who do you think you are?" The man wagering took his coin pouch back into his palm from the counter and pushed another patron out of the way. He got to Shen, and stared him down with a raised brow, looking to the bronze sword strapped in scabbard at Shen's back. "Think you're so tough with your sword, huh? I wonder how fast you can pull that out."

"Don't harass my customers. I'll have you out of this tavern so fast you won't be able to tell which way you were going," the owner said, slamming her fist down onto the bartop with a *thud*.

"You're right. You're right. I got a little out of control there, huh," he said, a devilish smirk still playing about his lips. "I won't be putting her in danger, directly at least, since you mentioned. She's going to have to pass through whether you or anyone else likes it or not." His attention was turned back to the woman behind the bar, looking to her with that smile still plastered onto his face. "So, how about our friendly little wager?" He brought his coin pouch back out, dropping it onto the countertop before the woman.

The woman pondered for a moment to herself, setting her fingers to her rugged chin. After a few more moments, she looked to the man and nodded, putting her fist to her chest in salute. "It's a deal."

"I knew you'd come through." He left back to his table, drinks scattered all about, with the coin pouch at his side, tied onto the side of his trousers with a fine piece of string.

"You'd wager money on a person's life?" Reina questioned, leaning back in the wooden stool she sat in.

"Idiots will be idiots. Not my fault if I make a little coin from them," she said. "Now, are you just here to sit and stir, or did you come for a meal? Maybe a room?"

"A room, for the night," Shen interrupted, both irritated with the man who'd left, and curious with the prospect of this Nettle spirit everyone seemed to know about one way or another. "We have plenty of coin."

"You and the girl?" The woman asked, gesturing her head toward Reina, who had now stood up and fixated the sword at the small of her back in a more comfortable position.

"And the boy, too," Shen added. Lao stepped up and stood with the other two, standing just behind Shen.

"Whatever makes me money. That'll be 10 Yin, up front if it's any difference," the woman said. She seemed bored of them, utterly apathetic to their queries, as if the clinking sound of coins against wood countertops was the only thing to rouse her. Shen pulled from the bag at his side the hefty coin pouch he held and reached in for a handful. Once he felt ten little silver coins in his fingers, he took them out and dropped them softly onto the bar counter. "Thanks. Up the stairs, second door on the right." She turned back around and approached a barrel, taking a wooden cup into her hands and filling it to the brim with the bubbling honey liquid she'd given to Reina.

"Thank you," Reina said, which was echoed by Lao, and the three of them filed up the stairs. Shen remained silent, thinking to himself. He wondered what exactly the Nettle was. It sounded like any other spirit he'd heard of, with the same shroud of mystery around the stories only merchants and unfortunate souls might have the capability to tell. He felt any sort of tiredness that he had drift away, as the thoughts of this spirit crawled around the depths of his thoughts. "You're awfully quiet," she said just as they entered into the room.

"I'm thinking. Can't help but worry about that man's cousin, and whether or not this 'Nettle' spirit is any real danger, if it even exists in the first place." Shen walked to a corner of the room and took the little firestarter into his hands from off a table. He clicked the little device's arms together and a spark was produced, which lept to the surface of the candle wick, the red wax candle melting a bit at its top.

"You really think it's that big of a deal?" Lao asked.

"Enough for those soldiers to guard the roads. You heard what the woman said, and you saw just how many of them were scattered across the town." He walked over to one of the beds, of which there were two large ones and one smaller one, and sat down on its cloth surface, amongst the pillows. "What do you two think?"

"I think we shouldn't worry about it," Reina answered.

"It sounds dangerous. We've faced spirits before, but they weren't quite like what this one sounds like. We could actually die," Lao said. "I don't want to die, Shen."

"I know, Lao. I won't let anything happen to you, you know that, right?" Shen got up and walked over to the candle, letting the skin of his hands soak some of the warmth from the little dancing flame. He walked back to the bed, and with a great sigh he sat back down against its surface. "But, this Nettle. I'm intrigued," he added.

"What's there to be intrigued about? Sounds like a fairly normal spirit to me," Reina said.

"Perhaps a little less normal than it's letting on," Shen said, trailing off, scratching the dark stubble along his jaw.

The night dragged on, and with a little slit in the wall nearby, Shen, who was still awake, could see the road alight by torches. They were posted to wooden poles, brightening the path, letting an orange glow wash over the dirt of the road. Clouds shielded the moon, and so its light was not shining upon the ground below as it had so many nights before. From the smell of the air, a rusty sort of scent with a chilliness to it, Shen figured it to rain in the near future. He looked around him, and his eyes rested on his two companions, situated in their beds, their forms undisturbed as they slumbered the soreness of their muscles away. Unable to sleep, he decided he might go and see this cart come into town. It had not already come through, nor had the sound of it been heard through the night's air.

Shen's thoughts were occupied with visions of the Nettle. There was this recurring image, of what it could possibly look like. He figured it some horrifying creature with a cadaverous form, longs limbs, fingers with needles poised under the fingernails, prepared to take down anyone unfortunate enough to come through. Soon, the thoughts in his mind got the better of him, and he scurried away out of the door, shutting it softly behind him while his feet carried him out of the tavern and into the middle of the road.

His eyes drifted, and they found their fixation on the eastern gate of the town. It was much like the one they entered from, but with many more guards than just the one. There were three of them, to be exact, and they stood like stone, still and strong. That is, until the sound of the cart rippled through the town's air. Shen heard it from behind him, and with a swiftness unlike any he'd demonstrated in a long time, he stowed off behind a small home nearer to the eastern gate. "The merchant's here, clear out," one of the guards said loudly. He was much bigger than the other two, who from the looks of their forms in the light of the torches were female.

"Yes, sir," they said in unison, and their voices were quite close to Shen. He felt his heartbeat pick up as the prospect of being found set into his being.

The cart lurched forward at a slow speed, guided by a single dimian, who looked to be a strong and formidable bird. As the creature came into torchlight view with the cart pulled behind it, it looked as if it wore a scowl on its feathered brow. Shen might've giggled to himself at the serious look of the dimian, had the cart not stopped abruptly. "Did you hear that?" One of the people with the cart questioned, the woman atop the dimian's saddle, presumably the man from the tavern's cousin. Apart from her, there were four others, men, which Shen figured were her subordinates. The guards had left, fled to the barracks on the other side of town, and the five of them and Shen were all that remained at the eastern gate.

"I didn't hear anything," one of the men muttered. He walked over to a tree on the outside of the gate, leaning up against its trunk. Suddenly, Shen heard what the woman was referring to. There was a rustling, and it came from up above, in the canopy of leaves that the patch of trees on the outside of the gate created. After the rustling subsided, Shen heard a low *thud* of something hitting the ground.

"Cai?" One of the other men said, and began walking near Shen. He walked along the inside of the gate, nearing the little alley where Shen hid behind the house, and stood, looking around. The rustling returned for a brief moment, before he heard three tiny bursts of air cut through the silence. Coinciding with these sounds, Shen watched the man carefully as three needles entered into different parts of his body. Little metal needles with little red ribbons dangling from the back of them, one of them stuck into part of the man's neck, one just above the knee, and the last into the arm near the bicep. The man was jolted in place for a moment, and then he quickly reached a free hand over and removed the needles from his body, pulling them out by the ribbons.

Immediately, blood began to pour out of the wounds, and before the man could even open his mouth to scream for help, his jaw locked up and his muscles tensed, his body falling to the ground in front of Shen, who was now hiding in a particularly large pot. He peaked out, and a shadow came down from above, descending upon the neck of the body before him. The figure was not as inhuman as he had figured. In fact, it looked quite human, wearing loose trousers, a wide leather strap holding them up at the waist, and a baggy tunic clinging onto their torso. Their head was wrapped in a cloth, hidden from view, but as it turned its head, a chilling sight came to Shen's eyes. Eyes stared back at him, piercing and blue, almost crystalline, the only thing that could be seen, since the other features were wrapped in the billowing cloth.

His heart dropped into the pit of his stomach. A thought crawled through his mind, as the eyes glinted in the torchlight nearby: 'does it see me?' His thought was soon answered, however, as the thing turned toward the cart and jumped against the side of the gate, kicking off and leaping up into the trees above again. Shen took this as a chance to move. He climbed out of the pot and ran across the road to the other side, hiding behind a little shed, ducking down to avoid being spotted. The other two men filed to the front of the cart after he'd done this, while the woman in charge came to the back.

There was more rustling from the leaves above, and a few of them floated down to the ground below as the Nettle came down on the two men. Shen could just barely hear the sound of the needles being thrown through the air, and then the subsequent sound of the two men dropping. The woman heard it too, though, and she pulled a dagger from a scabbard at her side as she turned toward it. Shen had full view of her, and luckily was still out of sight, as the Nettle came down right behind the woman in charge. "It's you!" She turned around and shouted, and swung her blade forward.

The spirit backed up, dodging the blow, and reached down to its thigh. With a flick of its wrist, a needle flew out of her hand and stuck into the ankle of the woman before it. The woman came down to the ground on one knee, and the Nettle took this opportunity to search the woman. It flipped over the woman and ended up behind the woman on her knee. In a strange sort of dance, the spirit brushed away the ponytail of the woman and tapped its fingers along her neck, and then, the strangest thing happened. The spirit's eyes went wide, as could be gleaned from the bright torchlight coming from a mounted flame at the back of the cart. The Nettle reached its arm around the woman's neck, squeezing tightly, kicking the dagger out of her hand with a swift motion, and held her there until the woman fell unconscious.

    Shen stood in shock. The other men that had traveled with this merchant were dead now, and yet this one was kept alive. However, he had little time to think on this point further, as three more figures came from all around. One came from the trees, one from a nearby building adjacent from Shen, and as was evident by the sound behind him, one from near Shen's position. They were visibly cloaked in fur garb, garments which were draped over the thin metal armor they wore, which glinted some of the torchlight off of it. Without any words, the figures began raiding the cart, taking wooden and metal boxes from its back. One of the figures even stripped the wheels and the bottom of the cart of the metal parts, screws, hinges, and the like.

    His position could be discovered at any moment, his fate made the same as the four men who had fallen to the Nettle, and as such, Shen decided to hurry back off to the tavern, only a short walk away. He turned for a brief moment, and his foot accidentally made contact with the wooden wall of the shed. His gaze darted to the Nettle, which stood in the middle of the dirt road, and his eyes met with the spirit's. They stared in his direction, not entirely at him, but just enough for him to affirm that it was indeed looking to him. In a split second decision, he used his abilities to lift a rock from the ground and flung it all the way across the road, striking another building. The Nettle's head jerked over to the sound immediately, and Shen took this opportunity to run back to the tavern.

    As he ran, he felt as though the spirit was trailing him. He felt like it was right on his heels, chasing him, which made his pace quicken even more than it already had been. His breathing remained steady, for fear that it might alert the spirit and its companions. He entered into the tavern to find it vacant. The owner, the older woman, was sat in a corner in a stool, leant up against the wall and letting a snore out from her nostrils. Shen took care to not make a single sound as he came up the steps, and even more care to not make too much sound when opening and shutting the door to the room. He came in, and his eyes met with Reina, up and standing by the little slit in the wall that served as a window. "And where have you been?" She asked, her hand poised on her hip.

Following

"Reina! I can explain this," Shen started.

"Don't bother. You went to go help the merchant, confront the Nettle, right?" She walked up to him, her hand still to her hip, a scowl painted onto her face.

"No. I couldn't help them. But I saw it. I did. I saw the Nettle. We need to leave, now." He began hurrying over to his bag, sat atop a table, shoving things inside of it that were lying strewn out of it. His rocks, berries, the coin pouch, all brushed into the open leather bag.

"You left us vulnerable? Me and Lao, alone in here. What if the Nettle came to us, hm? You should've stayed behind." She said it in a sort of shout whisper, to get across to Shen the gravity, the seriousness of the situation, without waking the sleeping Lao nearby.

"I went to see if this was something to be worried about, and it is," Shen snapped, trying to keep low in his anger, hoping not to wake the sleeping boy on the small bed nearby.

"What were you even thinking?" Reina said, shaking her head at him.

"What was I thinking? I was thinking this thing can be a real threat, Reina. I can't just stand idly by and watch it take all these lives. Not like that." He scratched at his jaw, creating a crunching sound as his nails brushed against the dark stubble.

"We already have a real threat, Shen. Zhi-Ming? Remember him?"

"Yes, but I-"

"But nothing, Shen. The Council is counting on us. We have bigger things to worry about. We have our journey, Lao, our own lives. We can't just rush into everything to save a few merchants. What happened to the Shen who wouldn't take on the Faceless at first? That Shen was determined to keep moving."

"Don't. Don't remind me of that day. That's a moment I will regret for a long time, even if you and Lao changed my mind in the end." Shen finished placing his things in the bag and closed it up, then sat atop his bed next to where his sword rested. "It was a moment of weakness I feel the greatest shame for."

"But you had the right idea, just bad timing." Reina walked up to him, slowly, and placed her hand on one of his shoulders. "There will come a time when we can help more people, maybe even stop the Nettle. But we already have one spirit to deal with. We'll leave first thing in the morning. It's too dark to leave right now."

Shen looked to the window, the open frame, and was met with darkness. The sky was still incredibly dark, and the stars provided no such light as the moon did. But, moonlight was shrouded now, blocked away by a rolling tide of storm clouds, sure to be the climate for the continuation of their journey in the morning. Without a word, Shen pushed his sword in its scabbard off the bed, letting it fall to the floor with a soft *thud*. His quarrel with Reina was ended, yes, but the feeling of it, the tension clinging to his chest and his heartbeat, was all still present.

Reina walked to her bed, which had been pushed close to Lao's, and she too was plagued by the prospect of their argument. As things slipped away from her tired mind, she soon fell into a light sleep that would be roused quite a few times before the morning sun arose. But, the morning sun did not rise as expected. The clouds were much too dense, and the rains poured upon the land like a typhoon. Houses began to flood, and once the water level reached to just halfway up the stools in the tavern's bar, the door to their room swung open with a loud *bang* as it hit the wall next to it. "Get up," the owner's voice shouted through the room.

Reina was the first to wake. She hadn't truly slept as much as the others, tossing and turning all night before her body rested at all. The softness of the bed, the waterfowl feather stuffed pillows, were not much to fight against the thoughts that clashed and whirled around in her head. "Yes, ma'am." She said, and the woman left back downstairs. Reina walked to Lao's side, gently shaking him awake. "Hey, Lao, wake up. It's time to go," she said softly.

"Reina? What is it?"

She walked to Shen next, and stood by his bedside as Lao sat up and swung his legs over the side of his smaller bed. "Morning time. We gotta get going if we want to reach the next town before nightfall." Reina leaned over Shen much like she had Lao, but instead of nudging him awake, she roughly pushed him off the side of the bed to the floor.

He fell to the floor and his limbs clattered, his head bumping into the bamboo wall, waking him from his sleep in a short bout of pain. "What! What is it?" He got up, and as his legs straightened out as he stood, the pain in his temple setting in. "Ow, what in the- what pushed me?" He asked, turning around to Reina and Lao, who were up now, gathering their things together they'd left on the floor.

"That'd be Reina," Lao said with a giggle. He picked up his tunic from off the ground, the greenish cloth one with the hood Shen had given him so long ago on Yedao. As he looked down at it, the washed out colors, the worn fabric, there came a little ache of soreness from his shoulder. He reached his hand over to it and brushed it against the bare dark tan skin. His eyes drifted over to it, to the pale scar slightly fading, missing bandages that must've fallen off sometime on their journey. He slipped the tunic back on and the inside was just as silky smooth and soft as it had been when he'd first gotten it.

"You pushed me?" Shen questioned, blinking his eyes.

"You wouldn't get up when I shook you, so I figured pushing might've helped. Come on, let's go," Reina said plainly, grabbing her sword from the table and putting it in the hold at the small of her back.

Shen looked to Lao, sensing that Reina was lying, still clearly irritated with him from the night before. "What?" The boy said, and stuffed the little bag of soap berries back into his pocket he'd gotten from the stream. Shen shook his head and walked around his bed to the table next to it. He reached down and grabbed the scabbard with his sword locked in, slung it around his arm and shoulder, as well as his neck, and let it rest at his back. Next, he grabbed his bag, and proceeded to tie the strap around his waist with the bag calmly at the side of his thigh.

"Who's riding Ping?" Shen asked.

"I am," Reina said without skipping a beat, and took to the door, walking out and down, getting a head start to the stables just across the road from the tavern. Shen begrudgingly followed after her as he stuffed back into his bag the pouch of Yin that had fallen from his bag onto the table in the night, and Lao chased after Shen in turn. By the time they caught up with her, Ping was already hooked up to the covered cart outside of the stables, the fidgety little man who owned the facility nowhere to be found. "Ready, boys?" She asked hopping onto Ping's saddle.

"Wait, are you actually going to just take the reins without asking me if I want to?" Shen asked, a little irritated with her.

"Hm, yes," she snapped, and Ping looked to Shen with his wide eyes, then let out a *squawk*, so loud and jarring that it made Shen step back a bit. Lao, who was already in the back of the cart, laughed to himself upon hearing the big bird make such a noise once again. It'd been quite awhile since his ears had heard it. Without any more words, Shen stormed off into the back of the cart with Lao. Reina looked down at the map in her hands, beginning to soak up a few droplets from the steadily increasing rain that was falling, and set her eyes on the smaller town of Lin-Hao. With a tug on the reins Ping set out on the road and out the eastern gate, headed onward once again.

Time seemed to slow to a crawl as the cart inched across the road. The rain poured in steady intervals, washing over the cloth covering of the cart, and once it began to seep in, the dripping started. Ping was much more irritable, letting out a bothered chirp each time a hefty droplet of rain landed on his feathers. Being as irritated as he was, he was much slower than he'd been before, and the trip that might've taken the group just under a full day's light, arriving at Lin-Hao at nightfall, it instead took more than that time, and they found themselves in the middle of the road as the nighttime darkness seeped into the sky. Reina, perceptive as she was, noticed the rain, coming down from the sky like whole pebbles, and spotted an overhang of rock upon the side of a nearby hill, and decided they'd stop there for the night.

Ping graciously obliged to the tugging on his reins, and brought the cart under the cover of the overhang. Fortunately, it was just enough to cloak him and the front half of the cart, while the back half of the cart was stuck in the rain. "Boys, you still awake in there?" Reina said, turning in the saddle and tapping the wood of the cart behind her.

"Yes, we're awake," Shen said, "sopping wet, and awake," he muttered afterward, wringing a few droplets from his dark hair.

"I told you not to sit so close to the leak," Lao said.

"Which you only said long after the leak started, might I add," Shen snapped back. He opened the back of the cart, and his eyes rested upon the sky, the darkness that engulfed the space around them. No stars showed their light, no moon bore its face upon the world, just an ever growing darkness that loomed over them with the rain. "Nighttime already?" Shen asked aloud, wiping a few droplets of rain from his face before ducking his head back into the cart cover.

"Yes. We're about halfway to Lin-Hao, the next named town over from Qianma. I'm going to get some rest, and you do the same, you'll be taking the reins in the morning," Reina muttered, and shuffled to the side of the cart cover. She opened up a little flap that lay there, and her hands grasped her sleeping roll, soft cloth untouched by the leak in the cover.

"Take it easy, alright?" Shen said, but got no response, as Reina was already laid down in her sleeping roll. Ping too was asleep, crouched down with the cart harness still hooked onto his saddle, moving only when his chest heaved air in slumber. Shen rolled over in his sleeping bag he'd already gotten set up, as he tried to fall asleep. He looked over at Lao and noticed how quickly he got to sleep. It was a strange sight, watching this young boy fall asleep so quickly. Shen thought why it was he got to sleep so quickly, before the thoughts changed to wondering why it was he himself couldn't fall asleep as quickly. But, when it presented itself, Shen figured it was the nearby noise that was keeping him awake.

It wasn't too intrusive, a mere scuttling in the puddles of rain on the ground around them, but it was loud enough for him to hear. His first thought was that it was just Reina, up and about in her restlessness. But this was nullified when from the quiet Shen could hear well and good her voice, muttering soft and incoherent words in her sleep. As such, his next thought drifted far from her, and found itself fixated on the spirit from the night previous. In his mind he saw the Nettle, stalking, creeping around the cart to throw its deadly needles into them. So many soft slapping sounds echoed in his ears as the night went on, and only when they finally faded into the background noise of the rain did Shen get any real sleep.

Once the morning came around, Reina was up and less irritable than she had been the day before. Her mind was well-rested, as the nightly sounds of the rain had lulled her into a slumber that couldn't be roused. Shen, on the other hand, was wide awake when the morning came around. He woke up from his short bout of sleep as the sun peeked behind graying clouds, and the drizzle of the rain hung over the land, dripping softer than before, and much more sparsely than it had been falling. The cart cover swung loosely as the wind brushed past, and once everything was packed up into the cart, Shen walked toward the now awake Ping.

Approaching the dimian, crouched down onto the ground, head darting around while eyes peered at dripping rain from the overhang, Shen noticed something faint in the ground, subtle, but apparent. Footprints. They weren't all too deep, and their were several sets of them in the mud. Clearly they were not from sandals or the leather shoes worn by more opulent individuals from the upper northeast side of the Batung Mainland. Rather, they looked to be just feet, without the outlines of the toes apparent, as if the feet were wrapped in bandages or cloth. It was this that led to Shen's idea of the Nettle and its companions. The thought raced in his head, bouncing around the confines of his mind, wreaking chaos. His nerves were twinged, strung high, and he hopped onto the saddle quickly. Someone was following them.

The cart crawled along the road at a steady pace, and soon the dirt of the pathway turned to scarce gravel and dust. What once was a light drizzle now turned into nothing. No water came from the skies, nor hung on their skin or the cloth of the cart cover. Lao and Reina watched from the back of the cart, from the pulled back flap of the cover, as the sun shone from behind hills and let its light flow out onto the land. Puddles quickly dried as they barrelled along the road at a fair pace. The more sandy consistency of the dirt gradually lost the water that it had soaked up the day and night previous, and now the path was more wide, the dwindling of it now no longer so.

  Ping kept his pace up more and more as Shen tugged upward on the reins. Reina, noticing this, tapped the side of her silver arm armor onto the wooden frame of the cart by where Shen placed his back. "Shen, what's the idea? You can slow things down, you know. Ping can only take so much exhaustion," she said.

  "I know, I know. But I think we're being followed," he snapped back.

  "What?" Lao perked his head up, raising an eyebrow, as his heart started to pick up its pace.

  "You're paranoid. We're not being followed, Shen," Reina said rolling her eyes.

  "I heard it, last night. And this morning, footprints, in the mud right by where you slept." Shen said frantically, scratching incessantly at the stubble on his jaw.

  "Now that you mention it, I saw a few footprints by the back of the cart," Lao said.

  "Those were my footprints, Lao. Shen is just paranoid, about the Nettle." She looked through the hole in the cloth cart cover near Shen's shoulder and looked ahead, to a few buildings that stood on the horizon, split by the road. "We shouldn't be discussing this, anyway, we're at the town," she said.

Shen looked ahead, and indeed there stood the small village-esque town of Lin-Hao. Buildings were made from bamboo, with wooden roofs that had become darker with the leftover rain that had been soaked into the beams. Sunlight glinted off the polished tips of tilling tools soybean and tea farmers held in their hands. They bent over at their fields, raking the finely darkened dirt around the plants, the green of them brilliant and visible from even so far away. As the cart entered into the town, some of them lifted their heads and smiled, saluting with a fist to their chest as they passed by. "Where to first?" Shen asked.

"I'm sure Ping could use some apples," Lao said, picking up the sack which normally held their apple stores. Inside there only sat three measly apples, smaller ones, which the dimian tugging the cart would not eat. "We're running low."

"General store it is then," Shen said, trying his best to cheer up and shake the nervous feeling which held in his body. He turned a bend in the road through the town and brought the cart to a stop just in front of a larger sized building which read 'Xin General Store' at the front above the door. "Let's hope they have enough apples for you, buddy" Shen said as he hopped off Ping's saddle, patting the dimian on the side of the neck, feeling his calloused fingers glide through wetted feathers, just now beginning to dry.

They walked in, and the building, which seemed fairly sizeable from the exterior, was all the more so on its interior. Paintings decorated the walls with little pieces of parchment reading their prices pinned to the wooden frames of them. There were images of the Batung hills, the mountains, forests, even plains landscapes with carefully brushed ram-horn deer stood stoically in the foreground. Reina took to these almost immediately, hoping to catch a glimpse of the rural countryside of Batung she'd mostly neglected to admire in her travels in the country. Shen, in spite of his companion, took Lao with him to the front where transactions occurred.

A man with an intricate tattoo upon the back of his light tan neck, similar to those the old monks of Vasai bore, finished getting a fine helmet from the man at the front. It was golden, with little white gemstones pressed into the forehead, clearly made for show, considering how malleable gold truly was. The man turned around to get to the door, and was met with Shen. As he looked to the man before him, Shen could tell by the bluish-hazel eyes, like gleaming gems, and of course the light tan skin, that this man was indeed from Vasai. There was something about him, though, that looked awfully familiar to him. Shedding this consideration for the moment, Shen pushed forward to the man at the front.

"Care to take a look around? I can almost guarantee we have just about everything, anything you can wish for," the man said. He too bore the light tan skin of the Vasai people, but there was a twinge of Ogon paleness in his skin that threw Shen off for the moment. His hair was a strange mix of the two as well, a color of mixed brown and auburn.

"I'm actually looking for something in particular. You wouldn't happen to have any apples, would you? Our dimian is quite hungry, and we could do with a few to satiate his," Shen trailed off, a picture drifting through his mind of Ping choking down an apple, "more monstrous hunger."

"You're in luck, stranger, just got a shipment in this morning. Straight from the east to you!" He knelt down behind the counter, getting down on one of his knees to reach the bucket of apples that laid there. While he did so, Shen looked around, keeping to himself mostly, and something caught his eye. The Vasai man from before, the one who'd purchased the helmet, was sat in a dark corner of the large shop. He took to covert ways, talking inaudibly to someone, looking back every once in awhile to where Shen stood.

The longer that the man behind the counter took with the apples, the more irritable Shen became. A number of things ran through his head. For one, he seemed to have quite a stature about him. He was muscular, lean, and formidable dressed in robe-like garment. There was another thing, which served to strike the last nerve Shen possessed, that stood wrapped around the man's wrist. Shen saw it as it came into the light of the sun peeking through the window nearby. It was a cloth, quite flowing, much like that which the Nettle wore around its face.

Shen stormed over to the man, stomping his bare feet on the ground, feeling every bit of resistance as the loose wooden floorboards pushed against his weight. "You! What are you playing at? Are you following us? What is it?" He shouted frantically.

"Shen!" Reina cried out, dashing to Shen, pulling him off the man by the back of his tunic. "What is your problem?"

"No! No, sir! I don't know you, any of you! Please, I'm sorry, if I've done anything, I sincerely apologize!" The man pleaded, and once he was free of Shen's grip, he took to the door with his helmet in hand, and ran for a building fairly close to the shop.

"Hey! What's the problem over here?" The shopkeeper, the man from the front, came to Reina's side as Shen stepped back, free from her grasp. He heaved as the blood rushed through his body and stoked his nerves. Before him stood a horrified Reina, a shocked Lao nearby, and the confused shopkeeper. Reina, who had already paid the man for the whole bucket of apples, which had been transferred into a sack, reached out for Shen. She hoped to calm him, but he ran out of the shop and into the sunlight before a single word could be uttered.

"Shen," Reina muttered, and sighed to herself. Lao, taken aback by his leaving, ran after Shen. "Lao, wait!" Reina cried out, and followed behind him out the door, the sack of apples swinging at the ground in the grasp of her hand. They came out of the door to discover they need not walk far, as Shen sat just before them, sat on his rear against one of the back wheel's of the cart.

"Shen, is everything okay? You freaked out back there," Lao said. He knelt down and then sat with him, laying a hand on Shen's shoulder.

"I'm sorry. That man… I shouldn't have done that," he muttered.

"Why? Why did you do it?" Reina pleaded with him, her eyes fixated on his form sitting there.

He lifted his head, his eyes had been to the ground, but were now set right on Reina, who stood in front of him with a strong stature. "You were right, Reina. Paranoia. That's the only way I can describe it. I couldn't risk… I couldn't risk him hurting you two."

"Hurting us? What are you talking about?" Reina said. Lao sent a look both Reina and Shen's way, as if echoing what she had said.

"The Nettle. I think it's following us. That man, he gave off this air to him, and it ate away at me," Shen said. He stood up and kicked a few puffs of dirt from the sweaty soles of his bare feet. The cloth cart cover behind him flapped lightly as a gust of wind brushed past them, supplying a cooling air to their skin.

"The Nettle? Are you serious?" Reina snapped.

"Yes! We have no idea what it can be capable of. The Faceless were able to do things any Mystic couldn't even dream of doing, right? What's to say this Nettle can't do anything like that, or worse for that matter?" He began to shout a bit, raising his voice as the wind began to blow ever more through the little town of Lin-Hao. "We already know the Nettle has been traveling in this direction."

"That doesn't mean it's after us, Shen. We have bigger things to worry about, anyway, even if it was following us." She paused for a moment, before a realization suddenly struck through inside her mind. "And come to think of it, we don't even know if what you saw was really a spirit. That's to say if you truly saw anything at all!"

"What do you mean, Reina?" Lao piped up.

"Shen snuck out two nights ago, when we were in Qianma. He went to help the merchant." She said.

"And what's so wrong about that?" Lao protested, standing up himself, taking a strong stature of his own, his shoulders poised forward assertively.

"It's impulsive!" She shouted out loud, and the wind that had been blowing strong before stopped. The cloth cover of the cart stopped flapping and the air around was quiet. "We… We need to go. The sun's going to be setting soon, and we need to get back on the road and find a place to make camp," she said, rambling, her voice wavering.

No other words were spoken, and the three packed into the cart, Reina at the reins and Shen and Lao stuck in the back, sheltered from the sun's light by the cloth cover. After Reina fed Ping two apples, a sufficient amount to bring the dimian's spirits up and poise him to utter a cheerful *squawk* in satisfaction, they took off back onto the road. By the time the night rolled around, the blue sky replaced with a black hue speckled with thousands of white dots and the moon chief among them, they had found camp near a small forest grove and a stream.

While Lao went out and got firewood, Reina set up a circle of rocks for which they would place the fire, and cook a few filets of Ailfish from one of the metal ice boxes in the back of the cart. The fish came from Vasai, a popular one among fish markets, and the pungent smell of it reminded Reina of her home somewhat. Shen had just finished setting up the cooking spit, when he decided to break the silence.

"Are we not going to talk?"

"What is their to talk about?" Reina muttered, putting a few logs into the circle of rocks. She took the firestarter from her bag and struck its mechanism together, producing a large spark, which she fanned with her breath to grow the embers that jumped against the bark of the logs.

"Everything."

She put the firestarter back, reaching her hand into her bag, and felt around in it for something. After a moment she brought her hand back up and in her palm there sat the little device Councilwoman Kaishi had given them. "Tell me, which way do you figure north is?" She said.

Shen thought for a bit, and Lao still had not yet returned. "Since we came from the west, and that way," he said and pointed toward the thicker trees in the grove they were situated in, "is east. So, I imagine north is that way." He pointed toward the stream, where a baby ram-horn was busy drinking its fill of water, before scampering away into the trees. "Now, are we going to talk, or what?"

"What do you know, this little thing really does work!" She exclaimed, and stared down at the little bowl-like thing, tapping against the glass cover with her thumb, smiling at it like a curious child.

"Reina!"

"What, Shen? What do you want me to say? 'Oh, it's okay, Shen. I know you're not *really* a paranoid man with the thought we're always being followed.'" She put the device back into her bag and looked to him with her eyebrows furled. It was there that the conversation ended. Shen could not muster up anything to say. He wondered if his actions were truly defensible, and the thoughts remained in his mind as the fish cooked after Lao returned with arms full of firewood and twigs. The thoughts swirled around in his mind like a whirlpool as the fire died out and the other two settled in their sleeping rolls. And, even more so, the thoughts remained in his head as the night dragged on and he could not even get close to falling asleep.

Caught Off Guard

The night air was stagnant and silent. It seemed as though the usual nightlife sounds, the bugs that danced around in the tall grass making their creaking and chirping sounds, were not to be found. Perhaps birds had snatched them all up, or they were swept away by the rains the day before. But regardless of the method, they were nowhere to provide the air with any semblance of sound. As such, Shen had difficulty with getting to sleep. On top of his stress and his regret for the events earlier in the day, he couldn't fall asleep with such little noise. The silence was unsettling to him.

Many times, when he'd first been placed in the camp, just twelve years old, he found that he couldn't fall asleep unless there was some sort of sound. The silence meant the calm before the storm that was another day of hard work, whipped and beaten to keep moving along the dirt to the next forge. But, the sound, whether it was the quiet mumblings of the other Mystics, or the smooth lullaby his father would sometimes sing to him, Shen could not get to sleep without sound. And now was not any different.

But, while the silence was unsettling, it wasn't constant. Every once in awhile Shen would hear a low rustling in the bushes or the leaves of the canopy of trees above them. It seemed, at first, that these were caused by small gusts of wind that blew through the little grove they were staying in. These sounds weren't enough to lull Shen to sleep, though, and only served to tug at his nerves even more. Soon though, there came a new sound. This one was eerily familiar, and once it truly cemented itself in Shen's head, as he lay in his sleeping roll next to the cart, he jolted up and out of it. Footsteps.

Shen looked to Lao, who was curled up in Ping's feathers, his sleeping roll warming his legs while he slept. His head then darted to Reina, who he could just barely see lying in the light of the last few embers of the fire they had made, her sleeping roll sat near it. Shen made sure not to make too much noise as the footsteps neared ever closer to his position, as well as grew in frequency. He thought to move to the cart quickly, search for the glowing rock and the bow and arrows Reina had brought on the journey. But, this was soon ruled out as an option. A figure approached, and entered the light of the embers, and he could just barely make out the head wrap around their head.

His heart jumped in pace, and he quickly pulled a few rocks from the ground, flicking his fingers upward in front of him, to grab at their ankle and fasten them to the ground. The figure stopped, and with the time he now had, Shen reached into the cart for the firestarter. He took it into his hand and ran over to the flame's embers, clicking it, and up the flames shot and began illuminating all around them. There stood the figure, small and thin, and Shen began to take notice of the other figures around their camp as he tossed the firestarter to the ground. "You!" Shen cried, and laid a firm punch into the jaw of the figure, covered in the tan-colored head wrap they wore.

"Shen? What is it?" Reina shot up out of her sleeping roll, and immediately grabbed for the sword at her back as she noticed the figures closing in on them slowly from the trees.

"The Nettle! It's the Nettle," Shen began, but, as the figure recoiled from the pain of the punch, Shen saw a glimmer in their eyes. Unlike the Nettle, who had crystalline blue eyes, this person's were a mix between hazel and brown. It was not the Nettle. This was a person, not a spirit. She seemed to be a Vasai woman, tattoo on her face like the ones he'd seen on the man from the shop in Lin-Hao, and skin almost exactly the same tone as Reina. "It's not," he mumbled to himself.

"I don't care who or what it is, Shen, why are they here?" Reina said, swinging her sword toward one of them, who was emerging from a bush. There seemed to be about ten of them. They all looked to be merchants, though more equipped like mercenaries than traders, holding swords in their grip and even a few daggers strapped to thighs or chests.

"Why are we here, you ask?" A familiar voice called out. From the darkness, the shadows of the trees that swung in the light of the fire, two more figures entered. "You cheated us." The meek voice was unfitting of the image, as the burly frame of Mao Xinyi stepped into the light. Behind him, there stood the man Shen had confronted at the shop, tattoos completely visible in the light of the flames that flickered and sputtered as they grew.

"Cheated you?" Shen asked. There was a sense of shock settling into his mind, and he could only play along with what the merchant before him was playing at.

"Zhi-Ming was our business to handle. And nobody, I mean nobody, messes with a merchant's business." He cracked a few of his knuckles and reached for the weapon at his back, the fastened trident that glimmered in the light of the fire, as an arrow whizzed past his head into a tree behind him. "What the," he started, and his head darted up to find Lao standing nearby the cart, awake, blinking his eyes incessantly.

"Shen, do something before I have to shoot this thing again. I'm not a very good shot either, so there's no telling what or who I'll hit." He was tired, dizzy and dazed, and he dropped the bow onto the ground, running for the back of the cart.

Shen reached his hands to his sides, and grabbed at a few rocks to throw at Mao and his group with his powers, while Reina fought off two of them nearby. The light of the fire was just enough to let Shen see what he was doing, As a consequence, however, it was more than enough light for Mao, busy with dodging the oncoming rocks, to see what he was up against. "You! You're a Mystic!" He smirked, pulling his trident from behind him, gripping it at his side. "That's rich. Now I have absolutely no qualms about killing you." He dashed forward, stabbing at Shen with the trident's tips. "Scum!" Shen jumped and moved out of the way each time, only getting scratched at his side once.

The scratch, though superficial, still served to send a pain shooting through his nerves. He reached his hand down and brought it up to see as his eyes beheld a glimmer of blood on his fingertips. "Good hit," he said, grunting in a bit of pain, "but you'll be lucky to get any more than that."

"Try me," Mao said. Two of his companions came from the bushes and stormed for Shen, who was ready with a few more rocks and another surprise up his sleeve. They came at him with their swords poised, one of them wielding one longsword, the other carrying two short swords, one in each hand. As Shen could see, between dodging and launching a few rocks into their chests, they were indeed the same group that he'd seen with Mao in the Council meeting. As for whether or not they were the figures he had seen with the Nettle in Qianma, he couldn't tell. They certainly had the stature, being quite muscular and capable of the combat they had in mind in taking him down. But, that was a thought for another time, as a few more of Mao's group shuffled over toward Lao.

Lao, still dazed and tired from the rapid shift from slumber to waking, jumped around the cart, avoiding the blades of the mercenaries assaulting him. "Hey! Can't we talk this out?" He joked. His heart though, was not as humorous as his mind, pounding inside his chest. Soon he was short of breath, and found himself with an arrow in his hand and the bow nowhere to be found. "You wouldn't kill a kid, right?"

"You don't look so much like a kid to me. And besides, we won't kill you. But that doesn't mean we won't hurt you," one of them said, closing in on him, before being knocked across the ground. He gripped at the dirt, having chunks of the ground burst in his hand into dust, as he looked up to see what had bested him. It was Ping, standing gallantly with his big eyes poised on the other mercenary in front of Lao.

"Nice birdy," she said, and was thoroughly distracted by the dimian, enough so that Lao could get in close. He came up behind her and jabbed her in the arm with the arrow, stabbing right through the flesh and muscle, seeing the blood spurt out in the minimal light. "Gah! You little brat," the woman said, dropping her dagger on the ground. Ping took this chance to charge at her, knocking her into the side of the cart. She struck the side of the cart with her head, and was knocked out cold, fallen to the ground, unconscious and unable to move.

Lao jumped for the dagger, and grabbed it just as the mercenary from before returned. "Thanks for the help, buddy, do you think I could get a little more?" He said. The dimian, as if understanding what the boy said, looked to him and let out a loud *squawk*, then charged ahead for the mercenary. "I'll take that as a yes," he said, and fled for the side of the cart where he dropped the bow, determined to use it better now that he was much more awake. In a matter of moments he seized the bow, and turned with another arrow in his hand, fumbling with nocking it onto the string.

Elsewhere, Reina had already killed one of the mercenaries that had gathered to her, and she was beginning to chip away at the other two. One of them constantly jabbed at her with the spear in his hand, while the other slashed at Reina's side with his sword. She blocked the blows from the sword with her own, but the tired muscles in her arm were beginning to wear thin with every hit that *clanged* into the air. The spear-wielder was largely inaccurate with his hits, but every once in awhile he would get a hit in, which would pierce lightly into her skin. Each time this happened she could feel her nerves weakening and her muscles getting sore, and she grunted in pain when it would sting. Soon, though, she got a burst of energy, and lashed out at the spear-wielder with her sword.

"I've had it with you," she cried out, and sank her blade into the neck of the man before her. But, once the energy wore off and she was once again tired, the mercenary with the sword lunged forward, slicing at the side of her thigh with the blade. Blood came from the wound and fell to the ground, and she got to her knee as the pain set in. Before he could get a finishing blow in, however, he was struck in the side of the head by a rock. "Shen!" Reina called out, and looked to see him nearing her, raising a few pillars of dirt from the ground to block the sword swipes from the oncoming mercenaries. "I can't hold them off for much longer."

"You won't need to," Shen said, and struck the mercenary in front of him in the stomach with a hefty rock, knocking them back on their rear. They heaved a breath in, but their lungs pushed extra hard to get the air inside. "It's just the other two of them and Mao left."

"Three Shen!" Lao said, firing an arrow aimed at the mercenary in front of him's head, though his poor aim landed the arrow square in the shoulder of the man. He fell back and hit the ground, and Ping rushed over to stomp on his chest, knocking the breath out of him. He found that his senses were falling away from him, his vision fading, and he finally fell unconscious. "Now two," he joked, running over to Reina's side with the bow, no arrows anywhere to be found in his grasp.

"Shouldn't you," Reina started, and breathed heavily as the blood dripped from the gash in her thigh down her leg and onto the ground, "have some arrows for that," she said.

"I'm not the best at aiming them. I figured I could just hit them with the bow, anyway," he said. Part of him was joking, but another part actually longed to be able to smack one of the mercenaries down with the bow, given there was no imminent danger of death he could be in by doing so.

"Lao, stay out of this," Shen snapped, turning to them as he got to their position, launching a few more rocks at the two closing in on them. They looked fierce, scowls painted on their faces, daggers at the ready as Mao came from behind them with his trident poised to stab at the three against him. "I won't let you get hurt."

"I've got a bit of backup, Shen. Don't worry," Lao said, and looked to Ping, who sat upon the unconscious bodies of the mercenaries he'd gathered together in a little pile. He let out a happy *squawk* and snapped his beak down at them, waiting for things to be settled so he could sleep once again. "But, it looks like my backup is busy taking a nap."

"This isn't the time for jokes, Lao, this is serious." Shen said, throwing another hefty rock into the chest of one of the mercenaries.

"I don't know, I sort of like the kid. Cracking jokes will be a good way to go for him," Mao quipped, and dashed toward Reina with his trident pointed toward her. His shrill voice was a strange contrast to his muscular physique, but it wasn't enough to minimize the aggressiveness of his attacks, as one of the prongs of the trident pierced Reina in the side. She yelped in pain and in a jerking reaction, she sliced her blade down and severed one of his arms at the elbow, loosening the trident from his grip until it dropped.

"Now, Shen!" She shouted as she tossed her sword to the ground, grasping Mao's trident and stabbing him in the legs with it as he writhed on the ground, pinning him to the dirt.

Shen followed the lead and jumped toward the two mercenaries left, swinging their daggers toward him. He brought his arms to his side and threw them forward, two dirt and rock pillars coming up from the ground and striking the mercenaries both in the center of the chest. They were knocked back into thick-trunked trees, and as their heads hit the wood, they lost consciousness and fell to the ground with a *thud*. "You," Mao mumbled. "You'll be killed by them," he trailed off, slipping in and out of consciousness, "the Council will have all of your heads."

"Just be quiet, and thankful that we're letting you live." He pulled his bronze sword from the scabbard at his back, and walked over to the flames that had been dying down since they started their fight. They climbed and crackled though as Shen brought the blade of his sword into the fire, and quickly felt the warmth of the metal gather all the way up to the hilt, where he felt the heat through the leather grip. "I'm going to need to do this, and it's going to hurt, but you'll thank me later," he said, keeping the sword above the flames as it began to glow with heat. "Reina, grab the waterskin and wash off his wound."

"Which wound," Reina said jokingly.

"The one you inflicted, his arm, of course. We can't let it bleed out or get infected." He pointed to the cart, the cloth covering of which flapped in a gust of wind that blew by. "It should be by my bag, right by where the icebox is," Shen said. Reina walked back over to where Mao laid after retrieving the hide waterskin, and unscrewed the cap to pour over his wound. Mao yelled out in pain as the blood and water fell to the ground and stained the dusty dirt below. Shen then walked over and placed the blade of the sword, burning hot, to the wound.

"Gah! You scum! I should've killed you myself, all of you!" He screamed, as the steam rose from his wound, carrying the smell of burning flesh with it. Soon, he passed out from the pain of it, and the screaming stopped, as did the bleeding from his wound, and the silence returned to the air more uncomfortable to everyone than it had ever been before.

"There. Reina, get the rope from the cart and tie them up. I need to sleep," Shen said plainly, walking back over to his sleeping roll and curling up inside it. The warmth of it was enough to bring his nerves down. Though, there was something irking at them, as the word 'scum' ricocheted around in the confines of his mind. It had been long since he was called such. But, it was not so much as to keep him awake, as after Reina had finished constraining Mao and his group, he fell into a deep sleep that wouldn't be roused until the sun rose in the morning. Lao had fallen asleep too, safe in the bed of feathers of Ping's side, his feet again warmed by his sleeping roll. Reina too fell into her slumber, her sleeping roll now set farther away from the fire that raged on into the night and died out when morning came.

As the sun rose from behind emerald hills lightly dotted with trees and flowers, a light came upon the camp of the three which illuminated a scene in contrast to the sounds that fluttered through the air. Despite the dulcet tones of birds which bustled in and out of trees, there was a horrid sight of death all around the camp, which Shen and Reina beheld with horrified looks. "Get Lao. Keep him away from this."

"Shen, he's seen death, we can't-"

"Just do it. He won't see this. I won't let him," Shen pleaded, and in a moment of emotion, he almost spoke wrong of the boy still waking up nearby.

He'd almost called Lao 'brother.' It was something he hadn't said of someone in such a long time, and he couldn't help but feel a burning tear jerk at the corner of his eye at the thought. But, he held his tongue, in majority due to the problem at hand. Before him sat Mao, precisely where he'd been left, along with his other companions, tied to the thick trunks of trees with bulky rope from the back of the cart. But, they were all but gone from what he could see in the light of the sun leaking through the leafy canopy around him.

In the neck, near the knee, and just above the elbow in the bicep, in each of the bodies sat before him, there stuck out metal needles, shiny and glimmering silver in the light of the sun. At the needles' backs were streaming red ribbons that blew in gusts of wind that passed through the trees in the grove they camped in. From the necks up, there sat purple veins, darkened and deepened in the different skin tones of each of the bodies. Whether in the light tan of the Vasai of Mao and some of his group, or the dark tan of Batung of the remaining mercenaries, the marks were ever apparent. Their eyes were bulging and bloodshot, rife with looks of horror set into their face after death. But, one of them did not wear this look, and instead hung his head in a tired stupor. From what he could see, his chest rising and falling softly with just a bit of air, Mao still lived.

"Mao," Shen clambered toward him, looking on as blood fell from the man's lips, "what happened?" Kneeling before Mao, Shen waited for a response from the weakened merchant as Reina kept Lao busy, sorting through boxes in the back of the cart.

"You." Mao spoke low, and for once, his shrill little voice was gruff. It seemed like his time on the plane of the living was coming to an end, as blood vessels in his eyes popped and brightened red, and the veins on his neck bulged and shifted into the sickly purple of his companions that laid dead around him.

"Why do you care?" He asked, coughing up blood onto his tunic. His hand looked to have gotten free in the night, his trident lying just out of reach as his muscles refused to move any longer. "Want to know what did what you couldn't?" As the man looked on at Shen, he smirked, blood staining his white teeth.

"What did this, Mao? You've done things, yes, but you're still a person, like me."

"Ha. You idiot. You're nothing like me. Mystic waste like you belongs in my spot, dying, bleeding like a weakling." He coughed once again, and more blood pooled at the back of his throat, irritating his mouth.

"I don't care what you think about my kind. Just answer me. What did this to you, to all of you?" Shen grabbed at Mao's tunic collar. "If I can't save you then I can at least hope to tell your story and save others from the same fate."

He paused, but then spoke low. "A spirit. Nettle. Happens to kill merchants like me and my group," he said, and trailed off as his mind began to slip away from him. Shen's face drained of color as he felt his senses numbing. Mao seemed to notice this, as his eyes lit up and the smirk returned to his face. "Heard of it, have you?"

"Mao. I won't let your death be in vain."

"Oh save it, Shen Jin. There's no need to run the self-righteous drivel by me. I got all that from you and your companions' speech at the Council," Mao stopped abruptly, though seemingly wishing to say more, despite how the strength of his lungs was giving out. The purple of the veins on his neck was now the darkest it could be, and his eyes began to bulge from his skull, until Shen could no longer see the breath rise and fall with his chest. Shen stepped back, standing now, and looked on as the sun's light shone bright into his eyes from behind leaves which swung away in the wind.

Silently, Shen walked back to the cart, and climbed into the back of it. He lifted and dropped the cover once he was inside, to find Reina and Lao simply sitting down, huddled amongst the boxes and bags. "Shen. What happened? Is everything okay?" Lao asked, his eyes wide.

"Fine. Reina, do you mind taking Ping's reins for the day?" Shen brushed off the question quickly, redirecting his gaze to Reina who sat adjacent to him.

"That shouldn't be a problem," Reina started, and climbed from out of the cart to hook Ping's harness back up to the pull mechanism at the front of the cart. "If I remember right, the next town is Sheteng. Ping needs more apples, anyway. I'm sure we can get there by sunset," she finished. She reached her hands to Ping, who chirped lightly and questioningly, until she grabbed at the leather straps that fastened onto the pull mechanism. The wood ground against the metal hinges, and then loosely settled as Ping shook around, letting a loud *squawk* escape from his beak.

"Perfect. Lao and I will rest in the back," Shen said. He dropped his bag from the side of his thigh, and reached back to grab at the scabbard which held his sword. He took the strap of it from off of him and dropped it down amongst the boxes. Reina hopped atop Ping's saddle and grabbed at the straps of the reins, tugging on them, and he bolted off at a great speed.

"Shen, what happened to Mao and his group? Are we just leaving them there?" Lao asked. But, he gathered no response from the man sitting across from him in the back of the cart. He was more preoccupied with the surroundings which were fleeting past as he stared through the hole in the cart's cloth cover.

"Reina, you said Ping needed more apples, right?" Shen shouted out to her, dodging Lao's questioning.

"Yeah. We've gotten through the good ones. The only ones we had left I tossed with the mercenaries, they were all rotten," she said.

"Rotten?" Shen pondered for a moment. Were they already rotten when they got them? Or, did they rot quickly in the warm confines of the sack they were stored in? Either way, it was a strange thing indeed, as apples could last a few solid days in those sorts of conditions, in the sort of weather it was during that season. "Odd."

"Shen. What happened to them?" Lao pressed on. He was near to grabbing Shen by the sleeve, tugging incessantly until he got the answer he felt he was entitled to. After all, he was a part of the group, too, and it was clear to him that Reina knew something or other about it.

"They're gone, taken by soldiers that came by," he said, lying straight through his teeth. But, before Lao had even the time to see through the falsehood laid out before him, Shen spoke again, firmly. "May I tell you a story, Lao?"

"Yes," Lao spoke softly, content with hearing another story to pass the time, though still slightly irked by the prospect of Shen deflecting him in such a way.

"Have you ever heard the story of Heijian's Sword?" Shen raised his eyebrow and let a smile creep onto his face, leaning toward Lao, welcoming the boy's answer.

"No. I haven't heard all too many stories," he said.

"Well then, I'm sure you'll enjoy this one," Shen started, and relaxed in the crook of a few boxes and Reina's leather bag, sort of like a pillow. "In a land far away from here, or Vasai in the south, or even Ogon to the east, there lived a young man. He was a bright and charming man, with fair skin and shining green eyes." Shen thought of his own eyes, but in his mind, this man he talked of had a light in the green of his eyes, where in Shen's there was an absence of light. "This man had a name, but his name was forgotten, swept away by the tides of time. He was simply known as the herald of the sword."

"The sword? Like your sword?" Lao questioned, and the childlike curiosity Shen knew from the first look in the boy's eyes returned.

"Somewhat. But, the herald's sword was much more powerful, much more important than this sword." Shen grabbed for the scabbard, and as an act of theater of sorts, he pulled it from the scabbard and held it up. Light from the sun leaking through holes in the cart's cover bounced off the bronze of the blade and danced all around the darker shade under the cover. "The sword of the Dreadking Heijian, as it was called, held a special power. It housed a spirit, an incredibly powerful spirit, the almighty lord of all spirits, in fact." Shen lightly moved his wrists around, swinging the sword around slowly. "This sword would be used to fight off a new evil, an army from the young man's rival nation, led by an evil general."

"A general. What was he like?"

"He was very fierce. He wanted to conquer the young man's nation to add to his land, so that he may one day rule the whole world. But, this general was no mere human like you or me. He had a great power that the herald of the sword had to seal away."

"What happened?" Lao was enthralled with the words that escaped from Shen's lips, leaning forward almost right off the edge of the wooden crate he sat on.

"The herald and the general met at a great tower, a huge and tall structure that touched the sky. They fought at the top, as storms raged and thunder crashed around them, they fought to a standstill. The herald brought his hand back as the general poised to strike him, and swung the blade of the sword of Heijian into the heart of the general's chest." Shen brought his voice up with the last of his words, and then fell quiet. "But, then a crash rang out through the whole of the world as the blade *broke*."

"It broke?" Lao shouted, hopping up, standing in the back of the cart in front of the crate.

"Yes. The blade shattered into three pieces in the herald's hands, and fell to the ground." Shen dropped his blade with a clatter to the floor of the back of the cart, and looked to Lao again. "The handle, the hilt, and the blade itself, lie before the herald of the sword. The general threw his head back and laughed at the hero, but his laughter was soon quelled, as the storm raged even more furious than ever before."

"What happened? What happened?" Lao pleaded, anxious and excited as he sat back down.

"Heijian, the evil spirit locked away in the sword, had escaped. He wrought his own kind of havoc on the world, and soon had most of the world conquered." Shen grabbed the sword and placed it back inside the leather scabbard at his side, then set it down atop a few of the wooden crates nearby. "Faced with total defeat at the hands of Heijian, the herald and his overseers allied with the general and his armies, to stop the Dreadking Heijian from taking the whole of the world for himself and his kind."

"Did they stop him?"

"Yes. But, it was not an easy task. Many lives were lost from both the armies of the general and the herald of the sword. Spirits were sent back into the objects they were freed from, stuck in their prisons forever, never to be unleashed again. Heijian, though, was the hardest of them to imprison, as he had been the first time." Shen relaxed his muscles, and settled even more into the backrest he had made. "After a long and grueling fight, the general was able to hold off Heijian long enough for the herald and his overseers to seal him away. The general, though, despite the evil and misery he had dealt to the herald and his people, sacrificed himself to stop Heijian and save them."

"He died?" Lao asked, shocked, his eyes wide and his jaw dropped.

"He could take Heijian's wrath no longer, and passed just before the evil spirit was sealed away. But, it let the herald stop him, and bring peace to the world." Shen concluded his story, and to him, there was a deeper meaning which Lao perhaps didn't get yet, one he might not ever truly get the way Shen felt it. Shen, though, smiled as he saw Lao simply happy.

"That was great! And the sword, what happened to the sword?"

"Its pieces could not be entirely rid from the world, and were instead hidden away far from the tower where the sword broke. Those pieces were never found again, and the world rested away in harmony as the spirit of Dreadking Heijian was split between those pieces of the sword."

"Wow! Is it real?"

"Is what real?" Shen asked.

"The story! Did Heijian, and the general, and the hero, did they actually exist?" Lao had hope inside his eyes, twinkling like the light of the sun that shone through the holes of the cloth covering of the cart.

"I don't know if it's truly true. I suppose it could be. But, there's no real way of telling, don't you think?" Shen asked, and smiled as he recognized how very enthralled he had brought the boy to be with his story, a story that Shen himself was told a few times as a young child.

"I guess so," Lao said. There was a feeling at the back of his mind, a want, a need for more information. He was so excited as the story engrained itself into his mind. It would remain there for many years to come, he thought, the images that flashed through his head of Heijian's sword breaking and a dark force shooting from the pieces, of the great general cackling as the hero fell, and the valiant death of said general that would overcome evil to combat it. But, as he looked out onto the trees that flew away from them, sitting in the cart while Ping pulled it along, he fell into a light sleep.

  Time crawled away from them fast, as the road depleted and lost its way. Not for long, however, as the road returned into view, graveled and dusty, leading right into a great town bustling with people. This town though, was strange for two reasons which were immediately apparent to Reina, who sat atop Ping's saddle. The first, none of the buildings were crafted from the typical bamboo or even wood that Batung architecture was known for. Even in the capital, this sort of style could be seen, no opulent bejeweled buildings or ones built from the most precious of metals only found in the caves of Ogon. These buildings were crafted from stone, raised right from the ground like huts and boxes into bamboo frames, with holes in the sides functioning as windows.

  The orange sunlight that emanated from the glowing orb in the sky was on the descent, just barely touching the horizon in its fall, came through the windows in the stone buildings and lit up all sorts of scenes on the insides. There were families gathering for dinner, setting tables with wooden bowls and plates, topped with meats, soybeans, and even a few treats for the children in the families. The light reached the farmers tending to large expanses of tilled farmland, field after field of soybean and tea plants being poked at with tools by older men and women dressed in loose tunics.

  They arrived at the front gates, unguarded, not a single soldier in sight, though there did stand a rather wiry woman. She had bloodshot brown eyes and dark tan skin caked in dried dirt or mud, from what Reina could tell, and immediately assumed she was a farmer like most others in the town. "Hello, ma'am, may we enter for the night? We need a place to stay." Reina said it low and warmly, smiling to the woman whose eyes darted around the cart before her.

"And your name?" She spoke up.

"Reina Yamato. I have two others with me, Shen Jin and Lao," she paused, as she'd not been acquainted with the name of the boy she had been following along with for days now. "Jin. They're brothers," she said, remembering what Shen had said before as a cover, trying her best to mask the uncertainty in her own words.

Shen and Lao came from out of the back of the cart cover and approached the woman with smiles on their faces. "Hello," Shen said. Lao, still tired from the events before, and unable to get a sound nap with the images of Heijian's Sword burrowing into his thoughts, simply put his fist to his chest in friendly salute. They were eyed up rather rudely by the woman, looked up and down and circled by the woman that stood coated in a thin layer of dirt before them.

"Why do you have that sword?" She asked coarsely. Her voice wasn't necessarily raspy, but neither was it smooth, a strange middle ground that nipped at Shen's ears as he heard the question.

"Protection. Many bandits and spirits on the roads, we've come to find out," he said plainly and with a warm smile. While it didn't seem like much, it was enough for the woman, and she hobbled over back to what was assumed to be her own home, also dusted with a bit of dirt at the outside walls. "Let's get to the inn and get some rest. We have to keep moving," Shen said, and the three of them slowly moved through the town, Ping lazily dragging the cart along the stone road through the town.

Silent Watcher

     In the night before, Shen and Reina had brought Ping out in the front of the inn, tied to a post by rope. The cart, however, was left at the back of the inn, guarded by a man hired by the innkeeper. There were several other carts, stocked to the brim with mainly produce either coming into town, going out of town, or simply passing through to get to the chief destination. While Ping rested safely outside of the inn, Shen, Reina, and Lao took to one of the inn rooms. With a payment of just six Yin, little silver coins engraved with images of tea leaves on one side and a water lily on the other, they received a room for the night and a meal for each of them. The people seemed generous, with the exception of the woman who they met at the front of town.

     As night turned to day, and the sun came up from its rest to shine on the farmland, most of the people left their homes and took to the fields for their day's work. Shen and Reina though, now wide awake, thought to stay in the town for just a bit longer. "Can't I go outside and look around? Just for a little bit," Lao asked them, also wide awake now that his mind and body were well-rested.

     "No, Lao. It's too dangerous," Shen said.

     "But how come?" The boy said back, urging to jump out the door and run around the stone houses of the town, meet new people and maybe make quick coin by selling some of the soap berries he'd kept stuffed into his pocket.

     "We were almost attacked the night before last. I hate to say it, but it's just too dangerous to be running around for fun. We have no idea if we might be being followed," Reina added in.

     "I'm not some little kid, Shen! I can handle myself." He said.

"I think the scars on your shoulder would beg to differ," the man said with a furrowed brow.

Lao rubbed at his shoulder and could feel next to nothing. His wounds had healed and they no longer bled like they had when first healing, but they still had a strange feeling to them that irked him every once in awhile. "I'm alive, aren't I?"

"Lao. It is my responsibility to look after you, don't you think?" Shen said.

"And mine too," Reina interjected.

"It's not! I'm not some little kid! Why do I have to keep telling everyone that? I can handle myself, and I don't need protecting." He began to get angry, and Shen, noticing the anger fuming up into his core, sought to calm him.

"Okay," Shen began softly, and he could see Lao get calmer with just the single word. "I think if you bring Ping with you, and the sword, then you'll be alright," he said. There was something in his mind, though, that was nagging at him. Even the way he said it could easily be construed as reluctance, but no one in the room perceived it as such.

"Really?" Lao exclaimed.

"As long as you don't make me regret it." Shen said. He got up off from the bed he had been sitting on, and walked over to a table where his hip bag and sword rested. He took it into his hands and felt the leather of the scabbard, smooth and fine in its creation, and brought it over to hand to Lao.

"The sword! This is so cool," Lao gushed.

"You need to be careful with it. Don't use it unless absolutely necessary, you understand?" Shen asked.

"Mhm, yeah," Lao said, occupied only with the craftsmanship of the sword's handle and hilt, the shining gold of it and the jade gemstone at the pommel.

"Lao, he's serious. A sword is not a toy to play with," Reina added. "It's something to take a life, or save one, or both in the same blow. Can you handle that?" She said, getting up and affixed her own sword into its hold at the back of her waist. Standing at the window, she looked out and watched as people walked the stone road, heading from one building to another.

The gravity would soon sink into the boy's mind, and with a stoic expression, he answered her and Shen. "Yes. I understand. I won't use it unless I have to," he said. Heavy in his hold, he put the scabbard strap over his shoulder and his neck, letting it rest loosely at his back. "Can I go now," he asked, eager, itching to see what the town had to offer.

"As long as you stay out of trouble, yes," Shen said, and before he could utter the boy's name, he was out the door and flying down the stairs of the inn. "Be safe," he whispered.

"He'll be fine, Shen. I think you worry too much," Reina muttered.

"I don't think I worry enough. You weren't with us when he got those scars on his shoulder."

"Yeah. I'd thought about that when you'd mentioned it. What exactly were you talking about?" She asked, sitting in a wooden chair she'd pulled up by the window to admire the morning sun.

"When I first met Lao, on Yedao Island, he was attacked by a hookbeak. Cursed thing clawed right into his shoulder and nearly sliced his neck up." Shen was tending to a small pouch of jerky he'd kept with him for a long while, and as hunger ate at his stomach, he chewed lazily onto it.

"How did he take it?"

"While it may have been the blood loss, pretty well. He was more concerned with me shouting at him for it than his own safety, or whether or not it would get infected."

"He's strong, Shen."

"I know that. But he's not as strong as he thinks," Shen said, and he too looked to the window that Reina stared out from. He watched as Lao took off down the road atop Ping's saddle, holding onto the leather reins for his life as he bounced along with the dimian's movements.

"Well he'll never get strong if you keep protecting him all the time. He handled himself well against Mao and his mercenaries. You should've let him keep fighting."

"He got lucky."

"What is your problem with him? He's growing. If you don't let him prove himself, he'll never be more than the scared little boy you think he is," Reina snapped, and she was out of her seat now, standing before Shen.

"I won't let him die, not when I can prevent it. I've watched what happens when people too young overestimate their strength. I won't let that happen to him," Shen said. He sulked for a moment, hanging his head as the rising sun's light came through the window and shone on one side of his face. The other side, though, was shrouded in shadow, hidden away.

"And is that why you didn't let him see what the Nettle did to Mao and his group? Because you were worried he'd get himself killed?"

"I won't let him see such horrible things, Reina. I won't let him see things like I had to see at his age. I wouldn't wish that on anyone," he said, and his face came into the light. He wore an expression of anger muddled in sadness. It was as though past was coming back, scratching at his mind like an animal trapped in a cage. "Not him."

"He needs to, Shen." Reina came forward, and her voice was far less snappy, almost motherly in its calmness. "If he wants to grow strong, he needs to stare those sights right in the face, and not let it break him."

"But what if it does break him? What then?"

"It won't. I'm sure of it," Reina said, and her head turned toward the window again, as if to see the boy, who had already bolted off far down the road on Ping's back now.

Elsewhere, somewhere near the gate opposite to the one they'd entered from, Lao found himself searching the treeline for something interesting. In the morning time, there was a chance for particular little creatures to come rising from the earthy and dew-doused ground. Little metallic bugs the size of a finger, they came only in the morning and quickly flew off to hide in the bushes for the day, awaiting smaller bugs to fly into their grasp. He hadn't seen them since he was but five years old, and he hoped with everything in him that he'd see them this morning.

But, he didn't see them. Perhaps they'd already left for the morning, or they were nowhere in the area to begin with, but in either circumstance, Lao's attention was drawn to something else beside the dirt. Near a thinner-looking tree with peeling bark, in a small patch of tall grass, there was a great bit of movement he could see. "You see that, boy?" Lao asked to Ping, pointing to where the movement transpired. The dimian, unassuming, was preoccupied with a tiny beetle crawling along the ground. His beady little pupils fixed on it, he snapped his beak at the insect trying to get a quick little snack. The rustling in the patch of grass soon moved, moving throughout the tall grass that went around the town and even trailed inside until it reached the edges of the soybean and tea fields. Soon the little movement was snaking all throughout the town, and Lao was determined to follow it, possessed by some sort of unknown drive.

He chased after it on Ping's back, laughing and smiling as the people in the street jumped from the boy's way. Some of them simply found it charming, particularly the younger ones, but the older people made snide remarks as the dimian was out of earshot. The movement in the grass shifted over into a fairly expansive section of farm field. Lao tried his best to avoid the crops, watching as the old farmers stormed over with tilling tools gripped in hand, but there were a few bits the big bird stepped in while he kept after the creature in the plants. "Hey! Get out of here!" One of them, an older woman with brown eyes, shouted.

"I'm sorry!" He shouted, with a huge smile across his face. For a moment, as his eyes fixated on the movement he was following closely behind, he caught a glimpse of it. To his astonishment, there was a glimmer to it. It seemed as though a muted green glow emanated from its back, scales reflecting the brilliant sunlight shining on the town. At first he thought it nothing more than an overly glossy lizard, maybe someone's messenger lizard from town. But, as he got even closer to it, and it peeked its head above the plants, he noticed fur. Light gray fur bounced around as the creature kept on through the field and now into the town.

People were moving all around, walking from building to building with bags at their sides and coin pouches in their palms. Wooden carts and their vendors selling produce and trinkets moved along the sides of the roads as Lao stormed into the town on Ping, tugging on his reins in hopes of slowing him down. But, to no avail, as the dimian stormed on chasing the little creature in the tall grass that ran through the town. "Ping, slow down!" He shouted.

While all of this transpired, on the other side of town where the commotion couldn't quite be heard, Shen and Reina packed up their things in preparation to leave. Reina was finishing up wrapping their sleeping rolls, which she kept in her bag for the time being, while Shen still looked out the window. "What's got you down?" Reina asked.

"Hm? What do you mean?"

"You keep looking outside. Worried about something?" She came to the window, and looked out to see a frail old woman across the street, sorting a few heads of cabbage within the confines of her little vendor cart. "Eyeing up the produce, I see."

"Do you think he's alright?" Shen wore a look on his face, somewhere between nervousness and sadness, one which he couldn't really shake off, though he wanted to. "Lao, I mean."

"I think he's fine, Shen. But I can tell that won't do any good to calm your nerves, will it?" She walked to him and brought her hand up to her other shoulder, scratching at the scar of where her right arm once was, an itch nagging at the burned skin.

"The Nettle must've been following us, right? It couldn't have just been stalking Mao and his group. It had to have been after us, since we'd left Qianma."

"There's no way to tell for sure. We just need to keep moving, right, not stay in one place for more than a day?"

"I guess so." He looked away from the window, and brought his gaze over to Reina who stood near him. "What do you think he's doing?"

"I can't even begin to imagine. He's probably just exploring. He's a good kid. I don't think he can get into too much trouble, right?" Unbeknownst to her and Shen, however, the devious Lao was getting into all sorts of trouble, barreling through the town toward the inn at a great pace.

The little creature was now fully out of the tall grass, and Lao could see just what it was. It looked to be a simple gray-furred weasel. He'd often see them in the time between the crisp Zong-Se season and cold Bai-Se season, when the air could still get a bit warm, but the grass did not have nearly enough nutrition to live and instead died and dried out. But, this one had a glaring difference to the others he'd seen when he was on the streets a few years ago. There were shining green scales on its back, and glowing black eyes that every once in awhile darted back to look at the boy and dimian chasing after it.

It seemed as though the little creature was smiling, a cunning grin that Lao only saw as the thing looked back or turned a corner on the road. As he chased it down he noticed the other people in the town only paid attention to him. Granted, he was the one bursting through the town, breaking up crowds of people and carts. The little weasel turned another corner getting closer to the inn and Lao froze in the seat of Ping's saddle as a cart came out in front of him, pushed lightly by a little old lady. "Watch out!" He shouted. But, the old lady was too late in her reaction, and the cart was toppled over as Ping and Lao bursted through it. The little weasel they'd been chasing had run right under it, and was now gone from sight.

"Young man! Are you insane?" The old woman shouted, and nearby, Shen and Reina came down the stairs and out the front door of the inn.

"Ma'am, what's going on?" Shen asked, coming to her side and resting a calm hand on her shoulder. The old woman pointed to the mess that had been made of her cart. Cabbage fell apart in leaves all over the stone road, getting dusted up with dirt, all around the pile of wood that once was her cart. Under the rubble though, there was a bit of movement. Out from under it, there came a familiar face. "Lao! What are you doing?" He shouted, his anger building.

"Um, I can explain," the boy said.

"Where's Ping?" Reina walked up behind Shen, a bit humored by the whole situation, with the boy smiling as he picked a few splinters from his tunic.

Her question was quickly answered, as Ping raised his head and neck from out of the pile of wood. He darted his head around, the big yellow eyes and beady black pupils staring at nothing, and let forth a bellowing *squawk* with his beak open wide. "Haha! Found him!" Reina giggled, and looked to Shen to see if he too was chuckling. But, to her dismay, it seemed he was fuming. His face grew red, and he breathed heavier and heavier as Lao helped himself and the dimian from out of the wood.

After some persistent apologizing by Lao, forced upon him by Shen, the old woman was given a few wooden crates of cabbage the three of them kept in the cart as payment for Lao's mess. The rest of their time together was spent in silence. Not a single word was spoken as the three of them shuffled off to the back of the inn where the cart was left. Even as they pushed off with Ping pulling the cart, they spoke no words about what had happened or what Lao had done, or even how quickly the sunlight seemed to fade away from the sky. Beginning to get fed up with all the silence, Lao spoke up. "Shen, are you mad at me?"

"Yes, Lao. I'm furious with you."

"Why?" The boy asked.

"Because you didn't listen! I told you to stay out of trouble, and what did you do?" He turned back, sitting in Ping's saddle with the reins in his hands, and shouted into the cart where Lao and Reina were sat atop wooden crates. "You went off and you destroyed some old woman's cabbage cart! Do you know how much damage you did?"

"I know! I know what I did wasn't good, but we paid her back, right?" Lao protested.

"And you also stomped on about five other farmers' crops. You can't just do that, Lao, there are consequences." Shen said.

"I said I was sorry," the boy snapped back.

"Sorry isn't enough! How can I trust you with my sword, when you can't even keep from trampling someone's plants?" Shen reached his hand back and adjusted the strap around his torso that kept the scabbard at his back. "You won't get it again for as long as I decide. And you won't be getting into anymore trouble like that again, either. End of discussion." He finished, and as he readied to say something, Lao lost all motivation to. Instead, he silenced himself, and the rest of the trip was spent in the same silence as it had began in.

Painful Memories

The silence reached a pinnacle, and no one in the cart could deal with it any longer. However, as a surprise to both Reina and Lao, it was Shen who broke the shattering silence. The cart came to a stop just before a large forest, with a stream that bore through the land out of the many trees and around a bend by the hills to their side. "We should get some hunting in before the night falls," Shen shouted back to the two in the cover of the cart, and pushed on further with Ping until he reached a spot on the left side of the forest that was just clear enough from trees and bushes, that he could let Ping rest at with the cart. He hopped down, petting the dimian softly on the neck, to which the bird responded by dropping onto the ground, tired and sitting with his beak in his chest feathers.

Lao was the first to come out of the back of the cart's cloth cover, anxious to get some fresh air. Reina came soon after, but as she stepped down on the step-like fixture at the back wheel, she missed, and came falling to the ground on her side. "You alright? Are you hurt," Lao asked, coming to her side quickly.

"Ha," she laughed to herself, "yeah, I'll be alright. Just my pride." She started to stand, putting her right foot firmly on the ground, and expected to use her right arm to push herself up. But as she sat with her left leg bent behind her and her left arm at her side, she had the sudden realization that this obviously wasn't going to be the case. Every once in awhile, when she hadn't gotten that much sleep, she'd get a sort of twitch where her right arm would be. It was as if it was still there. But, this of course was not the case. She shook off the feeling in a matter of seconds, though, and placed her left foot on the ground in place of her right, pushing herself up with the left arm. "You think there are any ram-horns in that forest?" She asked to Shen, who was already walking a few steps into the treeline.

"I'm not sure. This place seems sort of familiar, for some reason. But, I don't think I've seen this place on the map, at least not this particular forest. There might be fish in the stream though, which is what I'm hoping for," he responded, pushing branches from his view and looking around the ground.

"Let's not get too much. We've already got some in the ice box, and it's starting to stink if we don't cook it," Reina said. "Unless of course that's just Lao's armpits."

"It is not!" The boy protested.

"Enough joking around. Let's get going, the sun's almost down." He was not wrong in the slightest. The sun was just barely touching the horizon, and it wouldn't be long before it would fall even farther below it, the light going back to the glowing orb in the sky. As such, they hurried off into the forest, only hearing the occasional snap of twigs, most likely from some small rodent scurrying across the forest floor. Soon they reached the deepest part of the stream. It was situated in a little clearing where the dwindling light of the sun reached especially well. Such light allowed for water flowers to grow at the sides, lily pads with the colorful water frogs swimming underneath them. Little silver fish swam through, too, and there was one larger than all the rest with a particular shiny coat of white scales.

"Look at that one," Lao pointed out, looking toward the white fish.

"That seems to be the target," Shen said with a slight smile forming at the corner of his mouth. He stepped a foot back and flicked his wrist up knocking the fish into the air, up out of the water with a little splash. In a quicker motion than the previous, he brought a few sharp rocks from out of his pocket, and launched them into the fish. At the same time, though, there came another sound accompanying the limp fish smacking back against the water.

"Hey! You there!" A booming male voice shouted from behind them. The three turned around with whipping heads, and to their horror, there stood a sizeable group of Batung soldiers, six of them as Shen and the others saw. They weren't much like the guards they'd seen in the towns or the cities, or even the capital. These ones wore armor fastened to their chest in plates, tied together with thick rope in a neat pattern. This sort of design was made for the armor on their thighs and shins as well, along with their shoulders. Instead of helmets, they wore nothing upon their heads, and there black hair was tousled around by the breeze that came through. But, the most daunting part of it all, was the look on each of their faces, and the swords at the ready in their hands.

"Stop right there!" Another one of them shouted, a woman with a scar on her brow, pale in comparison to her dark tan skin the rest of them shared.

Shen's heart sank quickly into his chest. It dropped deep into the pit of his stomach and nearly knocked the breath out of his lungs. "Get to the cart, now, Reina," Shen said. "Take Lao with you." He began to run further into the forest, leaving behind the fish he had killed with his powers. Four of the soldiers followed after him, chasing him through the trees. The other two followed after Reina and Lao, and even the cart, as it took off deep into the forest in Shen's direction.

By the time Shen had figured he'd lost the soldiers, the sun was finally behind the horizon. It had fallen much quicker than nights before, and the darkness that flooded the land around him was almost palpable. He had found shelter in an abandoned building, a stone one with bamboo frames, much like the houses and other buildings in Sheteng, from which they had departed earlier in the day. From what he could tell, the soldiers were still around, crunching along through the twigs and shed leaves from trees. Soon, though, the sounds got closer to him. The footsteps approached the building he was in, and he reached his hands out to pick up a few nearby rocks he felt, until the faces came into view in the doorway at the back of the building.

"It's us," Reina whispered.

"Don't attack, Shen." Lao whispered too. In his grasp, there was a little glowing rock, the one Reina had had purchased back in the capital. It's surface was like salt rock, a bit dusty, but the light that came from it reached a little past their feet. It glowed with an orange light that reminded Shen of a dying fire.

"Cover that. Hurry. We can't let them see it from outside. Do you want to die?" He was beginning to ramble, and almost got louder than a whisper.

"It's alright, Shen," Reina said, covering the glowing rock in the boy's palm with a little square of cloth, presumably cut from the cover of the cart. "We're not going to die. Not tonight at least," Reina joked.

"This is no time for jokes," Shen said, his heart practically bursting from his chest as it beat furiously within him. "Where's Ping?" He asked frantically. "The cart, Ping, where are they?"

"They're fine, Shen," Reina pleaded. "Ping is a little bit into the forest with the cart. The soldiers gave up trying to find us in a couple minutes." She walked to him and put her hand on his shoulder, as he stood up anxiously with his knees bent, ready to run. "We'll stay here for the night. No sense in fighting in the dark, right?"

Though she expected a worried response, Shen had no words for her. Lao was too tired to say anything, put off by Shen's aggression, and instead took to a corner of the room in the building, sleeping with his sleeping roll over top of him. Reina and Shen, though, gathered in the center of the building on the floor, back to back against each other. Neither of them got a single wink of sleep. Shen insisted he stay awake to watch over Lao. Reina, the same idea in mind, wished to look after Shen. In both cases, they anticipated fighting off the total six of the soldiers, if they entered.

    But, none of the six soldiers entered in the night. The night wasn't all quiet, and some creatures prone to the darkness revelled in it, calling out to their kind in shrill cries. As Lao awoke to the sunlight flooding into the building, he brought his eyes over to Shen and Reina who still sat in the center of the floor. Shen was staring intently toward the doorway he walked in from. Things were much more dangerous now, the light easily giving away their position if the soldiers even just walked by the building. As such, Shen was quick to his feet, and made for the front entrance again. "Let's go. No time to waste," he said. Reina and Lao followed out next. Lao hadn't the time to fully roll up his sleeping roll, and carried the messy bundle of cloth out with him.

    Immediately as he came into the light, into the center of the clearing the building was in, which was large and expansive, he realized his surroundings. There was not just the one building, and instead a number of them, nine or ten, all in a circle around the clearing Shen now stood in. He looked to the ground, and he found the dirt dusty, old, and reddish. It stained his sweating feet. His head shot up and he became frantic. He knew where this was, where they were, and it was not good. As Reina and Lao watched him confusedly, Shen turned on his feet and looked all around the circle at the buildings. He'd seen them before, he knew that. Many years ago he'd been here. Confirming what he thought, as he looked to the west of the congregation of buildings, he found the gate. It was crafted of wrought iron, and in wrought iron letters at the top it read "Shi-Li." Memories long suppressed came back in a great flood, and Shen fell to his knees, his eyes on the reddish and dusty dirt.

When his eyes came back up, he was in the same place as before. However, things were much different. Reina and Lao were gone from view. Instead, there stood hundreds of people crowded by the buildings around him, with chains around their ankles and wrists. They wore tattered clothing with dirt spattered all over. Their faces were painted with looks of fatigue, sadness, muted anger, and not a single one of them had joy across their face. Suddenly, a familiar face came into view, and pulled Shen up from the ground. "Get up, son, we need to go."

"Father, I can't." Shen was no longer the age of thirty, and was back to a child of twelve years old. His mind had sunk deep into memory, and as Reina and Lao tried to bring him out of his state, he relived the past in vivid clarity.

"You have to, Shen, please."

"I hate it here!" Young Shen shouted.

"Hey! You there!" A soldier came through the crowd of people shuffling around them, sword pointed in their faces. "What's the hold up? Keep moving," she said. Her face was one of anger, fury even, and visible even under the shade of her wide-brimmed helmet.

"Please, ma'am. He's being difficult. I'll get him up in a bit," Shen's father said.

"Don't be proper with me," she laughed to herself. "Look at you now. Now your kind is no more powerful than the dirt under my feet," her face changed to a kind of devious joy, as she kicked her boot forward. A puff of dirt and dust bursted from the ground and onto their tattered clothes. They quickly got up from the ground and joined in with the group closest to them.

"Shen, you need to get up when they need us to. You can't keep sitting around like that."

"Why, father? Why are we here?" He looked to his hands, to the shackles around his wrists. "Why can't we get out of here?"

"Because we're Mystics." That sentence was the last thing they'd say to each other in some time, as the rest of the time with the others was spent in silence. A large group of maybe twenty of the prisoners left to a building, with little Shen and his father among them. They filed into a smaller stone building than the others, with flags of the Batung Council upon their exterior, and rows and rows of small beds on their interior. Shen and his father were the last to enter the little building, and so were unable to get beds next to each other. Instead they settled for the only empty beds, which were on opposite sides of each other. Dirt and bugs made up the ground, and as the night fell, there came no moonlight in from the windows. The skies were cloudy that night.

"Father," Shen said. It seemed like the others in the building with them were already fast asleep, or just not in the mood to bother with caring about some young child calling for his father in the dead of night. "Father," he called louder.

"Yes, Shen. Please. Keep quiet," his father called from across the building.

"Why are we here?" He asked.

"I told you before, Shen, because we're Mystics."

"But why would they want to keep us here? Did we do something wrong?"

"I don't know, Shen. I don't know." Shen's world was shattered. His father had always known everything. Every time he'd ask a question, whether it was about his powers or even what made the birds sing in the early morning, his father always had an answer. He never knew whether the answer he gave was honest or even true, but there was always an answer. Until now, Shen had never heard his father say he didn't know.

Just as quickly as it began, he was brought from his memories and returned to the present, and his surroundings again were different. Reina and Lao were back, but not in the positions they were in before. They were closer to him, with their backs turned to Shen as he sat on his knees in the dirt. "Reina? Lao?" He spoke up. Before they replied, he saw what they were looking toward. The soldiers from the day before, swords ready, stood in a line before them with valiant looks on their faces.

"You'll turn over the Mystic right now, and perhaps you'll live to see the inside of a cell," one of the soldiers shouted, a man with a broadsword in his hands and a pale birthmark on his cheek.

"You're not taking him anywhere," Reina yelled. She held her sword tightly in her grip, looking to the soldiers, eyeing up all of them and wondering in her mind what their moves might be in the next few moments.

"You know it is against international rule to harbor a Mystic. Turn him over now, or you will be killed along with him," a female soldier shouted plainly.

"You don't have to do this," Lao shouted, desperation laced throughout his voice, and Shen was thrown right back into the fray of his memories. He went back to his last day in the camp, the day he escaped, all alone at only sixteen years old.

"Please, why? Why are you doing this? You don't have to do this," a young boy said. His hands restrained behind his back in chains, he looked toward the ground and the green mark on the back of his neck was visible as young Shen looked to him, even through the dark tan of his skin. The boy didn't get an answer from the soldiers hovering over him, and instead remained sat on his knees in the line that each and every other prisoner of the camp did.

"Shen," a voice spoke.

Young Shen looked to his right and found his father on his knees next to him. From behind his father's head, his long black hair tied up messily at the top, he could see the glowing sun. It was a beautiful day. There sat no clouds in the sky, gray or white, that could taint the blue that was ever so inviting. Birds were like specks flying up above the prisoners and the soldiers and camp Shi-Li.

"Are we going to die, father?"

"Don't say that, Shen. Please." His father pleaded, and tried to think of something to say to his son that might calm his nerves. But, the time for that would pass in mere moments, as the sounds of people dying rang out into the air. Shen dared not look around, but his father did, and he saw what was to be expected. All the people from their building they'd slept in all these weeks were all lined up in chains, sat on their knees on the dusty dirt ground. Soldiers went through the lines and slashed at the backs of their necks, the visceral sound echoing in the air and against the surfaces of the stone buildings, bouncing back into Shen's ears.

"Father, what's happening?" He asked frantically.

"Don't look up, Shen, please," his father said. He too was becoming panicked. As more and more of them dropped like animals, cut down so quickly their voices were not heard, there came a rumbling from beneath the ground. While this rumbling came and grew, the soldiers got quicker. The sounds of children crying filled the air and were quickly silenced by the sound of blade cutting through flesh. This crying Shen came to know well from the nights in the camp. Him and his father would always keep the children quiet with their stories, but now there was no point in telling any stories. There was no point in saying anything, and yet Shen's father spoke still. "Please, Shen, listen to me," he started.

"Don't do this," someone shouted from close by, and there voice was quickly cut off by the sound of the sword and blood splattering against the dirt.

"Listen to me," he started again, and Shen, who kept his head down and facing the ground, began to listen to his father. "You're going to make it out of this." Shen couldn't have known what his father meant, but he couldn't find any words to say and instead simply listened along again. "I need you to run. Find your strength, break those chains, and run. Don't look back." His father was talking much faster, and by the sounds of the boot-laden footsteps, Shen could tell the soldiers were coming so much closer to the two of them now, slowly but surely. "When the gate blows, just run." His father began to cry, tears coming up to his eyelids in huge amounts, and his voice began to waver. "I love you, Shen. Don't look." Before he could say anything more, his voice was cut off and the sound of Shen's father's blood hitting the ground filled his ears. Shen was left wondering what it was his father was talking about.

"Don't, please!" A woman shouted near Shen, and was quickly killed.

"I don't want to go. I don't," another voice shouted, a child probably around Shen's age.

All of these voices were pounding on the inside of Shen's head, and he finally lifted it to look forward. He saw the gate, the wrought iron letters reading "Shi-Li" he'd come to see every single day in the camp. A soldier came from behind him, lifted their sword, evident to Shen as the shadow of the blade in the air was visible against the ground, and he closed his eyes.

"Now!" Someone shouted, and their voice came from outside the camp, outside the gates and the buildings. Just then the front gate exploded and fell to the ground in a huge puff of dirt and dust. The rumbling in the ground became so vicious that even some of the soldiers were falling over.

"Get them! Now!" One of the soldiers shouted from behind. The soldier behind Shen, however, was determined to finish off the boy before them. The blade came down, and suddenly, just before it could come close to him, he felt something surge through him. He lost all sense besides the power flowing through him, Batung's power. With his newfound strength he stood up and began to stand and step forward just as a jolting pain shot through the small of his back. His sense of pain quickly faded, as he spun around and kicked his leg up, sending a pillar of dirt into the stomach of the soldier, knocking them backward.

"I did it!" Shen shouted, in shock from his escape. He stood and bent over, bringing his shackled hands under his legs as he stepped over the chains. With a flick of his hands, a spike of rock came from deep underground and broke the chains at his wrists and ankles. When they separated, the chains fell to the ground, and the shackles remained around his ankles and wrists. Unconcerned with such things, he turned toward the gate and ran, and a few others followed along. He was fixated on the path out of the camp before him, runnin through the trees and the patches of bamboo, he lost track of the others who'd escaped in the chaos with him.

He finally made it to a fairly large tree on the outskirts of the camp, and the ground still shook. No sounds from the camp could be heard this far from it, and young Shen was partially glad for that. The ground shook under his feet and things began to set in. He wanted to reach to his side and grip tightly the hand of his father. But, as he tried in vain to grab for a hand no longer there, he felt the heat build up in his eyes. Tears came, and he fell to his knees once again. He was free now. But, here he was, on his knees, screaming in tears for his father.

He would not receive a response, and as the ground shook with what little power there was left from the others at the camp, Shen inadvertently made the ground tremble himself.

It was then that Shen was brought right back to the present. From out of his memories he opened his eyes and beheld the soldiers coming ever closer, forming a circle around the three of them. "Get away!" Shen screamed. Reina and Lao were close to him, knowing the two of them couldn't take on all six of the soldiers around them.

"Shen, help, please," Lao said.

"Get away! Get away! Now!" Shen shouted, and he stood up now. His fingers curled and his elbows bent, he looked up to the sky and screamed and the ground began to shake violently beneath them. The soldiers, taken aback, looked around and lowered their swords in confusion. "You killed him!" He shouted, and his arms straightened out, hands to the ground. He shook his arms and quickly raised them, shooting spikes of hardened rock right through the legs of all the soldiers.

"Shen!" Lao shouted.

"Agh! You monster!" One of the soldiers screamed. Each and every one of them was unable to move, held in place by the many rock spikes stabbing through their legs. They looked down, and all of them began to lose consciousness, feeling the blood pour from their wounds as the shaking ground brought them to passing out.

Shen was finished, and after letting forth one more scream into the air, he fell to his knees again. He looked down at the ground, and a few droplets of blood fell from his nostrils to the dirt. "I'm not a monster," he trailed off. He couldn't move his arms, they were much too weak, and his legs remained fixed in their position. "I'm not a monster. I'm not," he said over and over, "I'm not a monster." He said again, and Reina bent down to hold onto him. She hoped she could bring his nerves down, but he just kept saying that phrase. "I'm not a monster." He said it a few more times, getting quieter and quieter each time, until he finally fell into a deep sleep.

Aftermath

By the time he awoke, the morning sun was already arising, and Shen fluttered his eyes open to the sight of Lao. "He's awake! He's awake!" Lao shouted with glee, and ran all around the building they'd stayed in the night before last, a fire just barely lit sitting in the center of the room. "Shen, is everything alright?" He asked, and got closer to the man on the floor.

"Lao? Yes, yes I'm quite alright. What's going on?" Shen began to move a bit, trying to get up from his lying position in the sleeping roll on the floor, but his muscles ached far too much for it at the moment. "Agh, what happened?"

"You had quite the episode yesterday," Reina said, coming into the building from the front entrance. "They're still alive, you know," she said quietly as she walked past him.

At this, Shen brought a hand up to Lao's shoulder. "Lao, will you get my waterskin for me, I'm so thirsty," he said, and with his other hand he beckoned Reina over to him.

"Yeah, sure!" The boy said, and ran off to a corner of the room where Shen's leather side bag sat. He rooted through it and searched through all the odds and ends, herbs, tea leaves, little pouches of nuts and berries, even a few Yin coins that had fallen out from the coin purse. All the while he did this, Shen spoke softly and quietly to Reina in the center of the room, near the fire.

"Reina, I need you to do me a favor," he whispered.

"Of course, Shen. Anything."

"Get rid of them. The soldiers. Do what you can without Lao seeing, and I'll distract him." He began to sit up and fight through the pain of his aching and sore muscles. "Lao," he spoke up, and the boy turned his head toward him.

"Yeah, Shen?"

"Why are you making such a mess of my things?" Shen said with a smile, his attitude much more bright than the tone he'd taken with Reina just moments before. "The waterskin is under my bag. I swear, if I'd asked Ping to do it, he wouldn't have made nearly as much of a mess as you."

"Hey! That's no fair," Lao said, and grabbed the half full waterskin out from under the leather bag he'd made a mess of. "I'm not even sure Ping could look you straight in the eyes long enough for you to ask anyway," Lao said with a chuckle.

"Yes," Shen agreed with a sincere chuckle of his own, "I suppose you might be right." With the smile still on his lips, Shen looked to Reina, and then the smile faded away. He nodded with a stoic look on his face, and the woman understood, pulling her sword from its place at the small of her back and walking out the front door.

Lao came back over to Shen and handed him the waterskin, which he gladly took from the boy, and he looked to the doorway. "Where's Reina going?" He asked, his head almost tilting. He took a seat next to Shen, his legs crossed, the dark tan of his skin vibrant in the shimmering light of the flames nearby, and the light of the sun that leaked through cracks in the stone walls.

"She's going to get some meat from the cart, maybe even hunt for some. She tells me you and her found some ram-horns on your way here."

"Really? I didn't see any."

"You must've been too occupied with those soldiers." Shen stopped his voice for a bit, feeling the dryness creep up into his mouth, and finally grabbed at the waterskin next to him. He grasped it in his hands and unscrewed the finely crafted bone cap on it, putting the mouth to his lips. Cold water came into his mouth as he lifted up the bag. The feeling was unreal to him, so pleasing to his throat as the liquid went past his teeth and smoothed out the dryness that he couldn't help but let out a relieved breath. Lao thought to himself for a moment as Shen finished off the last of the water, setting down the waterskin next to him.

"Shen. Can I ask you something?"

"Of course. You know you can ask me anything, right," Shen said to the boy. He gradually stood up from his spot, crawling out from his sleeping roll and letting his legs stretch out. The soreness was leaving from his legs like a steady stream, and he couldn't help but let out another sigh of relief as he walked around the walls of the room, the last of the soreness fleeting from the muscles in his body.

"No, I know. It's just that, this place, you've been here before, right?" Lao asked softly. There was something in his voice which wavered, throwing off his usual curious tone.

Shen thought for a while longer than needed. He thought about everything he had been through, and how that could mess with the head of young Lao. After all, Shen himself was around Lao's age when he first arrived in the camp they now stood in. "Yes, Lao." He might've said more, gave an oral history of what he encountered, but he couldn't. For one, he thought it too much for Lao to handle at the moment, too much suffering inflicted by his kind that could bring Lao into sadness like Shen was. And for another, Lao didn't give Shen the time to say anything at all.

"Can we take a walk around? Maybe you can show me what you remember?" He said, and the curious tone and the usual expression on his face was back. Lao had wide eyes which glinted in the sunlight from the windows, and a big smile that Shen revelled in.

"I think we can do that." Unable to contest the boy's curiosity, Shen figured it a fine idea to walk around the complex, maybe see what it's become over the years since he'd left it. The memory was painful in his mind, yes, but not cripplingly so. "These buildings are connected to each other, you know." Shen continued to walk around, and his muscles were near completely free of the pain, and he had quite a bit of his strength back. He walked to the corner of the room where his bag sat and stuffed everything back inside, leaving the map for the last, in hopes that it wouldn't tear or wrinkle too much. After everything was inside, he lifted the bag by the strap and tied it around his waist, the bag resting at its usual position at the side of his thigh.

"What is this place?" Lao asked, walking along with Shen along the walls of the building they still remained in.

"A camp, actually. I'm not sure if you remember, it was when we first met, I told you I knew a boy named Lao in my childhood."

"Yeah! I remember that, you had told me you went to camp with him. Is that what this place is?" Lao practically bounced with this question, his face lighting up like the morning sun.

"Yes, exactly." That was all Shen said, as it was all he could say. He hadn't the heart to tell Lao that he never knew whether or not that boy he knew made it out alive. For all he knew, he was taken from the world the day he escaped, or even another day entirely before that, when the other prisoners of the camp were busy with field work.

"Let's go to the next building," Lao said, and moved along to the side of the room, where there sat another open doorway, "come on!"

Shen followed along and they both entered into a building with a much larger space than before. There were long tables of wood, a bit rotted from time and perhaps a few little wood-eating beetles, with wooden plates and bowls sprawled all around. Some of the dishes were thrown all around, broken on the floor, and some were set neatly atop the tables, as if they hadn't moved since they were placed down many years ago. There were no traces of food, whether fresh or otherwise, as the scraps of it had long been picked away by scavenging animals like hookbeaks and wild dogs. "I remember this place."

"You do? What was it?" Lao walked around all the rotted tables and chairs, the wooden plates and bowls scattered about, aimlessly and without a care.

"If it is what I think, then it's the old mess hall. We'd eat our food here when they called for us, around sunrise, before we'd get to work." He tried his best not to speak on how horrible things were back then. It took most of his fortitude, his courage, to keep from saying all the things he went through. But, that's not to say he couldn't share anything of what he experienced. "And the food, I'll tell you, it was horrible."

"Really?"

"Oh yeah," he started, and sat down at one of the tables. He looked around and reached his arm behind him to fix the scabbard strapped to his back. The leather of it was smooth and cold to the touch, which made the hairs on Shen's hand stand up. He brought his hand back up to rub at the stubble on his jaw and thought to himself as his skin crossed over the black hairs. It seemed like they had gotten longer since the last time he felt them, and he wondered what he looked like. It had been too long since he last saw his reflection. "It was always either stale bread or cabbage that had already been chewed on by mice."

"Ugh. And they fed that stuff to you? Why?"

"Probably couldn't afford anything too gourmet, I guess." Shen laughed to himself and got back up, looking toward one of the windows nearby. The walls were chipping, crawling with dying vines, the leaves of which were falling off and gathering below the walls on the stone floor.

"Gourmet? Like what, fresh bread and ripe cabbage?" Lao quipped, a smile on his face as he kicked a broken off piece of a wooden bowl across the floor.

"Yeah, I guess so. I never really ate too much of that stuff, so I guess I couldn't get too used to it. I much prefer the berries I've found and even hookbeak to that stuff." Shen moved around to where the food was kept, and found several wooden crates. They'd been busted open with rocks protruding from the ground, crumbs spilled out by the splintered wood. Despite these signs, there was no actual food left. It hadn't looked like it was eaten gradually, either, by rodents or bugs, but taken long ago by people, Mystics that had been kept there in the camp.

"Hookbeak is definitely something I might eat again," Lao said. "It beats stealing scraps of stuff," he said again, and walked further across the big room to a doorway, the broken wooden door still attached to its hinges. With a push from his hand it swung open a little, creaking, and on the other side there lie another building's room.

"What are you looking at?" Shen asked, turning and walking toward where Lao was.

"There's another room back here, I wanna check it out," he said, and scurried off into the room. The floor there was much more neat than in the one before, not speckled with leaves and vines, but cracked and chipping all the same. Shen followed in afterward, and the first thing his eyes fixated on were the beds along the walls. Their backboards were made from darker wood which had been rotting away for some time, and were pushed up against the walls on each side.

    Shen figured there was about thirty of them, with fifteen on each side in a row. The blankets that probably once sat atop them were not to be seen, probably raided by bandits or even the fleeing Mystics all those years ago, when Shen himself left with nothing but the ragged clothes on his back. "I think this is the guards' quarters." He looked again to the beds, and noticed a few of them had large wooden trunks sat next to them. The locks on them were bulky and silver, brushed with a fine coating of dust and dirt.

    "Guards? What kind of camp was this?" Lao asked.

    "Some sort of military sleepaway camp. At least, that's what my mother told me when she dropped me off here," he said confidently, lying of course. He thought to himself, and sat on one of the trunks, whose lock was busted and lying on the floor in front of the trunk. As he shifted around on the seat he took notice that the trunk was much heavier than he had figured an empty wooden trunk would be. "Lao, can you check those chests over there for any broken locks," he said.

    "Um, okay," Lao said with an inquisitive tone. He walked over to the trunks and looked over the locks. Most of them were intact, strong and hard to break, but two of them were busted, the pieces of which were missing from view. He bent down and opened the first trunk to find nothing, while Shen got up from his seat and opened the trunk he had been sitting on.

    "Find anything?" Shen said, and looked inside. He found a helmet worn by the soldiers from the camp. It was made from wood, a strong thin wood weaved together into a helmet similar to the hats the farmers wore. But, this one was wrapped around the edge in bronze, and decorated with a bronze embellishment at the pointed top. From the top there came a long green ribbon, which rested along the wideness of the helmet. "Wow."

"Woah, nice helmet!" Lao said as he got to the second open trunk. Inside, he found a plethora of things. There were bronze swords, plain and a bit damaged, and even a shield with markings like the Batung capital building had on its interior. But, he only pulled one thing from it, and brought it over to Shen. "Here, try these on," he said.

"What?" Shen looked down and put the helmet atop his head. It rested, fitting perfectly onto his skull, and he grabbed the objects from out of Lao's grasp. They were shin guards, made from plates of bronze weaved together with thick rope, with leather straps and silver buckles where they were to be put onto the wearer.

"Figured you could use a bit of armor. That way you won't get hurt as much, right?"

Shen looked up from the shin guards in his hands and to Lao. A smile came across his face, and he gladly put the armor onto the front of his shins. "Thank you, Lao." He tightened the straps and hooked them into the buckles, hearing the clinking as they rubbed up against the bronze plates. His hand went up to the helmet's brim, and he slid his fingers across the metal trim, feeling its smoothness. Upon the front of the wooden part of the helmet, there was a symbol painted in black.

"Hey," a familiar voice came from the front doorway of the building they stood in, and Reina poked her head in.

"Reina, everything okay?" Shen asked.

"Yeah, everything's alright. I came to tell you something, couldn't find you in that other building, so I just kept looking around," Reina said, wiping a few droplets of blood from her face.

"Reina!" Lao shouted, and closed the trunk, a little bronze dagger he'd found tucked into the back of his trousers, hidden away from Shen's view.

"Hey, Lao. Shen, I did what you asked." She said, and walked in. She sniffed at the air and her face instantly changed, her eyes scowling and her nose twitching. "Ugh, smells like dust in here," she said with a cough.

"You got more food?" Lao asked, walking over to where Shen stood.

Reina wondered what the boy had meant, and then looked to Shen, who gave a little nod. "Uh, no, couldn't find anything to hunt. But, we do still have some meat in the cart to cook up." Reina looked to Shen again, and raised an eyebrow. "What's with the armor?"

"You like it?" Shen asked with a smile. He turned around quickly and the green ribbon from the tip of the helmet swung around as he did. "Lao helped me find it, thought I could use the protection."

"Now, that's a smart kid. You certainly could use it," she said with a little chuckle.

"Hey, what's that supposed to mean? You think I can't hold my own?" Shen retorted.

"I said no such thing. That was all you, you're thinking that," she said.

"I can handle myself," he said, and Lao let out a little giggle from his lips. "I can, you know! I am perfectly capable of protecting myself."

"All I'm saying is it's a lot harder to cut you up when you're protected by a good layer of metal," Reina said. She took her hand and balled it into a fist, then knocked a bit on the front of the silver chest armor she wore, the specialized leather strings fixing it to her muscular frame.

"And that is why I'm glad to have the armor now," Shen said. He walked out of the building past Reina and into the sunlight. "Even though I would be fine without it." He looked around and to the ground, to the light brown dust, the dirt, stained with only a little bit of blood from the soldiers' legs, from Shen stabbing the rocks through their thighs. The soldiers themselves, however, were nowhere to be seen.

"What's the plan, Shen? Are we staying the night here again?" Lao said, coming out of the building next.

"Thank you for reminding me, Lao." Reina pulled her map from the bag at her side, pushing the little glowing rock and Councilwoman Kaishi's directional device out of the way to get to it. She opened up the map and pointed to nearby where they would be, if her idea of how far they'd gone was right. "There should be a town directly east of here. I say we head out after eating and stop there for the night."

"Yes, Yangshan. I've been there before. We should be able to get there by sundown if Ping can go even two-thirds of his fastest speed. Not a problem at all," Shen said, and he walked back in and toward the doorway between the building they were in and the mess hall him and Lao had left. "The fire should be ready to go up at our little camp. I'll get it going. Lao, can you and Reina get the meat and some firewood for me."

"Yeah!" Lao shouted, and ran out of the doorway to the outside, where he would run even further to the trees all around the camp.

"Shen," Reina shouted to the man, who popped his head back into the room.

"Yes, Reina?"

"You're going to have to tell him what this place is, what it really is, at some point."

"You don't think I know that?"

"I think you'd rather keep forgetting to tell him than ever have the idea come up." She walked to the doorway Lao had bolted out of, and leaned up against it on the side of her missing arm, her right side.

"I am, Reina. I'm scared to tell him. What will he think when he learns his own people tried to kill me, killed so many others like me?"

"It's not your place to worry about that." She began walking outside, but turned her head to say one more thing. "He needs to know at some point, what people are capable of," she said softly. She left from out of the building and headed back toward the cart, leaving Shen to think, and to go back to the fire.

In no time at all the two who had left to retrieve wood and meat had returned to the building they'd made camp at. The sun was high up into the sky, a little past directly above them, and shining its light down onto the ground with minimal clouds in the sky. Blue was the blanket that covered the world, dotted with white clouds above them, and darker, gray clouds further off to the east. Shen got the fire crackling wildly, the flames swinging as they climbed up at the spit he had built out of more thick twigs. He grabbed to meat, some saved ramhorn from the metal ice crate, and tied it to the main stick of the spit over the fire. The fire jumped at the hunk of meat, and began to cook it as the heat licked at its surface.

"Smells good." Lao laid back on his sleeping roll with his arms behind his head, using it as a headrest. "Do you have any spices or something you can use to season it, though?"

"Picky much?" Reina said, tapping her boot against the stone floor as she sat up against a wall by the fire.

"What? I can't ask for a little seasoning? Meat is good, but it's even better with a little kick to it," Lao protested.

"Yes, Lao, already ahead of you on that. I have some herbs and spices in a pouch in my bag, which I save for special occasions."

"What's the occasion?" Reina asked.

"Yeah, I'm wondering that too," Lao added.

"Well, after Yangshan, it's right off to Daoyan Caverns. Our destination is almost upon us," Shen said with a smile. He untied the hunk of meat carefully and flipped it over on the stick, then tied it back up as the flames nipped at it. The string was beginning to blacken, and the meat would soon be ready. He reached into his side bag and grabbed for the lightest leather pouch inside, until his fingers met it. The thing was pulled out, and with a little pinch of its contents, Shen sprinkled the seasonings atop the meat and watched the food cook until it was done.

"Oh that does smell really good, even better than before," Reina said.

"I told you! Seasoning makes everything better," Lao said, and sat up from his lax position.

"Has Ping been fed lately?" Shen asked.

"I gave him one of the last apples we have left. We'll have to pick up a few when we get to Yangshan, since we couldn't find any in Sheteng," Reina answered.

"Perfect. Then let's eat too," Shen said. With a few careful slices from his sword, Shen split the meat into three even sections, one for each person. They ate quickly, Lao especially wolfed down his food until he was content, his stomach warm and full.

The three of them finished everything up and began getting ready to start heading back to the cart, led there by Reina. Their things were packed away in bags and their sleeping rolls tucked under their arms as they stood up. The fire was put out, stomped on by Reina's foot, the embers kicked until they were finally extinguished, no more light emanating from them in the slightest. Once everything was cleaned, even the traces of there ever being a fire, they left the building and the camp, moving through the forest back to where Reina and Lao had left the cart and Ping, soundly snoozing away. Shen looked back one more time, at Camp Shi-Li, at where his father was taken from him and from the world of the living. A warmth built up in the corner of one of his eyes, and Shen tilted the brim of his helmet down to hide the tear that came sliding down his cheek.

To Tell a Story

Ping was excited to see Shen when he approached the cart with Reina and Lao. The dimian hopped up and fluttered its little wings that served no other purpose than an ability to flap a short distance forward, if needed. He let out many little happy chirps and one big *squawk* as Shen placed his hand on the feathers of his neck. After a few soothing words from Shen, Reina came around and fixed Ping's harness to the mechanism of the cart, and the whole thing shifted a little as the dimian got comfortable. He stomped his foot against the ground and a little puff of dust came up, and he let out another *squawk* as he stared forward with his huge yellow eyes, the beady black pupils staring in almost opposite directions ahead.

Once Shen and Lao were situated in the back of the cart, under the canopy of the white cloth cover, Reina tugged on the reins and turned the whole cart around to face the east. She had brought it just outside the trees of the forest, and there lay nothing but wide field before them. With one more pull of the reins, Ping took off into the field and they were headed all through the tall grass and fields, bound for the small town of Yangshan, not even named on the map. Though, that's precisely what Reina wondered as she rode atop Ping's saddle harness. How was it that the map was unaware of the name of the town they were headed to? How did Shen know the exact name of said town, and how did he know the time they'd get there? It was true he had said he'd been there, but what was it that took him there? For the time being, Reina made it out to simply be another place he'd visited in his travels, of which Reina had only the slightest inkling.

The landscape around them was beautiful, a wonder to be beheld only by the eyes and which words could not do justice. Fields were tall grass, emerald and swaying in the wind, with little beetles hopping out every now and then. They were plentiful, but only jumped from the sanctuary of the grass in little clusters, maybe of about five or six bugs. Red ones, green ones, even golden beetles, all hopped from one section of grass to the other as they passed by. Grass parted out of the way as little field rodents scurried through it. Lao, curious and attentive to the landscape as much as anything else, noticed another creature while looking from underneath the cloth cover.

There was a field thrush, large and mostly flightless. It was a big bird, probably the size of a log of firewood, and it sat patiently on a gray rock by a patch of taller grass. Waiting, it seemed to be sleeping, but Lao learned what it was doing in just a matter of seconds. It hung its head low, and as a movement in the grass near it showed itself, a group of three field rodents hurrying through, it pounced. The little field rodents, thin fur on their bodies, made no sound as they were snatched up and eaten whole by the field thrush. Once the little animals had been devoured, the bird moved around to the side of the rock it had been sitting on and hid under it, presumably in some sort of underground nest it had fashioned.

Another thing caught Lao's gaze next, and this was not like the field thrush or the bugs had been before it. The field was speckled with brilliant flowers, yes, but he noticed something about a few of them. They appeared in the grass in large patches, swathes of yellow or orange, but some of these patches were marked by rot. Some flowers had started wilting, dying off, turning brown from what would appear as old age. "Shen, should the flowers be dead like that?" He asked, his head still peeking from beneath the white cloth cover of the cart.

Shen brought his head from out of the cart as well, and his green eyes found the dead flowers too, the sickly brown look of them, hanging low like solemn souls. "No, not at all. That's odd." Shen thought for a moment, and his mind jumped around for what could be the cause of the wilting flowers, which by all means should have been vibrant and lively. His first thought, though, took priority in his mind. Zhi-Ming, he thought, was the cause of this, especially this close to where he made his home. But, Shen stayed silent on the matter, and the trip continued on.

After a while, the sunlight faded away from the sky, and the landscape began to become enshrouded with shadow. The light gray clouds encroached on the light and took up the sky, and soon the rains started. It wasn't a downpour as it had been a few days prior, but the incessant drizzle was irksome to say the least, especially for Reina, who had not a helmet with her to shield from the droplets. "Shen, do you mind if I borrow that helmet of yours?"

"Why for? Don't you already have enough armor?" Shen jested.

"It's raining, and I would prefer to make it to Yangshan with as little water as possible in my hair," she retorted.

Shen peeked his head out from under the cloth cover once again, his wide-brimmed helmet grasped in his calloused hands. A few little drops of rain pattered against his head, and dripped softly down the bridge of his nose. "So it is." He brought his head back in and pushed back the area of the cart cover right behind where Reina was sat, just enough for the helmet to fit through the opening. "Here you are," he said, and handed the helmet over.

She grabbed it and quickly put it on, letting the long and thin green ribbon at its tip dangle down to her right side. "Much appreciated." She smiled to herself, and Shen closed the opening he had created in the cloth cart cover. Reina looked out to the landscape ahead as the rain droplets hit the helmet and slid off, dripping down from the sides of the brim. While she had never been in these parts of Batung before, and it was different than most other places in the country, there was something familiar about it. Perhaps it was the way the hills curved along the horizon and bent away in the valleys where the streams flowed through. It almost reminded her of her home, of Vasai, the rivers that barreled through sand and rough dirt. "You said you've been here before?"

"Indeed, I have. Why do you ask," he responded.

"Well, you said you knew Yangshan, and that you'd been there before. I'd thought I'd misheard you for a second." She shifted around in her seat, her rear end getting a bit sore from sitting in the saddle seat for quite a long while. "Personally, it reminds me of home."

"You mean Vasai, right?" Lao asked, resting his head against his sleeping roll, pressed up onto a wooden crate like a pillow.

"Something like that. Now, the landscape here is much more different than in Vasai. Not as many open areas of field like this as much as dense forest. But, nonetheless, it has a weird welcoming quality to it," she said. "Maybe it's just the rain, though. We got a lot of that where I grew up," she said quietly, and let out a little laugh to herself.

Things became quiet after that, and uncomfortably so. Shen thought over what Reina had said earlier in the day. He loathed having to tell Lao what he had encountered in his childhood, in the camps, even after that, while he was on the run and surviving only on what he could catch. But, there was one thing Shen could count on, whether it was to distract Lao and Reina, or distract himself from the thoughts. "I think I have a story."

"Another story?" Reina asked, almost snappy in her tone.

"Oh! Another story! What's it about?" Lao, excited as always at the prospect of a story, nearly jumped from his seat at the words from Shen's lips.

"Well, perhaps if you'll listen, I'll tell you the story," Shen said, smiling slyly.

"I'm listening! I'm listening," Lao repeated, and settled in, quieting down and awaiting the new story that would come from Shen's mind to him.

"In another world not unlike our own," Shen began, "before time itself, there were three beings." He waved his hands in the air in front of him, and from out of the bag on his side, there came out three similar looking rocks. There was nothing special about them, simple brown and rugged rocks, but the way they gathered in the air in front of Shen made them seem mystical. "There was Wei-Fu, the weaver of dreams," he said, and one of the rocks floated forward a bit, before floating back in line with the others. "Yanjing, watcher of dreams," and the next rock floated like the one before it with those words, "and Zei, the stealer of dreams," he said, and the last rock did the same just as the two others had.

"Dreamstealer? He sounds bad," Lao said, raising an eyebrow, his dark brown eyes looking to Shen.

"I suppose it does. But, from his perspective, he was simply misunderstood. But, I will get to that soon. Wei-Fu, the weaver, was to create the fabric that people dreamed in. Whenever they would dream of beautiful sunsets or of wild adventures, or even of terrifying nightmares, Wei-Fu would make the thread which would become the dream." He took a breath, and then continued with his story. "Yanjing, the watcher, was very wise and smart, and knew all things. He would preside over the people's dreams and make sure they were pleasant. If not, and the dreams were evil, scary, or dark, he would tell Zei, the stealer."

"He would steal away the bad dreams?" Lao asked, and even at the saddle in front of them wondered, though silently.

"Exactly, Lao. Zei had the most trying task of the three of them. He would take the negativity, the darkness of the nightmares, and keep it away from the innocent people. But, this made only a problem for Zei. With all of that negativity residing inside him, he found his being corrupted, and he succumbed to his inner feelings of jealousy. You see, Wei-Fu took the form of a beautiful woman, and Yanjing and Wei-Fu quickly cultivated a love of each other. Zei, unable to connect with either of the two, and seeing Wei-Fu's beauty for himself, became envious." Shen took another moment of breath, and then continued once again with his story. "So, one day, Zei began to steal away the good dreams of the people, and leave the bad ones."

"But why would he do that? Wouldn't he have to only collect the bad ones?" Lao asked.

"After being holder of the people's negativity for so long, he became almost like them, corruptible and capable of mistake. He took away the good and soon he became better, but the people were furious, and Wei-Fu and Yanjing would have to confront their companion." Shen raised the rock he had used to demonstrate Zei before, and floated it in front of him. "But Zei was no longer his negative self. He had become positive with all the good dreams he had stolen, and was unsure that he had even done anything wrong. But, all the same, Wei-Fu and Yanjing decided to banish Zei to the realm of mortals, where he had taken the dreams from the people before."

"So he was done with taking people's dreams?" Lao asked.

"Not entirely. Every once in a while, Zei would look in on sleeping people, in the night, and if they were tossing and turning with nightmares, he would steal them away. He did this for many years until he could no longer handle the negativity, and he disappeared into the mountains," Shen finished his story, and lowered the rock back down to the floor, then floated the three of them back into his bag.

"What? That's it? Where did he go? Did he die? What happened to Zei?" Lao asked so many questions, but Shen simply laughed and stayed silent. After a twinge of annoyance passed by him, Lao stopped asking his questions and laughed too, then waited in silence with Shen and Reina as they reached the outskirts of Yangshan.

Shen, who had been peeking his head out of the cart a bit, beheld an abandoned house. It was broken down and the bamboo rotting away a bit, but it seemed sturdy enough to withstand the light drizzle that came from the gray clouds above. "Stop the cart," he said.

"What? Why? We're almost to Yangshan, just beyond that house," Reina questioned.

"I think we should stay in the house for the night. We got surprised by those soldiers before, and the Nettle could still be following us. It'd be best to lay low for our camp," Shen said, and Reina nodded silently, bringing the cart to a stop up at the abandoned house. Lao jumped from the cart and walked to the house, noticing its state.

"Looks just about as rundown as the one on Yedao. Right, Shen?" Lao joked, with a little giggle escaping his lips.

"Maybe better," Shen said, "or worse," he said, this time with a good laugh behind it. "Reina, can I have my helmet back, or are you going to keep it with you for the rest of the day?" Shen said with another laugh.

"Oh, right. Sorry. Almost forgot I was wearing it," Reina said, and reached up with her hand, grabbing the helmet by the brim and handing it back over to Shen. "Do you need it for something?"

"Yes, actually," Shen said, and put the helmet onto his head, fixing it comfortably in place. "I was thinking of bringing Lao with me into town. We've gotta get apples from the market, right? Since Ping's running out."

"Right, right," Reina said.

"If it's not too much trouble, could you get the fire going and get everything settled in while we're gone? We won't be too long, I'm sure, and we can help you when we get back," Shen said. He felt an itch build at his forehead, and reached his hand up to push away a tuft of his dark hair from his brow.

"Fine by me." Reina and Shen exchanged no further words, and she filed off to the house, inspecting it and bringing the sleeping rolls over.

"Come on, Lao. Let's grab those apples," Shen said.

"Right!" Lao smiled, and the two of them left toward the town, all while the light rain steadily fell down from the sky, the darkening clouds hanging above them.

The night would soon be upon them. Sunlight from behind the clouds was dwindling, making them seem darker and more like storm clouds. But, this was not the case, and was simply just the night sky nearing closer to full darkness. They reached the town and the first thing the both of them noticed was the absence of torches. There still stood wooden and bamboo poles, where there would usually be placed a sconce with torch lit and flaming with light. But, instead, there was a glowing rock its place on each short pole. They were similar to the little one Reina kept with her in her bag, but these ones were much larger and much brighter in their orangish light.

People were scarce in the dirt roads, but there were certainly a few. Most of the ones that were outside of the homes and the inns, the shops and any other building there might be, were under leather awnings that sat over doorways, jutting out and shielding them from the rains. They looked to the two entering into the town and eyed them up. This was no farming town like those the three of them had visited before, and instead seemed to be a town mainly involved in trade. The other people outside were merchants, their carts they pulled themselves decked out with all sorts of things to sell.

"Travelers! Oh boy, oh boy! Over here!" A voice called out from near the side of one of the buildings, a bamboo structure which looked to be an inn. Shen and Lao looked to each other and raised their eyebrows, then looked all around to try and find who the voice belonged to. "Yes! You two! I know you've got some shiny Yin in those pockets, and you must be looking for something here, so come on over!" The two looked to each other again, and almost simultaneously, they shrugged their shoulders, walking over to where they heard the voice. "Come on, the side of the inn," the voice said again. The two walked around the side of the bamboo building, until they came upon a man. He sat cross-legged on the ground with a huge bag strapped to his back, with many shelves fixed to the side of it which held all number of things. On the ground at his side there lie several buckets of things, including a bamboo one with apples nearly spilling out of it. "It is I!"

"And who are you?" Lao asked.

"What?" He jumped up and spun around, shocked, his eyes flaring wide. "You don't recognize me?" He had brown eyes, simple and similar to most of the population of Batung. But, his eyes had a weird look to them, a bloodshot look around the white of his eyes, as if he hadn't gotten any sleep in weeks. He wore tattered clothing made from thinly pressed hide, with an embroidered design upon it, and a big cloth coat over that. His hair was missing atop his head, but there were tufts of black hair on the sides, above his ears, crazy and unkempt. He was short too, only a little bit taller than Lao was.

"Not a single clue," Shen said.

"It is none other than," he braced himself, spinning again, and throwing his arms up in a theatrical pose. "The great Wan Yingbi! Merchant of the Eastern Shores!"

He waited a moment for a response from his audience, but Shen and Lao just looked upon him with amused confusion. "I still don't know who you are," Lao said.

"And I neither," Shen added.

"Agh!" Wan cried, and fell backward, sitting back down onto the ground with his legs crossed, just as he had before. "Well, you do still have Yin, don't you?" He asked in a defeated tone, his eyelids drooping over his eyes. "Yin you'd be willing to spend?"

"We do, as a matter of fact," Shen said, and Wan's eyes lit up, the dark tan skin of his face brightening. "About ninety-eight coins of it."

Wan smiled widely and started to show off everything he had with him. "What do you want? What are you looking for?" He brought a wooden case from off one of the shelves on the side of his bag, and brought it up to Lao's face, that stood right in front of the little man sitting there. "Rings? Jewels? I have good prices!" He opened up the case and there sat a few silver rings, some gold ones, and a good amount of differently colored gemstones.

"Um, no, not really," Shen said.

"No trinkets or jewels, huh? Maybe you'd want some weapons? I'm sure I've got something you could want," he said, and opened up his coat. Along the inside there were little knives made from different metals. There were dark iron ones, bright silver ones, a few gold daggers, and even one made from crystal, no doubt crafted by a long-dead Mystic blacksmith, the only individual capable of creating such a weapon. "Come on, take your pick."

"We don't need, or want for that matter, weapons either," Shen said. "We're just here for some apples, that's all."

"Apples!" He brought the bucket they'd seen before around from his side, and a few of them fell out. "Take the whole bucket! Please! They're fresh from the orchard just a few miles from here," he said, and continued his rambling on. "You know, they haven't had that good of a harvest in weeks. The apples just fall right off the trees and rot right on the ground in just three days! Nasty thing, too, smell that'll travel through solid rock if you had a bunch of them. But, these ones, oh no, not these apples." He patted them, and the rain that had been slowly dripping down made them shine. "These ones have been fresh-picked and perfect! And they've been that way for weeks, I'd reckon."

"Please, you can stop trying to sell them, we'll buy." Shen reached under the flap of the bag, his hand grabbing for the leather coin pouch, filled with little silver coins. "Just tell me how much and I'll be sure to pay you."

"Ah, well, these fresh babies will run you about 22 Yin," Wan said.

"What? Twenty-two! That's preposterous! For this many it'd be 15 Yin!" Shen protested, shouting at the little man before him.

"H-hey! Don't get too angry about it. Fresh apples like these are hard to come by these days." He grabbed a small pouch from a shelf on the other side of his bag, and brought it forward. "Hey, I'll throw in these spices from the next town over, they're famous in the mainland Batung! Honest!"

"Hm," Shen said, and thought for a moment. Lao wound his leg back and placed a firm kick into Shen's shin armor. "Ow! Hey, what was that for?"

"You can't pass up that offer! Those seasonings have got to be premiere, Shen! And I'm pretty sure we've still got a good amount of meat left to use it on," Lao said, his mouth nearly watering at the mere prospect of the seasoned meat.

"Alright, alright, I'll pay it," Shen said.

"Oh my! Thank you so much, sir! You won't regret this, not one bit," Wan said. "Just twenty-two little silver coins and you can be on your way."

"Yeah, yeah. I know. Just take the money and you can be on your way." Shen reached his fingers into the pouch in his hands and counted eleven coins in his palm. He pulled his hand back out and gave the coins to Wan. Then, he reached his fingers right back into the pouch and seized eleven more, handing them over again to the little man waiting patiently with his hands open.

"Oh thank you, thank you, thank you! Oh my little shiny babies. Look at you," he mumbled his words in a high-pitched voice, and ran the tip of his finger over all the little silver coins in his hand.

"Um, thank you?" Shen said. Wan was preoccupied, eyeing up his coins, and Shen took this time to take the pouch of seasoning and place his own pouch of coins back into his bag along with it. "Lao, grab the apples and let's go, before he notices we've left," Shen said. With a little chuckle, Lao grabbed the bucket of apples with the both of his hands and began to carry it away. The two of them walked out of town slowly, and unlike their steps, the sun fell beneath the horizon quickly. It was full night by the time they arrived back to the abandoned house, and the only way they found it was by the light of the fire on the inside.

"Reina, we're home!" Lao shouted, and lightly kicked open the door of the house.

"Lao, quiet down," Shen said.

"Oh stop it, Shen. I think we're safe enough to bust this house up, busted as it already is," Reina said, and poked at the fire with a stick. As Shen looked to her, he noticed something which had changed about her since the first time he laid eyes on her. The two dark blue horizontal lines that were once painted upon the bridge of her nose, they were gone. He figured they'd been washed away by the rain, or by sweat, or most likely had been washed from her face when they bathed in the stream with the soap berries. "I took out a bit of Ailfish from the icebox. I figured we could cook it for a meal, it's light enough."

"Sounds like a good idea to me," Shen said with a smile, taking out the pouch of seasonings he'd bought from Wan.

"What's that?" Reina asked.

"Seasonings!" Lao shouted, and set down the bucket of apples. He took one of them from the top, a fine-looking one with a good shine to it in the light of the fire. He walked from out of the house and brought the apple to Ping, who gladly gobbled it down in one chomp.

"You got more? Where'd you get them?" Reina said, getting up and grabbing the Ailfish set atop an old table Reina had cleared off.

"Don't ask," Shen said, and took a seat in a rickety old chair in a corner. He shifted around in the seat and a creaking sound came from under him.

Lao came back inside and the three of them continued to pass the time. The Ailfish finished cooking and after Shen had thoroughly seasoned it, they each got their shares of it, and ate it all in no time. Full from the food, Lao began to get tired, and soon he settled into his sleeping roll placed in the corner by Reina. He fell into a deep sleep, like Ping who slept just outside, and even snored a bit as the other two still left awake conversed.

"You still haven't told him," Reina said, "about the camp."

"I just can't, Reina."

"And I've noticed something, too, that you've done time and time again." She relaxed in her seat on the floor, atop her sleeping roll she had laid flat on the wood. "Why do you tell him all those stories?"

"What do you mean?"

"On our way to Sheteng, you told him the story of Heijian's sword. And, just on our way here, you told him that story about the dreamstealer. He's told me before that you tell him all kinds of stories, even before I joined you two." She looked him in the eyes, her hazel eyes glinting in the light of the flames, and his glimmering green. "So why do you do it?"

"When I was a child, I'd tell my brother stories to keep him calm and get him to bed. When I was in the camp, my father used to tell the children stories, especially in the nights when things got dark." He looked to the fire, and sat in his sleeping roll on the floor too. "It kept them distracted from what was going to happen to them."

"And what is that, exactly?"

"Reina, you know good and well what would happen to them. You yourself were a witness to what they did to my kind."

"I know."

"What did you do, anyway, after you lost your arm?"

"You're deflecting again, from the subject," Reina said.

"Just answer the question. Hey, you can even tell a story of your own," he said, a smirk across his face.

She settled in and reached her hand up to her neck, where the spirit mask she once wore would have been. But, her mind wandered and remembered she had left it in the back of cart. "After I lost my arm?" She asked. Shen nodded softly. "Well, after I lost the arm they put me on leave. I got to look over the operations on all the Mystics they rounded up and killed in Vasai and Ogon. I knew firsthand just what they were doing," she said. "There came a point where I couldn't handle it anymore. What had these people done to me that I'd have them killed? They never did any harm to me. So, I packed all my things, reported to General Hatsu, and left for Batung."

"That's it? You just up and left?"

"I suppose so, yeah. I traveled by boat to the mainland. When I first got here, I'll always remember this, I got stopped by a man. He said his wife and daughter were Mystics, that they had lived in Vasai before they were taken away by my team. Apparently, he recognized my armor and my mask, which is what we wore when taking in the Mystics." She reached her hand to her hair and pushed away a bit of it, and turned around a bit. Upon the back of her neck, there was a big scar Shen hadn't noticed before on her light tan skin, pinkish from fading. "Took out a knife right there on the street and slashed at me from behind."

Without any words, Shen got up and took off his tunic. He felt the soft cloth glide over his tan skin until he held it bunched up in his hands. On the small of his back, which came into view as he turned around, there was a huge scar in his skin. Reina could tell it had been deep, and if there were any more focus put into the slash it came from, Shen would've been nearly dead or paralyzed. "I got one too." Shen had gotten it from the soldier, the one that was to slaughter him, but missed the chance just as the camp's gates were blasted open.

"Looks like your kind and mine are even," Reina said with a smirk.

Shen put his tunic down onto the ground next to his sleeping roll and settled back into it, sitting with it up around his outstretched legs. "That man, the one who gave you that scar, he was a Mystic?"

"No. No he wasn't," she said.

After that, things were silent. Shen couldn't find any other words to say, and Reina had already quickly fallen asleep in the warmth of her sleeping roll. Shen, though, was awake with thought. He thought chiefly of his brother. Just mentioning him and telling him stories, he could get a clear picture of him in his head. Blue eyes, black hair, and tan skin like his own that was perfect and unblemished. It had been so long since he last saw him. Shen looked to the fire, and whether it was from its light, or its warmth, or the longing to see and hold his little brother again, he let a few tears drip from the corners of his eyes. He sat there for awhile, clutching his tunic in his hands, with his brother the only thing on his mind. After that he too fell into sleep, and the night passed on like nothing, the rain tapping on the roof of the house lightly as the three of them slumbered.

The Last Stretch

  The morning came with the sound of tapping at the wall of the house. Shen and Lao got up first, and the first thing either of them noticed was the sound of the rain. It had picked up quite a bit in the night, almost reaching a downpour, and Ping had come to the house to get out of it. As Shen came to the wall where the tapping sounded, he noticed it was Ping making the sound, pecking at the wood with his big beak. "Now, what's that for," he said with a yawn. The bird looked at him, head cocked, with a blank stare for a few moments, then belted out a *squawk* that nearly shook the rickety old house. "Good morning to you too, Ping. Lao, would you get Reina up. We'll need to leave right quick to get to the caverns by dusk."
  "Shen, are you forgetting something?" Lao asked, Shen's tunic held in his grasp.
  Shen felt a little warmth build up in his cheeks, and walked speedily over, grabbing the tunic from out of Lao's hands. "Yes, can't believe I forgot to put it back on."
  "Put it back on?" Lao wondered.
  "I had taken it off in the night, couldn't sleep, it was getting too hot for me," Shen said. He walked over to a chair right by Reina where he had placed his bag and grabbed it. As the weight was lifted from the wood it let out a mighty creaking, which seemed to be enough to rouse Reina enough from her sleep.
  "Would you keep it down, I'm trying to sleep," she mumbled. After a few seconds, the realization of their ongoing journey set in, and she hopped right

up and out of her sleeping roll. "Wait! I almost forgot what today was. We're finally getting to Daoyan!"

"Excellent recovery, Reina," Lao jested.

"Oh shush, kid. You would've forgotten too if it weren't for that celebratory meat he made us," she said.

"Hey! You know you liked that stuff just as much as me." Lao looked to her pouting, while his hands were occupied with rolling up his sleeping roll. Once it was all in a little bundle he walked out the door and settled into the back of the cart.

"Are we going to talk about last night?" Shen wondered aloud.

"I don't see any reason why we would need to. You gave me your side of the story, and I gave mine. I'll tell you, I can see why you do it, you're good at it." She grabbed her sleeping roll and rolled it up into a neat bundle too, then stuffed it under her arm. Carefully, she grabbed for her hip bag and let the sleeping roll fall from her grasp. With her hand now free, she fastened the bag onto herself, where it sat dangling at her hip. She then reached back down to the floor and took the sleeping roll again.

"I have just one question, and you don't even have to answer me. I've just gotta ask."

"Anything, Shen."

"Did they suffer? Those soldiers at the camp, did they suffer before you ended it?"

She deliberated for a moment. When she had done it, took the lives of those soldiers, she had considered making them suffer. She had thought about dismembering them for the things they might've done, the horrible things they supported. But, she decided against it. She had thought to herself, that if she made them suffer, she would be no better than those she loathes. "No. I didn't. I couldn't bring myself to do that," she said, her head lowered and her tone muted.

"Thank you. I feel awful for making you do it in the first place. I just couldn't bring myself-"

"Hey. Just drop it. We don't have much time to feel bad, we've gotta get going," she said. She was looking right at him now, and there was a smile on her face. It was genuine, and Shen could see that, from the glint of joy in her hazel eyes.

"Right." He said softly. "Lao!"

"Yeah, Shen?" The boy shouted from outside, his voice muffled a bit.

He walked outside once he'd rolled up his sleeping roll and held open the flap of the cart cover. "Make sure you're not forgetting anything. We won't be coming back here."

"I'm not! Now, can we go? I'm ready to take on Zhi-Ming already!" The boy said, an excited glimmer in his brown eyes. He reached his hand back and scratched at the back of his neck, where the shaved down black hairs were slowly growing back.

"Oh, now don't get ahead of yourself. You won't be doing much fighting," Shen said.

"What? Why not?" He said.

"Zhi-Ming, in case you hadn't gathered, is an incredibly formidable spirit. I'm not letting you get yourself killed because you want a bit of fun. I wouldn't be a good caretaker if that happened, would I?" Shen said.

"I guess not," Lao muttered.

"Alright," Shen said, and began walking over to where Reina was tending to Ping, and the front of the cart. He had expected her to be standing next to the dimian. But, to his surprise, she was sat atop the saddle, the reins held firmly in her hand's grip. "Hey, what are you doing?"

"Painting a beautiful self-portrait," she joked, "I'm driving the cart. Is that not what it looks like?"

"You brought it here. Your butt's gotta be at least a little bit tired from sitting in that saddle all this time," Shen said.

"You still need to get some rest. And in any case, who are you to speak for my butt?" She smirked, and raised an eyebrow, a few heavy droplets of rain dripping down her brow.

"Alright. But after this whole Zhi-Ming thing is over, I'm taking the reins," Shen said.

"Sure. That is, if you have the strength to take them from me," she said snappily, and the smirk got wider on her lips. A bit irritated, Shen walked to the back of the cart, and settled under the cloth cart cover with Lao.

"She take the reins from you?" Lao asked, letting out a little giggle.

"She called me weak," he said, crossing his arms.

They took off through the town of Yangshan, heading southeast, with the aid of the device given to them by Councilwoman Kaishi. She made sure to let the little rock arrow inside it point to the chalk indication of north. From there, she went the direction that would be southeast, gleaned from using the northward point as a reference. Reina felt a good sense of pride as she guided the cart in the direction of Daoyan Caverns, until the feeling of dread set in. The fight ahead would be a perilous one, and she would have to be prepared for whatever might end up happening. She felt her own personal endangerment, and then took to worrying about her two companions.

Soon, though, she would need to worry about something else. Since Ping was going much slower, brought to a mere walking speed by the rain, the surroundings were much easier to look to. There seemed to be signs that they were being followed. No tracks or anything, as that would be foolish of the ones that were following them. But, she noticed that as they moved along the path of dirt and mud that cut through the grass and parted two sections of trees, birds would flutter up out of the trees. This would be no cause for concern, but it was the timing of them that threw her off. They would fly up and away with a beating of their wings behind them, after they had already passed through. It was as if there were others in the trees, following the cart just behind, stirring up the birds as they trailed them.

"Shen," she whispered back.

Shen pulled back a part of the flap of the cover. "What is it, Reina?"

"I think we're being followed," she said.

Shen let go of the flap and moved to another end of the back of the cart. He lifted another section of the cloth cover from the bottom, and the muted light of the sun came to him. As he could see in front of him, they were passing by whole droves of forest, tall trees and patches of bamboo that climbed up toward the little light the dark clouds let loose. But as they moved along the path, he too noticed the birds taking off from out of the trees. In his mind, he knew they were being followed, and he thought just who it might be that would follow them in this manner.

"I hate to say it, but I agree with you," he said. "I think it's the Nettle and its companions."

"Nettle? You think it's caught up with us? Even after Mao?" Reina said.

"Yes. I think it's been trailing us since then."

"What do you propose we do?" Reina asked, and Lao began to get worried. He looked to the bow and arrows he had used against Mao's mercenaries, and feared he might have to use them again.

"I think we can trap them."

"Are you crazy?" Reina snapped back.

"Think of it like this. They don't know we know they're following us, right?" Shen said.

"I suppose not. They wouldn't be able to tell from that far away," Reina replied.

"Precisely. I think if we can make them think we've stopped for whatever reason, maybe I act sick, we can trick them into getting caught." He let a smirk creep across his face as he let go of the cover he was holding up, and came back to behind where Reina sat.

"You think that'll work?" She asked.

"It's worth a try," he said. "This might be our only chance to get close enough to catch the Nettle for good." Shen grabbed for his helmet, brushing off some dust from the surface of the wide-brimmed, flattened cone-shaped helmet. The metal that wrapped around in two bands shined with a bit of the rain it had gotten on it, dripping down from Shen's face.

"What should I do, Shen?" Lao asked. "Can I help? I can take on a few of them!" He jumped up from his seat on one of the wooden crates, punching at the air as if there were an opponent before him. "I think I can get a hang of the bow."

"You won't be fighting. We can't risk you getting hurt," Shen said.

"What? Again?" Lao whined.

"Yes, again. The Nettle is an incredibly dangerous spirit. We won't be fighting it and its companions, we'll be trapping them, and you can't be getting in the way of that," Shen said. "You might be killed."

After that there was silence, not another word from Lao or Shen, or even Reina. She brought the cart a bit farther down the path until they reached a fork in the dirt road. The road they had followed diverted into three separate paths. The leftmost path led through the forest and splintered off into many other paths, going to all kinds of towns, and most likely even leading to the capital. The middle path led through the two sections of trees and bamboo, and just a bit more to Daoyan Caverns. The rightmost path, though, led right into the trees and bamboo, presumably to a town on the other side, where the path would then divulge into many other paths. These would most likely run even more eastward, to where the port town of Gangkou stood.

    Deciding quickly, Reina steered Ping and the cart down the rightmost path. The cart slowly crept into the trees and bamboo, and soon they reached an end of the path, finding where they'd make camp as a few more clusters of birds flew up into the air further behind them. Reina pulled on the reins in her hand and Ping slowed down to a complete stop. He let out a few low chirps as the rain came dropping down onto his feathers, and as Reina jumped down from the seat of the saddle. "Shen. Come on, we've gotta set up camp. Start acting sick," she said.

    Shen and Lao came from out of the camp with Shen's arm draped over the boy's shoulders. Shen put forth hefty coughs, covering his mouth with his other hand, and hobbled over to a tree. No words were spoken, and instead, everyone was busy setting up a small camp. The sleeping rolls were taken from out of the back of the cart by Reina, and she even grabbed a large swatch of cloth to make a little tent for Lao to pretend to sleep in. She hung up part of the cloth on a branch of a tree, and let the rest of it hang diagonally, providing shelter from the rain. Once that was set up, Lao handed Shen over to Reina and grabbed his sleeping roll. The boy brought it over to his makeshift tent, and set it inside, letting Reina tend to Shen at the back of the cart.

"You think they're buying it?" Shen asked, letting out another fake cough.

"Considering you're actually a bit weaker than usual, yes, I think they are," Reina said with a laugh, holding a wet piece of cloth to his forehead.

"Would you give that a rest? The joke's not funny anymore."

"Really? Because, I'm definitely laughing," she said with another chuckle. After giggling a little more, she relaxed herself and continued rubbing the cloth along his forehead. "You think pulling into the trees was a good idea?"

"Perfect actually. The Nettle seems to take to the trees and pick off the opponents it can see."

"And hiding us in the back of the cart, and Lao in the tent, that makes it so that it can't see."

"Exactly. Now the Nettle has to get close, close enough for us to get the drop on it."

"What about its companions? You mentioned it kept a few other spirits with it to help."

"No. It seemed like the other ones were only there to tend to whatever the Nettle had left behind. Scraps. We shouldn't have to worry about them unless we get apprehended first." Shen let out another cough, and looked outside the cart cover at the rain steadily falling from the darkening clouds above. The rains began to pick up pace, and the sound of it nearly drowned out all other sounds.

Soon, though, a new sound surprised the two sitting at the back of the cart. It was the sound of wings flapping. Were it not for the closeness and ferocity of the sound, Shen and Reina would have dismissed it as the Nettle getting closer, more birds flocking away from them. But, the two could not move fast enough to avoid what was making the sounds. The cart cover was suddenly torn apart and the culprits, four adult hookbeaks with glaring beaks and glinting eyes, beat at their faces with their wings.

The feathers smacked against them and some flew from the wings of the creatures, floating down to the ground and the floor of the back of the cart, as the hookbeaks screeched. Reina tried to reach for her sword at her back, but a hand grabbed her by the wrist and twisted her arm behind her back. Next thing she knew, there was the feeling of cold metal pressed to the skin at the front of her neck, and someone standing behind her. "Now, wouldn't want to do anything too drastic, would we?"

"So, you were the ones following us," she said through gritted teeth.

"Guilty," he said. "But now we've got you."

She looked around, and two other figures came from out of the patch of bamboo nearby. They were bandits, cloaked in tattered clothing and geared up with rugged swords. Shen, still in the back of the cart while she was walking away from it, was held by point of another of the bandits' sword, and ushered out of the cart. "Shen!"

"Don't, Reina." He said.

"Listen to the man, will you? One wrong move from you and I'll have your blood spilling out of your throat faster than my hookbeak can catch a mouse." The bandit behind her smirked, and one of the hookbeaks that attacked them settled on his shoulder.

"Alright. Alright," she said, pleading. She held her arm still in the grip of the bandit behind her, trying not to do anything that might set the bandits off. Her hazel eyes darted around and counted out four bandits, including the one bringing her over to a tree by her arm, each of them with a hookbeak on their shoulder. When she was brought over to one of the trees, along with Shen, they were both promptly tied up and secured. They would be unable to move, and as the bandit wrapped a thick rope around their heads and had them clench it between their teeth, Reina and Shen were unable to make a sound louder than a muffled grunt either.

"There. Can't have you screaming for help now, can we?" He said with a dirty grin.

Elsewhere, Lao heard the bandits shuffling around in the back of the cart. Thankfully, Shen's bronze sword was out of sight, hidden at the way back of the cart inside one of the larger crates. But, unfortunately, that would mean it was only a matter of time before it was found and taken. He worried too if they would just up and kill Shen and Reina. They had them right where they wanted them, at their mercy, and it would take barely any effort to take their lives. Lao thought and thought, holding his breath quietly. He had to devise a plan, something fast, something that would save his two companions and get the upper hand on the bandits. He poked his head out from his little tent, and like he'd figured, he saw Shen and Reina tied up to the tree.

He had to think of something fast, faster than the bandits could either find their valuables or him. Peeking his head out from the cover of his little tent, he saw the four bandits. Two of them had a hookbeak on their shoulder and their backs turned to the boy, looking instead toward the two prisoners tied to a tree. Another of the bandits, one with a deep and glaring scar upon his left eyebrow that was pale against her dark tan skin, was walking about aimlessly. The last one though, was occupied with rooting through the cart's contents. He shifted through everything with his torso under the cover, and his hookbeak perched atop the cart, looking out toward the other bandits in their group. Both the creature and its owner were facing away from Lao, giving him perfect opportunity to sneak by.

Readying himself, he reached his hand to the back of his trousers, and grasped the little bronze dagger he'd gotten from the camp. He held its handle in his grip and carefully walked over, crouched low to the ground, each step incredibly slow. His plan was to sneak up behind the bandit with his head in the cart, slice at the back of his knees quickly, and then jump into the cart to retrieve the sword. That was as far as he got with the plan. He held a clear picture of where the sword was, held tightly in its leather scabbard, sat behind one or two wooden crates. It was out of view of the bandit, but if he didn't move quick enough, that would change.

He came up into the treeline, directly behind the bandit and many steps behind, and realized something. The hookbeak was no longer facing away from him. Before setting off the bandit, Lao turned and ran into the trees behind him, taking to the left, where he'd come from. The hookbeak screeched wildly and took off, flapping its wings briefly before landing on the dirt and grass and bolting into the trees after the boy.

"Hey, Zhe, what was that?" The female bandit with the eyebrow scar shouted out, twirling a silver dagger in her hand.

"Just my hookbeak," the bandit rifling through the cart said, still under the cover, pushing away a few crates smaller crates.

"What set it off?"

"I don't know, Qiao," Zhe snapped, "probably a mouse or a weasel, or something."

"Alright, alright," the female bandit whined, and then took back to walking aimlessly

In the trees, Lao ran around the trunks quickly, as the hookbeak that followed him in climbed upon them. Its sharp talons scratched off pieces of bark, and Lao dodged frantically as the bird got close and snapped its beak or swiped its talons at him. He had to think of something. It was too late for him to catch this thing by surprise, it was already hot on his trail, its ratty tail whipping around and gripping onto the thin tree trunks as it came after him. There had to be some kind of opening for him to slash or stab this creature. To his luck, as he looked at it, dodging out of the way, he noticed a pattern with its hunting of him. Each time it would wrap its tail around another tree trunk, it would swing around and take a snap at him with its curved beak.

    Armed with this new knowledge, he quickly put into action his new plan. When the hookbeak whipped its tail around a new thin tree trunk, and right after it snapped it him with its beak, he slashed the creature in the tail. The blow left a mark in the tree, and it even brought the creature down to the ground. Without even thinking, Lao jumped to the creature while it was writhing, and wrapped his fingers around the beak, shutting it from snapping open at him. In his other hand he held the grip of the bronze dagger, and brought the blade down into the neck of the hookbeak, spurting out blood as the creature squirmed around. He stabbed it once again in the neck, and then another time in the chest.

    After just a few moments, the hookbeak stopped moving, and its eyes rolled back, the beady black of them that once glinted with animal rage now extinguished. He pulled the blade from out of the bird and only then realized the weather, as hefty drops of rain fell down from the leaves above and splashed onto him and the bloody dagger in his hands. Soon the rain even washed away most of the hookbeak's blood left on the blade, and when Lao snuck back to his position behind the bandit, the blood was barely stained. He moved forward, and his footsteps were unheard by Zhe, the bandit in the cart. Once he was within striking distance, determined Lao with his heart pounding leaped forward.

    In a quick whipping motion of his arm, he slashed deep into the muscle at the back of the bandit's knees. The man dropped backward down to the ground, and Lao jumped into the cart, dropping his dagger in the process. "Gah!" Zhe screamed. "Tang! Lang! I need help!" He shouted, and the twin bandits watching Shen and Reina rushed over to him. Lao was out of sight inside the cart, hurriedly pushing crates out of the way until he came upon the sword. It sat on the floor of the cart at the way back, near the metal icebox and where Shen left his helmet in his acting sickly, and Lao grabbed the weapon frantically. He took it from out of the scabbard, tossing it to the side, and held the weapon in his hands, then moved to the side of the cart by where his two companions were being held.

"Zhe! What happened," The bigger of the two bandits asked.

"I don't know! There must be a third of these idiots. I think they're in the cart, get them!"

As Lao heard those words, he jumped from out of the cloth cart cover and rushed over to Shen and Reina. His hands twitched and shook as he removed the rope at their mouths. "Reina, no time, do the hookbeak call!" The woman before him moved her lips a certain way, positioned her tongue, and blew air out. A familiar call filled the air, and the sound of the three other hookbeaks taking off joined the sounds of rain and footsteps in the air.

"Over by those other two! Go!" Zhe shouted, and soon all three of the other bandits were gathered around Lao.

"Think you can run," the smaller of the twin bandits said.

"You wish," the bigger one said.

"I'm not sure how you eluded us, but you're going to regret you did," the female one said. Each of them carried a different weapon. The bigger of the twins carried a wooden club, the smaller one a thick iron sword, and the female bandit of course wielded her dagger.

"Lao, I need you to listen to me" Shen said.

"What? What is it?" Lao pleaded, his heart beating furiously inside his chest.

"Lead them over to me and I can grab them with my powers. But I need you to focus and lead them to me, got it?" He thought for a moment and then furrowed his brow. "Do whatever you have to with the sword, just get them to me."

"I thought you didn't want me to fight," Lao snapped back.

"That's not really an option right now! Just do it!" Shen shouted, and the female bandit lurched forward. Instinctively, Lao slashed at her thigh with the sword. The weapon was heavy, even in the grip of his two hands, but he managed to get a fairly deep cut into her skin. The tattered cloth of her trousers tore, and began to stain with blood. She yelped out in pain and became angry, dashing at the boy. Lao moved a bit next to Shen, and she was stopped abruptly by rocks at her ankles, clutching her firmly to the ground..

"Mystic! Watch out for the man, and don't get too close," she cried. She noticed Lao not paying much attention, and threw her dagger at his leg. He shifted, though, and the blade only nicked him in the ankle.

"Ah!"

"It's alright, Lao, stay focused," Shen yelled.

While Reina was fidgeting her hand behind her, trying to free herself from the rope, Lao had a tougher obstacle to face now. The twin bandits were now after him, at the same time, and on top of that they now knew of Shen's abilities. The smaller one swung his sword slowly downward at him, and Lao rolled out of the way. Fortunately for him the blade embedded itself into the ground, and Lao had time to slash at the bandit's leg. But, before he could, the breath was knocked right from his lips as he was sent into Shen by the bigger bandit's club. He felt along his chest with one of his hands, heaved his lungs, and finally regained breath as the bandit slowly walked up to him.

"Thought you could get the drop on my brother did you?" He smirked, but the look went away as he tried to take a step forward. Rocks and dirt gathered at his ankles, and he was unable to move. In a last ditch effort, he tossed his club at Lao, who had gotten back up. The boy, though, had other plans, as he ducked out of the way. The smaller bandit, sword in hand he'd finally pulled from the ground, ready to swing, was right behind Lao when he had ducked, and was struck in the stomach by his brother's club. Taking the opportunity, Lao stabbed the bandit through the leg with the sword as he lie on the ground out of breath. Pinned to the ground, the bandit was unable to move, and Shen quickly raised more rocks to lock his ankles down onto the ground.

Reina, finally free from the rope, stood up and surveyed the area. "Lao? Did you do this?" She asked. Without an immediate answer, she turned to the boy, who was sat on his rear and clutching his face in his hands. "Lao, are you alright?" She asked, rushing to his side, her hand on his back.

"I'll be alright," the boy muttered.

At the Mouth of Daoyan

"Lao," Reina shouted with a smile on her face, "you did incredible! You stopped all four of them all on your own?"

"It wasn't incredible, it was foolish," Shen said, shedding the scraps of rope that had once tied him to the tree. He rubbed at the red marks on his arms left by the ropes, more pinkish in color on the tan of his skin. "He got lucky."

"Lucky? That had to have at least taken some skill, right?" Reina said.

Shen thought for a moment with a hand to his stubbled chin, the hairs of which had been growing steadily since their time on Yedao. "Yes. I suppose he did do well enough before he needed my help." Shen walked around to the cart, not paying attention to his own sword that stuck bloody through the larger bandit's leg, through the shin, where the cloth of his trouser legs was ripped and torn.

"You, you pile of dirt," Zhe grunted out, trying to get close to them by crawling on the ground. He let his bloodied legs, the muscle still slashed at the back of his knees and aching with pain, drag lazily behind him as he creeped along the dirt with his arms. "Bring that kid over here and let me get a rematch. Come on, I'm sure I can get a few hits in," he muttered. His face was plastered with splotches of mud, and as he lifted his face from off the ground the rains that fell from the dark clouds began to wash it away.

Shen knelt down and looked to the man's legs, the blood staining his hide trousers and dripping from the fabric to the ground. "Zhe, right? I need only ask you one thing."

The bandit at Shen's feet spat out a wad of saliva, which landed right on the top of his right foot. "Bite me."

"Are you with the Nettle?" Shen asked plainly.

"Nettle? That spirit? Why would I be working with some spirit, those things hate humans more than I hate your kind," Zhe said with a smirk, his lips slightly stained with mud. "Never even," he grunted, "seen the thing."

"Let's go," Shen said. He flicked his wrist up and grabbed Zhe by the ankles with rocks, and the bandit moved forward no longer. Afterward, Shen reached into the bag at his side and pulled from it a few pieces of bandage cloth. He wrapped it around the bandit's wounds, only after placing down some herbs, and fixed it tightly to the backs of his knees. "There. The bleeding should be slowed just enough, and those herbs should help with fighting off infection. Your companions should be getting free from those rocks by the time we leave." Shen leaned close and spoke sternly. "Don't come after us."

He walked past and Reina walked after him. "Shen. We need to talk," she said.

Shen, who was stood next to Ping, petting the dimian's neck, feeling the softness of his light brown feathers. "No, we need to get on the road. We're already running slower than usual because of the rain and we need to reach the caverns by nightfall."

Reina lunged forward and grabbed Shen by the tunic, gripping a handful of the tunic. She dragged him to the side of the cart and shoved him into the side of it. "Look. I am getting sick and tired of your righteousness, alright? You've either gotta treat him less like a child, or quit acting like you're so above everything." She clenched her teeth and almost growled her words. "He took them down. Yes, he needed your help, and yes, it was reckless. But we wouldn't be standing here and talking right now if he just sat around like you want him to."

"What do you want me to do, Reina?" Shen said quietly, in an almost whisper shout. "He could get himself killed. I can't have that blood on my hands."

"Give him a chance. He uses that sword well, why don't you give it to him?" She said.

"What?"

"The sword. You can teach him how to use it, to protect himself. If you keep treating him like a helpless child, he'll always be in danger, but if you do something about it he won't need you to protect him all the time." She let go of her grip on his tunic, and took a step back. "He needs to know what this world is like, especially the cruelty. Only then can he be as safe as you want him." She walked to the back of the cart, and spoke something under her breath. "It's not like you use the sword much anyway."

Something seemed to change in Shen's face. He blinked his eyes a few times and walked straight away from her, over to the tree they had been tied to, where Lao still sat. While Reina was busy fixing the mess in the back of the cart, Shen pulled the sword from out of the big bandit's leg. "Gah! Oh, oh that stings," he cried, and the pain began to numb out.

"Shen, I'm sorry I didn't mean to steal it. I just, I had to-"

"Lao, it's fine. You did very well."

"Really?" The boy asked.

"Yes. I think… I think it's time that I teach you a few things," Shen said, and held out the sword in his hands. "Here."

"Okay, what happened to the real Shen?" He joked, a little smile upon his lips.

"I'm serious. You hate being treated like a child. You're not one, and I think I need to realize that. So, I'll teach you how to fight. But, you have to take this seriously. This weapon is dangerous and should only be used when you need to use it."

"It's not a toy, right, you've told me this before."

"Before you steered Ping right into an old lady's cabbage cart."

"Please don't remind me. I think I've still got a bruise on my hip from that," Lao said.

"Lao. After Zhi-Ming is dead, and he will be, and we get to Zhimai, I will start training you." Shen remained holding out the sword, and raised his eyebrows at it. "Go on, take it." Lao reached his hands out and grabbed it by the grip with both of his hands, just as the blood from the blade was nearly all washed away from the rain. The boy swung it around in focused strikes, his eyes lighting up, the rain falling and bouncing from off the surface of his skin, and Shen looked on at him. He wondered if it was the right thing to do, if letting Lao fight would be more benefit than not. But, there was not much more time to think of such things, as Reina had readied Ping's harness and returned over to the two of them.

"We're just leaving them here?" She asked, raising an eyebrow.

"We've got no choice. The further we get, the easier it will be for them to get out of those rocks, my power's hold on them will only weaken." He walked over to the cart and reached under the cloth cover, feeling around with his hands, until he pulled them back out with his helmet in their grip. "We should be long gone by the time they can get after us," he said, and put the helmet on his head. The rain fell steadily from the sky and hit the surface of his helmet, some of it soaking into the strong wood and other droplets sliding down off the wide, flat cone shape of it.

"Good. I'd like to get a good nap in without having to worry about them again. Though, I'm pretty sure I could take them all on again," Lao said as he climbed into the back of the cart, under the shelter of the cloth cover.

"Being all cocky now, are you? Guess the shock of it finally wore off?" Reina joked with him, following into the cart after the boy.

"I wasn't in shock!" The boy whined, lying down against a wooden crate, his sleeping roll acting as a comfortable neck pillow behind him. "I was just trying to catch my breath."

"Sure you were," Reina said with a roll of her eyes. Shen took a look at his map, and the area looked familiar to him. He had traveled it before, though without a map, but each look at the map only cemented the terrain in his mind. After fixing the direction through the trees they'd need to go to reach Daoyan, turning Ping southeast, he tugged on the reins and then moved forward at a pace just faster than Ping's usual trot, reserved for the nasty weather.

"You try taking a club to the gut without any armor!" He rubbed at his stomach with his hand, using the other to grab for his new sword's scabbard, which he found next to another crate, where he'd tossed it before. "I still get a little ache every time I inhale."

"Is that whining I hear from the great warrior Lao?" Reina jested again.

"I'm not whining!" He shouted, his voice faltering, raising in pitch. "I'm going to get some rest," Lao said, turning over in his spot. "Wake me when we get to the cavern." After Reina let out a little chuckle at the expense of her young compatriot, she too settled against her sleeping roll to get some rest for herself. Her eyelids grew heavier and soon were closed, her mind wandering off into the realm of dreams.

While his two companions fell into a deep sleep, lulled by the rhythmic motions of the cart going through mud and rocks, Shen looked on into the trees.

The ribbon at the tip of his helmet swayed on the side of the brim while the rain came down and bounced off its surface. He looked to the treeline nearby and saw a little pack of wild stub-horned dogs. They were small, less furry than the domesticated ones they'd seen on Lujing, their coats thin and short. Some were gray, others brown, and the largest of them was a light gray more akin to white, and they walked carefully under canopies of leaves of bushes. The rain soaked into their fur, it seemed, and they appeared to walk slower and more sluggish than otherwise. There were five from what Shen could see and as soon as they heard the cart come by they dashed off into the bushes.

  Ping went ever forward, as slow as his pace was, and Shen's mind ambled around within itself. He looked down to his legs, where the sound of the clinking bronze plates of his shin armor jangled around with each bump onto a rock in the road. Mud splashed around underneath the wheels as they dipped into declines in the dirt, and soon Shen began to notice something. He figured they were getting close enough, as the way in his mind from the map foretold, but he began to notice something peculiar. There was a smell that hung in the air, somewhere between the smell of a burnt out fire and a bit of metal. His nose to the air, he was unaware of what lie ahead until the cart's front wheel nudged into something.

  Ping stopped in his tracks and stomped the ground, splashing mud up onto his scaly, thick legs. "What is it, boy," Shen said aloud, and let go of the reins. He hopped down from the seat of the saddle and climbed down to the ground. Nothing was out of the ordinary by Ping, but, as he looked to the wheel, he found what it was. He was taken aback, stepping backward in surprise as the body of a Batung soldier lay just in front of the right front wheel. Were it not for the blood splattered across the neck of him, from the deep gash along his neck,

Shen would've flicked his wrist and caught the soldier with every rock he could pull from the muddied ground.

"Help... help me," a voice came, and Shen jumped back again. For a moment, he thought it was the body talking, but that was quickly done away with for obvious reasons. "Please, help," the voice came again, hoarse and strained, and Shen could clearly hear it coming from a tree nearby.

He walked over to where the voice seemed to be coming from, some trees up a small hill beside the road, and he saw that just beyond the trees ahead was the entrance to the cavern. It was huge, the dark abyss like the gaping maw of the beast that lived within it, and the stone part of the mountain it was born from glistened with the dripping of the rain. Shen broke his sight from it and brought it to the tree where the voice came. All around it were more bodies, male and female Batung soldiers alike, sat up against trees with their armor broken and split, wounds bloody. Flies and beetles climbed along their faces and limbs, along their dark tan skin. "Who's there?" Shen said aloud.

"Over here, please," the voice called, and it was closer. It was coming from one of the bodies he'd thought was dead, their wound a slash across the chest where there was no armor to protect them.

Shen hurried over to him, a younger looking soldier with skin the same tan shade as his own, unlike the dark tan color of a pure Batung person. "Okay, calm down. You're going to be alright, okay? What's your name?"

"Fu. Fu Min."

"Okay, Fu. My name is Shen. I'm here to help." He talked quickly, reaching into his bag and pulling bandage wrappings and herbs to fight off infection. "What happened? Animals? Hookbeaks? Bandits?"

"No, no," he pleaded, his breath wavering and his vision fading in and out. "Soldiers. Soldiers... There was an ambush."

"Okay, alright, don't strain yourself. Batung soldiers did this?" He said, and begun to rub the green and brown dried herbs along the wounds where the man's tunic was torn.

With an exhale and grunt of pain, the soldier felt the sting of the herbs reacting with his blood and muscle. "No. No, Vasai. Silver armor, spears, one of them wore a spirit mask." He began to lift up his hands, moving his fingers as the feeling returned with a twinge of aching pain. "They came from the trees, all around us, we didn't even see them until they were already on top of us."

"Why were they here," Shen asked. He gripped handfuls of Fu's tunic in each hand, and tore it apart as he tossed it to the ground next to him. The rain came down from the dark clouds above and dripped along the man's bare chest. His form was frail, not much muscle on him and no fat whatsoever.

"I have no idea." Fu grunted again, and let Shen wrap the bandages around his chest, over and over, a bit of the dried herbs sticking to the blood and being pressed down against the wound by the steadily tightening bandage. "I think they said something about a gauntlet, some treasure in that thing's den," he said.

"Zhi-Ming, you mean?" Shen said.

"Yeah, exactly."

"And what were you doing here?" Shen said, turning his head to the side to reach into his bag again, for one of the sharp rocks he kept to cut bandage.

The question seemed to catch Fu by surprise, as he got abruptly quiet. In reality, he had seen the mark on the back of Shen's neck. The covering the old man had put on Shen's neck had been washed by the rain, and now the green mark was easy to see against his tan skin. But, the soldier shook it off, and instead replied to his savior's question. "Routine patrol. Our navigator, Gong, she lost the map and we got all turned around. We were just supposed to rally here, it was our landmark, but that's when the Vasai came."

Shen finished wrapping Fu's wound with the bandage and sliced the last length of it with the sharp rock he pulled from his side bag. After tying it as tight as it would go, he put what was left of the herbs and the bandages back into the bag at his thigh, along with the rock he'd used. "Alright. You're all patched up. Now, we need to get into that cavern, and you need to keep that healing."

"Wait, wait, you're going in there?" Fu said, reaching up and gripping Shen's tunic loosely.

"My group and I were sent by the Council to slay the spirit Zhi-Ming."

"Well, you'll need to watch yourself in there. Not just around Zhi-Ming, either. The Vasai soldiers we got ambushed by ran in there just before I blacked out." He let go of the grip on the tunic, rainwater squeezed from its fabric on his palms. "They're probably still in there."

"We'll be prepared," Shen said with a soft smile.

"Shen!" Reina's voice came from below, where the cart was left.

"Reina, up here! Bring Lao! I've found the cavern!" He shouted, and soon the other two of Shen's band of nomads came running to his side. Fu was taken aback by the sight of Reina, as she wore her spirit mask on her face, the rain bouncing off her silver Vasai armor. "Fu! Fu, it's alright. She's not going to hurt you."

"What's with him?" Reina looked around, Lao too, and their eyes scanned over the bodies of the other Batung soldiers around them.

"Vasai soldiers. An ambush," Shen explained.

"Where are they now? Are we going to have to fight them," Lao shouted out, pulling the sword from the scabbard now strapped to his back.

"The cavern, probably. Just one more thing to worry about before Zhi-Ming," Shen said.

"Just like fate to screw us over. Never truly at the end of this, are we?" Reina observed.

"I guess not," Lao replied.

"Fu. I need you to listen to me, alright?" Shen started.

"I'm listening, Shen."

"I'm going to bring you to our cart. There's cover from the rain, and I'll need you to look after it while we're in the cavern. You should be alright to move soon. If we're not back by afternoon tomorrow," Shen said, and looked to the sky. The clouds were much more dark, signifying the quickly encroaching night. "You take the cart and you go to the nearest town. Alright?"

"Alright. Anything. I owe a great debt to you, for saving my life," Fu said, and tried to move his legs, but felt a great aching in his muscles.

"Don't try and run now. I'll get you just fine," Shen said. He bent down and placed one arm under Fu's neck, the other under his knees, and carefully lifted him from the ground. Fu grunted a bit as the ache in his wound came back for a moment. "Just a bit more pain, that's all, then you'll get your rest." He brought the soldier through a few trees and down the little hill, and over to the cart where Ping was. Delicately, Shen set Fu down on the back of the cart and pulled away some of the cover. "There you are. Should be safe from the rains for the time being," Shen said, and as the words hit the air, the rain began to fall even faster. It tapped furiously against his helmet, dripping off the brim in large quantities.

"The rain's been awful here lately. Storms too." Fu settled into the seat, while Shen went around to the side of the cart, digging his hands under the cloth cover.

"It's Zhi-Ming," Shen said, pulling from the cart his bow and quiver, a mess of arrows still left inside.

"Pardon me?" Fu retorted, raising a bushy black eyebrow.

"Zhi-Ming. I think he can sense we're getting closer, and knows his end is near. He's getting angrier and angrier lately." Shen slung the strap of the quiver over his shoulder and did the same with his bowstring, slinging it in place on his other shoulder.

Fu was able to lift his arm somewhat now, and ran his bloodied fingers through his thick black hair, tied up at the top with a thin piece of string. He brought it back down to his face, and once his eyes rested on the blood coating them, he shook his hand to get some of it off. "That's a weird way of thinking about it."

"My thinking can be a bit old-fashioned." Shen walked back over to the bottom of the little hill, and turned back to Fu with a smile. "Anyway, I'll leave you to the cart. Keep Ping over there company and everything. We'll see you in no time," Shen said, and before Fu could let out any parting words, he was gone up the hill.

Soon he came back to his two companions, and they looked on ahead to the cavern. "Any idea why Vasai would be this far in mainland Batung?" Reina pondered aloud as they walked forward.

"I've no idea. But it doesn't seem good. Fu says they were looking for some sort of gauntlet. Any clue on that?" Shen asked.

"Beats me. Either it was beyond my position, or this is a completely new revelation. Or, it could be something entirely different," she said. "Either way, I've never heard anything about a gauntlet."

"Not sure if I've got anything to add, but, if we do find any sort of gauntlet, I vote we keep it," Lao said, the bronze sword held lax in just one of his hands.

"Mighty fine idea if you ask me," Reina said with a smile. "What do you think, Shen?" She turned to Shen, who stopped abruptly as they reached the entrance of the cavern. The dark stared right back at them, almost endless, and as Reina pulled the little orange glowing stone from her bag, even its light was barely bright enough to pierce it.

"I could use a gauntlet," he said. He looked to Lao, and a smile came across the boy's face. Shen too smiled, seeing the glint of curiosity and wonder in Lao's eyes, in spite of the darkness of the clouds, and the rain, and the path that lay ahead. With no more words, they entered into the cavern, valor in their hearts and nothing more than an inkling as to what they were to face.

Labyrinthian

It took but a mere few steps into the entrance of the cavern that the darkness began enshrouding them. It was immense and almost palpable. Each of them felt the crushing weight of the darkness, the only sound that of a steady drip of water outside from the rain, and the thought that nearly anything could be lurking in the caverns ahead of them set in. Reina, tense at her surroundings, gripped onto the glowing rock in her hand so tightly that its light wasn't let from the confines of her fingers. Shen turned his head to where she was when they walked in, and spoke up in a low tone. "Reina." It was nothing more than a whisper, but the emptiness of the cavern echoed the sound of it all around. "You still have that little rock?"

As she heard the words, she shook a strange weight from her mind and again felt the odd semi-rugged texture of the stone in her grasp. "Yes. I've got it, right here."

"Give it here," Shen said. Without question she reached her hand, palm upward and fingers unclenched from the object within them, letting the light leak out so that Shen could see where she was exactly. He grabbed it from her and held it in his hand. Looking down at it, it was not any bigger than an eye. But, the light it produced, when unobscured, was bright and glowing a smooth orange like fire.

"How are we gonna get to Zhi-Ming if we can't even find him?" Lao said in a whisper, and then thought again about his words. "Forget that, how are we gonna fight if we can't see!" He shouted, and the sound of his voice shot down the path ahead of them, bouncing and veering off into numerous paths.

"Just watch. I think I have an idea," Shen said. He held the stone carefully between just two of his fingers, so that the light could shine to its utmost potential. It did, the orange light glowing all around, and soon it reached the walls closing them in on the cavern path like a corridor. But, the glow rock Shen held was not the only light, as more were revealed to be embedded into the cavern walls around them. They could see ahead now, at where the path went, where it stopped and split off into three separate ways.

"Well isn't that just great? Now we gotta make a decision, and the wrong one could set us back hours," Reina whined, her voice raising and lowering in volume as she was made aware of the sheer echo too much noise made.

"Hey, what's that?" Lao asked, and pointed ahead.

Luckily, what lie beyond his pointed finger was within reach of the glowing rocks' light, and as Shen beheld it, he walked closer toward it. Along with him went the light, and with the light the other two followed close behind, almost afraid they would be left behind in the monumental darkness. "Spirit statue," Reina whispered as she saw it. Before them was a person-sized statue, carved from a finer stone unlike that of what made up the caverns. It stood menacingly, right next to the opening to the leftmost path diverting from the entranceway.

"Indeed it is," Shen whispered. It looked unlike any spirit they had seen before. Upon its collar and neck, and all the way down its back to where a tail rested, coiled upon the ground, there were scales. They seemed to have been painted green, but time had weathered them away to the same color the stone the rest of the statue was crafted from. Its face was mammalian, with a small, sharp-toothed grin of a mouth.

Lao looked around it, and it seemed to look more and more familiar to him. It looked like just a weasel-like spirit, perhaps one taking the form of the slippery rodent, but as he looked closer and his mind wandered as it did, he realized. "Hey! This is the thing I saw back in Sheteng!" He said.

"What? What do you mean?" Shen retorted.

"When I ran into that lady's cart, I was after this weird little mongoose with glowing scales on it. I think it was this, a spirit," he said, and bent down to where its feet were carved. It stood upon a pedestal of the same fine rock, and on the front of the pedestal there was etched in a name. "Shasha," Lao read aloud.

"Shasha? Never heard of that one before," Reina said.

"We don't have time for spirit stories," Shen said, "we have to keep moving." He looked closer, and inside the statue's mouth there was a small bit of wood. "Reina, do you have a firestarter on you?"

"Coming right up," she said. She reached into the bag at her hip and pulled the little device out, kept dry all this time in spite of the rains outside.

Shen gripped it in his hands, wiping away some dirt from the metal, and placed the tip of it to the wood. With a squeeze of his grip there was a spark, and then another, and as Shen blew a bit of breath into it, the wood was aflame. "There." He stood up straight, and looked ahead to see the path. Curious, he held out the glowing rock again, and its light reached further and touched a few other glow rocks embedded into the cavern walls. Ahead, quite a few more steps, there stood another spirit statue, almost identical to the first. Against it, there sat another Batung soldier, reaching her hand up toward the light from the fire in the spirit statue.

"Shen, there's someone down there," Reina said.

Shen quickly began walking down the left path and the other two followed behind him. "It's alright, ma'am, it's gonna be okay," he said as he got to the soldier. "How badly are you hurt?"

"What… what are you doing in the caverns?" She muttered out.

"We're here to kill Zhi-Ming. Now, I need you to answer my question," Shen said kneeling down. He reached into his bag and felt around for his bandages again, before his arm was grabbed. Turning his head, he saw the soldier's hand gripping his arm tightly.

"Don't bother. I already patched myself up, hours ago," she said. "Keep moving." She said, letting go of her grip on his arm.

"We found one of yours, Fu Min, we'll come back for you." Shen said.

"Fu? Ugh, he must be hating me right now. I'm the one who got us lost and ambushed in the first place." She brought her hand up to her forehead and gripped her temples. Shen pulled his hand from out of his bag with a pouch of berries and nuts in his grasp, his eyes looking to the soldier's wounds. She had been slashed in the legs, and the nerves were destroyed, blood everywhere. Shen knew, and was sure she did as well, that it was unlikely she'd be able to move her legs again.

"You're the navigator? Gong?" Shen asked handing over the pouch. "Here, it's food, the least we can do."

"Yes! Did he say something about me?" She asked frantically, her eyes widening, her attention away from the pouch of food in Shen's hand.

"Just your name, and that you lost the map. He didn't seem all that angry." Shen reached and grabbed her hand, placing the little hide pouch into her palm, then closing her fingers around it. "Take the food. Please."

"Thank you. Thank you," she said with tears forming in her eyes. "Tell him I'm sorry. Please, you have to," she said.

"No need to worry about that," Lao butted in. "We'll be back in no time at all." He gave a great big smile which almost shined in the light of the glow rock in Shen's hand. "We are coming back, right Shen?"

"Of course," he answered.

"No need for it," she began, putting a few fingers into the little pouch and shoving a few berries and nuts into her mouth. "Get back to Fu. Tell him where I am, and then ask him to put out a signal." She spoke with her mouth full, before chewing quite a bit and swallowing down the food, then continued. "He'll show you how to create a signal fire. The next town over should be able to see it from here, and any soldiers stationed there."

"And you're sure this will work?" Reina said, the spirit mask pulled down onto her collarbone, the leather strap dangling loosely on the back of her neck.

"It's the best option we have. Fu will know what to do." She finished off the rest of the nuts and berries quickly, and handed the empty pouch back to Shen. "Now go. Those Vasai soldiers might be back here any minute."

"What are you going to do if they catch you?" Lao asked.

"I'll fight them off," she said with a smirk. "Still got enough in me for a good fight."

Lao couldn't tell, but Shen and Reina heard it in her voice. She was lying. Nonetheless, Shen brought the firestarter back out and placed it into the mouth of the spirit statue before them. Again, the flames were alight, dancing around inside the statue's mouth, and the path was lit up and shown to divert once again, this time into two more ways.

They moved forward, saying their goodbyes and good lucks to the soldier Gong. When they reached the diversion of the path, they were now in a larger opening of the cavern. It was almost like a room, a much more wide open space than the confines of the paths. There was no way to tell which path to go down, but soon, there was a sound. Footsteps, quick and clanking in armored boots, came up from the path on the right. "Ready yourselves," Shen said.

"Shen, I have an idea," Reina said.

"An idea? What are you talking about?" Shen asked.

"Lao and I will fight them," she answered.

"You'll what?" He shouted, and the footsteps became louder and grew closer.

"Over here! I think I hear someone!" A voice called from down the right path.

"He needs the practice. He'll stay close to me, and I'll show him what to do. If things go wrong, you use your powers to help." She explained, and still it seemed Shen was wary. "Please. We can't avoid them," she said. She reached behind her with her arm, and pulled her sword from its hold under the small of her back.

"Fine," Shen said, and backed up to give them room to fight.

"I see them! Look for the light up there!" The voice called again. Shen looked to the glow rock in his hands, then around to the other glowing rocks embedded in the stone of the cavern around them. Quickly, he closed his hand, and the light was gone, apart from the dim light of the fire behind. "Where'd it go?" The voice called again, and in the scarce flame light, two Vasai soldiers stood at the entrance to the path on the right.

Reina and Lao stood in the shadows, unable to be seen. Lao's heart pounded in his chest, as he was close to one of the soldiers. Reina however, was on the other side of the right path's entrance, with the two soldiers in between her and Lao. She gripped the handle of the sword in her hand and looked to the soldier closest to her. He was small, frail, with patchy stubble and short black hair. Lao gripped the handle of his bronze sword with both hands, his fingers almost shaking, waiting for some kind of signal to attack.

"I hear something," one of the soldiers said, the one nearest Lao. He had a scar upon his shoulder, where his armor was absent. His silver armor only covered his legs, upper chest, and his forearms. Lao could only assume he'd heard his heartbeat, as it seemed to be near to bursting out of his chest.

"Now!" Reina shouted, and lunged forward with her blade ready. She and Lao each swiped their blades at the lower chest of the soldiers, and they were quickly taken by surprise. The one near Lao fell immediately, blood splattering across the stone wall nearby, and onto the floor as he fell. However, the one slashed by Reina had only been hit in the side, and was merely knocked back.

"Gah!" He shouted out, and looked to Reina, now in the light of the fire that came down the path and into the little stone room like a beam. "You! I'll kill you!" He shouted, but was abruptly silenced as the blade of Lao's sword stabbed him through the side. The soldier let out a cry of pain once again, and Lao pulled the blade from out of his flesh.

"Shen!" Lao called out.

"I've got them!" Shen shouted, and lunged forward, flicking one of his wrists up. Rocks came from off the ground and fastened the soldiers to the ground by their legs. For good measure, he flicked his other wrist downward, and a few small rocks came down from the walls and smacked into their heads, knocking them out.

"We did it!" Lao said.

"Yeah," Reina said, trying to catch her breath.

"What was that?" Shen said, walking up to her.

"What?" She replied.

"You hesitated. You could've easily killed him, but you didn't," he said.

"I didn't hesitate, he moved out of the way too fast. You need to relax."

"I need to relax? You could've been killed. Lao could've been killed!" He shouted, and his voice again echoed through the path which the soldiers came up from.

"Shen, I'm fine," Lao interjected. "I took one of them down! All by myself."

"I know, Lao." Shen trailed off, guilty of himself.

"Come on," Reina said shaking off a few drops of blood from her blade. "Let's keep moving."

"Which way?" Shen said.

"Left path," Reina said quietly.

"What makes you think so," Lao asked.

"Well, they seemed lost, and were just now coming back to the surface." Shen listened, and it seemed to make sense to him. "Plus, if they had run into Zhi-Ming, they probably wouldn't be coming back alive," she said.

"Fair point," Shen said. He brought the glowing rock out from behind him and its light once again shined out. It reached partially down the paths in front of them, and it bounced off the glow of the other rocks in the walls of the cavern. "You want to lead?" He asked, holding out the rock to Reina.

"No," she said. "Better you lead." She kept her sword in her hand, and she looked to Lao. In her mind, she was worried about the boy. It wouldn't be easy for someone as young as him to go right to attacking someone, let alone killing them, and yet he seemed unfazed by it. Perhaps it was his hardened demeanor from living on the streets. Either way, there was nagging worry at the back of her mind.

"Alright then. Let's keep going." Shen said, and looked to his two companions. After a few moments, he turned back to the path ahead, and continued on downward.

They walked on, coming to more statues of the spirit Shasha, lighting them with fire along the way. Each time they encountered one, the path seemed to diverge into different ones. But, each time too, Shen held out the orange glowing rock and the light climbed across the walls and lit up other rocks, and reached another statue. The ways came and went, and each time there was a statue which seemed to indicate the right way. Down certain paths there were other statues, ones of warriors long past, with torches in their hands. But, he kept on looking for the statues of Shasha, and he was led down more and more paths, deeper and deeper into the caverns. The caverns twisted and turned, but something about the statues compelled Shen to follow after them.

Soon, they reached a large chamber in the caverns, with only one path. Strikingly, this one had a statue too, right next to the entrance to a last path on the opposite side of where they came in, and this one was already alight. Its eyes shined with light of the glowing rocks in the cavern stone and in Shen's hand. However, what struck Shen and the others worse than the sight of the statue, was the sight of three more Vasai soldiers coming from out of the path's entrance.

"Travelers?" One of them called out. She wore the silver armor much like Reina's, and the bridge of her nose had painted on two thin horizontal lines in dark blue. "You!" She called out. "You're Vasai military. I recognize that armor anywhere, and that mask."

"No! Not anymore, I'm not," Reina shouted out, gritting her teeth together. "And I will never be again."

"You. You found those soldiers, didn't you?" Another of the soldiers said, a man with only a single dark blue streak of paint, which lay horizontal on the bridge of his nose. "If you tell anyone, we'll be at war. It will be all our fault," he said frantically.

"They're not going to tell anyone," the third one said. She was large, muscular and fierce, with a big spear in the grip of her scarred hands. On the bridge of her nose were the same markings as on the first soldier that spoke, and which Reina had once had, before they were wiped away.

"What makes you so sure of that?" Reina snapped at her.

"You've just an unarmed hermit and a child with you. And you're missing an arm. We're leaving here alive, and you're not," the soldier said, and the other female pulled a small trident from behind her back which had previously not been seen.

"I'm not a child!" Lao shouted out, and his voice bounced all around the stone walls and came back to him, seemingly somewhat high-pitched.

"We're going to kill them?" The male soldier cried.

"Of course we are, Netsu, you coward. Get your sword ready." The big soldier snapped, and lunged forward at Reina with her spear poised forward. Reina slashed upward with her blade, aiming for the handle of the spear she thought was of wood, but was taken aback as the clash let out a mighty *clang*. "Not what you expected?" She said with a smirk.

The other female soldier, the one with the trident, ran forward past Lao and toward Shen. "You can't leave here alive, none of you can. We can't risk the Council finding out." She stabbed again and again, but Shen kept jumping from out of the weapon's way. "That's why you're here, right? Those old bums sent you?"

"Precisely," Shen said, and reached his hand up. He flung it down quickly, and a large rock dislodged itself from the ceiling and struck the soldier in the back.

"You… You're a Mystic!" She shouted, a rage building in her eyes, her breathing becoming heaving, angry. "Now I don't have *any* problems killing you," she shouted again, and lurched forward with her trident. With this jab, one of the outer prongs sliced Shen in the side, and he quickly spun his body toward her, swinging his arm around and smacking her in the face. She fell backward, landing on her rear on the ground. With one quick motion of his hands, flicking his wrists upward, rocks came from off the ground and grabbed her legs by the ankles. "I'll kill you. I swear it," she said, struggling.

"Shen, I could use some help here," Reina said, her blade held up, fighting off the strength of the larger soldier.

"I can't," he said, strained.

"What do you mean you can't? Use some rocks or something and knock out this one," she said, pushing the soldier off her with a foot, turning to slash with her blade. The strike missed, however, and the soldier moved around to stab at her again.

"I can't, Reina. If I overuse my powers, my strength starts to go. I'll need all of it for Zhi-Ming. I'll keep this one restrained for now." He said, and pulled another rock from the cavern wall, throwing it into the restrained soldier's head, knocking her unconscious. "Where's Lao?"

"Over here!" Lao said, jumping away from the swinging sword blade of the male soldier. "Sort of busy," he said again. The soldier was haphazardly swinging, no real aim, and Lao quickly saw an advantage this. In an act of quick wit, Lao turned and ran toward the bigger soldier fighting Reina, and the soldier, Netsu, followed suit.

He slashed and slashed, and soon accidentally sliced into part of the big woman's side. "Gah! Netsu, you idiot," she shouted. She spun around toward him and stabbed nearby him with her spear, holding it in her grip with just one bulky hand.

"I'm sorry, Yama. I was only after the kid," he said.

"You should really," Reina started, and ran up to the back of the large woman soldier. She got low to the ground and spun around, anticipating a stab of her spear, and held her sword upside down in her grip. With a single stab, Reina plunged the blade straight through the soldier's side, at the ribs where the silver armor didn't reach. "Watch your back," she finished. The soldier fell to the ground with a thud, and her spear hit the stone with a great clatter that filled the big cavern chamber they stood in.

"Yama!" Netsu shouted. "Yagh!" He shouted again, and fell to the floor. He'd been slashed in the back of the knees, and in the small of the back, Lao standing above him with his sword in both hands as he huffed and breathed heavily.

"That's," Lao said with a breath, "what you," he paused once more to breathe, "get." He choked down a hefty amount of air, and finally caught his full breath. "For standing still," he finally said with a smile. Unable to move, and not truly wanting to, Netsu submitted and stopped moving.

"Do we need to kill them? Well, the rest of them," Reina asked, looking toward the body of Yama, slowly bleeding out and paralyzed

"No. We've done what we can to stop them. They aren't a threat anymore," Shen said.

"You don't think they'll report us, report you for being a Mystic?" Reina said.

"Yeah. If the Council finds out, we're all," Lao trailed off, "well, you know."

"They won't." Shen said with confidence.

"Why are you so sure?" Lao asked.

"If they go to the Council, they'll have to explain what they're doing on Batung land. And besides that, the only other person they can report us to is the king of Vasai. And this seems to be outside his jurisdiction." Shen said it with a smile, and held the glow rock firmly in his hand, clenching his fingers onto it.

"That's a fair point," Reina said.

"Makes sense to me," Lao echoed.

"They won't follow us," Shen said, and walked on into the last path of the cavern. Lao and Reina followed along, their weapons held lax, walking behind Shen. They continued on with the light of the glow rock, the light of the flames of the statue's torch dwindling into nothing behind them. The glow rocks in the walls began to become much more scarce, and that only left the light from the one in Shen's hand left.

Zhi-Ming's Fury

Just before they entered into the chamber at the end of the path, Reina stopped, and backed up a bit. "What is it?" Shen asked in a quiet tone, walking back with her.

"Do you think this is all too easy?" She said low, looking to Shen as Lao kept on walking, slow as it was.

"What do you mean," Shen replied.

"Getting here, to Zhi-Ming. You'd think with how prolific he is, all the might and danger, you'd think it wouldn't be this easy to get to him," she said. "What if we're walking into our deaths here?"

"Now, don't say that," Shen retorted.

"Tell me you haven't worried."

"Worry? Reina, what do you mean?"

"Tell me that you haven't once thought we might die taking this on. I mean, did you really think there wasn't a danger when you decided to do this?" Reina asked.

"Guys, I found the chamber!" Lao shouted from ahead.

"We'll be there! Just making sure we have everything. Don't go too far ahead!" Shen said. He moved the glow rock around in his hand, the light bouncing around and hitting a few of the other ones inside the walls around them. "Reina, of course I've worried. I'm worrying right now. But, I can't let that stop me," he answered to her in a whisper.

"So you've been worried, scared, but you're still going to do it?"

"Why are you so pressed on not fighting him?" Shen asked.

"I'm not. I want to. Do you?" Reina said, and Shen went a bit quiet, dropping his eyes from her.

"No. I don't really want to. But, I don't have a choice," Shen said. "This is the fastest way to get closer to him, to my brother. I won't pass this up," he finished, and turned, walking further down the path to where Lao stood, just in front of the chamber. Reina followed after him, just on the heels of the glowing orange light. "Lao," Shen spoke up.

"Yeah, Shen?" The boy gripped the handle of his bronze sword in one hand and lifted it up over his head. It was heavy, but he managed to lift it up just enough to slide the blade into the leather scabbard on his back.

"Did you get a chance to look inside?" Shen asked, as Reina walked up behind them.

"No. It's too dark. I got one foot in, and I couldn't see a thing." He looked down and saw the orange light shine upon a rock on the ground. Curious, he kicked it into the cavern chamber ahead of them, and the sound echoed all around for a few moments.

Shen walked in with the glow rock held out in the grip of two of his fingers, and the light only got so far. Just a few steps in, the light barely reached, and didn't touch any of the walls. Hoping to get a grasp of how big the room was, Shen took to one of the walls closer to the entrance, Reina and Lao following behind him single file. He started walking against the wall all around the room. It had a jagged circular pattern from what he could tell, curved all around, and had stuck upon it torch sconces in a few places, though absent of wood to light. It was a few minutes until they reached the entrance to the chamber again, after they'd traveled all the wall, though they were moving fairly slowly.

Along the way, there were three things Shen had noticed along the walls. For one, there were claw marks along the wall in certain places. Areas in the wall had been indented with claws and stained with dried blood. He could only assume this was the work of Zhi-Ming, but where was the beast himself? The second thing he noticed were the cave paintings along the wall. They were painted on in a pale white chalky substance, and depicted several things. There was an image of mountains crumbling, of villages flooding, of plants and crops dying, animals overrunning a town. But, one caught his eye, a huge army of soldiers, with the giant visage of Zhi-Ming stood behind them. He couldn't remember where on the wall he'd seen it, but it was in his mind nonetheless. The third thing that caught his attention, though, were several bodies along the wall.

There weren't many of them, and they weren't human. A few were hookbeaks, slashed open with feathers scattered everywhere. Blood stained the floor, but it was long dry. There were also two larger bodies, the carcasses of ram-horn deer, with their stomachs slashed open by vicious claws. Innards were nowhere to be seen though, and Shen had assumed they'd been devoured by the creature that killed the ram-horns in the first place.

"Unless the thing's stalking us in the middle of the room, this isn't the way we should've gone," Reina said.

"No, it is, I know it," Shen retorted.

"How do you know," Lao asked, sticking close to Shen at the entrance, enveloped in the light of the glowing rock.

"I just do. There's something about this place. We need to look for an entrance, it's probably blocked off," Shen said.

"Well for that we're gonna need light," Reina said.

"Why don't we just build a fire?" Lao wondered aloud.

"Two things wrong with that plan, kid," Reina started. "One, unless we go all the way back up to the surface, we've got no wood to make the fire. And two, even if we did, in an enclosed space like this, a fire that big will end up smoking ourselves out."

"Oh, yeah. That makes sense," Lao said with a half-hearted chuckle.

"In that case, we'll need more of those glow rocks that we passed," Shen said.

"I was just thinking of that. I think I have an idea for those, beyond just brightening up this room," Reina said.

"Alright then. You wouldn't mind getting them then, would you?" Shen asked.

"I'd be delighted," Reina said with a joking smile.

Shen handed over the glow rock to her, and the orange light around them shifted just a bit. "Take the glow rock with you. Get as many as you can stuff into your bag, and be back here as fast as you can."

"You got it," she said.

"We'll stay close to the entrance so you can find us," Shen said.

"Works for me," she said, and walked back up the path to retrieve the rocks. As she walked away, the light moved and faded away from the chamber Shen and Lao stood in, leaving them shrouded in the darkness, unable to see anything but black.

"You doing alright, Lao?" Shen asked.

"Yeah. Why?" Lao replied, gripping onto the side of Shen's tunic to keep close.

Shen sat down against the stone wall, and Lao did so too, taking his seat right next to Shen, right up against the side of him. "You fought off those bandits, and those soldiers. That must be a bit taxing for you, right?"

"Yeah, I guess so." Lao dropped his eyes low, and was thankful Shen couldn't see him. "I was scared the whole time. I didn't want to hurt them, or kill them or anything, but I had to."

"You know that's okay, Lao." Shen reached his hand over, despite the dark, and placed the palm of his hand on Lao's shoulder. He gripped it softly with his fingers, and Lao's nerves began to calm. "We're protecting ourselves. You're protecting yourself."

"But, what if they have families? Or friends? What if they're like us?" Lao asked, and his nerves began to tense again.

"Well, Lao, that's for you to think about. You can accept that what you're doing is for your own safety, that there's no other way." Shen rubbed the boy's shoulder softly, and he began to relax. "Or you can do what I do and try your very best not to kill them."

"Have you ever killed anyone?" He asked, naivety in his very voice.

"No, I don't suppose I have," Shen said. "But, people have died because of my actions, one way or another."

"Do you feel guilty about it? I mean, when I hurt that soldier, I think I killed him. I've been feeling bad about it all this time."

"Lao, guilt is inevitable. Whether it's rational or not, we're always going to feel guilty."

"So how do you get past it?"

"Keep moving. Know that in your heart, in your mind, you're doing what you must to stay alive."

"Will you get mad at me, if I kill someone?" Lao asked, and even through the darkness, Shen could tell he was looking into his eyes.

Shen squeezed the boy's shoulder again, reassuring him. "Never. If you know you did it to protect yourself or others, then that's perfectly alright with me. The world is a scary place, you know."

"Don't have to tell me twice," Lao said with a little chuckle. "The streets aren't a fun place for a thirteen-year-old kid."

"I know how you feel, Lao. I've lived on my own since I was sixteen," Shen said. "Things can get difficult."

"You're not on your own now," Lao said, and Shen could practically hear the boy's smile through his words.

"No, I suppose I'm not," he said in return with a smile.

After that the two of them stayed quiet, simply waiting for Reina to return. The room was cold at certain points, but it went unnoticed by the two as they were relatively warm sitting next to each other. Lao found himself resting his head against Shen as he had done on the boat to Lujing. Shen, though, fiddled with the bow slung onto his shoulder, making sure it was ready to be used. The fight with Zhi-Ming was ever present on his mind, and the worry of what might happen right along with it. But, the comfort of Lao was a welcome feeling apart from the anxiety. Soon, the two of them heard footsteps returning, and were greeted once again by the warm orange light of the glow rock in Reina's hand.

"I got a whole bunch of them, probably enough to light up the whole room twice over," Reina said with a smile, visible now in the light of the rock.

"Good. I saw empty sconces around the walls, could you hand over a pile of them?" Shen said.

Reina handed over the rock for a moment, and the light shifted around as Shen took it into his hand. She unfastened the bag at her hip, and it fell to the ground. The flap opened up upon hitting the stone and a few glowing rocks spilled out. "Help yourself, but save a few. I'll need them for your arrows," she said.

"My arrows?" Shen reached a hand to his shoulder and slipped off the strap of his quiver, reaching out to give it to Reina. "Take it, I'll go and put the rocks in the sconces." He reached down and grabbed Reina's bag, taking it with him to one side of the room, guided by the light of one of the glow rocks.

"Perfect," she said, and took it into her hand. "Lao, I think I'll need your help. Sound like a plan?"

"Yeah!" Lao replied, and walked with Reina after taking a good amount of the glow rocks with him. They walked along through the center of the room, aided by the orange light, until Reina bumped her foot into something. Their eyes went down, and rested on a wooden table and a chair. There were many books, leather-bound with nothing on the covers, and strewn about all along the surface of the table. "What's this doing here?"

"Your guess is as good as mine, kid," Reina said. "But I won't say no to a good seat." She set the quiver down onto the table and sat down in the chair. It produced a fairly loud creaking, which echoed throughout the stone chamber.

"What was that?" Shen asked loudly, his own voice bouncing through the room.

"Found a chair. Seems the wood's a bit weak," she said.

"Don't break anything," Shen replied.

"You calling me fat, Shen?" She asked aloud, and got no response from Shen, who was steadily going around the walls of the room, placing the glowing rocks in the torch sconces. Light began to slowly come into the room, and Reina smirked a bit. "That's what I thought."

Lao set all the glow rocks he had brought down onto the table next to the quiver, and their light shined brighter than ever. "What's your idea, Reina?"

He asked. As Reina was about to answer, there was a strange sound coming from nearby. It sounded like a great huff, a whooshing of air pushed from the mouth or nose of someone snoring. "What is it?"

"Nothing. Thought I heard something," Reina said, forgetting about the faint sound.

"Oh, okay. So what's your idea? You didn't answer."

"Right, well, first, grab me one of those arrows." The boy did as he was asked and pulled the arrow from out of the leather quiver. Its arrowhead was made from chipped rock, razor-sharp, and the fletching at the back was crafted from thick feathers. "Now, get one of the glow rocks, just a bit bigger in size than the arrowhead," she said. Again, Lao complied, and grabbed a small glow rock from the pile. Reina reached her hand down and pulled her sword from out of its holding place. She brought up to the table above where the glow rock sat, and held it with the blade up, the pommel facing downward to the table. She began chipping away at the sides of the glowing rock, and pieces broke off easily. It was very brittle, and soon, Reina had pounded out the rock into an arrowhead shape.

"You're turning them into arrowheads?" Lao asked.

"Exactly. Shen's gonna want to know what he's shooting at, and there's a good chance that Zhi-Ming likes the dark." She grabbed the arrow and handed it over to Lao. "Could you untie the arrowhead from that and tie the glow one on it? The same way it was tied on, if you can."

Lao took it into his hands and his little fingers quickly untied the thin string. Despite its thickness, or rather the lack thereof, the string was made from a very strong fiber. He took the glowing arrowhead and fixed the stem of it where the previous one had been. Without any prompting, he tied up the arrowhead to the shaft of the arrow, tighter even than it had been done before. "There," he said, and handed over the newly-crafted arrow.

It glowed with a more muted light, as the pieces lay glowing and scattered on the table. But, it was a good amount of light, and Reina marveled at it in the grip of her hand, after she'd set her sword down next to the quiver on the table. "Wow. Where'd you learn to tie this so well, Lao?" She asked.

"Picked up a few tricks on the streets. Met a really nice hunter I stole some Yin from. Showed me how to make arrows, even offered to teach me to hunt."

"You stole from him?"

"Needed money for food that day. Not one of my best moments, though. He was so nice," he said.

"Alright. Well, think you can do that again," she looked into the quiver, counting out the number of arrows left in her head, until she got the exact number. "Fourteen more times?" She put the arrow down onto the table, and picked her sword back up.

"I certainly can try," he said.

While they continued on creating the glowing arrows, Shen was still occupied with lighting the room. He'd gotten the whole half of it, placing the glowing rocks into the sconces, acting as torches of their own. The light wasn't terribly bright, but it served just enough to light up some of the middle area of the chamber. He continued walking along the wall, placing more rocks into the sconces, until he came upon something toward the middle of the room that wasn't visible before. The light crawled from the wall and along the floor, resting at the feet of a human body.

Shen walked over toward the center, and he still carried with him the glowing rocks, and soon their light illuminated the body of a traveler. They had long been dead, as tattered clothing and armored boots clung only to bones of their skeleton. The body was sat up against a big rock, right next to a rotted chair, and held something in its hand. Shen knelt down and grabbed for it, feeling the leather cover of a journal. In their other hand, as Shen quickly noticed, there sat a dagger, embellished with images of flowers upon the handle and engraved into the silver blade. Shen opened up the journal, and as his eyes scanned up and down the pages, the writing in hasty black ink, he read through what it detailed.

The first few pages had detailed much of the traveler's journey before arriving at the caverns. He had been traveling with two others, his sister, and a friend of theirs just a fews years younger than the both of them. During this time, it seemed to Shen, Zhi-Ming was rarely confined to the caverns of Daoyan, and instead roamed free. He quickly learned that the body sitting before him was once an Ogon man. His name, Shen discovered, was Valkyr Igarok. Valkyr, along with his companions, had been sent off by his village to travel Batung, in search of ways to render their fields fertile.

Valkyr set out with his sister Ilse, and their friend Sigtur, and sailed by a small boat into the port town of Gangkou, just on the eastern shore of mainland Batung. They arrived and were greeted by friendly faces in the town. They were treated to a great feast on their first night, with meat and fresh vegetables, and even mead, which had been a commodity in abating then, rarer than gold. The local innkeeper of Gangkou allowed them a free stay and helped them off to a blacksmith where they would get their weapons. As Valkyr described it in his journal, 'the man we came to know as Heng showed us kindness befitting of family.' It nearly put a smile to Shen's face as he read, and he flipped the pages of the journal more and more. A few more pages detailing their acquisition of daggers and even a sword were passed quickly, and then the real journey started.

They would travel from Gangkou to forests and other towns which hadn't yet names. Each time they were greeted with friendly faces. But, there came a point where the towns stopped appearing, and when they did appear, they had arrived as the town lay in ruins. They had no other choice but to turn back and return to the last town they had visited, curious as to what had happened. 'Zhi-Ming,' they were told, 'had unleashed his fury upon humankind wherever possible.' Shen shivered, partly with cold, and partly with a slight fear of the very name. Zhi-Ming felled entire villages with his mighty claws. His roars filled the nightly air as he lay waste to houses as people fled, and soon the towns around Daoyan became too overfilled.

Valkyr, Ilse, and Sigtur had spent enough time in their town, and were determined to move onward. As such, Valkyr thought Zhi-Ming a threat to be taken down. They left after one last night of safety, and set out in the early morning sun to reach Daoyan Caverns, with the knowledge in their minds that Zhi-Ming was resting there during the colder Bai-Se season of Batung. The trip on foot took nearly an entire week, and they encountered droves of vicious creatures along the way. There were hookbeaks, river weasels, even some spirits had made targets of the three of them.

Despite all the obstacles however, the three Ogon travelers arrived at Daoyan Caverns. They were very tired, and made counsel to determine whether they would make camp. Ultimately, they decided to make a fire at the mouth of the cavern, and go in for battle the very next morning. The fire was made, they settled in just inside the entrance of the caverns, and slept the night away. As Valkyr awoke, he did so to the sound of crashing rain. A huge storm was raging outside the caverns, and even still there came another shock. Sigtur was gone from his place of sleep, and Ilse lay on the ground with her throat slashed open.

Valkyr was immediately overcome with grief. The pages went on for long about how perfect she had been. It detailed the curvature of her face, the paleness of her skin, the beauty of her blonde hair up in a braid atop her head. It was clear Valkyr had loved her, and soon Shen could tell the grief turned to rage just as strong. He read further, and it seemed Valkyr was bent on killing Zhi-Ming in the most gruesome fashion he could imagine. The caverns were treacherous, but the lone Valkyr easily traversed them and arrived in the very chamber Shen now stood.

Valkyr had gone through the doorway and into Zhi-Ming's chamber, as Shen read, and was armed with only his dagger. The odds to him need not matter, and the only thought on his mind was that of revenge. Valkyr had attempted to slay the spirit beast in his sleep, but he had missed a fatal blow. The writing in the pages described their battle, how it went on for what seemed like eternity, and how the ferocity of Zhi-Ming could be matched by no one, not even himself. Soon Valkyr had crawled back into the chamber previous, where his body now rested, as Zhi-Ming sealed off the entrance to his sleeping chamber with a giant boulder. It was clear that what Shen was reading were the last pages of Valkyr's journal, and that it would soon end as his life had.

With the little time he'd had, Valkyr wrote of how he thanked his sister for coming along with him. He pondered in writing where Sigtur had gone, whether he was the one who'd killed Ilse, or whether he was simply cowardly enough to run away from whoever did. He wrote of his home, the sprawling mountains and the snowy plains which wooly cattle grazed upon. His writing began to get more sporadic, and words would pick up off the page and appear back again, indicative of Valkyr's fading consciousness. Soon, the writing stopped abruptly, and Shen turned over the rest of the journal's pages, wondering in his mind if there was anymore to be read. But, not surprisingly to him, there was nothing more.

He closed up the journal and put it back into the hand of Valkyr's body, the bone fingers simply holding the book against them. Shen went back to where he'd left off with the glow rocks and continued moving along the wall. It curved around and he noticed a small crack in the wall, where it seemed to be indented. He moved on from it, and filled the rest of the sconces with glow rocks. The light shined amongst the whole of the chamber, and even reached the table where Reina and Lao were finishing up their work on the arrows.

"Glowing arrows?" Shen asked, bringing over a few extra glowing rocks that he was unable to use.

"Yeah! Reina thought you might want to use them," Lao said with a smile. He finished tying up the last arrowhead to the arrow, and it was completed.

Shen took them all into his hands, looking them all around, the light of them glowing up upon his face and the bottom of the wide brim of his helmet. "These are well crafted. How'd you make them?"

"Apparently glow rock is super brittle. I found that out when I was getting them, further back in the tunnels," Reina said. She brought her sword down, but neglected to place it back in its hold at the small of her back behind her, and stood back up. "Lao, ask Shen what you were talking about earlier."

"Oh yeah. Shen, do you think you can control the glow rocks, I mean with your powers?"

"I'm not sure. I haven't tried it yet. Do you have one I can try it out on?" Shen asked. Lao took a small one from off the table and handed it to Shen. He grabbed it from Lao, holding it in the palm of his hand, and began to search it out with his powers. For a moment, there was nothing, but soon there was a burst of light in Shen's mind, and a pull, and he grasped it. Soon the glow rock floated up slightly above his palm, before falling back down. "It seems I can. But, not as easy as the other rocks, unfortunately."

"It's cool anyway!" Lao said, a wide smile on his face.

Reina cleared her throat for a second, and then spoke up, leaning to one leg and placing her hand to her hip. "So, Shen, any luck finding how to get to Zhi-Ming?"

"No. There was a crack in the wall, but I think it might just be natural," Shen answered.

"Did you hear anything from it?" Reina asked.

"Nothing I could remember, why?"

"Humor me. Where's the crack?" She asked again.

"By an indent in the wall, I'll take you over if you want," Shen said. Reina nodded and the three of them walked over to where Shen had found the crack. Strangely, Reina immediately put her ear up to the crack, her hand holding her sword up against the stone wall where it indented. "Reina, what are you doing?" Shen asked, raising a bushy black eyebrow.

"Quiet. I need silence." The two looked to each other and shrugged, then silence fell upon them. In a brief time, there came a sound, one which Reina immediately recognized, especially since it was louder now. "There. Did you hear that?"

"Yeah," Lao said happily. "What is it?"

Shen's eyes went wide with the realization, and his heartbeat jumped a bit. "Breathing."

"Exactly. And there's only one thing I can think of that'd be big enough to make that much sound breathing," she said. "I think Zhi-Ming is behind this wall."

"But how? Do you think one of the other paths leads into it?" Lao asked.

"No. This is the entrance, but it's just sealed," Shen said.

"You're sure?" Reina asked.

"Positive," Shen assured her, and stepped back from the indent. "Get out of the way of the wall. I'm going to move it," he said. They did as he said, walking back and getting behind him. He held his hands up, arms bent, and hands open. His powers felt around for what exactly it was blocking the way, until they found the outline of the boulder on the other side. He braced himself, but with only a single push of his powers, the boulder was moved. It had surprised him. He had moved boulders similar in size before, and that would put much strain on him, but this felt different. He shrugged it off, however, and with a flick of his arms to the side, it moved over as quietly as possible, and the light from the chamber they stood in leaked in and rested on the sleeping beast. Zhi-Ming was found.

The Chamber of Zhi-Ming

They stood there for a second, just staring at the hulking beast in the chamber. The chamber they stood in itself was gigantic, two, perhaps three times larger than the one they came from. Stone pillars rose from the ground up to the ceiling, rugged and clearly shaped by Mystics, Shen could tell. Boulders and piles of rocks sat around the chamber's floor. Blood splattered the floor and the walls, the rough stone coated in splashes of red. Near the beast's body there lay several skeletons, hookbeaks and ram-horns, and one human skeleton clad in light armor of silver with their jaw hanging open. Their identity was impossible to tell, their soul lost to time itself, to the beast their body now lay near.

Each of them looked to the beast and eyed up all of it, frozen in place, their feet unable to move. The way he slept had him facing them, and the size of his head alone was massive. It was about the size of Shen, bulkier even, and the fur was thick and coarse. Gray colored fur covered most of his head and his body, but there were tufts of dark red fur on the top and back of his head, and going down his spine like a mane. His chest rose and fell with each slumbering breath he took. He was similar in appearance to any other badger you might find making its den in the forest, but at the front of his muzzle there stood two long fangs. Thick and pale-yellow, they seemed to be as sharp as any blade from the finest blacksmith.

They looked on, and it seemed Zhi-Ming was deep into his sleep. Lao started to step in at first, but Shen put his hand out to stop him. "Don't get ahead," he whispered, incredibly quietly. "Let us lead for now. There's no telling what might happen." Lao stepped back and Shen moved forward with Reina at his side. She held not her sword in her hand, but a glow rock, the same thing both Shen and Lao carried with them. "Keep your fingers around the rocks and focus the light forward," he said.

"What? Why?" Lao asked.

"It keeps the light from spreading everywhere," Shen started.

"Lesser chance of Zhi-Ming seeing it," Reina finished.

"Exactly," Shen said.

They were all speaking in the quietest of whispers they could while still being heard by each other, and as Reina and Lao followed after Shen, he widened his stance and bent his arms. He grabbed onto the boulder with his powers and lifted it with great ease back to its place, and left just enough of a crack to let in only a sliver of glowing light from the previous chamber. "Hey," Reina snapped, "what'd you do that for?"

"It's our best option," Shen said.

"Option of what, keeping us trapped in here?" She retorted again.

"No. Firstly, the light might've woken Zhi-Ming if we let it keep glaring like that. And, I've got a sneaking suspicion, that if we're to get the upper hand on him, we need to take away any exits he might use as well," he said.

"What if we need to use it, Shen?" Reina said a bit louder than their tiny whisper.

"Be quiet, Reina, I'm not arguing with you on this. Besides, it's not like you can move that boulder away yourself," Shen snapped at her.

"Are you mocking me?" She questioned.

"Not mocking if it's true, really."

"You are such a child," she said.

"I am not a child."

They went on, bickering amongst each other, while Lao strayed away from the two of them in the dark. Guided by the light of his glow rock, focused into a dull beam in front of him as he cupped his hands around it, Lao moved around one of the pillars and walked aimlessly. He found himself wandering all around the chamber until the light of the glow rock came to a fantastic sight.

Before him there lay a huge mound of treasure. Goblets of gold encrusted with jewels of red, blue, and green, sat atop piles of ornate golden plates. There were weapons, knives of sterling silver and of polished copper, even a sword made from the finest gold Lao had ever laid eyes on. His mind raced with how much these would all sell for. He then looked around the more noticeable items, and his heart practically leapt out of his chest. Among the items themselves, their lay piles upon piles of Yin. Leather pouches laid on top of thousands of little silver coins, stuffed with even more of them, and they glinted with the light of his glow rock as he neared closer.

Without thinking, he began to grab handfuls of the coins. He stuffed them into his pockets, pushing the confines of them, moving the fabric all around as the weight of the silver coins added up more and more. The sounds were getting louder and louder, but Lao didn't seem to notice it, too busy filling his pockets with Yin, and filling his head with fantasies of being rich. He would never live on the streets again, never have to steal from anyone, not even those deserving. He could repay that hunter for teaching him how to make arrows, or the old woman for the sword he now had strapped in scabbard to his back. But, something changed in a moment, as a sound filled his ears.

With a low growl from in front of him, he brought his eyes up and his hands stopped moving, frozen in front of the treasure. His eyes met with a single solitary eye, giant, red and glowing with a sharp, thin almond-shaped pupil. "And who are you?" The voice boomed.

"Lao!" Shen shouted, and lifted a rock from off the ground quickly, launching it at the now awake Zhi-Ming.

The creature stood up, its sword-like claws tapping against the ground as it moved around the treasure mound. Lao ran back over to Shen and Reina, where he could see their light. Zhi-Ming simply moved to the side in a fluid motion, the rock flying past his body. "Oh, nearly tickled the hair on my back." He spoke with a smooth, booming voice, with just a hint of ruggedness to it. "It's been many years since I last got to kill any travellers."

"You won't be killing anyone!" Reina shouted, pulling her sword from behind her back.

"Please, darling, I wouldn't have slept if I'd thought you were a threat. I didn't even have to prepare for your arrival," he said. "I got much needed rest waiting for you," he seemed to snake around, and his tail whipped past a nearby pillar. In the light of Shen's glow rock, it looked serpentine, dark gray with scales all along it.

"You heard us coming into the caverns, didn't you?" Shen questioned through gritted teeth, Lao standing next to him with his sword drawn, both of his hands gripping the handle.

He came somewhat into the light, and his red eyes glinted. Shen noticed a mark on his forehead, white fur in a spot pattern, but it was quickly shadowed as he went back into the darkness. "Oh, no, I've known you were coming for quite a time before that. My little friends have been watching you rather closely, after all," he said, and barely any of his enormous frame was visible. The three only really saw his silhouette moving throughout the dark, with glowing red eyes staring back at them.

Shen thought for a moment, and he remembered the statues they had followed down into the caverns. "Shasha," he said angrily.

"The little weasel spirits? Like the one I chased after?" Lao questioned aloud.

"Precisely. Shame, they weren't supposed to get that close to you, or get spotted. But, I suppose they do have something of an alluring sense about them to humans. They did what I asked of them, anyway," he had a conniving tone about him, a way of speaking that was malicious but suave.

In a quick moment, Shen unslung his bow from his shoulder and pulled a glowing arrow from his quiver. He pulled it back and fired. "Reina, get around to his side! Lao, stay close to me, and don't do anything unless I tell you."

"Got it," Reina said, and ran around behind one of the pillars on one side of the beast.

Zhi-Ming felt the arrow pierce into the flesh of his left side, and looked down at it for a moment. He reached a giant paw to it and slashed the arrow shaft with a touch of his claw. "Hm, you seem to be able to hurt me." Glowing yellow, almost golden blood poured slowly from out of the wound, alighting a small bit of his gray fur. "No matter." The great beast leapt from his place toward the pillar Reina hid near.

"Reina, get out of the way!" Shen said, and flicked his wrist all around, sending pieces of the pillar flying off and into Zhi-Ming's face.

"Hold still, now, we can make this quick that way," Zhi-Ming said. Reina had jumped from out of the way, running around to Zhi-Ming's blindspot, near where his back leg was.

"Take this!" She shouted, and slashed at the fur. To her shock, the sword bounced a bit as it struck the beast, and only a small cut into its hide was made. "No!" She shouted.

Zhi-Ming's tail whipped back, knocking her over onto her back. "You little nuisance. Haven't sharpened that blade of yours enough, hm?" He stood up on his hind legs for a moment, before slamming his arms down, causing the ground to tremble. Reina, trying to stand up, lost her footing and fell back again.

"Get away, Reina! Regroup!" Shen shouted, and hid with Lao behind a nearby stone pillar. He pulled another arrow from his quiver, quickly firing it into Zhi-Ming's back, then another, firing it into the spirit's foot.

"You will all meet your end. But it is rather enjoyable to have this sort of fun beforehand," Zhi-Ming said, and let a grin creep across his muzzle. His nose twitched, as Reina ran out of his reach, to the pillar where Shen and Lao were. They were out of sight, but not for very long.

"What do we do?" Reina asked, heaving her breath.

"I don't know. I can't think of anything to slow him down, let alone get in close to kill him," Shen said.

"You think you're so clever? May I remind you, I can see you, and you're completely blind," he let out a laugh, and Shen and Reina's discussion was interrupted as the pillar they leaned up against was struck by Zhi-Ming's claws.

"Get out of the way!" Shen shouted, and Reina ran over to a further pillar, taking Lao with her. He lifted his arms and bent his elbows, and his powers seized the larger chunks of the pillar in the air. For a moment, it was enough to bear, but soon the weight of it was pushing his powers to their limit. He quickly threw his arms in front of him, where he'd thought Zhi-Ming was. But, the rock merely crashed into the ground ahead, echoing throughout the chamber.

"Oh, what a show of power!" Zhi-Ming snaked around another pillar nearby, looking toward Shen with something of a respect. "Never have I faced one of Batung's kind with such formidable skills." While the spirit was admiring him, Shen ran over to where he'd guessed Reina and Lao went off to. As he was running over, he noticed puddles of glowing yellow blood that had fallen from

Zhi-Ming's wounds. It provided a bit of light to guide him, and he soon joined back up with Reina and Lao.

"Shen! Are you alright?" Lao asked worriedly.

"Yes," he said, and paused for a breath, "I'm fine."

"Shen, I think I have a plan," Reina said.

"No time to question it, just say it, hurry," he said, as the sounds of Zhi-Ming's encroaching footfalls neared closer and louder.

"You and Lao distract him. I'll try to get back into his blindspot and crawl under him. From there, I think I can slice open his stomach," she said, and she started moving to another pillar. The other two followed after her, and Zhi-Ming kept his rather slow pace toward them. "If that isn't enough to kill him, it'll at least give us some light to see. That blood of his seems to glow."

"I've noticed. You think it'll work?" Shen asked.

"I guess we'll find out. Now, go," she said, and ran to a further away pillar on the other side of the chamber, away from Zhi-Ming.

"Stay close to me," Shen said.

"I know," Lao replied. They ran out from behind the pillar, and began waving their arms in the air, unsure of where exactly Zhi-Ming was. But, soon the red eyes revealed themselves, bright and glowing, and they saw him in front of them. "Hey, ugly! Come to see us?" Lao shouted.

"You little brat. You think you can speak like that, after trying to steal from me?" Zhi-Ming flashed his teeth, and swiped his claws in Lao's direction. Shen quickly turned his hands over, and flicked his wrists up, sending a wall of rock up from the ground before Lao.

"No!" Shen shouted, and felt his body getting weaker.

"You Mystics, always getting in people's way," Zhi-Ming muttered. "Why do you think they came after your kind, hm?" He wiped the scowl from his muzzle, and it was replaced with a smirk.

"Shut up! You don't know what you're talking about," Lao screamed.

Shen just stood there, making sure Zhi-Ming came no closer, waiting on Reina to get close enough to him and do something. "Oh? Don't I?" He looked to Lao and him only, and his words came again. "You don't know anything about the cleansing, foolish child, do you?"

"I'm not a child!" He screamed again.

"But you are. A child unconcerned with what the humans do to Mystics, what they've done. You're only concern is stuffing those greedy pockets," Zhi-Ming said, and Shen could tell Lao was getting furious.

"I'm not greedy! I only steal when I have to!"

"But do you? I have a hard time believing that," Zhi-Ming said.

"Don't listen to him, Lao. He's just trying to get you to attack him," Shen said.

"Oh? So the scoundrel wants to speak on my actions, hm? You think because you've just a tiny portion of the blood of the earth god flowing in your veins, that you're some kind of force?" Zhi-Ming grinned with malice, his red eyes glinting with light. "Your blood is nothing. The gods don't matter anymore, and neither does their kind, none of you Mystics. I'm not sure it would be worth anything more on the floor of my chamber than it would coursing through your veins."

"Don't talk to him like that!" Lao screeched.

It seemed like the distraction was working, but Reina hadn't anticipated Zhi-Ming to be this cunning. Nonetheless, she got into her position and readied her blade. She ran forward, approaching the blindspot she'd struck before, her blade poised to stab through the spirit's side. But, something came in the way. Zhi-Ming had heard her steps, the clanking of her boots on the ground, as he wasn't sufficiently distracted by the other two. He whipped his tail around toward the noise, and Reina fell back onto the ground.

Zhi-Ming quickly spun around, and Shen could tell how enraged the spirit was becoming, his body heaving with angry breaths. "Reina! Get away! Now!" Shen screamed as he readied another arrow, but it was no real use. Reina stood up, and before she could act, Zhi-Ming swung his paw into her, knocking her across the chamber into one of the stone pillars. "Reina!" He shouted. He fired the arrow, and then another, and continued moving around the ground firing arrows.

"You all are such a bother! None of you are leaving here alive!" Zhi-Ming shouted, taking the arrows. He lunged forward, claws poised and ready to strike, and Shen grabbed Lao, jumping over to a nearby pillar out of the way. "You can't hide for very long, you little rodents," Zhi-Ming muttered.

"Lao, I need you to stay here," Shen said hurriedly.

"What? Why?" Lao said, his voice frantic.

"I need to go help Reina. She's still alive, I know it."

Zhi-Ming crashed through the pillar, reckless, throwing his body into the stone while Shen and Lao moved out of the way to another. "You can't see too much, can you?" His glowing yellow blood dripped from a new wound he'd gotten, and fell near the two, lighting up a small area of the chamber. "But I can. I can see everything here in the darkness, as if it were a day without a cloud in the sky," Zhi-Ming said.

Shen stepped a bit back from Lao, and put his hands out, his palms upward and his fingers bent. "There's no time. I'm putting up a dome of rock to protect you. You'll be safe from him until I can come back."

"But-" Lao was promptly cut off, as thick walls of rock came up around him, sealing him inside with only a few cracks in the rock for him to breathe through.

Finishing Blow

With Lao safely entrapped within the confines of the rock, Shen rushed over to where he'd imagined Reina had landed. Unfortunately, the chamber of the cavern was still much too dark to see in. But, around where Reina had been struck, there was just enough of Zhi-Ming's blood on the floor glowing yellow to see which direction she had flown off in. He ran past a few more puddles of the glowing stuff, when he heard the steadily approaching stomps of Zhi-Ming crawling over. Claws scratched the ground as they neared him. And Shen could just barely see a pair of stone pillars standing next to each other. "You can't outrun me, Mystic filth," Zhi-Ming echoed.

Shen ran through the two pillars, and as Zhi-Ming was right behind him, the beastly spirit was knocked back by the pillars, not running quite fast enough to break through them. "I don't have to," Shen said, almost cracking a smile, and continued running as fast as he could toward the other end of the chamber.

Zhi-Ming had had enough of dealing with Shen, and turned his serpentine tail to get at the rock fort Lao was shrouded in. Shen kept running, and as he got closer to the wall of the chamber, things got much darker. Zhi-Ming had not shed blood on this side of the chamber so the darkness was impossibly thick. Shen reached into a pocket on his tunic, still gripping his bow in the other hand, and felt around. When that yielded nothing, he reached into his bag, feeling around again, until he came upon a rugged little object.

He pulled it from out of the bag quickly and the light shined out. His eyes drifted ahead and he saw he wasn't quite close to the wall, either that, or the orange light of the glow rock was not nearly as bright as he'd thought it might be. He took a few steps forward, and his bare feet felt cold against the stone ground. He'd gotten used to the feeling of rocks on his soles, the roughness, the bumps that would bruise the skin and ache for weeks. Soon he came upon the wall, but there was no Reina to be seen. "Reina," he called out loudly.

There was no immediate answer. He didn't know which way to go, to the right or the left, or she may have been nowhere near him. But, a faint sound came from nearby that dismissed any kind of that thought. It was low and incredibly quiet, but Shen could easily make out that it was the sound of shifting metal. He rushed over to where he heard it and eventually the orange light in front of him fell on Reina, lying on her side, nearly slumped over against the wall. "Reina," he said, kneeling down to her and setting the glow rock on the floor.

"Shen." She whispered, her voice strained and grainy.

"Reina, are you alright? You're alive. Oh, you're alive."

"Yeah, I'm alive," she said. For a moment she tried to stand up, but a piercing pain shot throughout her chest and her legs, and she fell back down. "Gah!" She yelped, and relaxed back down on the ground with a whimper. "I can't stand up. My ribs… I think some of my ribs are broken."

"Alright. Alright, I think I can keep you from getting any more damage. Give me a moment." Shen reached into his bag and felt all around frantically, his heart beating violently against his chest.

"Shen. Shen, you… where is Lao?"

"He's safe, Reina. He's safe."

"That's not what I asked, moron" she winced as more pain shot through her system. "Where is he?"

Shen took out a few herbs and a small wooden bowl, the only one which he carried in the big bag on his side. "You need to relax," he said, and began to grind up the herbs with his fingers.

"I am relaxed, Shen. Where is Lao?" She looked ahead, past where Shen was kneeling in front of her, and saw a glint of red. It was Zhi-Ming's eyes, and they were far away from the two of them.

On nearly the other side of the chamber, Lao was becoming further and further frightened, despite being held in the safety of Shen's rock fortress. "Little child, you can't hide in there forever," Zhi-Ming said, circling it. He lunged forward and slashed at it, but his claws simply bounced off it, like the rocks had their own force pushing back on him.

"I'm not a little kid!" Lao shouted from inside.

"Oh? You're not? Then why do you act like one?" Zhi-Ming said again, and he skulked around the fortress slowly, looking on with a smirk across his razor-sharp teeth, his two prominent fangs hanging down.

"I'm… I'm not acting like a kid," Lao shouted meekly.

"No? Then why do you hide, hm?" Zhi-Ming jumped forward and slashed at the rock again, and a piece of his claw chipped off. He grunted as the pain of it set in, but shook it off in moments, stalking around the fortress once more. "Those other two. So valiant, aren't they? Real heroes if you ask me."

"Of course they are!"

"Oh yes. Yes they are. But you? Oh, you on the other hand hide and don't fight, do you?" Zhi-Ming taunted.

"That's not true! They tell me not to, or I'll get hurt."

"Yes, yes, that's what they say. But, deep down, you don't want to fight," he paused, and came right up to the fortress, placing his big glowing red eye up to the crack where Lao would see it. "Do you?"

"I do want to fight," Lao said. "I want to fight and prove I'm not just some little kid who can't do anything!"

"Oh, but you are. You're so helpless. Just a coward, right?" Zhi-Ming backed away from the fortress and walked around again, then braced to hit again. He wound up one of his hind legs and swung it around, placing a firm kick into the rock with his palm. The strike did nothing, however, as his leg was knocked back by the force of the rock and Shen's powers, and he clambered to the ground. He growled for a moment and then continued walking around the fortress.

"I'm not a coward!" Lao said, nearly to tears.

"Oh but you are, child. Just a street rat coward. No regard for anyone but yourself. That's why you came here, isn't it? All that treasure."

Lao thought back to the Council, their meeting in the capital where their quest first started to kill Zhi-Ming. He remembered smirking as the thoughts of treasure filled his mind. The sight of the coins entered his head too, and those weapons, the goblets and the plates, all the things he could sell for huge amounts of Yin. "No, that's not what I am anymore."

"You think you can change, boy?"

"I have changed!"

"No one changes. That woman with you, nothing more than a murderer, not unlike those other Vasai soldiers wandering around in my caverns. And that man, that filthy Mystic. Why, he's no better or worse than Batung himself, lazing about, so self-righteous."

"You're wrong! Shen and Reina aren't like that," Lao cried out, and his eyes began to water, the tears falling down his cheeks.

"Deny it all you want. You know deep down that I'm right," Zhi-Ming said with a smirk on his muzzle, and he slashed again at the rock. Inside, Lao cried and screamed, and banged against the rocks with all his might, even pulling his sword from the scabbard to slash at them.

Meanwhile, Shen was still tending to Reina. He had finished grinding the herbs, and mixed them with a drop of his blood he had gotten from a cut on his side that hadn't fully healed. He wondered for a moment where he'd gotten it exactly, but it wasn't a pressing matter, and quickly expelled it from his head. "What, what do you want me to do with that?" Reina asked.

"Eat it. The blood is a little unsavory, I know, but it makes everything work stronger." Shen wiped off his fingers on his tunic, bits of green and purple herb staining the tattered fabric of his tunic.

"You want me to eat this?" She asked, raising an eyebrow.

"Yes." He reached the bowl out to her, and scooted a bit closer to her. "Do you think you can sit up? It'll make the herbs go down easier."

She tried to get up, moving her arms, but just that motion alone brought a searing pain into her stomach. "Agh," she cried out.

"Reina, don't-"

"Shut up, Shen, I don't want to hear it," she said, and moved again. She moved her arms up from her lying position, and with gritted teeth, held back a scream as she lifted herself from off the ground for just a moment. With a turn she sat up against the wall of the chamber, and her eyes watered. "You," she paused to take a breath, letting tears fall from her eyes, "you owe me."

"Yes," Shen said with a chuckle. "Yes, I guess I do." He handed over the bowl, and Reina brought her cracked lips forward. Shen tipped the bowl forward and the clump of herbs and blood rolled around, where Reina waited for it. It went to her lips, and she inhaled the thing, chewing on it for a moment before choking it down. For a second, Shen felt something, a kind of twinge of pain or force against the inside of his head. He winced for a second, and Reina took notice.

"Shen? Something wrong?" She asked with a grunt.

He winced again, as another pound struck against his brain. "Yes," he said, and put his fingers to his forehead. "Yeah, just my powers."

"Your powers? What," she paused to breathe, "what do you mean?"

"The rocks, Lao, I need to keep them strong," he stopped briefly and winced even more in pain as his nose began to leak with blood. The pain returned, pounding and pounding against his skull as Zhi-Ming slashed at the rock fortress. It shot through his head and down the back of his neck, and he gripped at his head with both hands, dropping the bowl on the ground. It burned, it shook his brain, but it soon abruptly ended all in one second.

"Shen," Reina said.

"It's gone. It's gone," he said, and wiped the blood from his nose and his upper lip, staining his tunic sleeve. "The pain, it's all gone."

"Shen, we have to go, now," she said.

Shen looked back, as the sound of stomping came toward him. Zhi-Ming's eyes, red and glowing, stared back at him. He looked on past the quickly approaching spirit and he saw, in the light of yellow glowing blood, the large pile of rocks that was once Lao's fortress. "No!" Shen shouted. Zhi-Ming lunged forward at them, and Shen stomped his foot on the ground. A rock pillar came up from the floor and struck Zhi-Ming under the chin, knocking him over.

He stumbled back, and Shen took this opportunity to divert the beast's attention away from Reina. Shen ran away to another side of the chamber, as fast as he could, while the angry Zhi-Ming clambered toward him. "You insolent rodent! I'll have your blood on my fangs in no time, I'll promise you that."

"Where is he? Where is Lao, you disgusting monster?" Shen shouted, jumping over a large rock as Zhi-Ming lunged forward at him. He turned, and kicked up another chunk of rock from the ground, launching it into the side of the spirit's head.

"Oh, the little coward?" Zhi-Ming leapt forward again, shaking off the shock of the blow, and crawled around a stone pillar near where Shen stood in waiting. "Why, you must know what I've done to him."

"You're full of it," Shen said. He waited, and lifted a hefty rock from the ground, ready to launch it once again.

"Oh, am I?" Zhi-Ming came round the pillar, and Shen launched the rock. It flew past the spirit, and crashed into a wall, where it broke apart into tiny pebbles from the sheer force of the throw. "Or are you too afraid to confront the truth of the matter?"

Shen reached his hands out forward, and felt around for something specific. Zhi-Ming rounded the pillar again, to where Shen had moved, and snapped his jaws as he leapt forward. Shen bent his fingers, and gripped one of the glow rock arrowheads with his powers, pulling it from out of Zhi-Ming's side. With a flick of his wrists he pierced the arrowhead back inside his skin and twisted it around. "Gah! You filth!"

"Reina, I can't keep this up for very much longer," Shen said.

"Oh, talking to your friend? She's not perished yet? I can change that." Zhi-Ming hissed out the words, and snaked around another pillar, his glowing yellow blood dripping from his wounds. He lunged forward, fiercely snapping his jaws, and Shen flicked his wrists up. A large chunk of rock from the ground jumped up and lodged itself in between Zhi'Ming's sharp teeth.

"He's got to have a weak spot, Shen," Reina shouted out, since Shen was quite nearby her now.

Zhi-Ming bit down, as he couldn't open his jaw wide enough to release the boulder. It shattered into pieces and he quickly spat it out onto the ground with a clattering sound. "You think I have a weak point, do you?" He ran forward and Shen twisted one of the glow rock arrowheads in its wound. Zhi-Ming cried out in pain again and his red glowing eyes darted all around the chamber. "Ugh, that blood of yours, those abilities, such a pain in my tail."

Shen backed up, as he couldn't bear the weight of using his powers for much longer. He was up against the wall of the chamber, feeling the rugged stone against his back through even the fabric of his tattered tunic. "Reina, stay away," he said.

"Always the hero, aren't you?" Zhi-Ming crept ever closer, slowly, his red eyes glaring at Shen. Pain was setting in, and it distracted him from any other feeling, including the one which crawled up his back. "I fought a man like that, many years ago." The feeling kept climbing up his back, pulling on the hair of the red strip of fur starting at the back of his head.

"Valkyr," Shen grunted through gritted teeth.

"Precisely. You've heard of him? Last I saw he was crawling out of this very cavern with his guts hanging out of his stomach. Finally, the feeling kicked in past the pain, and Zhi-Ming felt something on his head, but it was too late. "What is that?" He asked aloud, and Shen looked up at the beast's head to find a familiar face.

"Lao!" Shen cried out with joy.

"What?" Zhi-Ming shouted, enfuriated. "How could you possibly have survived that, you brat? I crushed you!"

Lao finished crawling up the spirit's head, and in one hand he gripped the bronze sword. His limbs were getting tired, the climb rigorous, and the sword heavy in his grasp. But nonetheless he clambered all the way to the top of

Zhi-Ming's head, clinging onto the thickly packed gray hair on his head, the red fur of his mane extending down his neck. "I'm not a coward!" Lao screamed.

"Get off of me you insufferable wretch! I'll claw the entrails from your tiny body slowly, bit by bit." Zhi-Ming shook his head all around, thrashing the little boy about. "You can't kill me! That little sword of yours will do nothing to me!" Zhi-Ming screamed and wailed, moving around the chamber and slamming his body into stone pillars. One of them crumbled and a tiny piece of it flew by Lao, scratching him in the cheek.

"Lao! Get down from there!" Shen called out.

"No, Shen! I can do this," Lao shouted, holding onto Zhi-Ming's fur for dear life.

"You can't! You won't," Zhi-Ming cried. "I'll kill you without a question! Your body will be the next thing to rot away in my caverns, I can promise you that!"

"I'd like to say the same to you!" Lao shouted, and as Zhi-Ming slowed his thrashing, tired and bleeding glowing yellow, he gripped the sword's handle with both hands. His fingers wrapped around the leather binding and Shen watched as he plunged the shining bronze blade, glinting with a bit of light Zhi-Ming's blood gave off, deep into the spirit's forehead.

All of a sudden there was a flash of light, and it showed both Shen and Reina that Lao had stabbed through the white spot of fur at the center of Zhi-Ming's forehead. Yellow blinding light shone from out of the wound, shooting rays of it everywhere, and soon the light began to fill Zhi-Ming. "No!" He shouted, and the light filled his mouth. His red eyes lost their sharp pupils and their glow turned to a shining yellow blast. In one last flash the light abruptly ceased, and Zhi-Ming came crashing down to the ground with Lao on the back of his head.

The Bronze Gauntlet

In the minimal light glowing from Zhi-Ming's yellow blood, Shen could see Lao gripping onto the sword lodged in the beast's head for dear life. Quickly the body of the spirit began to fall, his head swinging back, and Lao was coming down too. "Lao!" Shen shouted, almost out of breath. The boy let go of the sword as Zhi-Ming's head swung forward and he flew up into the air. Shen swiftly brought rocks up under his feet, and launched himself up way above the ground, where he flew into Lao. He grabbed onto the boy, he wrapped him in his arms tightly, and continued flying forward. In a moment he turned his body around, using his powers in hopes of softening the rock below. He landed flat on his back on the now dirt-hard patch of ground he'd softened.

"Shen. Shen, I did it," Lao said softly, and then got up from Shen's grasp.

Shen felt his breath steadily flying away from him, his lungs desperate for air, the wind knocked out of him, until it came rushing back. Part of him wanted to shout at Lao, to lambaste him for his recklessness. But, he took a few more breaths and then spoke up in a raspy voice. "Yes, Lao. You did it," he said softly.

"Are you okay?"

"Yes. I'm just, out of breath." He reached his hands out and pulled Lao into a hug, holding him tightly to his chest. "I'm so glad you're alright. I thought I'd lost you," Shen said softly.

Lao was taken by surprise, but clutched Shen's tunic in a hug back. "It'll take a lot more to take me down, Shen. I'm just that good." They held onto each other for just a few moments longer, before Shen let go and the two of them stood up. "Where's Reina? Is she okay?" He asked frantically. "She got hit really hard."

"She's alright, Lao. She should be nearby where we came in, resting. Once we get to Zhimai we need to take her to see an herbalist to fix her up," Shen said.

"What? Do we need to hurry?"

"No, no, Lao, it's fine. Don't worry so much. Just a few broken bones, nothing she hasn't endured before, I'm sure." He began walking over to where Zhi-Ming's body lay, and Lao took this chance to return to the pile of treasure the spirit had been sleeping upon. He grabbed for one of the coin pouches he'd seen, and started to stuff it with coins of Yin. Once it was full he grabbed for another one, doing the same and placing it into his pocket.

While Lao was busy looking through the treasure, Shen hobbled over to where the body of Zhi-Ming lay. He looked upon it, his green eyes scanning over the fur matted down with yellow, glowing blood. Shen laid his hand against his stomach and felt a growing pain, as he tasted a hint of metal in his mouth. Blood. He looked to Zhi-Ming, and now the mighty spirit no longer looked so beastly. In fact, he looked as pathetic as he'd made the three of them out to be. He walked around to where Zhi-Ming's forehead rested and beheld the sword, its bronze metal glinting in the light of his blood.

Shen reached his other hand out and wrapped his fingers around the leather-wrapped handle of the sword. He pulled, and there was little give, so he pulled again. The sword was lodged deep within Zhi-Ming's skull. It felt as though it wouldn't come out, but with a few more tugs and the help of his other hand, Shen pulled the blade from out of the spirit's head. A splash of glowing yellow blood came from out of the wound and Shen had an idea. He dragged the bloodied blade along the ground, creating a trail, and made his way over to the treasure pile where Lao sat waiting patiently.

"Looking for this?" Shen asked, lifting the sword up in front of the boy's face.

He held something in his hands behind his back, and he brought it forth into the light glinting off the treasure and the glowing blood nearby. "I'll trade you," Lao said, holding it in his hands in front of him to Shen. In his grip there was a piece of armor. It shone in the glow of Zhi-Ming's blood in puddles on the ground, made from a fine bronze metal. A gauntlet, to cover the upper half of the forearm, as well as the whole of the hand, besides the fingers. All along the metal were engravings in a language Shen couldn't understand, and Lao neither. But, strange most of all, upon the back of the hand portion, there sat a smooth green gemstone.

"Where'd you find this?" Shen asked.

"In the pile of treasure. Had to toss a few golden plates, maybe a couple daggers, but I eventually found this."

"Lao, you don't need to give me anything."

"Oh don't give me that. It's a good enough trade for the sword. And, if it's not, consider it a payment for the awesome training you're gonna give me!" He practically jumped up in joy, and Shen smiled softly.

"Alright, alright," Shen said. He handed over the sword, and Lao took it with one of his hands, the heavy blade weighed down, hitting the floor with a *tink* sound. Shen reached out and took the bronze gauntlet from Lao's hand, and looked at it all around. He read over the strange language on the engravings, the embellishments like beautiful patterns on the metal. Almost all of it was illegible, save for one word, or rather, a name. There was the name Batung engraved on the side of the forearm section. Paying it no mind, he slid the piece of armor onto his left arm, and suddenly felt a rush of energy pulse through his veins. For a moment, it appeared as though the green gem glowed in the gauntlet.

"Shen, did you see that?"

Shen thought for a second, the pain in his chest fading, the taste of blood in his mouth nearly all gone, and then spoke. "Yes."

"What do you think it is?" Lao swung his bronze sword up and placed it into the scabbard behind his back.

"I don't know," Shen muttered.

"Maybe it's like the glow rocks in the rest of the caverns. But, instead of orange, it's green." He tilted his head a little inquisitively, raising an eyebrow.

"Could be." Shen reached down into his side bag and grabbed for his large coin pouch, filled with a few of the little silver coins. He pulled it from the bag and stuffed it with more of them, grabbing handfuls from the treasure pile and dumping them into the hide bag. In a few minutes the bag was filled nearly to the brim with about 290 silver coins. "Let's get back to Reina. I'm sure she's worried about you." Lao nodded and tucked away his own coin pouches, filled with a total of exactly 174 Yin.

The two of them made sure they each had everything and knew where it was. Shen checked to make sure his bow and empty quiver were still slung over each of his shoulders, which they had been, and that the bag at his side was still fastened on tightly. Lao reassured himself that his newfound coin pouches were in their places in his pockets, and that his sword rested firmly in its scabbard on his back. Once everything was confirmed secured, they walked calmly over to the other side of the chamber, where Reina sat up against the stone wall, her head tilted down, nodding off.

"Reina," Shen said. There was no answer, and it seemed as though she was fast asleep. "Reina, you need to get up. We need to figure out a way out of here," Shen pleaded, louder now. At the same time as his need to wake her up, he wished not to disturb her. After all, she did look rather peaceful in her resting state.

"I got this," Lao said quietly. He cupped his hands around his mouth, and belted out a hefty yell. "Reina! Wake up!"

"I'm up!" She shouted, and tilted her head back up as if nothing had happened. "You don't gotta yell, kid, I'm awake." There was a glint in her eye from a nearby puddle of Zhi-Ming's glowing blood, and it highlighted the irritated look she wore. "I've been awake, you know," she said settling down, wincing a bit as she shifted around in her seat, still in pain.

"What? Why didn't you just answer me the first time I said your name?" Shen protested.

"Because I wanted to see if I could get a bit of shut-eye before we got out of here, grumpy."

"Don't call me grumpy. I am not grumpy."

"You sound grumpy," Lao said.

"Exactly." She tried to get up, moving her arm, but there was too much pain. It shot through her chest and through her stomach, like a burning rivaled only by actual fire.

"Don't try and get up on your own, Reina. You're entirely too damaged, and weak."

"Well then, thanks for the confidence boost, Shen," she said

Shen rolled his eyes. "So, did you have any ideas on how to get out of here while you were resting your eyes?" Shen asked.

"Not that I remember. Of course, my mind's been blacking out at weird times from the pain, and who knows what I could've come up with in those moments," Reina said, and let a smile crack onto her face.

"Enough joking around. We need to get out of here and back to Fu and the cart."

"I know, Shen, just relax," Reina said.

"Can't Shen just use his powers to move the boulder back from the entrance?" Lao interjected.

"I'm not so sure." Reina nodded her head in the direction of where the doorway they entered from was. In the light of Zhi-Ming's blood, there could be seen not one giant boulder anymore, but several more smaller ones toppled down around the original one. "Even if Shen wasn't weakened, which he is, when Zhi-Ming died he seemed to cause a rumble from falling that broke off parts of the ceiling."

"That's not from just him falling, either. I remember a couple times I heard a few rocks chip off from the ceiling," Shen said.

"Oh," Lao muttered to himself.

"What do you mean weakened?" Shen said.

"You were nearly coughing up blood. The last time you were in that bad of shape, it was back at that camp, and you had to sleep for nearly a half a day in order to function," Reina said.

"I don't feel like that anymore. Definitely not as bad as coughing blood," Shen replied. "Shouldn't we at least try it?"

"No, Shen." Reina looked to him with a bit of a scowl, her hazel eyes glaring. "We can't risk you knocking yourself unconscious, not when we're stuck in here at least."

"Alright, then what do you suppose we do?" Shen took a few steps near her, and sat next to her up against the wall of the chamber.

Lao ambled around the ground for a little bit while the other two sat silently, thinking to themselves. He had his head tilted down, looking at the ground, at all the pebbles and rocks, at the puddles of glowing blood that had dripped from Zhi-Ming's many wounds. Lost in thought, he hadn't noticed he was walking toward a wall. He was taken aback as he bumped his head into it, and looked up to come face to face with the wall. In a moment he'd thought of an idea. "Hey, guys!" He shouted, unsure of where exactly his companions were.

"Lao! Where are you?" Shen called out, standing up from his seat against the wall.

Lao followed after his voice and came back to where the two of them sat. "I think I have an idea on how to get out of here."

"Well don't leave us hanging. What is it?" Reina asked, as Shen sat back down next to her, the two of them looked up to Lao, awaiting his response.

Lao smiled, and he reached his hand out toward the wall. He balled his fist and proceeded to knock his knuckles against the rock. "Follow the wall around." He brought his hand back and let his arms rest at his sides, putting a lax lean onto one of his legs. "Like we did in that other chamber, when we were trying to find the entrance to here. Just follow along the wall and look for another way out."

"You think there's another way out?" Reina asked.

"It's worth a try."

"Zhi-Ming might've blocked off any other exit from here. I mean, he did block off the one we came in from," Shen explained. "I think it's leaps better than just sitting here forever."

"Not sure if you boys know, but, I can't really move," Reina muttered.

"Well aware, Reina," Shen said.

"You can be our meeting point!" Lao said, and the two before him looked to him with confused faces. "We start off here, where Reina is sitting. I'll go one way, Shen goes the other way, and we meet where Reina is against the wall, after meeting up in the middle anyway, I mean."

"I think it works better than anything else we could come up with right now," Reina said. "I'm not at my best, though, so that's not really saying much."

"Well then," Shen said getting up from his seat, standing up next to Lao before Reina. "Stay close to the wall and don't leave it, alright?" He asked Lao.

"I think I can manage that."

"Don't go away from it. You could easily get lost in the dark in here, and I don't want you hurting yourself because you tripped on a rock," Shen said with a little chuckle.

"I won't, Shen. You don't give me enough credit," Lao said. He tapped his sandal against the ground, finding a pebble, and he kicked it along the ground. The sound of it tapping against the rock echoed out quietly.

"I suppose I don't." Shen flexed the muscles in his bare feet, feeling the aches and the bruises, and looked to the side, along the ever expansive wall of the chamber. "I'll take this way," Shen said with a point toward Reina's left side, where her only arm stood. "You take that one?" He questioned, and pointed to Reina's right, where the tunic under her armor was tattered and torn from when her arm was burned and amputated. "Okay?"

Without a word, Lao walked off in the direction Shen indicated, placing his palm against the wall, and Shen dropped his pointing arm in confoundment. "What the," he said to himself. He let out an exasperated sigh and Reina chuckled in response. Shen shot a scowl her way, with a furrowed, dark brow.

"What?"

Shen shook his head and went the opposite way that Lao had gone. He lifted his arms and placed his calloused palms up against the rock wall of the chamber. The ruggedness of the wall felt coarse upon his skin as he moved along the wall. His senses were sort of numbed by it all. There was not much to see, unless he came upon a puddle or drops of Zhi-Ming's glowing yellow blood, and the only time he could hear was when he'd stepped upon a pebble. Of course, he could feel things like the rocks and the wall. But, there was of course nothing to taste, and the only smells were the sweat staining his tunic and occasionally the metallic scent of the aforementioned blood.

He walked along the surface of the wall and felt around with the tips of his fingers for anything that could indicate an exit. He felt around for indents like the one they'd found before. In addition to that, he felt for cracks. If he found even a small crack in the rock, he would place his cheek up against it, trying to see if there was a draft coming onto his skin. Unfortunately though, there was no such feeling among any of the times he'd tried, and no indents could be felt anywhere in the wall that would warrant anymore investigation. Having found nothing, Shen returned back to where Reina was sat, in the light of the glow rock that was set down near her legs.

"So, are we saved?" Reina asked, lifting her head up.

"Very funny," Shen muttered.

"I was being serious."

The two looked to each other with plain faces, sort of taken by surprise at Reina's tone, until she let out a stifled chuckle. Shen rolled his eyes and continued on. "I couldn't find anything that seemed like a way out. Not even a crack that would indicate another section of the caverns."

"No boulders or anything blocking a way?"

"Not that I could tell," Shen said, taking a seat next to Reina, making sure she was staying awake while resting her eyelids.

The two sat next to each other for just a few minutes longer until Lao returned, as it seemed he'd gotten off track. "Did you stray away from the wall?" Shen asked.

"No," Lao retorted, "I was just going really slowly, you must've passed me at some point without realizing it."

"I guess that does make some sense. I stepped away from the wall a few times," Shen answered. "Well, did you find anything?"

"Unless Zhi-Ming has an entrance way up high where I can't reach, nothing. I didn't even really feel any cracks in the walls," Lao replied.

"Looks like we're right back where we started," Reina muttered, dropping her head down, partially in disappointment, and another part because her muscles were beginning to tire. "So, what now?" She moved her arm only slightly, placing it over her lap, and a surge of pain shot through her limb.

"We could sit here and enjoy our time together before we die here?" Lao said with a sly smile, sitting down on the other side of Reina.

"Lao!" Shen protested.

"What?" The boy crossed his arms across his chest, feeling the soft fabric of his tunic against the skin of his arms. "I'm only joking."

"At least the kid's got an idea," Reina said, rolling her eyes, her eyelids drooping over them.

"Reina, I've already suggested I move the rocks," Shen interjected.

"And I've established how bad of an idea that is."

"I've got to try. There's nothing else we have to do right now. We can't just dig our way out, and we've already tried to find another way out." Shen stood up and walked toward the rocks. "It's the only thing we've got."

"I think you should at least try, Shen," Lao said.

"Shen, there's no way you can move that first boulder alone, not when you're weak like this," she protested. "Even if you could, it's bound to knock you unconscious again, and then that just leaves Lao to move the rest of the rocks."

"I don't feel weak, though. I did before, but, now it's like I'm as good as new." Shen walked forward a few more steps, and was now facing the pile of boulders blocking the entrance they came in from. He lifted his arms, looking to the bronze gauntlet clinging to his forearm and hand, and curled his fingers. Soon, he felt of the rocks at once with his powers.

"Shen, what are you doing?" Reina said, trying to get up, but the searing pain in her torso brought her back to the ground.

"Relax, Reina, I can do it." He lifted the rocks up, and all of them moved at once, hovering high above the ground, casting shadows upon the glowing yellow from the puddles of blood, and the orange from the glow rock by Reina and Lao. In one quick toss they all flew far into the other side of the chamber, crashing into the rock wall. He took a breath, and things seemed fine. He'd felt better than he'd had in awhile, in fact.

"You... you did it," Reina muttered.

"Yeah! Nice one, Shen!" Lao shouted.

Shen took a step back, and he was met with the glowing orange light from the glow rocks he'd set in the sconces along the wall of the other room. "Alright, we should get moving. There's no telling what time it is, and we need to get Reina to a healer as quick as possible," he said. He shuffled over to Reina and crouched down. He put one arm behind her neck and the other under both of her knees, lifting her up in his arms.

She wrinkled her nose and furrowed her black brow in pain, wincing. "This is so degrading," she said softly, resting her head on Shen's shoulder. She reached her arm up from against his chest, and draped it over the back of his neck, and a small bit of the pain in her chest faded. For a moment, she could feel a warmth building up in her cheeks.

"Oh hush," Shen said back.

"Come on! Lets go!" Lao said, and led the two of them into the previous chamber, set on snaking through the paths they'd walked before.

Gangkou Port Town

Lao nearly ran forward back through the previous chamber they'd been in. The orange glow from the rocks washed over them and eased their muscles for just a moment, their eyes scanning around the room. Nothing had really changed, the table and chair near the wall right where they'd left it, the body of Valkyr as Shen noticed, his journal still tucked within the bones of his fingers. Reina shifted for a bit, and leaned her lips closer to Shen's ear, shaking off the pain that gathered in her stomach. "What is it, Reina?" Shen asked, watching as Lao ran ahead of them.

"You did good, Shen. Look how happy he is," she whispered quietly. Shen raised his eyes and he saw Lao, practically bouncing around and giggling. "See? You can have him be safe without being overprotective."

"I know," he said, trailing his voice off as he walked forward. He shifted his arms, carrying Reina a bit more comfortably. "I'm still ridiculously worried about him. But, you were right. He's not just a helpless child."

"He took down the big bad spirit, too," Reina said with a chuckle, followed by a wince in pain. "More than you could do."

"Hey, I helped," Shen said, and he let a smile come along his lips.

They quieted down and moved on through the paths of the caverns. As they entered into the next section of the cavern they'd already been in, they discovered one of the soldiers they had beaten. Yama, the large and muscular woman Reina had fought, laid dead further away from them, at the entrance to the chamber they'd fought in. The other two soldiers, the other woman with the trident, and the bumbling man, seemingly had escaped, nowhere to be seen.

They retraced many paths lighted by the torches of the spirit statues, and all of them just led further and further up toward the entrance.

Continuing on, they reached the other paths, to the small chamber where they ran into the other two soldiers. Here, the light of the fire from the Shasha statue up ahead shone on the body of the man Lao had slashed. The other soldier was gone, presumably having fled, leaving her companion to bleed out in the chamber. He had, the blood pooling underneath his body, showing the trail he had made crawling toward the path out of the cavern. Lao looked to him, the soldier he'd killed, and was overwhelmed with a strange feeling.

It was like a weight was placed against his chest, and then added onto more and more as he walked forward, Shen with Reina in his arms following after him. He knew it was what he had to do. But, that thought alone couldn't dispel the guilt that washed over him. He hadn't even known the name of the soldier, whether he had dreams or aspirations, or family like Lao had Shen and Reina. "Lao," Shen spoke up.

Lao shook his head, finding himself stopped in place near the last path, the light of the sun leaking through down to them. "Yeah, Shen?"

"Are you alright?" Shen came up behind the boy, Reina resting her eyes in the grip of his arms.

"Alright?" Lao thought back to the soldier, and he suppressed the feelings that bubbled up in his chest. "Just a little tired is all," he said.

"Well, luckily for you, you'll get to nap plenty in no time," Shen said.

"Yeah," Lao muttered.

The three moved up the path and reached the mouth of the cavern, the sunlight a delightful change from the glowing orange rocks they'd gotten used to, though it stung their eyes a bit at first. It seemed to be about midday by the position of the sun that hung bright in the clear blue sky. All the storm clouds that had gathered before were completely gone. There was still the echoing sound of dripping water, leftover from the rain, dripping down from the rocks at the mouth of the caverns onto the rugged rocky ground. Lao and Shen stepped forward from out of the cavern, and their feet sunk partially into the soft dirt.

    A breeze came over the landscape as the three of them continued forward, and the trees swayed like dancers as their branches caught the wind. Shen's eyes drifted down from the tops of the trees, and rested at the trunks, finding a familiar sight near the path through the forest. At the side of the trees there sat the cart and Ping at the front of it. Fu, who had been entrusted with the cart, sat up against a tree with his legs outstretched. He wore a helmet on his head, with greenish feathers upon the front, made from a bronze metal. Ping was quite curious of it, it seemed, the dimian pecking incessantly at the top of it.

    "Fu!" Shen shouted, and walked faster with Lao, reaching the soldier and the dimian at the cart.

    "Shen," he muttered in an unamused tone. "You actually did it, didn't you?"

    "Yes. Zhi-Ming has been slain," Shen said.

    "What are you doing here? Weren't you staying with the cart down there," Lao asked, pointing ahead toward the downward sloping hill, where the cart originally sat on the dirt road.

    "I brought the cart here to look for my helmet." He looked upward, and he felt Ping's beak tapping against the metal. "Found it," he mumbled.

    Shen thought for a moment, and remembered the Batung soldier they'd encountered within the caverns. "Did you see Gong? We ran into her in the caverns," Shen said. "She told us to get help, have you a build a signal fire."

    "Yes, I saw her. She's alright." Fu said, and stood up, his injuries less apparent than they'd been before. "She found her way out of the cavern, headed off that way to the nearest town, Anquan." He pointed toward the north, and then walked forward to the three of them, away from Ping, who tilted his head in confusion at the soldier. "She was very adamant about making sure you were safe."

"She made it out?" Shen questioned.

"She was incredibly slow with it, but yes, she hobbled all the way out of the caverns." Fu took his helmet from off his head, inspecting the surface of it for dents, and found none, tucking it under his arm. "So, what now?"

"The Council said we'd need to get to Zhimai to finish out the task, but that's really all," Shen said.

"Zhimai, huh? Well, the only real way to get there is through Gangkou."

"The port town on the shore?" Shen questioned.

"Exactly," Fu replied. "If we go now, we should reach the town just in time for nightfall, when the last few ships leave the docks." He walked around to the side of the cart. "If you'd let me, I can lead the cart to town, I know the way well enough."

"That won't be necessary," Shen said. He walked up to the back of the cart, reaching his arms out, setting Reina down inside the cart's cloth cover. She grunted for a moment as the shift agitated her wounds, before relaxing, lying against her soft sleeping roll. "You, Lao, and Reina will stay back here and look after each other. She's incredibly injured."

"There should be herbalists on Zhimai. I know a little bit about the art, from my training. I'll do the best I can to help her," Fu said.

"Thank you," Shen replied.

"You know the way to town, right Shen?" Lao asked, climbing into the back of the cart after Fu, who had settled in next to Reina.

"Yes," Shen said, and walked to Ping, giving him a loving pat on the side of his neck. The dimian chirped quietly, almost smiling at the gesture. "My map has the road to Gangkou mapped out nearly perfectly." He climbed up onto Ping's saddle, grabbing the reins, savoring the familiar feeling of the leather in his palms.

As the cart bumped along the rocky dirt path, Reina thought to herself. She silently cursed herself for being in such a state, weakened, battered and broken by the spirit that was taken down by a mere boy. But, that boy was Lao, and she supposed that was better than anything else. Through the pain present in her chest, the broken ribs inside her poking around each time she shifted position, she let a smile come across her face. The look soon faded though, as the wheel of the cart bumped into a particularly large rock and caused her pain to flare up strong once again. She couldn't get any real rest, and instead looked to Lao, who stared from out of a hole in the cloth cart cover.

Lao's eyes drifted across the sunlit forest, and as the cart came from out of the trees, his brown eyes met with expansive fields. He saw a smaller town, not any larger than five houses, and a giant patch of farmland. There were people tending to the crops, soybeans and tea plants poked at with long tools. The emerald green of the plants nearly gleamed in the light of the sun catching the dew still left on the leaves of the crops. Every now and then, one of the farmers, usually an old woman or a young man, would look up from their work and wipe the sweat off their brow. They would look up, and bring down the brim of their wood farming hat to shade their eyes, and then get right back to work.

Shen, who was also looking to the farmers and their fields, wore his helmet on his head with the shade covering his eyes. The sunlight was piercing and warm against the skin of his arms and his neck. Under the gauntlet, however, the skin of his arm remained untouched by the warmth. He looked down to it and pondered to himself, mainly about where exactly the armor had come from, and whether it was of any real importance other than protecting his forearm. The shiny green stone glinted in the sunlight, and seemed as smooth as any fine silk.

Fu, situated comfortably against Shen's sleeping roll near the furthest back of the cart, shifted around and itched at the wound on his stomach. "We should get there just before nightfall if we keep this steady pace," he spoke up. He brushed off a bit of dust from the surface of his bronze helmet. "It works out, actually, since we'll have to take the nightly ferry. That's the safest passage for Mystics, without getting caught, I mean," he said.

Shen's heart dropped, and he immediately pulled on the reins. Ping stopped in place, and Shen hopped down from his saddle, walking to the back of the cart. "What did you say?" Shen commanded.

Fu looked around him in the back of the cart, and he saw that Lao had now placed both of his hands on the handle of his sword. Reina wore a scowl, her eyes wide and the bags under her eyes dark, her hands poised to attack if she had had the strength. "What? What's the matter?"

"You know what I am?" Shen said. "And what are you planning on doing?"

"Please, whatever you think I'm going to do, you're wrong."

"Prove it to me!" Shen yelled. "You want to kill me? Or, would you rather turn me and them into the Council, have us killed and try to haggle yourself a little reward."

"Shen, please, I'm not going to do anything like that." Fu pleaded, his hands up in front of him in defense. "Just listen, okay?" The man, tan, bearing the same skin as Shen who stood outside the cart before him, looked nearly terrified. Shen lowered his hands and straightened himself out.

"Explain yourself," he demanded hesitantly.

"I saw your mark. But, I don't care, Shen. You saved my life. Why would I want to turn you in after that?" Fu seemed genuine, his tone sincere and his eyes warm.

"Because of what I am. What my blood means for my life," Shen muttered.

"You're no different than me," Fu said. "I have no reason to hate you like that. Yes, they tell us you're evil, like monsters, but obviously that's not true."

Shen thought back to Shi-Li, to the soldiers, the ones who thought nothing more of him than dirt. He thought of how they spoke about his kind, calling them monsters. In a moment, there built up a warm tear in the corner of his eye. He reached his hand up to his face and wiped it away. "Thank you, Fu," he said.

Lao lowered his hands from his sword, and Reina relaxed herself, her eyelids slowly becoming heavier. "I'm sure we'll have enough time before the ferry to get a warm meal. I know a good place, my father owns the shop."

"They serve ram-horn there?" Lao asked.

"Fresh as it can get, the town is near a forest full of them," Fu said.

Lao gripped his stomach, feeling the growl of hunger build up inside. "That's what I like to hear," he said.

After adjusting the gauntlet on his forearm, checking the map over a few times, Shen grabbed the reins once again and continued on down the dirt road. For a long stretch of time the inhabitants of the back of the cart rested their eyes. Even Reina got a bit of rest, despite the pain still present in her chest. Soon night was upon them, and just in time, as Ping pulled the cart right into Gangkou, as indicated by the sign at the front gate. One of the soldiers standing guard at said gate came from out of a shadow into the light of the torches outside the houses and other buildings of bamboo.

"You there," the soldier shouted, walking up to the cart, "on the dimian."

"Yes, sir?" Shen asked.

"I'll need to examine your cart, as well as your necks. Mystics around here, it's protocol, you know?" The soldier said.

Just then, from out of the cloth cover of the cart came Fu. "Hey, Min," he said.

"Fu? Is that you?" The guard responded.

"Yeah. We had a little trouble over by the caverns, Vasai ambush," Fu explained.

"So I heard. Gong came by earlier," Min said. "She said you'd be looking for her."

"She walked all the way here from Daoyan?"

"No way. The way she tells it, sounds like she caught a ride from a travelling merchant, some guy who frequents this place. Think she said his name was Zexian," Min said.

"I think I've heard the name around here."

"Heh, yeah. I still haven't gotten used to this place. Can't believe we got stationed here while the rest of the guys in our squad got sent to western mainland," Min complained, rubbing the back of his neck with his palm.

"It's not so bad," Fu said, and quickly changed the subject. "I forgot to say, I already ran through the mark thing with him and the other two in here. He's just a traveler trying to get to Zhimai."

"That makes my job a whole lot easier. Much appreciated, Fu."

"Don't mention it, Min." He went back into the cart cover for a moment, then poked his head back out. "Oh, you know if my dad's got his shop open yet?"

"It's rush hour. Better get in quick while he still has the bar open," Min said with a laugh.

"Yeah. Thanks, Min."

"Sure thing. And, sir, I wish you and your companions in there good luck on your journey," the soldier said with a warm smile.

"Thank you, sir." Shen tugged at the reins and Ping moved forward once again, until they came to a stop at the front of what Fu had said was his father's restaurant. "Fu, what was that all about?" Shen asked as Lao was waking up.

"Ugh, my head. Last time I nap against the icebox," Lao muttered.

"Shen, just because I think you're not worth killing, doesn't mean Min thinks the same way. I wasn't going to take the chance." Fu climbed out of the cart and outstretched his arms to Reina, offering to carry her.

"No thank you. Shen'll carry me. He owes me that much," she said, as Shen came around to the side of the cart where she rested.

"Oh? I thought you said it was degrading," Shen said with a smirk.

"Well, I can't really walk, you know. And you definitely owe me this," she said.

Shen picked her up as he had before and brought her to the front of the restaurant. Fu walked up behind them, with Lao following in tow, and rested a hand on Shen's shoulder. "You can stay out here with her, while the little one and I go get the meals."

"Really?" Lao said. "Shen, is it alright if I go in with Fu?" He asked.

"I suppose it's no harm," he turned to Fu. "You have helped us tremendously so far," Shen said.

"Don't worry, I'll keep him out of trouble," Fu said.

"Hey!" Lao protested.

As the two of them went inside, Shen and Reina stayed outside, Shen setting Reina down in a bamboo chair. Reina was a bit more uncomfortable than she would have wanted to be, but it wasn't nearly as bad as the bumpy ride of the cart. Shen came back over to her after feeding Ping a fresh red apple, and sat down in a chair next to Reina. "So, what do you plan on doing once we get to Ogon," she asked.

"I'm not sure. We should really be focusing on getting those wounds of yours fixed up. Zhimai should have a good herbalist for that," Shen said.

"Will you stop your worrying? I'm going to be fine," Reina said with a roll of her hazel eyes.

"Yes, I know." Shen sat back a bit in his chair, relaxing his muscles. "Are you alright with it?" Shen asked.

"With what?"

"Returning to Ogon, after what happened to you, what happened there."

Reina thought for just a moment, and then spoke low. "It's not that big of a problem, Shen. What I did was of course horrible, and will I ever make up for it? Probably not." She tilted her head down, looking toward the dirt road in front of her. "So, I suppose it'll be a fitting punishment for me to return to Ogon."

"You did what you were told to do. That's loyalty, no matter how awful."

"That doesn't excuse what I did, Shen. You of all people should know that."

"I know, but if you keep dwelling on it like that, then you'll never be able to move past it, become better than the things you did." After those words, the two went silent. They remained silent for a long while, staring out at the citizens walking through the buildings. There was a small market where the merchants would peddle their things, fish or other meats, cattle steaks, some jewelry from more noble merchants, even a few weapons being sold by a person who was once a blacksmith's apprentice.

Soon Lao and Fu came back from out of the shop, warm wooden bowls nestled in their hands, one in each palm. "Hey, we brought some stew over rice for the both of you," Fu said.

"I already had a bite of mine. It's probably the best I've had in all of Batung," Lao said, still chewing on a piece of tender ram-horn deer meat.

"It didn't cost you much, did it?" Shen asked, standing up to retrieve his and Reina's bowls.

"Actually, the kid here paid for it. Any chance he lifted all that Yin off of Zhi-Ming," Fu joked, taking a seat near Reina.

"Maybe, maybe not," Lao said, sitting on the ground up against the front of the shop, his mouth full of meat and broth and rice.

"Haha, don't worry, your secret's safe with me," Fu said, chuckling aloud.

The four of them ate their meals in silence. Though, there came times when Lao would break from scarfing down his food to say a few words of warmth to Ping, who stood stomping his feet lightly at the smell of the broth that wafted up from the bowls. As the night carried on, they finished up and Fu began to tell them of the nightly ferry he'd have them take to Zhimai.

Raid at Sea

    Fu led the three of them to a building just near the docks. Here, he stood and let the three of them listen, Shen and Lao standing side-by-side, while Reina rested in the grip of both of Shen's arms. "Alright, this should go all according to plan if you just follow it," he started. "The nightly ferry has no guards, but does require one to send it off, by nautical law."

    "That's where you come in, right?" Reina asked, coughing a bit, the taste of metal creeping up the back of her throat.

    "Exactly. I heard Mystics had been using the ferry to get safe passage to Zhimai, especially from Ogon, if my information was reliable. Now, the important thing about it is that the ferry won't be checking you for marks on the backs of your necks, which only Shen really needs to worry about," Fu said, and his voice was trailing off toward the end.

    "I'm sensing a 'but' coming," Lao said.

    "*But*, you will be checked once you get to Zhimai. If only by one soldier, you're still going to get past them."

    "So what do we do then?" Shen asked.

    "You need to talk with the other Mystics on board. I have absolutely no clue how to avoid capture once you get to Zhimai, but the Mystics already on the ferry have to have some kind of plan to keep from getting found."

    "And what about you?" Lao asked.

    "Well, I forgot to mention that you won't be able to take your dimian with you on the ferry. Weight limits and all that. The ship they use is purely for human passengers, not cargo," Fu said. "Where do the Council have you going after Zhimai?"

"Ogon. We were granted passage there in return for killing Zhi-Ming. It'll get us that much closer to where we're ultimately going," Shen answered.

"Well, it'll be incredibly hard for me to get your dimian all the way to Ogon, across the water and everything. They'll probably take you through Aegir Port from Zhimai, and from there you'll need to get the dimian and the cart over more water to reach the Ogon mainland." Fu placed his fingers to his chin, scratching at a tiny bit of stubble forming.

"I suppose you have another solution?" Shen asked.

"Well, sort of. Is there anyone on the mainland or an easily accessible Batung territory you trust to take care of the dimian while you travel?"

Shen thought, and his mind jumped across all the people they'd met. Mina and her sons in the capital, but they were much too low on space to house both Ping and the cart. He thought back to Lu Min, the old woman, Quan, that Shen had met. But, this wasn't a well enough option either, as he didn't want to burden the people he, Reina, and Lao had saved. Just then, he was reminded of their time on Lujing, and instantly an answer was found. "On Lujing, the woman we'd gotten Ping from. Her name is Xue Yimu. I think she'll be delighted to look after the dimian before we can get back to him."

"Xue Yimu?" Fu asked.

"That's correct. Owns a stable in a no-name port town, a really nice place."

"Alright. I'll see to it myself that Ping makes it there completely safe." He stopped, and looked again toward where the cart and dimian stood. "I'll be sure to try and send some supplies from the cart to Zhimai with your name on them."

"You're not coming with us on the ferry, Fu?" Lao asked, his smile going away a bit.

"No. I should stop in the capital and report to the officer of the Guard Brigade, Commander Teng." Fu rolled his eyes a second, almost annoyed by just the utterance of the name. "Last I'd heard, she was taking a leave to Doshi market to shop and to talk with the Council."

"She sounds like a riot," Reina said with an unamused tone. "I've had my fair share of bothersome commanding officers I had to report to," Reina said.

"The Vasai ones any better than Batung's?" Fu asked.

"I'd bet a hefty amount of Yin they're about the same."

"Well, regardless, I've gotta tell her about our ambush at the hands of the Vasai. There's no way I can keep that kind of information from her and the Council." Fu looked back from the road and saw a large wooden ship with giant sails, of which were made from white and yellowish cloth, and fashioned so that they looked like the dorsal fins of fish. In the light of the torches on the ship, the sails were able to be seen. "We need to get going quickly, they should be boarding the ferry now."

Fu hurried them down the road right to the docks, where several smaller wooden ships operated not by sails but by oars were docked, tied up to the wooden poles of the dock by rope. They arrived to the ferry and were greeted at the boarding platform by a welcoming face. It was a man, fairly old in his appearance, his dark tan skin wrinkling and his black hair sprinkled with hues of gray. "Hello, I take it you're the soldier sending us off tonight," he asked. From behind him, people came close and hurried onto the ship without any notice by the man that greeted them.

"That's right," Fu said. "Brought you three more passengers too, looking for safe passage to Zhimai."

"That's what I'm here for," the man said.

"I take it you're the captain of the ferry," Shen said aloud.

"Yes!" He was very happy to be called captain, it seemed, and Shen was almost taken aback by his eccentricity. "Dui Zhang at your service," he said, and placed his fist to his chest in Batung salute, something Shen and Lao hadn't seen in quite some time.

"You'll have to excuse me, but my hands are a bit full," Shen said, while Lao graciously returned the gesture to the man before them.

"Sorry about that," Reina said with a strained voice, pain radiating within her chest.

"It's quite alright, young lady, I don't take it personally." He stepped aside, and gestured toward the boarding platform leading them to the ship, where a few more people were getting on. "Please, let's go before the sun comes up, hm?" He said, and gave a warm smile.

Fu turned to the three, and he wore a solemn expression on his face. "Well, it seems this is where our journey together is gonna have to end." He placed his fist to his chest in a firm salute, and smiled. "Thank you, Shen, for saving my life. And, thank you especially for defeating Zhi-Ming."

"We'll miss you, Fu," Shen said.

"Yeah. You think we can meet up again sometime later? We're going to have to come back for Ping anyway, and it'd be great to see you again," Lao said, returning the salute once again.

"Let's hope so," Fu said.

"Alright, come on, before the sun comes up," Reina said.

"Haha, okay. I'll let you guys go on," Fu said.

"Don't mind her, she's just cranky is all," Shen said with a hearty chuckle.

"Take care, and safe journey."

"The same to you Fu," Shen said, and Lao echoed the same sentiment.

With nearly no more words, the three of them walked up the boarding platform and onto the deck of the ship. Many more people came onto the deck, taking spots along the sides of the ship where they'd place their things, bags of food, waterskins, blankets and sleeping rolls, before the ship finally set out onto the water toward Zhimai.

As it cut into the water, sailing at a decent pace, Lao couldn't help but marvel at the night sky he'd taken for granted before. The light of the stars shone down on the water in vibrant arrays of light, and the sky was painted a luxurious dark blue that set his nerves at ease. Even the moon was more beautiful than it had ever seemed to be before. It watched over the sailing ship like a king of the night sky. The light of the torches around them was not any hindrance to the majesty that the lights from the sky portrayed to them. He stared just a bit more up at it for a few moments, before he broke his sight and looked elsewhere.

"Shen, is Reina alright?" He asked, looking to the woman who lay nearly motionless nearby him, sat up against the taffrail around the deck.

"You can just ask me, kid. And I'll manage, thank you very much," she said.

"Oh. Sorry. You sorta look," he began to trail off into thought.

"Dead. You can say dead."

"Oh hush, you," Shen retorted. "Lao, would you like to join me?"

"With what?" The boy asked, almost tilting his head in curiosity.

"Well, like Fu said, we'll need to ask around the deck for a way to get past the mark checkpoint." Shen looked around, and many of the passengers were already fast into sleep in sleeping rolls, while others huddled around food, wrapped in blankets for warmth against the cold night.

"And you think my dashing charisma might help you accomplish that?" Lao held his head high, wearing a smirk on his face.

"Not really," Shen said, and Lao brought his head back down, "I just thought you'd might want to join me."

Lao looked a bit disappointed for a moment, before the look faded back into a warm smile. "Well, at least you've got that right," Lao said. The two of them wished Reina some rest, to which she scoffed, and began going around to the groups of passengers. Shen found himself among a small, older group of four gathering in a circle, while Lao found a younger-looking passenger singled out from the groups. "Hi! My name's Lao," he said with an even wider smile than he wore earlier.

"Please, don't talk to me," the boy before Lao said, seemingly just a year or so older than him. "Just leave me alone." He looked out onto the water with his arms placed onto the taffrail. It was in this position that Lao could see it, staring at him in the light of the moon, a green mark on the back of his neck.

"It's alright, your secret's safe with me. I promise," Lao said. The boy turned, seeing Lao's smile, and he couldn't help but let a smile of his own form across his lips.

While Lao was talking with the young boy, Shen had his own conversations starting with the group he'd sat down near. "Please, don't be alarmed," he explained as the passengers appeared frightened. "I know what it is to be an exile."

"What do you know of exile? You look nothing more than another traveller, probably looking for coin," one of the older men said, a scar upon his jaw, pinkish as a contrast to the pale color of the rest of his skin.

Shen turned his neck around to them, in the light of the night sky, and displayed the green mark he'd had since birth, the sign that he was a Batung

Mystic. "Does this shed any light on the subject?" The old man with the scar showed his mark, reddish in color. "You are of Ogon, aren't you?" He looked around, and the other three members of the group showed off their marks, though they were different, seemingly burnt off and faded like scars. "You all are?"

"That's right," one of them said, an older woman, though not much older than Shen himself.

"All four of you," Shen said to himself.

"There used to be more of us, about fifteen when we first left Frigard territory," the old man with the scar said.

"And that was nearly two years ago, Kodvir," one of the women said.

"You've been travelling like this for two years?" Shen asked, positively enthralled by the four before him. "Why?"

"To be free. Free of fear, free of hiding and running like cowards." The man spoke with a muted anger, clenching his fist.

"Kodvir, stop talking like that," one of the women said, her hair short and pale blonde, a neat braid of it hanging down next to each of her ears, which were slightly pointed at the tips, as was uniform of Ogon Mystics.

"You know it's true, Ikfrid." The man pounded his fist against the ground. "We're like animals to them, weak, frail, just running around in circles until they can finally catch us."

"How've you escaped before? Obviously you've come quite a long way, and those marks aren't an easy thing to conceal."

"If you hadn't already noticed, only I've got the regular mark," Kodvir began. "The others have had theirs burnt off. It wasn't easy, but it was better than doing nothing or trying to find the Bregda."

"Bregda?"

"Nothing more than a myth. They say that on the southwestern islands, Sindmir family territory, there's someone who can surgically remove the mark," he said, and reached his hand to rub the back of his neck. "I won't hide what-*who* I am. So, I haven't even bothered with it."

"Then how have you gotten through the checkpoints?"

"Haven't. Just been taking sneaky ways around them. Nearly gotten captured ourselves plenty of times because of it," one of the women said, the younger looking of the three. "That's how we've lost so many."

"We just plan on swimming once we get close enough to Zhimai's shore. It's worked before," Kodvir said. "And, even if we tried, and we could mask our marks better than a burn, it's not like we can hide the pointy ears, you know?"

"Yes. Well, I appreciate the information." Shen said, and stood up. "Safe travels, all of you."

"The same to you, stranger," Kodvir said, and the gesture was echoed by the others in his company.

Shen walked back to Reina, sitting down against the taffrail next to her. "Anything?" She asked.

Shen put his head in his hands. "I wish I could help them, every last one of them," he said. "They're just like us."

"I know, Shen. But, for now, we've gotta keep moving on, focusing forward."

"Yes," Shen said. "You're right."

Elsewhere, at the edge of the ship, Lao was still talking with the young boy, though not as extensively as Shen had done with the group of Ogon Mystics. "You know you can trust me, right? I may not be like you, but I don't think like all those soldiers and other people. I don't think you're a monster."

"You're more kind than any person I've met before." The boy sat down with his knees bent, his head resting between them. "I can't trust that."

"I get that." Lao thought of his journey to Yedao again, his leaving his hometown of Zhaoyin and his father behind. "You're alone?"

The boy mumbled a bit, but then spoke up. "My parents are already in Zhimai," he said.

"That's great!"

"No!" The boy nearly shouted above the murmuring voices amongst the ship, but then settled down, lowering his voice again. "It's not. I don't know where they are. What if I don't find them?"

"I'm sure you will. You seem like the kind of guy that'd be really good at that."

"I'm scared." He looked around, worry filling his voice. "What if I can't pass the checkpoint, and I get captured? Or, or, what if I can't even find them because they've already been captured themselves?"

"Hey," Lao said, and placed a firm hand on the boy's back. "It's alright, just relax." The boy tensed up for just another moment, and then his nerves began to relax. "It can be hard to find family. I know. But, there's this connection to it, and that'll lead you to them everytime."

"You think so?"

"I know so. Even if they aren't my blood, I found my family, after searching for quite a long while."

"You're saying it'll take me years?" The boy asked, and his nerves flared up once again.

"No! No, not at all. All I'm saying is family finds a way," Lao said. "I meant to ask, how do you think you'll get past the checkpoint?"

The boy straightened his back a bit and reached into his pocket, seizing two small bags of what seemed to be powder. "My grandfather gave these to me before I left. Told me it was a specific mix of herbs, rub them on my skin and they'd mask my mark."

Lao's face lit up immediately. "Do you mind if I borrow one of those? My," Lao struggled with exactly what to call Shen, but came upon the thing he'd called him a few times before. "My big brother needs it to get past the checkpoint too."

The boy handed one of the bags, a warm smile on his face. "Take it."

"Yes! Thank you so much, I'll try and repay you somehow."

"It's alright. Your kindness was payment enough." With a lazy salute from Lao, in a rush to return to Shen, he took off, leaving the boy to stare out at the starlit waters once more.

Lao returned quickly, standing in front of the two as they sat next to each other. He held out the little bag of powder nearly immediately, and Shen looked at it with a raised eyebrow. "What is that?"

"The way past the guards!" Shen stood up and snatched it from out of Lao's grasp. "Hey!"

"Is this what I think it is?"

"If you think it's a healthy mix of herbs to mask the Mystic mark on the back of your neck, then you'd be right!"

Shen wanted to shout all the thanks he could to Lao, but something interrupted them. The boat abruptly began to slow, pulled back by some force, while the sounds of splashing water came from near the sides of the ship. "What is that?" Reina asked, trying to get up from her seat, but encountering the searing pain in her chest once again.

"I don't know," Shen said. "Lao, stay close to me," he said. For a moment he thought back to the boat ride from Yedao, of the sawtooth dolphin and shredfish that had attacked them, fearful that it might be those two animals again.

Soon the ship came to a full stop, and Shen looked all around the deck to figure out what was happening. He looked to the other passengers, who were just as, if not more put off by the sudden stop. Even the captain came out of his cabin, looking around in the same way Shen was. Obviously he hadn't done it himself, and in any case, the ship wouldn't have been stopped nearly this fast, or unannounced. "Is everything okay?" The captain shouted out. There was a clamoring of voices, as he walked around to each of the groups of passengers. "Did anybody see what happened?" As he came closer, something caught Shen's eye.

On the taffrail, subtle, but just as the moonlight hit it, it was visible. A hook, with a rope tightened and tied to the back of it, latched onto the ship. "No! We're being boarded!" Shen shouted out. Suddenly, the ship was swarmed with shadowy figures. They were cloaked in dark, billowing robes, and their faces were all covered by scarves of fine cloth. There was something entirely familiar about them.

"Grab anyone you can!" One of the figures shouted, their voice female, though muffled behind the cloth of their scarf.

The figures began seizing passengers, one for each silhouette that jumped along the deck of the ship. They placed their hand over their mouth, and it was almost as if the passenger was completely overcome by sleep, as they became motionless and easily dragged overboard. Shen tried reaching into his bag, to grab for the rocks he kept there, but he wasn't quick enough. Another figure jumped onto the ship right near them, and in a fluid motion, grabbed Lao by the mouth. The boy almost instantly went unconscious, one of the bags of Yin falling from out of his pocket, and the figure came nearly into the light of the moon. Their billowing robes and headscarf were visible, but what lie behind the scarf chilled Shen even more. Pale, crystalline eyes. The Nettle.

    With a twist of their body, the figure jumped from off the ship and down into a small wooden boat below. At the back of it there stood another dark figure, who waved their arms rhythmically, water seemingly pushing the boat from underneath at incredible speeds away from the ship. "No!" Shen screamed out, but it was too late. As the little wooden boat with the Nettle sped off into the night, Shen could have sworn he'd seen a glint of light bounce off a lock of blonde hair, braided down the Nettle's back. He looked around frantically, and the figures had all seized a passenger, taking them in the same manner as Lao had been. The rest of the little wooden boats below the ship took off with their captives, and Shen was left with Reina. "He's… he's gone," Shen said to himself, knelt down on the ground, clutching the little silver coins Lao had dropped, a fire burning in the corners of his eyes.

Made in the USA
Las Vegas, NV
07 November 2021